SLEDGEHAMMER: A ROCK & ROLL FABLE

Volume I

JUKEBOX HERO

Jason Stuart

BURNT
BRIDGE

BURNT BRIDGE
www.BurntBridge.org

Cover layout by Justin Adcock
Editing by Charlie Knight
Images used under license from Shutterstock.com

For my daughter, Larkin

Acknowledgements

This book is for everyone who loves the 80's, that wild, bizarre, awful, wonderful decade full of sheer and utter nonsense — that cocaine-fueled fever dream of Reaganomics, Cold War hysteria, pop culture, and pumped sneakers.

Also: special thanks to my editor, Charlie Knight, for sharpening and polishing this into the best it could be. Thanks to my cover designer, Justin Adcock, and his many drafts until we hit the bullseye.

Thanks to my beta readers: Juliana, Ashley, Charlie from Starkville, and Nick. You were all invaluable in shaping the early, unwieldy beast this was.

And thanks to all my friends who encouraged me to start writing again. It feels good to be back.

Somewhere in the '80's...

In a place without a name...

EPISODE I

"SISTER CHRISTIAN"
—NIGHT RANGER, 1983

THREE STANDING GRANDFATHER clocks gazed down at her that morning, ten years to the day since they found her wandering alone with no memory—not even a name.

There, at the corner of Elm and E Street, Molly Slater (the name they'd given her) gripped her Fender Stratocaster like it were a weapon forged for her hands. Her fingerless gloves whispered at the strings, ready to saw down some serious noise. Jordache jacket with the sleeves ripped off at the shoulder. Purple lipstick and double-earrings. Corvette red hair. Bette Davis Eyes.

The garage smelled like the early morning—no other sound but her Cons slapping the dewy concrete. She kicked away shorted out gizmos and various half-finished contraptions littering the cold slab floor. Hoyt, her foster dad, fancied himself the inventor. Any day now he'd invent their way into riches untold. Any day now.

Those grandfather clocks ticked at her as she plugged into the Peavey. More of Hoyt's tinkering, thinking he could set his machines by them. Each triggered a different chain reaction every morning. One fed the dog. Another opened the garage to the day. A third...well it never worked anyway. She stared at them, as did they her in return. They held no judgment, only the looming doom of the impending hour.

As the garage doors groaned, opening to the dim autumn light outside, she cranked up and twist-tuned her axe. She gave it a gooseneck and sliced right in. *Mötley. Halen. Bowie. Duran. Whitesnake. Saxon. Maiden!* Fluidly, she moved from one riff to another. She was totally, epically zoned.

She lived in that fifteen minutes.

Those granddads thundered their terrible news.

The parentals shouted.

"Shut that racket off! You're gonna be late, I swear to every god," the mother said. As if there were gods. Molly just shook her head, put up the guitar and grabbed her bag. "And put on a hat on that red hair. I don't want you getting murdered by that maniac!"

So dramatic. Like anything that interesting could ever happen.

She always knew it would be like this

I

"DON'T YOU FORGET ABOUT ME"
—SIMPLE MINDS, 1985

MOLLY SLUDGED HER WAY through a wet October morning, eager not to be late lest her Saturday detention become two. The whole thing was bogus to the max already because the vice principal had a total gear to grind when it came to her, and Becky de la Beckwith was nothing but a complete stain with Daddy's MasterCard. Besides, Becky deserved it anyway.

Molly's bowling-shirt collar was turned up, peeking out from her checked jacket. She knew she should have brought her scarf as she pulled more of her molten red hair over her ears. It was colder this year than last. Colder every year, they kept saying, though temperatures one way or the other never bothered her too much.

When she hit the smoothtop fresh sidewalk—this two-horse town had few such spots to boast—she laid down the banana board and put her All-Stars to work. She thought she caught a glimpse of the psycho newspaper kid on his bike who always hounded her for the subscription fee, like that was somehow her debt and not Hoyt and Clair's. She was late enough as it was.

The creeping Spanish moss hung like dead fingers reaching from the low, sprawling limbs of the live oaks peppered through the neighborhood. In the dense fog, this biting cold, the gray drizzle warned of no good thing to come. Molly sometimes had a sense of these things. Like the night before an exam she knew she'd biff. Only worse. Some "birthday" this was gonna be.

Not that it was her actual birthday. She had no idea when that was. Today was the day they 'found' her. Just two days after the night of the comet, they'd told her later, when she finally spoke. She remembered not even understanding words, at first—like the whole world was new to her. She'd been wandering around out by the highway, abandoned by some parent or other or both. *Jerks.* Whoever they were.

Today was always the worst day of the year, thinking of that and how she couldn't remember anything from her life before. The nuns at Our Lady had said she looked about eight or so. That made her about eighteen today. Or so.

Neither Hoyt nor Clair had even mentioned it before she bolted out the door. She wasn't in a hurry to remind them, either. Being legally eighteen meant their check from the state would cut off at the end of the month. She wasn't looking forward to that conversation. Life in this 'burb wasn't ideal, but it could be a lot worse if she were suddenly homeless.

She cranked the Gabriel on her Walkman. Power 108 was at least rocking this wet morning. Always crap weather on her 'birthday' too. Just an all-around ugly gray day, barely interrupted by the occasional flash of lightning in the far-off sky and some low rumbling. The cold, wet pattering of everyday nothing.

Becky de la Beckwith had got all up in her face and called her "coast trash" after she'd caught her ex-boyfriend Easton, not even her current boyfriend Blake, looking at Molly after school. Saw her standing in line for the bus and told her only trash rode the bus, and that's what she was. Nothing but some "fosty coast trash who couldn't get a real boyfriend any more than she could get real parents." Everyone always knew Hoyt & Clair's kids were adopted since Clair was black and only like one of their kids was—the oldest one, as Molly recalled. Sometimes Molly wondered about Becky. People knew the Beckwith reputation when it came to...*all that.*

"They left you here because you're nothing but trash. They knew it, and you know it!" Becky had yelled in front of everyone and then grabbed Easton practically by his groin and kissed him. Lips and everything. "And now you're dead meat, too, Coast Trash." She'd laughed as she threw down a wrinkled copy of the Coast's fishwrap of a newspaper. Just from the picture, Molly knew.

They'd found another dead girl yesterday. Another redhead. The third in as many years.

Becky had walked away laughing, triumphant, with her attendant escort of Bayettes, the elite cheer squad and dance team.

"Dead meat! Dead meat!" they chanted at her as Molly stood there, glaring at them.

So, obviously, Molly egged Becky's letter jacket the next morning. The one she "earned" from volleyball even though she never played and only went out for the pictures in the yearbook and their "cute uniforms." Her daddy was Bobby de la Beckwith—yes, *that* Bobby de la Beckwith who owned Bobby's Benz, and had his stupid face plastered all over half the billboards on the interstate. Like anybody here had money for that junk. And yet he always seemed flush enough. Bobby wrote plenty of checks to the school, so Becky stayed on the team.

Besides everybody knew Becky cheated on Blake every time they had an away game. And before Blake, she'd dated Easton and cheated on him with Blake. She didn't even make any big secret of it. It's almost like she wanted to get caught, to be seen necking with any boy in school that was worth more than $1 and had an even halfway kissable face.

And then there was Easton. Easton Braddock.

Easton was just... But seriously. He had that kind of unkempt almost long hair that fell down *that* way in the morning. Every morning. Sandy locks just long enough to curl into a wave that begged to be surfed. He had a kind of boyish face, not like his buddy Nguyen who looked older, like he should be in college. There was also a hidden maturity behind his softness. He had a sad smile that told only half its tale. And his cheekbones were sharp, strong, cut by some god who really knew what she was doing. Scotch brown eyes.

Not that Molly drank. Well, maybe sometimes. When Hoyt and Clair would take off to Mobile or New Orleans for their weekends away. Which was most of them, though they never stayed in NOLA overnight. Maybe she might sneak a swig or two of Hoyt's single malt on those weekends. Not that it ever did much for her. She didn't see what the fuss was about.

But, anyway, Easton was hot. The kind of hot you could bake with. Like *All the Right Moves* Tom Cruise, but without the weird middle tooth, hot.

It was Easton, really, who'd caused the whole thing. That icy stare Becky had caught him shooting at Molly. But the real transgression of it had been that Becky had seen *Molly* catch Easton staring at her.

He had never seemed to notice her before. In fact, she'd been the one most often staring at him, the way he rolled onto campus each morning with those brown eyes barely open, bags already forming on his young face, like he'd been up all hours the night before, every night. His piercing gaze had always directed itself anywhere but Molly, like he was trained to see every tiny detail of everyday life *except* for her. So much so it was weird when he finally had looked at her. Not like he liked her, or even saw her as a person. The way he looked at her, she felt like a thing. Some object. Like a homework assignment he hadn't finished.

And there he was. Front and center at the first table when she walked in the library to take her spot and serve her sentence. Becky de la Beckwith with her perfect perky blonde hair and her perky always-tan despite the cold face, was there too. Right beside *her* Easton, like he remained her property somehow. They'd all gotten detention over the whole thing because that's the kind of unilateral peckerwood Vice-Principal Lebeque was. Say what you will about his heinous and total lack of chill, he was at least fair and equal in his distribution of punitive banality.

But Lebeque's mustache totally had to go. Like totally. Made him look like an aging, bald Burt Reynolds hanging out at the playground.

"Just don't even, you bitch!" Becky hissed through her teeth and gave Molly the grimmest side-eye her perfect, plied-on lashes could stab at her.

Lydia Stiles, Molly's best friend and bandmate—their band being only the two of them so far—sat in the back, slumped over with her head face down on the table. Poor Lydia got a slip just for having the bad luck of standing next to Molly when it all happened, which she said was fine, really, because she would just as well come hang out in detention since she didn't have anything better to do. And besides then they could at least hang out and talk.

"They don't really let us talk," Molly, a veteran of Saturday detention, had said then and again now. "It's supposed to be punishment."

"Well, yeah," Lydia said, "but we could work on our face code! We have all morning, and we—"

"No talking!" Lebeque barked.

Molly sighed and resigned herself to a long morning of suck.

Lydia was already half asleep, swatting at the imaginary flies in her head. The others stared, which Molly returned with a death glare. Lydia might be a bit of a spaz, but Molly would still fight anyone who said so. Bless the poor girl's heart, she had on way too much eyeshadow and was dressed like a widow who slept in her funeral outfit but also had an expense account at the Army/Navy shoe section. She could rip a bass, though. Like nobody's business. And, always with the hats. And the spiked bangs. Always.

There was one other kid there, too. A Freshman. Wyatt Morrison. Except everybody called him Watts. One of Molly's younger "brother" Hurl's best friends who all held their top-secret meetings in the backyard shed. A supergeek. A skeezoid. He got it way worse from all the proper people than she and Lydia ever had. Lydia at least had her pickup truck with the KC lights that she "inherited" from her brother while he was... well...working for the state for a few years. So that got her a few extra cool points from the peanut gallery. Watts, though, he was one of those A/V kids that jumped a couple grades after he built some weird machine in his garage and then left all his friends behind in junior high. Now he was dead meat in 9th grade with guys like Track Parkman and Ty Williams—seriously, what asshole parents gave their kids names like that? She almost felt sorry for the kid, despite him being such a horrific turbo-nerd, always going on about 'millennium calibrated' this and 'force-powered trandroids' that.

"We know for sure he has a flying car, but I heard it can go invisible, too," she'd overheard recently, walking by their secret meeting in their 'inner sanctum' where they played their stupid dice games with their worksheets.

"Who has a flying car?" she'd asked before she remembered not to care.

"No one," one of Hurl's underlings snapped back at her, and then slammed the shed door in her face.

So, yeah. Almost.

"So, what are you in for?" Molly asked Watts. His eyes shot wide-open and stared at her like she'd fired a gun. She looked back at him with that same question in her eyes, shrugging her shoulders.

"Huh?" he squeaked out.

"I mean the rest of us are all here for the usual B.S. because Lebeque has that stick up his butt and can't get a girlfriend." She saw Watts' eyes get even wider and fill with a kind of dread/empathy that of course meant Lebeque was behind her and had just heard the whole thing.

"Thank you very much, Miss Slater. I'll be seeing you again next Saturday. Now sit down!"

"Great!" She grinned her meanest grin as she slumped down on the cold plastic chair at the back.

"Watch it, Slater! Or we can go for three!" Lebeque flexed his neck almost like he wanted to show off his black-collared shirt underneath his gray blazer. Dude was dressed for singles night at the Marriott lounge trying to put in the work on some not-yet-divorced, bake-sale-mom half down a gin martini. *As if.* None of it was going to make up for that tragedy of a slick bald head. All Mr. Clean in a disco jacket. Barf.

"Why not four?" she barked back. She just wasn't having it today. Dude had major damage.

"You got it!"

"Good!"

"Cut out it!" Becky yelled.

"What do you care?" Molly gave her the stink eye. Like it was anything but a boon to Miss Perfect for Molly to be sequestered away in detention, away from the world and Becky's harem of boyfriends past and present.

"That's enough out of you, too, Princess! I don't want to hear another peep out of this room. In fact, I want every one of you to write a two-page essay on what landed you here. I got you all til noon."

He walked back out toward his office, shooting a glance back at Molly just before he got out the door. She met it with a wink and a kissyface.

He shivered and bolted.

"You got major balls." Easton got an elbow to his own balls, or near enough, for that crack. Deviation from total worship of her Beckness would not be tolerated.

"Yeah what was that about?" Watts asked.

Lydia just chuckled, long the wiser on all matters of Molly.

"He's the one losing his Saturdays," Molly said. "I don't have squat going on, anyway. Besides, I get to read all morning. We are in the library, after all."

"Ew," Becky groaned.

Molly could tell her answer had pleased the nerd. More importantly, it appeared to have intrigued Easton; she could tell by the way he was totally staring in that not staring way that all boys tried to get away with but never did. Like never.

*

The hours stretched out like cold pine sap never all the way dropping, just freezing in place eventually—calcifying into that sticky gross crust. Every minute ached on with Becky all secret flirting with Easton up front just to shove it in Molly's face that she could get him back any time she wanted. And probably could.

Watts read three books at once. Like for real three. A science textbook because of course he was, a book on vampires and werewolves in America—if only—and one of those stupid dragon game manuals he and Molly's brother always carried around with them. Busy doing his worksheets for it, too. Rolling his 40-sided dice or whatever under the table.

"Doesn't count if you roll it into your hand," Molly whispered at him.

He grimaced and turned away from her. He side-eyed her, blushing red as a coke can. Busted. Totally had a crush. Totally. She giggled at the thought.

Lydia dozed, occasionally slapping the strings on her ghost bass. She wore her side-zip half-knee combat boots today along with her black skirt with the safety pins all up one side. Not to be confused with her other black skirt with chain link all up one side. That and her biker jacket. Spiked her bangs into blades today, too. Those looked rad.

"I think tonight I'm gonna do it!" she said. "I really am." Lydia was always threatening to run away to New Orleans and get a job selling shots at a metal club. Said her parents would freak out and send twenty rednecks and a battalion of pickups after her, though. Lydia's dad and brothers could be overwhelming, but Molly always found it charming how close they all were. Only Lydia stuck out and had to dress like it was Halloween every day just to be noticed amid the sea of six foot broad-chested men who always wanted to have a pickup football game or a surprise wrestling match. Sweet god, that family loved their wrestling. "You're so lucky. You don't have to deal with this stuff!" she added.

"Yeah. Lucky, that's what I am." Molly sighed.

"That's not...I mean...you know what I mean. It's just—"

"Yeah, I get it. Don't worry about it. And don't run away, either. I gotta get a ride out to Bebop to get some records. We can cruise the beach for tur-bros and get them to buy us lunch. Don't wear black."

"There's no one at the beach. It's cold," Lydia said. "And I'm definitely wearing black."

"The mall then. And there has to be at least one primary color in your outfit!"

"Red."

Of course.

*

Detention ticked by. Molly caught Becky pretending to read a book about Étienne LeCroiseur, a local legend and the lead singer of Darksiders who died right after their only album came out. As if Becky even knew what good music was. She probably heard Molly and Lydia talking about them in the halls—which they did a lot—and was just making fun of her. Mostly she shot dirty looks at Molly if she caught her trying to scope Easton. Molly tired of it and joined Lydia who'd wandered into the stacks of the library, to the "Witches and Cults" section, which Lydia always complained was woefully understocked. She said they refused to get anything that went against "their dumb Christian B.S." anyway. Lydia wasn't shy with her opinions on church. She skimmed a book about the witch trials way back when and kept showing the drawings of the ones they hung, as if Molly needed that in her head. It had plenty of torture already.

Molly found one book she thought sounded interesting called *The Sleeping God*. It had weird symbols on the front and was old—like falling apart old. She lost focus on it, though, as she caught Easton checking her out three times for sure and then at least one other time, maybe. Probably. She wished he'd make good on it and ask her out or something, not just sneak the free looks. But there was something almost unnerving about the way he looked at her. She couldn't put her finger on it. Not exactly checking her out, but something...*else.*

Noon approached. Watts completed a stack of his dragons worksheets. Becky had conspicuously dozed off on Easton's shoulder. *Barf.* Lydia was scribbling down ideas for spells she could try at home. Molly wished *she* was the sleeping god.

No one did their essay.

II
"COLD HEARTED SNAKE"
—PAULA ABDUL, 1988

OUTSIDE, EASTON'S FRIEND Nguyen met him in the Z28 convertible they always rode around in. Easton took the wheel, as usual. The car was cherry, which wasn't why Molly liked him, but it didn't hurt things one bit. That thing could scream.

Speaking of engine noise...she heard Lydia's Silverado dually 3500 fire to life just as Watts climbed into his mom's Pinto. Kid ducked for cover when he heard that gunshot exhaust.

Lydia reared her brother's dinosaur-sized pickup truck around the front of the school. Black with blue stripes and a galloping razorback hog painted on the scooped hood because her brother was a maniac and spent all his drug money on the big stupid beast. "It's mine to keep running until he gets out," she had said.

"When's that?" Molly had asked.

"1992."

So, it would be awhile. Lydia could not look less at home behind the wheel of the greatest hick-mobile of all time, but it gave them a ride to the mall or downtown anytime they needed to go. Wheels were wheels.

Becky de la Beckwith was in the girl's restroom in the library still. Probably making sure her makeup was super extra perfect for her super extra perfect boyfriend who was waiting for her, leaned all cool against his Porsche. Perfect was about right. Blake looked sorta like Easton, except in some plastic way. Like some dollmaker had looked at Easton and then made a mannequin of him but with straighter hair and sharper lines.

"Good afternoon, ladies," he said in a voice like whisky in a milkshake and tipped the white fedora he wore every day. His cool guy shades slid just right down his nose. Always too perfect. Like he worked off a script or something.

Everything about the dude was like that. Always trying too hard to be cool but just wasn't quite there. He'd scoped on Molly when he first transferred in this fall. She didn't know what that was about, but it had put Easton on the market when Becky dumped him for the "upgrade."

And money. Obviously from the Porsche, yeah. But the kid had dollars. His dad had bought the old bottling plant downtown and did...something or other down there, Molly wasn't sure. Sometimes she just wanted to shake him and be like, "Dude, just ease up one inch and you'll be solid." But she never did.

"You know there's a little get-together at my place later. Maybe you and," he motioned at Lydia, who was making mouth movements to what was surely going to be The Cure when she got in the cab, "your little friend here might swing by. No big."

Molly leered at him. "Yeah. Pass, Blake."

Blake Elvis. Maybe that's what made her skin crawl about him. The actual worst dude name of all bad dude names. *Ew.*

"You don't have to be such a b-word," Blake dangled his cigarette out of his mouth and turned away like he was smooth.

"Which one? Broccoli?" Molly smirked. "Beltway? Betelgeuse? Barnacle?"

"You know which word I meant," Blake snapped back at her. "Don't say words at me! I know every word!" He was out of breath.

"What's your malfunction, man?" Molly raised an eyebrow. Dude was fritzing like a madman's switchboard. Like total psycho.

Lydia jammed out in the cab of her truck watching the whole thing as Molly was being accosted by *Le Garçon Riche.* De la Beckwith finally emerged from her metamorphosis into the runway pageant queen she made sure everyone knew she was.

"Um. Why are you even near my property, trailer park?" Becky said.

"She doesn't live in a trailer park," Lydia shouted from the truck. Molly always appreciated the support, but, man, she really needed to work on her comebacks.

"God. Go to your drag race or whatever you skeeves do. Don't infect my weekend anymore, you total loss!" Becky climbed into Blake's Porsche and daintily but firmly slammed her door. "Dead meat!" she called out, just to drive home the point that started the whole debacle.

Blake put his head back together, smirked at his supermodel girlboss—er girlfriend—and passed one last look—almost kind but also not really—back at Molly before he jumped in his Porsche and legged it.

III
"MAN IN MOTION"
—JOHN PARR, 1984

MOLLY SCOPED HER CASCIO and cursed. She put the banana board to work behind Lydia's dually, then swerved up 25th at Downtown. She had to kick it, or she'd be late again for her shift at Tracey's Treasure Box. One more and she was technically "under review." Not that Tracey would, but still.

Molly liked Tracey Melnitz—one of the few grownups in the whole town she liked. Tracey was the exact right kind of funky-weird. She'd also put Molly to work at 14, letting her sweep and mop the place after hours, and do other odds and ends. She paid her a little, even back then, but had always given her a blank check expense account on anything she wanted in the store. For a foster kid that bounced from one trailer to the next all through elementary and half of junior high, that was like some kind of heaven.

And Tracey made use of it herself in spades. Every day she was a different person. One day she was 70's chic disco-tacular. The next she was headed for a cocaine-powered vampire ball in the B'Easy.

Today Tracey wore a white body hugger with slits along one side and a neon pink garden hat with visor shades. She was fully prepared for battle. She was also holding a bottle...of hair dye.

"How do you feel about blonde?" Tracey shook the bottle as Molly walked through the door.

"I think your hair looks great as is," Molly assured her.

"Not me. Of course mine is perfect, you dolt!" she sneered. "This is for you, ginger! I won't have your grisly murder on my conscience. And besides I hate closing." That part was true enough. Tracey liked to make happy hour at her favorite bar, St. Elmo's, just up from the shop. She also liked to tease and flirt with the bouncer, Dice. Molly was pretty sure they had a thing. Or once did.

"Do not even come near me with that!" Molly held her index finger up like a stop sign. People kept blowing this whole dead girl thing way out of proportion. Like, yeah, okay. There was the one girl from Central last year they'd found. And now this one in Bogalusa. But that was from like...seven or eight years ago they were saying. The hair was a fluke. People just liked to drum up drama. As if there wasn't already enough with the old New Orleans gangs creeping around the burbs these days. Whatever that was about.

"Fine. Your funeral, kiddo." She put the bottle away, but Molly eyed it, making a note to destroy it later. Last thing she ever wanted in life was to have anything in common with Becky de la Beckwith.

Tracey kept a little TV behind the counter to distract themselves with on slow nights, which tonight was becoming. The news had some image of Maggie Thatcher shaking her fist at Gorbachev. She'd become a much bigger deal since her boyfriend stateside got ousted by the handlebar-mustachioed longshot.

"What do you think about the old Iron Lady?" Tracey squinted at the beehive hairdo. The image cut to a missile test. Everyone was so ready to blow the world to hell.

"I mostly don't," Molly said.

"Yeah, me neither. Tell me something..." Tracey switched the set off. "Why are all men such children? Just little boys in great big bodies. Nice bodies, mind you, but still. Especially George."

Tracey pulled down her glasses to peek at Molly sternly.

"Oh, god. George. He was..." She stared off at the clearance racks that still needed organizing. "Well, I need a Gatorade. You want one?"

"No thanks," Molly said.

"How was the state pen?"

"Huh? Oh, detention. Yeah. I go back next week."

Molly slumped behind the counter. Pretty much all of life was a pill.

"You gotta stop bucking the bulls. Start clipping them into steers!"

Molly stared right at the walking pastel neon Cosmo ad. "I don't know what that means."

"I don't either," Tracey said. "Something my old grandmother used to say. She had cows. I think. Also, she was a pilot in the war."

"Which war was that?"

"I don't know. One of the airplane ones."

Tracey sashayed toward the break room, pausing at the *National Geographics* and grabbing one to read with her Gatorade.

*

Lydia stopped by just before Molly went on break.

"Got you this," she handed her a bottle-shaped brown bag. "You know. For your birthday or whatever you call it."

"My 'Found-On' day, yeah." Molly inspected the bag. "How'd you score this?"

Lydia laughed. "I rubbed my eyes red and made my voice go full demonic bass, and Zits at the counter was too scared to say no!"

"Really??"

"No, it's the last of my brother's secret stash." She shrugged. "But that'd be a cool story if it happened, huh?"

"Yeah. If." Molly stashed the liquor. "Still, this is boss. You're a proper friend. We gonna drink it at practice tonight?" She liked drinking with Lydia because they had fun, but Molly never seemed to feel drunk. Lydia might be stumbling, but Molly could walk a razor line.

"Why wait?" Lydia cocked an eye. The lazy one.

There were no quick shots on the sly, though, as time totally went bonkers when the doorway jingled and in wafted Easton Braddock wearing what had to be the raddest brown leather blazer rolled all the way up past his elbows. Like holy god. His hair danced in the frozen time, waving at her like breakers cresting off the sound. Robert Palmer went nitro in her head. Or was it the loudspeaker? Somewhere there was Palmer. Definitely Palmer. So rad.

So hot.

So—

"So, you work here?"

"So I what where who?" Molly vomited out all over herself. *Holy shhhhh.* "Huh?"

Easton smiled directly at her, the grin like a shotgun blast, the dastard. *Dastard? What? No.*

"Yes, she does," Lydia said, finally, to cut the air. "But she's off at 4!"

Lydia! Molly telepathed to her as angrily as she could. Lydia read it loud and clear and mowed right through it anyway.

"So, what can she help you find today? Some retro fat ties? Big collar paisley shirts?"

Lydia, I will murder your face and all your future children and burn your house down.

"New hat?" Lydia continued.

Lydia, I will summon the powers of seven realms and hurl you into an endless frozen void! And I will—

"Got any records?" he asked.

"Yep, In the back. By the books and magazines. You can't miss 'em. I'll be right here when you're ready. K. Good luck!"

Easton looked askance at her and then wandered toward where Molly's finger was still involuntarily pointing.

A long moment of terror entered Molly's unblinking face.

"What are you doing? You absolute biffed that. He's turbo into you!"

"The sick dog he is, my sweating butt!"

"Oh, he totally scoped your butt," Lydia chuckled.

"I'm will murder y—"

"Found an Ozzy," Easton shot into the conversation out of nowhere and Molly felt her body turning to stone from the ground up.

"Um...Ozzy. You like Ozzy?" Molly said. "I mean he can throw down. Have you heard Saxon? Or 'Phantom of the Opera' by Maiden? Or Lita? She can really tear it in half! Or old school with Zep. Nah, they're tired. Mercury! You like Rhapsody? Of course you do. Who doesn't? Right? Am I still talking?"

Easton chuckled.

He. Chuckled.

He was laughing! At her? With her?

This was all too much. Too heavy. *Is it hot in here? No?*

"Anyway, um, yeah! Those are all $1. Cash?"

Lydia grinned as he fished a buck out of his jacket. The cool brown jacket.

"She always like this?" he asked Lydia.

"Oh, her? No. Not at all. Usually she's way more spaz." Lydia face-coded Molly a full-on belly laugh.

Molly stared bolts of white-hot lightning into Lydia's soul.

"Anyway." Easton tucked the record under his arm. "I'm in this area a lot, too."

"Yeah," Lydia cut in, "I've seen you and your buddy what's-his-name coming out of that creepy old church on Sarter. What's that about?"

Oh my god, Lydia, if you don't just stop, I will summon wolf-riders to tear your bones apart!

"Oh, uh, yeah... that place." He stared off for a second, then focused back on her—mostly her hair. "We've been doing some renovations and stuff there. Us and some guys. But, anyway, I mean..." He sweated bullets.

Molly suddenly felt some weird tingle. Almost like she felt what he felt. But that didn't make sense.

"Yeah, we should hang out," he mustered the courage to say. "You seem cool. And you're funny. Maybe later tonight? Can I call you?"

Molly stared into the empty cavern of her own soul. It was as blank as her memories. He was an endless chasm that she'd never cross. She had fallen entirely out of reality. There was nothing. No one. Just the endless expanse. And that forever echo. Resonating. *Molly... Molly....*

"Molly!" Lydia shouted. "Write your number on his receipt. Jesus. Yes, Easton, She will hang out. She's free all night tonight. After 7 good?"

"Yeah, that's—" He chuckled.

His teeth — oh god his teeth, and the way his tongue flickered against them when he made sounds with his face mouth. *What? Number.* Molly wrote her number down. God mother all-mighty what was even real?

"Tonight? 7. I'll call you?" He smiled and walked out as quick as he'd come in. Poof.

Gone.

"Was that...?" Molly started.

"Yep."

"And did he...?"

"Yep."

"And we...?"

"7 o'clock!"

Molly stared away at nothing. Except it wasn't nothing. It was a purple cowboy hat with feathers dangling from the back and a fur, ankle-length coat flowing around the only human in three coast counties brave enough to wear it.

"Well?" Tracey asked.

Lydia told her everything and Tracey smiled wide as a stretched limo.

"Outfit!" they all said in unison.

*

What followed lived somewhere in the distance between a dream and the reality Molly knew. First of all, there was Madonna. Had to be. No other would do. Then began the frenzy of skirts. Pants. Skorts. Jorts. Ew, no. Sashes Scarves. Capes. Capes? Jeez, Tracey had literally everything. Hats. Caps. Gowns. No way. Heels? Sneaks? Boots? Boots. Most def. Colors. All of them. Azure. Crimson. Black leather! Chain mail? Why? Earrings. So many! Every length and shape. And her hair! It had to be perfect. It was too long. She'd meant to cut it. Should she cut it? There was no time. Tracey could mousse it into anything.

The person who left the store that afternoon was no one Molly could recognize in the mirror. Calf-length fake leather high-heel boots, an azure diagonal-cut dress with one sleeve and the other cut at the shoulder, one thick braid on the bare-arm side, and wicked come-get-some eye shadow. Who? Exactly.

Molly was more excited than she'd ever been since...since she could remember. So, of course, her foster mom told her she had to babysit as soon as she walked in the door at home.

IV
"HUNGRY HEART"
—BRUCE SPRINGSTEEN, 1980

"WHAT DO YOU MEAN BABYSIT??" Lydia yelled into the receiver.

Molly, deflated and back in her denim, winced at the sound squawking out of her handset. She wrapped the cord around her fingers and sank to the floor, along with any hope she had for the evening.

Hurl unfolded his massive game board, the one where they pretended to be knights and fought dragons or whatever, on the dining room table. His buddies were coming to play. She had the fabulous honor of supervising them, despite the fact that Watts was one of the group and he was only two grades under her. Yeah, sure, he was technically *their* age, but whatever. What good is skipping grades if you get stuck with a babysitter from your own math class? Or worse, detention.

Clair, her latest and, to be fair, best foster mom, unloaded a bunch of bags from their hideous monstrosity of a Truckster station wagon. Sweet wings of a banshee, it was ugly.

"I'm sorry. But I can't watch Howie tonight. We've got the engagement dinner and then a ton of work to get the bridal shower ready for tomorrow at the Ladies' Auxiliary. Your sister is counting on me and your dad," Clair droned on while walking around like a lost dog, glancing at every spot all over the house.

'Sister.' Just like Howie, aka Hurl, was her 'brother,' None of them blood-related. Clair and Hoyt couldn't have kids, so they made up for it by adopting every lost cause Our Lady had to offer. Molly barely even knew the sister getting married next month. *Cindy? Sally?* She'd met her maybe once.

"You know this was the only weekend we can get everyone together."

Right. This weekend. Only one. Not like anything else mattered this weekend. Like today. No big. Nothing else special about today. Whatever. It didn't matter. Just like *she* didn't matter to whoever dumped her by the side of the road.

"Let's see, where did I put my..." She went on.

"Yeah? Anything else you're forgetting about today, *Mom?*" Molly asked.

"Huh? Today? No, I got the cards. And your aunt Jackie doesn't even get in for another two hours! Oh, god, the airport? Jeez!"

Clair flipped out, grabbed the keys to their convertible, and ran to the door.

"I gotta go, left some money for pizza and the keys to the Truckster in case. Love you all. Bye!"

Clair was out the door right as Mike the Mic burst in, announcing his presence with the police radio his dad got him that he went nowhere without. Dear god, what a power-nerd.

This was the actual worst day.

"Molly! Molly!!" the phone was shouting from her limp hand. Lydia. Right.

"Yeah?" she said.

"So like...any hope?"

"Nilch."

"Bites."

"Like seriously."

"Well, look," Lydia started.

Here it comes, Molly thought.

"Like, I might go check out that party anyway."

"Yeah okay whatever," Molly looked at Mike the Mic jiggling Hurl's belly rolls into his radio to see if he could amplify the sound. "Keep me posted, K. I gotta go. I'm gonna hurl looking at Hurl's weird friends."

*

The dice games rolled through the hours as the nerdgang waxed philosophical about whether vampires and dark elves were the same thing. And whether either of them could beat werewolves or vice versa, or even whether vampires WERE werewolves, and whether some super guy named Copper Top or something stupid could defeat them and on and on and Molly was getting wrecked on it.

She eventually went to the garage to snag her Fender and some headphones and zonk out for the duration of the Geekcon. Tonight was baked. She pling-ed out some Henley — not too shabby if she said so herself — and she worked that into some Eddie V, then tried her hand at Alice Cooper. Somewhere in the midst she zoned all the way out.

*

"I'm telling you, man!" Mike the Mic whispered for once. He held up a short stack of comics to the gang. Hurl shook his head in denial. Watts reviewed the evidence, glancing back and forth from the comics to the sleeping Molly.

"It's difficult to determine. I mean, this one is just a drawing."

"You guys are dweebs, man!" Mike folded out a two-page splash of Red Sonja, skull in one hand, bleeding axe in the other. "I'm telling you she's spot on. Like she came right off the page. I've always said so."

"No," Hurl insisted. "Dude, she's basically my sister. She's a complete punk and as basic as it gets. No way."

"Screw you guys!" Mike said. "Hey, where's her underwear drawer?"

V

"TAKE ON ME"
—A-HA. 1985

A VOLCANO ERUPTED. A rocket of magma shot into the blackened sky. Smoldering cinders rained to the ground. There was a snake. A big one. It wound its way here and there as it came for her.

She felt it wrap around her and begin to squeeze. She wanted to scream, to cry out for someone, *one* she knew. But she couldn't name them. Couldn't see their face. Like it was held from her. Blocked. Walled off behind some secret door.

But there was a face. Some smirking goblin or creature, one of Hurl's "dark elves." It laughed at her. Groped at her. Reached its gnarled fingers toward her, its sharp, angular, veiny features sickening her. Then she got angry. She needed to fight. She had to fight. She wanted to fight. It was all she wanted, like it was a part of her. She reached for something that wasn't there. She couldn't feel it. Couldn't name it. It did not come. Why was it not coming?

"Molly!"

Was that its name? What was her name? Her true name?

"Molly?!"

She had to know. She had to remember. Why couldn't she remember anything from before? Where was she? This wasn't her home.

"MOLLY! Wake up!" Hurl shouted at her.

Molly snapped to. She'd nodded off somewhere halfway into some Clash. Watts held the phone, and Mike the Mic talked into his receiver.

"EARTH TO MOLLY. OVER. EARTH TO MOLLY. OVER. IT'S YOUR LOSER GOTH FRIEND. OVER. DO YOU COPY? OVER."

"I swear to god, Mike, I will take that radio and launch it into space, you damn nerd!"

"Whoa, language!" Hurl neenered. "I'm telling Mom!"

"To reach space, it would have to leave earth's atmosphere. The escape velocity from Earth is about 11.186 km/s. To reach that, you'd have to throw the radio with a force of at least—"

"Thank you, Watts. It was a figure of speech, oh my god!" How did she get here? Why was she here? She was going mad. "Just hand me the phone!"

*

Because *of course* Lydia had a major emergency. She always did. Because of course she had gone to the party with some boy. Some boy she didn't know. And *of course* she rode there with him. Which you never do. N E V E R. And of course it got weird. And now she was stuck. Trapped. With the weirdness. At the party. Blake's party. Blake the plastic face. Of course.

"Okay, here's the deal, nerds..."

*

They packed in and buckled up. The Truckster rolled out in all its wood panel glory, Watts jittery riding shotgun. She bribed Hurl with two of his chores the next week to not tell Clair. Mike the Mic packed a sack lunch for some damn reason. Shoved it down his backpack with his random other tools and half-broken gadgets, wires, and...a Cascio keyboard?

It was over thirty minutes to Blake's beach house, over the Bay Bridge and all the way down Highway 90. How did he even go to Bay High? Clair had ever so kindly left the tank on E so Molly swung the hatchback travesty into Bix's U-Fil-It on the other side of the bridge. Molly had a pair of wrinkled ones in her pocket and there was another sixty cents in the console. Hurl came loose off a quarter. That would just get them there and back. Hopefully.

"I thought Mom left some money," Hurl whined.

"Yeah well I forgot it. Don't be a waste."

Inside was quiet. Like weird quiet. No customers. Not even a clerk. Molly had half a mind to just bail.

"Yo!"

She wandered through the aisles, the temptation to snag some Funyuns and duck out rising in her. She gazed around, feeling like it was some weird test. Like the clerk would jump out and grab her if she did.

She walked toward the bathroom, glancing down each aisle, and heard something coming from the back office. Muffled voices. The door was cracked so she peeked in. Some waste with a terrible blonde rat tail mohawk was pointing a pistol at the bawling clerk. Another dude in a ridiculous red bucket hat was two-fisting a sawed-off shotgun. Both wore frazzled red jackets. This was bogus max. She'd heard about these guys. *Les Mutants Rouges.* Mutes. A gang out of New Orleans that crept this way the last few years.

"I said open, shitlick!" the Hawk said. The clerk kept crying.

"I can't! I'm telling you, I can't."

"Forget it, Biff. Let's just take the register and go!" Bucket Hat said.

Rat Hawk pulled back his hammer and slammed two in the clerk's chest.

"Jesus Christ, Biff!! What the hell?"

Time stopped. The image frozen in a single moment as Molly swore she saw the clerk's ghost jump from his body. She gasped. They both turned in her direction.

"Grab her!"

She didn't leave that option on the table.

Molly vaulted across the stocked shelves like an Olympic hurdler and shot out the door, glass bursting everywhere from the force. She hadn't slammed it that hard, had she? She ran at the Truckster, jumped the hood to the cockpit, and half slipped/half slid all the way across. Molly whipped into the seat and hit the gas.

"Holy Nikes! Was that a gun?" Hurl asked.

"Yeah? Was that a gunshot?" Mike the Mic said into his mic.

Molly reached back and yanked the wire out of its socket.

"I swear to the gods, Mike. Get down. Everybody get down!"

Molly's eyes peered into the rearview for headlights, barreling down the highway toward town. She saw the snake eyes dot in the distance behind her. Closing.

She hit the floor with it.

"Let's see if you bastards can do 90!"

"The Truckster can't do 90," Watts informed her. "It has a governor from the factory set at 70. They do it to save on gas."

"Thank you, Professor."

Molly held it to the metal all the same. The Truckster cooked along the blacktop the best it could go. *Nope. Don't lose it, Molly.* The drizzle from the day turned to a downfall. Lightning flashed. A crack somewhere not far off. That didn't help things. She heard the low rumblings in the distant sky. Maybe the storm could help her ditch the bangers before they got to Blake's.

Holy crap, the party! Lydia! What the hell was she going to tell her? What was she going to tell the geeks in the back seat? Clair & Hoyt?

This was heavy duty.

VI
"*OBSESSION*"
—ANIMOTION, 1984

THERE WAS NO MISTAKING Blake's house. Well, his dad's house. A wraparound, pillared behemoth up on stilts right off the sand on 90. Of all the bigshots at her school, it was Blake who was truly loaded.

From everything she'd seen of him since he showed up, he had more dough than the De la Beckwiths ten times over. So, of course they bought the biggest beach house they could find on the whole Coast. Even bigger than that Civil War loser's. They should burn that stupid place down for real, though. Screw that guy.

Cars were everywhere. Vettes, BMW's, and one very distinct Z28 convertible— the who's who of at least three high schools. Driving up and down the street, Molly begged the clouds for a spot hidden away. Somewhere they couldn't be seen. She couldn't tell if Rat-hawk and Bucket-hat had lost her or just held back, waiting for the right moment.

God, this was all too tense! What the actual? Like a full-blown murder. Should I call the cops?

She should call the cops.

* * *

Blake watched Molly and her unfortunate entourage walk through his door from the foyer balcony, a pleasant if unexpected turn of events. He had hoped for so long she would warm to him. Perhaps his tact had been working better than he thought. Easier to get a girl when you already have a girl, he'd heard.

He'd begun to think playing the heel was the wrong move. Some dullard he spoke with occasionally — Ty, Todd, something like that — had advised him as such. But he preferred flattery to rudeness. He decided tonight was the time to clench it.

He made his way down the rounded staircase into the foyer. The place was packed, music wafting softly in the background, and he held a martini glass lightly in his hand as he motioned some other kid aside. Becky was nowhere in sight, which was convenient. He didn't need her making a scene just as he made his maneuver. He would settle their arrangement later.

Blake shuffled toward Molly and the middle-schoolers, one hand shoved into his red & black smoking jacket. His perfect blonde ruffles danced in the breeze from the doorway. Lightning flashed in the background, illuminating the lines in his face and making him wince from the strobing effect. He didn't care for the weather tonight. In fact, it was the last thing he wanted to see.

"What surprise is this?" He extended his hand from his pocket, the other raising his glass before returning it to his lips.

"Hey, look, I know this is weird, but I just need to use your phone if I can," Molly blurted out. "Also, I need Lydia. I'm her ride."

"Indeed." Another flash from outside. Blake closed his front door. "What interesting weather you've brought with you. Shouldn't dampen our spirits too terribly, I hope."

The weather? Seriously? He was going with weather? Just what was this guy's deal? Molly twisted her head to reckon.

"Yeah. Stormy and gross. But, like, where's Lydia?"

"Yes," Blake began, "your, uh, compatriot. Indeed."

And why did he keep saying *Indeed?*

"Shall we begin our search together? I can show you around. It will be, doubly, a pleasure."

"What happened to me being the B-word?" Molly gave him the side-eye.

"Do accept my apologies. You see, with a certain someone nearby, I had to make, shall we say, appearances. But, I've been thinking of making some...changes."

Watts, Hurl, and Mike the Mic stood awkwardly by the door. Not only was this their first glimpse at a real deal high school party, but any party, replete with booze, almost certainly drugs, and probably even...*sex.*

Mike the Mic took the lead and led them right up to a table with an impressive pyramid of Budweiser cans, stacked nearly to the ceiling. He propped against the table to relax and survey the scene. Watts and Hurl nervously leaned back and tipped the table, sending the whole pyramid crashing down on top of three super-jocks from the weightlifting team.

"Oh, perfect, guys! Real good," Mike the Mic blurted out. "Way to go. I just...I can't even. Jeez." He walked off like a shot and eyed them to follow suit. They weren't eager to stick around, so they scarpered.

Easton Braddock caught the commotion from the beer can crash and saw the lite brigade bugger toward the kitchen. He grimaced, finding them odd. Kids at this party didn't please him either, though. The girl he'd just been chatting with, a redhead, took her exit. He scoped the area, snagged a glimpse of Blake leading Molly and her glowing red hair up the stairs. What was she doing here? She'd bailed on their date earlier. Now she was here? And with Blake, the very guy he was here to...?

Something was off. This couldn't be coincidence. He glanced to his buddy Nguyen who just returned it with a knowing nod.

Easton made his way toward the stairs, but was captured by Becky de la Beckwith, hammered as usual. She grabbed onto him around his shirt collar and pulled his face toward hers, way too close for his comfort.

"We need to talk," she slurred.

"Look, I don't—" he began, as she fidgeted with his shirt and reached inside his jacket to wrap her arm around him. "I just can't with you right now, okay?"

Easton did the best he could to detach himself from her clutches and follow Molly and Blake upstairs. He needed to know what was going on. If it was what he thought, it would ruin everything. Becky still had a grip on his belt, though, and wound up being dragged along with him. He passed by one of the keg stations and overheard one of the middle-schoolers bragging about underwear as he swallowed the last of his drink. He should probably shut that down, but Molly was the priority.

"Where we going? Upstairs?" Becky stumbled along behind him. He really didn't need her as baggage but maybe she could be the distraction he'd need to get Molly away from Blake and salvage the original plan. Becky *was* Blake's "girlfriend" after all — at least as much as she'd been Easton's or anyone's for that matter.

Next year he'd be free from this whole nightmare. At least he'd better. If he finished this job, he'd have respect. No more...*kid stuff.*

Upstairs, Blake took his sweet time pointing at boring paintings on the walls and talking about what dead boring artist painted all of them, as if Molly could ever care a single fluid ounce. She tried to press him on the urgency of her situation, but left out the whole murder bit. She didn't trust Blake for squat. Plus, she wasn't sure yet how to put it into words.

What was she going to tell the police? Would they even do anything? Had it really even happened? Maybe she imagined it. Maybe.... Maybe not.

"Yeah. Um...phone?" Molly insisted.

"Right this way." Blake motioned into one of the doorways and escorted her into a large, open bedroom. It had to be the master. There was a giant TV at one end, at least 40 inches, a full record player and stereo with a tape deck, and a bathroom on the opposite wall, bigger than her bedroom from the looks of it. There was yet another open bar in one corner. And, of course, the bed. A four-poster king or maybe even bigger.

"Is this your parents' room?" she asked. This was getting weirder and weirder.

"Do you see any parents?" He smirked and walked toward the bar, motioning her toward the old timey telephone on the stand by the bed. He started pouring more drinks as she raced to the phone, picked up the receiver, and started cranking the rotary dial over and over...

Nothing.

"It's dead."

"Probably this storm." He shrugged as though there weren't crazed killers about to murder her face any second now. "Should be working again soon." He sat next to her on the bed and offered...whatever he had just mixed up.

She definitely didn't need to drink tonight, given, well, everything. She could sure go for one, though. Like a whole bottle. Not that it would even give her a buzz.

She accepted the glass from Blake as he clinked his against it.

"Bottoms up." He took his down like a champ. He was so content with everything. So confident. So in control. Which wasn't the worst thing.

The door they'd left ajar creaked. There stood Easton Braddock. Molly's heart sank. Of all the last things she needed tonight, him seeing what this *totally looked like* was the absolute top of the list. Her heart slammed into her feet and she wanted nothing more than to vanish.

Then Becky rolled in like a bulldozer.

"This! This!" she was screaming. "Is this some kind of nightmare?! I'm having a nightmare. Trailer Park? Really? REEAALLY??? Blake?" She stomped toward them, twice almost tripping herself. She was way drunk, Molly noted. Becky went in for a full arm slap, and Molly dodged under it like she was programmed to do that. *Weird.* The slap arm kept going and Blake caught it just before it made contact with his own face, which it was just as likely meant for.

Molly booked for the door.

"Wait!" Blake shouted after her. Becky picked up the drink meant for Molly and tossed it in his face. It dripped off him, but he held himself steady, not losing control. Ever. Becky flailed her arms at him.

Seeing her chance, Molly zipped into the hallway, passing awkwardly by Easton.

"Thought you couldn't make it out tonight." His voice a knife.

"Look, I didn't lie to you, I swear," she said. "I'm in a lot of trouble right now. I'm babysitting those geeks downstairs, the ones that never should have set foot in here, but you try telling them that. I came to get Lydia before she gets herself in any worse trouble or I wouldn't have come. And, oh my god, could tonight get any worse? Look I like you. A lot. And I am still saying things out loud, aren't I?"

Easton relaxed and smirked. "You know what? I believe you."

"You do?" she asked.

"Yes. I don't know why...but yeah. Now let's find your friend and get you sorted out."

They checked the next four rooms on the hallway. *How many freaking rooms does this place have? Richies.* Who even needed something like this? For real. Finally, they walked into what looked like *another* master bedroom, complete with its own full bath again. There was some college-age dude sitting on the bed looking frustrated. Molly heard retching coming from the bathroom and ran to see.

"Look, she had a few too many I guess. Just started to barf, I swear."

"Yeah." Easton gave him the stink eye. "You're just up here, alone, seeing to her health, are you?"

"Look, what are you a cop?" the guy bowed up at Easton.

"Do I look like a cop?" Easton matched posture.

The guy smirked. "No, you're way too pretty to be a cop."

Molly returned from the bathroom practically dragging Lydia with an arm around her shoulders, all the worse for wear.

"Hey, look, we came here together," the dude started again. "I can drive her home."

Easton reared to deck the guy, but Molly was faster. She half threw Lydia into Easton's arms and went right for the dickhead's throat, pinning him all the way up against the wall off his feet. She stiff-armed him like he was made of paper and gripped him tighter.

"You don't ever come near her again, do you understand me?" Molly growled. Her eyes burned into his. Right into his soul. The guy wore black pants, but she could smell it. She could smell his piss. *So gross. What a wuss. Really?*

Molly dropped him to the ground, grabbed Lydia, and made for the door.

"Oh, hey, Mol, you made it?" Lydia muttered. "Can we go to Popeye's? They open still? I want some hot fries."

"Yeah, sure," Molly said, "we'll grab some hot fries. Let's just get you out of here."

Easton followed her into the hallway, clearing them a path to the stairs. Blake met them but didn't try to stop them.

"Look, let me help you get her down," Blake offered. "This was all just — "

"Not our best night, no," Molly offered. "Another time," she said, this time right into Easton's eyes.

She made her way down to the kitchen where the idiots were playing quarters for drinks. At least Hurl and Mike the Mic were. Watts, the king geek, stood like a dufe holding a Gatorade. Actually, that was handy. Molly snatched it from his hands and started pouring it down Lydia's throat.

"Hey, I was going to drink that!" Watts insisted.

"Oh god, grow up, kid," Molly said. "Look, we got what we came for, now let's get the hell out of here."

"What?" Mike spat out. "No way, this party's bodacious!"

"My foot's gonna be bodacious in your asshole if you don't book, Microphone!"

"You ain't the boss of me!"

Molly's face darkened, her voice again a low growl as her eyes locked contact with his. "Get your damn friends and get in the car, or I will peel the skin from your back and feed it to hellhounds!"

Mike, in a trance, did exactly as she said, even going so far as grabbing his friends by the arm and escorting them toward the foyer.

"Dude?" Hurl said.

"Do as she says," Mike said.

They moved toward the front door but Molly stopped them short, turned away quickly just as Rat-hawk and Bucket-hat walked through the door scanning for her. They must have spotted her car from the road.

Stupid. Stupid. God, this is all too real. What now?

"What's wrong?" Easton saw the worry in her eyes.

"Those guys." Molly motioned behind her, and Easton glanced at the punks. "They're trouble. Long story."

Blake rejoined them and overheard. "What kind of trouble?" he asked.

"The really, really bad kind. Look, is there a back way out?"

"Indeed," Blake said. "Follow me."

Blake led them through the kitchen then through another hallway, past a storage room and the laundry room, to a back door with coats and hats up on pegs and umbrellas by the door.

"Hold up," he said, taking off his smoking jacket. *A smoking jacket, really?* Molly stopped herself. He was being perfectly aces. Blake replaced his jacket with a long tan overcoat and picked up what looked like a fat cane with carvings at each end, one a purple, fanged snake, the other a flaring, gray wolf. Inside the mouth of each was some small orb or jewel. *So weird.*

"What's that for?" she asked.

"Just in case they're as bad as you say," he said.

"Yeah they're worse than *that.*"

"*I RAN (SO FAR AWAY)*"
—FLOCK OF SEAGULLS, 1982

MOLLY BUCKLED LYDIA in the Truckster while Lydia smiled and waved her head back and forth, humming the lyrics to "Boys Don't Cry" as she nursed what remained of the Gatorade. Hurl and Mike the Mic strapped up in the back. Molly turned to Blake and Easton to thank them for...whatever. She mostly just wanted to look at Easton one more time.

"THERE!" she heard someone shout.

Rat-hawk was out in the front yard pointing dead at her.

"Shit, that's them." She didn't even think; she tossed the keys to the Truckster at Watts. "You're up! Get them out of here! I'm the only one they know."

"I can't drive! I don't even have my permit," he protested.

"You're some kind of genius. Figure it out, kid. Look, go toward home and then cut up Paradise. I'll jump in with you there."

"What?"

"Just go. Now!"

Molly sprinted up the road, fast as she could go. This was a terrible plan. What was she thinking? Blake and Easton both ran after her. What were they thinking?

"What are you doing?" she hollered back. The bangers chased after all of them. Blake produced his cane.

"Don't be an idiot. They have guns."

"Guns?" Easton echoed.

Molly didn't linger to explain. She cut across the next yard from Blake's and hit the gas, leaping over a six-foot fence in one bound and thudding on the other side without losing a step. She baked through one yard after another, leaping fences, lawn toys, or whatever else crossed her path. She caught a break with a trampoline and used that to spring so high she flew across the next yard, inching closer to the street. She got within eyeshot of Paradise Avenue and cooked her legs even hotter.

*

Watts wove in and out of his lane, barely reaching the pedals. Lydia loopy trying to coach him.

"Steady," she tried to help him hold the wheel straight.

"Here she comes!" Hurl shouted.

"Whoah she's going fast!!" Mike the Mic scoped the speedometer and clocked the car at 35 and Molly was closing on them. "Like, *really* fast."

Watts hit the brakes and Molly swapped him the driver's seat. She shoved it back in drive and gave it all the Truckster had. She swerved off Paradise and hit

Township. Not a half a mile further, when the adrenaline slowed, she finally felt the tire slapping the road.

"Why why why? What now?" Molly jerked the wheel into the parking lot of some joint called The Bunker and got out. The driver's rear was flat. "Get the spare, quick!" she barked at the gang.

"There's no spare," Hurl said.

"What?!"

"Mom took it out to make room for all the wedding crap earlier."

This was a flawlessly orchestrated catastrophe. She couldn't have planned it better if she tried.

"Okay, think! Think! Think!" Molly looked around. The street was dead, quiet all around but for the juke joint. She spotted a small empty garage behind the building and got back in the car to limp it inside.

"Okay. We go in, use their phone, call the cops, and see if anyone can help with the tire."

* * *

Back at the party, Blake and Easton had seen Molly vault over the fence like it was nothing, then disappear into the void. Blake glared hard at that feat—as did Easton, who thought maybe there was more to *this* redhead than the others. The bangers doubled back and jumped in their car, a half-stripped Monte Carlo, and gassed it trying to follow the Truckster.

"We gotta go after them."

"Who, those bangers?" Easton asked.

"No. Molly," Blake said. "She will require assistance."

Easton thought Blake seemed excited by the prospect. He'd gotten himself mixed into this now, and the last thing he needed was all this attention on him.

"My Porsche is blocked. Do you have a vehicle?"

"Yeah, right over there." Easton pointed at his white, blue-striped Z28 with four on the floor.

"It will suffice," Blake said.

"I mean shouldn't we call for—call the cops?" Easton grimaced.

"The phone's out. Besides, I'm all she'll need. And I only need you for the conveyance."

Easton gave him the eyeball. "We don't know where they went."

"We'll find them." Blake noted the rain had stopped, the clouds above them dissipating.

VIII
"All Night Long"
—Joe Walsh, 1980

MOLLY AND THE GANG cruised into The Bunker as a monsoon fell outside. The place was half full of Jims, Bobs, Bubbas, and two or three Norma-Raes. There was an electric bull up in the front corner because why not.

The main guy behind the bar yelled into the phone while another guy cleaned up bottles around the tables. All eyes but the bartender's spied the kids who stuck out like fruit on a pizza.

"Damn bastards!" The bartender cussed as he hung up the phone and then picked it up, dialing again. He was older, maybe pushing sixty, with suspenders and those old man whiskers that were not quite a beard or quite anything, really.

"Excuse me, sir," Molly said to him.

"Name's Lester. What'll you have?" he asked, still cranking his rotary. "Jimmy'll fix you up." He motioned at the other guy clinking glasses onto the bar.

"No, uh, we're not here to drink," she said. "We're not even old enough."

"Ain't me says so. That was Commie Ron. The hell you want then, anyway?"

"We just need to use the phone, sir, if we can," Molly pleaded. "I need to call the police. We're in trouble."

The bartender frowned. "I'm using it. And we don't do cops here, you savvy? Now, you're about to be in real trouble. So, go on, git!"

Molly slammed her fist down onto the bar so hard it dented the wood.

"Look, Mister, I've about had a night from nine hells, and I've got a flat outside with no spare, and there's two Muties looking for us as we speak and hoping to close my eyes tight, you *savvy*? We could really use a solid if you can dig one out from wherever you've got one hiding because I'm out of options now."

The bartender stared her in the face, glancing over her sorry looking crew: Three geeks and some drunk hippy dressed like a vampire slumped over the kid with a radio on his belt.

"Look, kid, I believe you. I do. I don't think for a split second you'd walk in here with that sad sack of nuts behind you if you weren't hard up. But, here's the thing: we DON'T do cops here. Ain't gonna happen. And, I can prolly wrangle one of these ol' gearheads in here to slap a tire on for you, but I'm a mite busy at the moment. I got a big crowd be pouring in here directly — if they can slog through this sudden rain, that is. Saturday's our live show night, and my damn house band's done split on me at the last second. So, I'm busy trying to get anybody that *will* to come down here and play something so these maniacs don't start tearing holes in the walls. Or, god forbid, each other. So, unless you got anybody can sling the strings handy, I got work to do."

Molly scoped the stage all the way at the back of the dive. A three-piece setup: bass, lead, and a set of black keys all behind the chicken wire.

"Chicken wire?" Molly raised an eyebrow.

She walked back to her crew and gave Lydia a look over. Still loopy, but she'd have to do. Molly eyeballed the three geeks hard as she could.

"Tell me, for the love of everything sacred, that one of you can play music?" she prayed more than asked.

"Is that a Yamaha?" Mike the Mic indicated the keyboard. "I can lay you a beat down. Work in some synth if you let me at it a minute. I'm in junior band."

Of course he was. Bless his glorious nerdy heart.

"Okay, Mister Lester." Molly walked back to the bar with deal-making smirk on her face.

"It's just Lester." He dialed another number as they spoke.

"You got yourself a band. How's about an hour in exchange for that flat-fix?" Molly proffered. "And I'll owe you another one if you like what you hear?"

Lester the bartender looked down hard at the Mouseketeers and furrowed. The plucky shotcaller held her hand out like she was JR about to own half o' Texas. *Cocky little squirt. But there was something about her.*

"An hour and a half," he said, "and I'll get that tire on for you. But can your partner in the black duds cut her mustard?" He motioned at Lydia wavering back and forth to the George Jones coming off the jukebox.

"She'll be fine. She just needs some coffee if you got some," Molly said.

Lester turned to the other guy at the bar. "Jimmy! Let's make some Wake-Up Juice!"

* * *

"Mic check, two, three," Mike the Mic spoke this time into an actual microphone instead of his hand radio. "Check, two, three. We're good." He gave the thumbs up to Molly in front of him on the lead axe. Lydia gripped the bass. Whatever they fixed her up with was like pure cocaine. *God, it probably was cocaine*, now she thought about it. Great.

Molly gave her guitar neck a stranglehold and cut a few chords to get loose. Hurl and Watts sucked sodas at the bar fast as Jimmy would pour them.

"A'ight, y'all ready to go?" Lester asked, eager to get them going so his regulars wouldn't start fighting, at least not too soon.

"Yessir!" Molly assured him, giving it a little twang.

"Oh, and one last thing," he said. "None of that punkass hippy shit. This here's a country joint. Y'all know that, right?"

"Yep. No problem!" Molly smiled as he made his way back to the bar with more customers clambering inside.

It was a big problem.

"Okay, crap." Molly turned to Lydia and Mike. "What country do we know?"

"I know plenty." Lydia smirked.

"Huh?" Molly stared blank.

"God, that's all my brothers and dad ever listen to. You're the only one I know likes rock. It's why I dug you at first."

"Well alrighty. What country do *I* know, then?" Molly racked her brain.

The crowd sneered at her. She figured she didn't look their usual, what with her ripped jacket, blood orange Cons, and black tight jeans. She probably had a few too many earrings for them, too. Lester the bartender crunched peanuts waiting on her do play something, probably already thinking he'd made a bad deal.

"TV?" Mike the Mic said.

"Huh?"

"TV. Do you watch TV?"

"I mean, yeah, but..."

"*Simon & Simon?*"

"I gotcha, kid." Molly launched right into the guitar riff from the theme from the show. How the hell she had it down pat, she couldn't say. She was good at picking up a tune after a time or two hearing it, and she'd heard that one every week in the background when Hurl would turn it on. That kid watched a lot of TV.

Lydia was on her game with the bass, right in time. Mike the Mic kept the beat up on the keys and stayed with them. The crowd ate it up, even slapping their legs with it.

"What next?" she said when that was over.

"*Urban Cowboy?*" Mike said. "That movie? Know anything from that?"

"Bob Segar!" Lydia smiled. "Hell yeah!"

Okay, yeah, Molly actually had seen that movie because Travolta was way cute in that hat. And yep, she was about some Segar.

"'*9 Tonight'* on three...two...three." She cranked the guitar.

They rolled into it - the kid doing great, and Lydia a savior. This wasn't so bad. Well, except for the murderers, Molly allowed. But, still. They were slaying it.

* * *

Easton kept a steady 25 down Township. They'd been by this spot already. He knew Molly lived on the other side of the bay from here, at the corner of Elm and E Streets, in fact — among the other things he'd learned about her of late. None of this had been part of the plan for how tonight was supposed to go. And now Blake insisted they keep checking this area, though he had his eyes on the sky half the time. *The hell is he looking for?*

"What are we doing, man? They're long gone. And I haven't seen the bangers' car for that matter, either."

"Just keep looking. Check the parking lots. They must have hit some trouble. They're still around here."

"How do you know that? How can you know that?" Easton shook his head. The guy was dead weight and making this a lot more complicated than it would've otherwise been.

"Trust me, kid."

Kid? The hell was this guy's damage? Easton really hated his own boyish face. He wanted his beard to come in soon, like his dad's was. Then he'd be square and wouldn't be stuck...doing this.

"Look, I'm pulling over," Easton turned the wheel. "I've got her phone number. Maybe they made it safe and sound. At least let's check."

Blake agreed, and they wheeled into the first payphone they saw. The cord had been yanked out along with the receiver. This wasn't exactly the best spot in town.

"What's that sound?" Blake turned his head.

"What?" Easton looked around. "What sound?"

"It's coming from there." Blake pointed at some bar a half block down with plenty of cars in the lot.

"What about it?"

"Let's check it out." Blake walked that way, tucking his snake-wolf cane into his long jacket. Easton followed, wishing he could bring his own *items* but not with this dude along for the ride. He was still confused as to where they were going. Or why.

They walked inside and saw what Easton expected: a barn full of lumberjacks and dockworkers, all ready to burn a week's check on Bud and broads. There were worse ways to lose your money, but these guys looked like they would start a fight at the drop of a hat. It was only then it hit him.

Molly Slater lasered right into Easton's eyes from fifty yards. She owned the stage, chicken wire and all. The crowd was as locked to her movement as she now was on Easton's eyes.

Blake got a drink at the bar, like all this was just fine to him. *That guy. That freaking guy.*

Molly lit into her second rendition of the *Bonanza* theme for the night. They rolled through every western, bounty hunter, and detective show theme song Mike the Mic could think of at least twice, plus half the tracks off *Urban Cowboy* they could remember, even the Jimmy Buffet one — these hicks really ate that one up.

"Play some Jerry Lee!" some yokel shouted from the bullpen.

"Jerry Lee?" Molly looked at Lydia.

"Lewis?" Lydia mouthed back.

Molly racked her head. What did she know by— She locked eyes with Lydia.

"Are you thinking what I'm thinking?"

"Oh yeah."

Molly jerked her head back to Mike. "Do you know Iggy? 'Real Wild One?'"

"Do I?" Mike said and laid down the beat.

Molly sang out and wrenched her strings. Lydia echoed in monotone. Mike the Mic was a champ on the Yamaha.

The crowd was totally having it, and Molly crested. Never mind the rest of the night's chaos, and, well, murder. This was jamming. Easton watched her, jaw-dropped. She licked her lips looking at his. She was going to neck with him after this, no doubt. At the one-minute mark, she hit that sick guitar solo and ripped it. The crowd lit up like a firetruck in the night.

Molly felt something...strange. Like their energy fed her somehow. They couldn't deny the power of Iggy Pop. *Jerry Lee who? Damn right.*

MOLLY HUNG UP HER loaner guitar for the night. She had really done it. She'd played a full gig for a full crowd and they didn't roast her on a spit. She smirked at Lydia who felt it, too. They would get the gig for prom. She just knew it. They were gonna own it.

And Mike the Mic. *Who knew Mike the Mic was cool?* Well, sort of. No one who knew Iggy could be all bad. That kid could kick some synth, she had to give him that.

Molly cut through the crowd, some still half clapping for her, the rest going back to their drinks and darts. She zipped right for Easton Braddock, grabbed him in her arms, and twisted round and round with him like he was a doll. He sort of was, a little. *God, she could drink his face.*

Blake Elvis joined them, eager to garner some of that affection himself, she could tell. He went for a hug, but she laid him up for the friend high five. She tried to apologize kindly with her eyes. *Sorry, Blake. This just the way it's gotta be, though.*

"You were amazing!" Easton stared like he was just seeing her for the first time. That empty look he'd given her before was gone. Now he was like he was a different person—and she more than *homework.* She liked this new look.

"Thanks! Yeah, it's so weird. Like, he needed a band, and our car had a flat, and it all..." She stammered. "I don't even know anymore."

She had butterflies. The music. Easton. All of it. Her body felt like it would explode, like she could blast off into the sky or knock out a freight train.

"You should play prom," Easton said.

"Yeah, we're gonna," Molly agreed. "I mean, we're gonna go out for it, totally!"

"I can probably make that happen," Blake interjected. Of course, he had to move into the moment. *Like, take a hint, dude.* Luckily the old man bailed her out.

"Damn, that was some damn fine picking, kid," Lester said, walking up. "Bobby-John got yer tire all fixed up. Hell, I ought to pay you on top of it, that was so dang good!"

"Really?" Molly's face lit up. She didn't hate the idea of money.

"I mean I ain't gonna," Lester added.

Oh, well. Fair's fair. She was still giddy. That energy from the crowd coursed through her. She felt like she could soar. Or throw a truck into the sky. Knock down a mountain.

Molly turned to Easton. "I gotta get these kids and my bass player home safe. Can I meet you later? I really want to see you, if you're still hip?"

"Uh, yeah," Easton said, caught off his feet—she felt him feel excited, somehow. "For sure, yeah."

Blake grimaced as Molly fished her keys from her jacket pocket. She gave him the *sorry better luck next time* shrug and peeled off toward her crew.

"All right, trucksters, let's get trucking," she said. Mike the Mic chatted at some forty-something at the bar, and, *god, he was drinking beer again. Jeez, if their parents find out any single part of this, I'm super dead like stone cold dead.*

"Can you round them up for me?" she asked Easton. "I'll pull the car around front. I just want to get home quick."

"Yeah, sure."

Molly knew he dug her. He totally did. But he also felt...*something else.* And she still didn't understand how she knew that.

*

Lydia followed Molly to get the car, twirling as she walked. It was still parked in the garage where she'd left it. They really had torn one up. That juice did the trick. Molly hoped it wasn't cocaine, though.

Molly scoped the rear tire, and found it was tip-top. They were solid. Lydia went for the passenger door latch.

"You know, we should play here again." She opened the door to get in.

"Yeah, sure," Molly said. "A gig's a gig, I mean, but I don't know about doing more country. I want to play our set."

"PLAY THIS, BITCH!" rang out from behind her. Cold metal kissed the back of her neck. Twin barrels jabbed into Lydia's, leaning her head all the way to one side.

Oh, right...the murder.

A third guy rounded the corner, then a fourth. And a fifth. This was like a bad dream. *Please let it be a dream. Why? Why does this have to be?*

"We been waiting all night for this," Rat Hawk said. "Knew you wouldn't get far. How you think that tire went flat in the first place, you dumb skank?"

They all had red vinyl jackets in various states of disrepair. They were Mutes for sure. The biggest one, the last one to come around the corner into the garage, had the nicest. It still had its sleeves and cuffs in order.

Molly tried to get her head on straight. But this...all this? It just wasn't right. It couldn't be right. And some feeling, an energy, surged through her. The way the crowd had shouted for her. Called out to her as she played to them. *Praised her.* She still had that tingle in her body. That electricity. But now there was something else, too.

"Take them out back," the big one said. Rat-hawk, who had the shotgun to Lydia's head, dragged her by the arm.

"Ow! What the hell?" Lydia griped. He clenched his grip harder.

Bucket-hat was the one behind Molly with that pistol, the one she'd watch pull the trigger earlier in the night. How was she going to get out of this? She couldn't die now. Not *now* when she'd finally had a night worth being alive for.

"Where to, boss?" Bucket-hat asked.

"Across the tracks there. That old building. And let's make it quiet. Grab something here to do the job. The guns will get the heat on us. No more screw-ups from you two idiots tonight."

One newcomer picked up an eight-pound sledgehammer and another a crowbar. She felt inside them, like she had done with Easton. They felt hate, and fear, and malice. They *wanted* to hurt people. This was unreal. This was barbaric.

The gang took Molly and Lydia through the darkness into an abandoned old boathouse nearby. Lightning lit the scene with streaks across the clouds. The rain slammed down hard again. Everyone was soaked by the time they got inside. The boss fumed.

"Hurry up and get it over with. Then shove them in those barrels over there." He motioned at two fifty-gallon drums, probably still half full of boat fuel. Lydia sobbed. She had no idea what was happening or why. She'd only just woke from her stupor. Nevermind this was all kind of *her* fault. No. No, that wasn't fair, Molly told herself. It was random. It was all so random. She still couldn't believe any of it.

"Come, on," the boss barked. "Whack 'em in the head and let's scat."

"I don't think you want to do that," came a low, threatening voice behind him. Along with a thick, gleaming blade right at the boss's throat.

The boss freaked. He held both his hands out to the side, eyes popped and glued to that blade at his throat. The thing was straight out of fiction. Across his neck, a foot long at least, and shining like the moon itself. Another identical blade appeared from behind the boss. Then it shot out, extending itself, doubling its length out of nowhere. A hand gripped it expertly — at the pommel, a fanged snake's head just like on...

Blake's cane!

Blake Elvis's face appeared as the sky flashed, making him wince. Molly's night kept leaping from weird to weirder. And that energy bubbled inside her again, her eyes feeling too big for their sockets.

"If you gentlemen would like to keep this associate of yours in good health, I'd suggest you let go of those young ladies."

The gang looked to their boss for direction, not eager to cow to some preppy mall ninja.

"Y-You heard him," the boss said. "Let 'em go!"

"A wise decision, sir. I commend your leadership skills." Blake smirked. He was way too into this, Molly thought. *Just get us the hell out of here already, dude.* As soon as she was released, she backed away easy and steady with Lydia on her arm, moving Lydia behind her instinctively.

One guy in the back of the boathouse pulled up a big revolver with a long barrel. "I can tag him, boss," he offered. "I got a bead."

"You really want to try it?" Blake said, like it was all some movie. Like he sat around rehearsing crap like this in his bathroom mirror. *Christ, he probably did,* Molly thought. "You know your gun, such a crude device, is only a few centuries old, while the blade..." He twisted his arm, letting the sword catch the light from the flashing sky. "Such an elegant, yet simple thing, really. This is the child of aeons. Many more than you know, in fact. So what do you think, gentlemen?" he went on. "Do you like your chances?"

The rest of the gang pulled their heat, hammers clicking back like knuckles popping. They liked their chances just fine. *Idiot, Blake.*

Molly couldn't take it anymore. She couldn't breathe. In fact, she hadn't breathed in minutes. She'd just stopped. She gasped for air but couldn't get any. Like it came in and did nothing, as though her body didn't need or even want it. She clutched at her throat, terrified she would just die any second from panic. Nothing came. The hair on her arms stood straight up. Even the hair on her head stuck up everywhere and out to the sides. Why couldn't she breathe? Why did she even need to breathe? Did she breathe? Was she dead? Was this death?

Lydia's eyes widened, staring above Molly. Blake saw it too and dashed for her.

"NO!" he shouted, shoving Molly and Lydia both six feet away as a bolt of lightning slammed the tip of his silly sword and went right down through his body, lighting him up like the 4th of July.

The blast of the strike knocked the boss to the ground and scattered the gang.

"Outer freaking Limits, man!" Rat-hawk shouted.

Blake lay out cold on the ground, his dumb sword on the ground at his feet. *Who even has a sword? Really? Much less two.*

"Screw this. Light 'em up and let's git!" The boss scrambled to his feet.

Molly heard the pop.

Then nothing.

No pain. No hurt. No death. She'd closed her eyes on instinct and now peeped one open. Bucket-hat stared in disbelief. *Had he missed?* Lydia stared at her, too. Like she'd never seen Molly in her life. Like she was some kind of freak.

Bucket-hat popped again. And again.

This time she heard them. Little bitty plinks as the bullets hit her in the chest. The next one hit her square in the cheek, the lead flattening into an imperfect disc and then falling to the ground.

WHAT THE SH — the boss mouthed but couldn't make sounds come out.

Rat-hawk hit her with both barrels of his shotgun and ripped a fat hole in her favorite jacket. Still nothing.

But Molly wasn't scared anymore. Her mind snapped into some kind of other place. Some foreign realm where there was no such thing as fear. Foreign. Yes. Foreigner. She could hear them playing somewhere in the deepest creases of her head as she stood there. In the Rain.

The boss got his voice back and screamed, "Somebody hit her with something!"

The guy with the sledge ran at her, bearing down on her. Dead-center skull. Her hand seized the ball of the hammer just before it made contact. Molly gripped it so tight she dented the steel with her fingertips. Her head, low, rose to greet them all in the eye.

"My turn!" She took the hammer by its head and shoved the hilt into his gut, doubling him over. He groaned, holding his belly. Shock dripped off his face. Molly front-kicked him in the chest and sent his limp body flying thirty feet, slamming into the back wall of the building. She took the hammer in both hands and gripped it tight. It felt good. It felt right.

Two bangers rushed her. She held the hammer horizontal, one hand at each end and clotheslined the two dipsticks right in their foreheads. They stumbled backwards. She then flipped the hammer up and caught it upside down, gripping it like a baseball bat. She didn't feel like killing them, though. She wasn't a killer. Was she? Could she? But *they* were.

She Babe-Ruthed one right in the shoulder, heard the crack. Bones heal, she figured. She grabbed the other by his throat, lifted him in the air, and threw him all the way to the ceiling of that high-vaulted boat house. He slammed against the tin roof and came crashing back down. More pops and cracks. But he was crying. That meant he lived.

Rat-hawk and Bucket-hat, her two favorites—the very ones that started this whole fiasco—cowered, backing away from her.

"Please," Rat-hawk pleaded. "Please just let us go."

"Like you were going to do with us?" She picked him up with one hand and football chucked him all the way through the thin metal walls of the shed. She could hear his moans and whimpers. Still alive. Maybe bleeding.

Bucket-hat. He was a killer. She'd watched him kill. No. Murder. He was a murderer. She seized his throat.

"I won't beg like he did," he said.

"I don't care." Molly gripped his forearm with her other hand. She clenched and felt both bones burst. He crumpled to the floor when she let go.

She turned, feeling some kind of muscle memory kicking in, though from where she couldn't say. The boss was on his feet. She took that eight-pound sledgehammer up from the floor where she'd left it. He was at a jog now, just getting his bearings. She looked at the hammer's dented head, her fingers writing their mark in it forever now. The boss was at a full run, nearly across the field and back to The Bunker.

Molly held it just right at the bottom and sent the hammer flipping end over end like an airplane propeller flung off its axis, spinning it with shocking speed right at his fleeing backside. She heard the thunk of its hilt against his head and saw him go sprawling just as he touched asphalt. She could hear the skin of his face tearing as it slid when he fell. She could hear it? From here?

An eternity passed in a single moment. Everything swam down from the clouds back into place. Like time slowed to nothing around her. She felt the wind come back into her stomach. Had she only just now breathed again?

She could feel the air again. The rain had stopped. That was good, at least.

She heard voices. No. A voice. She knew the voice.

Lydia.

Lydia looked at her — just staring.

"Molly?" she muttered again as if terrified that, in fact, Molly wasn't there.

"So," Molly finally responded, "yeah. This is new."

X
"HOME SWEET HOME"
—MÖTLEY CRÜE, 1985

MOLLY CARRIED BLAKE back to the car like a sack of potatoes, Lydia following along like a zombie. Lydia cranked the Truckster while Molly walked to the bar.

"What happened?" Easton said. "I thought I heard shots?"

"Lightning," Molly said, still not quite believing her own truth as she said it.

"Huh?"

"He got struck by lightning," Molly insisted. "He's alive and breathing, but he needs a hospital. Can you take him?"

"Yeah, I...what?"

"Look, I've had a night. I've got to get these kids home. I don't know what else to do right now. I'll explain everything. Later. Somehow. I promise," she said, her eyes begging his to let it go. How would she explain?

"I believe you," he said.

In the car, with everyone and everything fully, finally squared away, Lydia stared into the speeding yellow lines that vanished underneath them. No sounds from her at all. The goofs in the back played bloody knuckles. So weirdly innocent. Like they knew so little of what went on.

Molly focused on the road, unsure of so much more now than she ever had been before. But at least it was over. For now. Tomorrow was whatever.

She turned up the radio. Mötley was playing. That sweet piano intro. Like warm chocolate.

She checked the rearview, watching the kids in the back then caught her own eye staring at herself. One tendril of flaming red hair danced in the light wind coming through her cracked window. She chuckled to herself a moment. If there really was some maniac out there coming after redheads, well...

Come get some.

In the back seat, Mike the Mic folded out his comic books and showed the other two. "I'm telling you guys."

EPISODE II

0
"EVERY BREATH YOU TAKE"
—THE POLICE, 1983

MOLLY FLICKED A PEANUT off her palm. Like a bullet it shattered the glass bottle she had set up on the back fence ten yards away. She shot another. And another. Shards burst into the grass all around. Hoyt wouldn't love that.

She calmed her nerves. Closed her eyes. Sat down. Folded her arms and legs. She reached into the back of her mind, as deep as she could go. Looking for... something. Anything. She breathed. In. Out. Deeper. One breath after another.

Breathing?

She stopped. She didn't even grab a last gasp—wondering how long she could hold it. So many questions swam through the muddled sea of her storming mind. The world she'd known, believed in, lived through, all that had vanished in a single gunshot.

Lightning surged through her mind's sky—like the lightning bolt that had slammed into Blake. She wanted to sleep and wake up and do the whole day over, detention and all—just so she could never set foot in that stupid gas station.

Minutes ticked by.

And yet more minutes.

She sat there. Alone. For over an hour. Searching for any memory she could find. Any answer.

All without another breath.

I
"I STILL HAVEN'T FOUND WHAT I'M LOOKING FOR"
U2, 1987

MOLLY TOSSED A BALL in the air with her right hand, watched it crest above her, and caught it with her left. Over and over. She had that line from *Dirty Harry* stuck in her head. Hoyt loved that movie. He'd made Clair almost miss a Ladies Auxiliary ball one night because it was coming on TV and he wanted to try to tape it with their new VCR, but ended up losing the first five minutes because he couldn't figure out how the damn thing worked and kept hitting rewind. Molly felt so bad, she walked up and hit Play+Record at the same time.

Maybe being a little more helpful would keep them from booting her. They still hadn't mentioned her turning eighteen.

"Jeez, Hoyt, how'd you guys win Vietnam?" She'd snarked.

"We lost Vietnam, Molly," Hoyt had said. "And your mother and I were flower power, baby!" He held up his two fingers like Tricky Dick. *Gross.*

"Could you, like, not?" Lydia slumped on the lawn chair opposite Molly in the backyard. Molly had gotten so fast with her solo game of catch that Lydia dizzied watching.

Molly didn't catch it the next time and let the 30-pound cannonball — one Hoyt had snuck out of the fort the last time they rode the ferry to the island — thud to the earth, sinking into the grass.

Lydia glared.

Molly slumped into her chair, fluttering out a sigh.

Lydia glared.

"What??" Molly blurted.

Lydia shook her head. She couldn't even form the words to her questions there were so many, so splintered, so broken. *Just what the actual even?*

"Well?" Lyd's face was wrought with lines of confusion, peppered with hurt and even a pinch of fear. The ball stunt unnerved her, the way Molly was just getting so used to it. Like it were any other nothing,

"Do we really have to do this?" Molly turned her face away from Lydia. She was terrible at this kind of crap. *Stupid B.S. Why do we have to talk? Talk talk talk.* It never made any difference. Like those nuns at Our Lady, all teaching her to act proper and the right way to pray to their stupid dead god. *Real gods didn't die. Only loser gods got smoked.*

"Yes!" Lydia stamped her foot.

"What, then? What do you want to ask that you think I can answer? You know as much as I do. You were there. Here we are. So, what? What big mystery shall we solve together?"

"How long have you..." Lydia didn't know how to finish the question.

"Since last night. Totally random. Totally brand new."

"Well..." Lydia just couldn't even.

"Never had anything like that before. But now it's like all the time. God, I slipped last night and caught myself on the wall and smashed right through it."

"Drywall?"

"Brick." Molly folded her bottom lip under her top. "I moved my Darksiders poster to cover it for now. Hoyt is gonna FLIP." Molly reached down to the ground, planted her hands, lifted both legs in the air, then held out one arm, balancing herself perfectly on the other. "This is kinda awesome, though, I'm not gonna lie."

"Stop showing off," Lydia pleaded. "What if Hurl sees?"

"He's at Mike the Mic's with Watts. They're going 'exploring' today in the swamps up north of the bay."

"Your folks?"

"It's Sunday. Boogie time!"

"Ew."

* * *

Upstairs in Molly's room, Lydia inspected the wall wound behind the big poster of Étienne LeCroiseur, the baddest guitar player and vocalist ever. Molly'd had that poster since she was little. The hole was just the size of Molly's palm, give or take. The brick and mortar caved in like with a...*well*, a sledgehammer. *Right.*

"I mean, admittedly," Lydia started, "it is kinda rad."

"I know, right?!" Molly flopped onto her bed a little too hard and snapped one of the legs off, rolling her onto the floor. Molly and Lydia both burst out laughing.

"So...I mean..."

"Yeah?" Molly already knew what this was going to be.

"I mean this has to have something to do with where you're from. Like where you're actually from."

Molly sighed. This again.

"I've told you so many times," she groaned. "I remember nothing — literally nothing — from before they found me."

She had told Lydia the story a dozen times. Found wandering around out in the woods south of Stennis, half covered in dirt and dust, just filthy. She didn't even speak for three days, just sat catatonic. The guys from social services called her Space Cadet. When she finally started talking it was just yes or no answers at first. She couldn't remember her name, her parents, where she was from, how she got there, nothing. Blank. Even the world itself seemed new, at first. Every animal fascinated her, made her smile — even the killy ones.

They put her with Our Lady of the Bay at first, but with her bright red hair, she was a quick one for the foster system, though the families tended to return her before 3 months was up. Always in trouble at school, fighting, spitting, "backtalking"...Molly was a pistol, true. Always had been.

"Hey, yeah, maybe you're an alien escaped from the space center!" Lydia blurted, way too excited about that.

"Oh yeah, sure." Molly rolled her eyes and lowered her voice like some radio announcer. "Last daughter of the planet Xenon! As if."

"Or a government experiment! Like that one guy, you know?"

"I doubt the government would just lose me."

"True." Lydia looked again at the poster covering the hole in the wall. Étienne LeCroiseur. Darksiders, easily the coolest band that had ever come out of anywhere near them — not that Bogalusa was super close, but close enough.

"Wait." She nodded at the poster. "What about him? What if you're Étienne's long-lost daughter?" Lydia asked. "They say he had a daughter. I heard that. I know I heard that once."

Molly sighed at her friend. "Sure. I just happen to have superpowers AND I wind up being related to my *second* favorite musician. That's a big *as if.*" Molly did leer at the poster for a moment and entertain the idea. For a moment. Just for fun. "Besides, Étienne was dark-skinned Créole. If I was his daughter I'd at least have a better tan."

"You're darker than I am." Lydia put her forearm against Molly's.

"Milk is darker than you, Lyd."

"Also, wait, second favorite?" Lydia pulled her arm away. She couldn't fathom this heresy against Darksiders in her presence. Molly nodded at the Mötley Crüe poster on the opposite wall and Lydia groaned. "Right. Well, what about that stuff you had?"

"Huh?"

"You said they found you with all that junk?"

"I told you. Just some trash whoever ditched me had me in. Just random nonsense."

"Let me see it."

This again. Fine.

"Mom!" Molly wandered into the hallway. Clair creaked her doorway and poked her head out, cinching her robe.

"Yeah?"

"Do we still have that box of my stuff? From Our Lady?"

"Yeah, in the attic. Why?"

"Lydia wants to play Nancy Drew."

"That's not what I—" Lydia folded her arms. "I just...ughh."

"Now, Molly, you know Hoyt and I love you very much truly as our own daughter. Don't we, baby?"

"We do!" came Hoyt's voice from the room.

"And we really do want you to think of yourself as our daughter. It doesn't matter how you start," she said. *Oh, god, here it comes.* "But how you finish! And you finish with love!"

Barf me out, Clair. Molly smiled through her teeth as she back-walked toward the attic pull.

Lydia shrugged. "I mean that doesn't sound like they're gonna kick you out."

* * *

Molly dropped the tattered cardboard box onto her broken bed. She needed to shove some old books under there later or something. She also needed to get a handle on this...whatever it was.

"Fur boots, grey skirt. Normal enough. *Flash Gordon* t-shirt. Vintage, too. Not bad. Obnoxiously wide fake leather belt with way too much dazzle." Lydia held it up to the light to inspect it further. "What the hell? A freaking Falcons hoodie? Are you joking?"

"Nope." Molly propped her feet on the bed, leaning back in her beanbag. "Like, eight sizes too big, too."

"Doesn't look *that* huge," Lydia folded it out.

"I mean back then, dufe!"

"Right. Hey, maybe you're from Atlanta?"

"Or maybe my folks were just fans. Who knows?" Molly strummed a beat on her air guitar.

"No one's a fan of Atlanta. Gross."

"Yeah, or it was thrift store trash." Molly was into whatever beat was in her head. "Like me!"

"That's not...you're not..." Lydia didn't finish. She was not about to offer emotional consolation to the girl with freaking superpowers, for holy mother's sake. "Oversized gold Mardi Gras beads, nice!" Lydia held them to her neck, posing. Molly laughed. "A French horn. That's weird. And...oven mitts. Oven mitts?"

Lydia held them up in her hands for confirmation.

"Dude your guess is good as mine." Molly shrugged.

They both stared at the wardrobe. It really didn't help.

"What about Blake?" Lydia said, finally, thankfully, moving on to a new topic. "Have you heard anything?"

"No. I mean he lived. That's something. Should we go see him at the hospital?"

"I mean, probably." Lydia shrugged. "He did kinda try to save us, I mean..."

"That stupid flipping sword!" Molly giggled.

They both roared laughter for a minute.

"Seriously, though." Lydia caught her breath and she held up the sweater again with a scowl. "Freaking Falcons?"

II
"BELIEVE IT OR NOT"
–JOEY SCARBURY, 1981

THE CREW RETURNED from their expedition bold and beyond. Tales abounded. Something about the perfect spot for their stronghold. Something about gathering tools and provisions. An entire treatise on fortifications and perimeter security. Rumors of a twelve-foot alligator. Was that big? Molly wasn't sure how big alligators got.

Lydia was no better. She'd gone through their entire collection of *World Book Encyclopedia* (missing I and U, of course, because Hurl took them to school for a project and they never found their way back home) looking for anything to give any sense to Molly's new *condition.*

"Anything?"

"Well, there is something here about adrenaline. Apparently, mothers have been known to become temporarily super strong when their children are in danger," Lydia informed her.

"Yeah..." Molly furrowed her brow. "I'm not a mother."

"I mean that's not the only example it gives."

"Yeah? Can they bend steel?" Molly scratched down an idea for a guitar riff. *Have to test that out later.* "'Cause I did that." She recalled her fingers pinching into the head of that hammer.

"I don't know. I don't know how hard it is to bend steel."

"Hey, Watts!" Molly shouted into the garage where Hurl's crew rummaged through Hoyt's tools. He was gonna kill them. "How hard is it to bend steel?"

"You'd need a force of at least 40,000 pounds per square inch," he stated without a beat.

Lydia winced. "How do you just know that?"

"Why did you ask me?" Watts gave her an eye.

"Because you'd know. But still," Lydia replied, then whispered to Molly, "Really, who just knows that?"

Lydia closed her book. She had *that* gleam in her eyes.

"What?" Molly groaned.

*

Another diesel giant lumbered down the tracks, passing them by as Molly followed Lydia along the old, worn down tracks at the far end of the downtown depot. Dusk crept on the horizon. This whole section in the old part of town was basically closed off now. They wouldn't be bothered out there. And hopefully not noticed.

"Okay, do something," Lydia ordered.

"Like what?"

"Like, super stuff, I don't know," Lydia pressed. "Break that big rock!" Lydia pointed at one of the big stones piled up near an old boxcar.

Molly walked up, picked it up, inspected it. She squeezed it between her palms, tightening her grip.

"Well?"

"Hold on," Molly gasped. "I'm still getting the hang of this."

She put more force into it, a good shove from each arm. The rock burst into dust and two smaller chunks fell to the ground by her feet.

"Cool. Now lift that train car!"

Molly stared at it. It was huge. A full-size rail car. "I can't lift that. "It's way too big!" She walked up to the rear of the car and squatted into position, got her legs and thighs situated. Didn't want to pull a muscle or anything. Could she even do that? Had she ever? She gripped the underside of the car. She hefted, tightening both arms and engaging her legs. The metal grumbled and groaned. She steadied her palms and wrapped her fingers around the bottom lip of the railcar. She stood, shoved herself and the whole car upward. Molly kept going, lifting the rear of the car up to her chest, then palm-pressed it all the way up over her head.

"Holy sh..." Lydia's eyes were baseballs.

Molly held her pose for a second while Lydia gawked. She thought it would be harder. She poofed out a couple breaths, not that she needed them, and let the car slam back on the tracks with a roar. The steel crunching steel rang out for miles. The boom rippled all the way through the sides of the car. Lights appeared beyond them, voices yelling.

"Time to bolt!" Molly grabbed Lydia and they took off.

* * *

Lydia drove to the emptiest part of downtown. Sunday night was stone dead. Not even the dregs scruffed about. The moon and the one or two working streetlights was all that lit their arena.

"Okay," Lydia had Molly down Fishbone Alley, the creep-darkest spot in all of downtown. "Can you fly?"

"What? No way."

"Try."

"How, Lydia? How does a person *try* to fly??"

"I don't know. Think about it, or something!"

"What? Happy thoughts, is it? Come on gimme a break." Molly rolled her eyes. This was dumb. And, besides, they should be practicing. Maybe they could get another gig at that juke joint.

"All right. Let's go up to the roof of the bank and you can jump off."

"I'm not doing that. I'm not jumping off a building. That's dumb. I'll just splat."

"Well..." Lydia racked her brain for an idea. "Jump really high from here. High as you can."

Molly shook her head. *Is this really necessary?* Although she had gotten curious now. She squatted. Got her bearings. Gave her legs a couple of practice springs. Good and limber. Check.

"Okay, here goes nothing!"

Molly shot into the sky like a bullet.

Lydia watched her rocket into the air. She was so high.

"Holy crap, you can fly!" Lydia gazed up but Molly got harder and harder to see.

Up in the air, Molly was giddy. She soared higher. She was doing it!

"Holy crap, I can fly!" she screamed. "I can fly!"

It was so amazing. This was the most kickass sensation she'd ever felt. She had just thought it out, jumped, and now she was soaring. She was almost to a cloud. She couldn't wait to fly everywhere. Home. The beach. No, screw those places. New York. L.A. The Whiskey A-Go-Go. London. Hyde Park.

She was flying. She was freaking flying. She was—

She was falling.

"Whoa what?" Molly twisted and writhed in the air. She had no idea how to aim, how to push herself in any direction. She clenched her face, closed her eyes, and willed herself to hover. *Nope.* Still falling.

She pushed with her legs against...nothing. She flailed her arms. Nothing. She got out just enough of a scream to call it one before her body slammed into the asphalt on the street not ten feet away from Lydia, crashing all the way through the blacktop, making the biggest pothole in the history of potholes.

Lydia's gut dropped, praying Molly wasn't dead. "Yikes! Did that hurt?" She gritted her teeth, squinting.

Molly climbed her way out of her hole and dusted off. More rips in her jacket and jeans. "Mostly my feelings," she groaned.

"Okay, what about laser eyes? You got those?"

"It's not like I came with an instruction manual." Molly felt all around her body to make sure she was all there. Surprisingly, nothing hurt. That was something. "Or if I did, who knows where it is now?"

"Well, stare at that trash can really hard!"

Molly focused, squinted, glared. Nope.

"This is stupid."

"Freeze breath! Freeze it!"

Molly pursed her lips and started to blow. Nothing unusual happened.

"Blow harder! Really go for it!"

Molly reared back, sucked in a huge breath, bigger than she ever had before, and let go with a blast. The air flew out with a boom and she just kept blowing. The breath knocked over the can and twirled in the air, forming into a full whirlwind gliding down the street, knocking over cans and flinging trash everywhere.

"Okay. Maybe not that one again."

"Can we go home now?"

"One more."

* * *

On the football field at Bay High, everything empty for the weekend, Molly let out the longest and deepest sigh. She wasn't tired in her body, but in her mind. She was so tired. She'd barely had a moment to process any of this, and Lydia was poking and prodding her like some bear in a cage. She just wanted to sleep now. Sleep? Did she need it? Or food? Drink? Water? Did she need any of it? So many questions.

"Okay." Lydia stared down at her watch. "And...go!"

Molly ran. She knew Lydia hoped for faster than a speeding bullet, but no dice. Molly cooked her legs hot as she could, but she wasn't breaking any sound barriers. She lapped Lydia, and again and again, and then she'd had enough. Her legs hadn't worn out. Just her patience.

"Okay," Lydia clocked it. "So, that was..." Molly watched her do the math in her head; she wasn't good at math. "Carry the one, and...like that was almost forty miles an hour!"

At least Molly wouldn't need to bum rides to work anymore. That was something.

III
"MANIC MONDAY"
—THE BANGLES, 1986

MRS. CLINTON SCRIBBLED something on the board about The Bay of Pigs or whatever, droning on and on about how some dude named Stalin killed eleventy jillion people, like way more than Hitler ever did, and it was all because communism took away their freedom of speech and that's why hospitals should only be for profit. Or something. History was lame. Also, Mrs. Clinton was a liar. Molly read the textbook the first week and had already caught her in three lies. Not that she corrected her. That was a short trip back to Lebeque's office.

"Do it," Lydia whispered.

Molly shook her head no. Lydia egged her on.

Fine. Screw it. Molly pursed her lips and blew a targeted blast of air right at Becky de la Beckwith's oh-so-perfect hair, swirling it all around her.

Becky glanced around. Lydia squelched a giggle. Molly smirked.

She needed the clock to say Three already.

*

They'd sat earlier with Easton at lunch, and did the best they could to avoid Watts for the moment, poor kid. Being the literal *kid* in high school didn't win him any popularity contests. He always sat alone. At least he was so small that the jerks kinda left him alone. Pantsing a nerd was one thing, but thumping an actual child was too much even for the tur-bros. Molly noted that from now on, she'd make a point to eat by Watts and try to be nice to him in the halls. But not today. She didn't need to him eaves-ing on what she had to ask Easton.

"So?" Molly observed Easton inspecting his country-fried steak with all the enthusiasm of a boy opening his sweater vest Christmas present from his aunt Belinda.

"I mean he's okay, I guess. I mean, I know people get struck by lightning, but like, I never saw it happen to anybody. So far out."

"Yeah, it was crazy!" Lydia eyed Molly. They needed to work on that face code. "Did he, like, say anything?"

"Not to me. But the nurses had a million questions, and I didn't know what to say. I think the cops may want to talk to you."

"Cops?" Molly widened her eyes. *No no no.*

"Yeah, I mean," Easton picked at his fries, then finally gave up on the whole meal, "it's all probably just their procedure, er, policy or whatever. I don't know." He fidgeted. Like his own words bothered him.

"I mean there's not much else to say." Molly noted someone had scratched *Étienne Lives* in the table near her. She stared at her meal about as energetically as Easton had his. Did she need to eat? She liked to eat. Eating was great. But, still. *What if she didn't?* How boring.

"Like, just like that?" Easton slammed his fist into his other hand. "Bam! Lightning? That's it?"

What's with the 20 questions, dude? Just eat your fries and look hot, jeez. She did like the way his eyes popped in that green shirt. There was that.

* * *

Hours ticked into days. Her shifts at Trace's, once the highlight of her week, became strange and dull. Tracey, always on about something, took notice of Molly's doldrums and put her in charge of setting out and designing the Halloween display and merch, thinking that would help. And at any other time it would.

Molly dug Halloween in her own odd way. Of course, costumes were rad and all. But it also legit gave her the creeps in some deep corner of her un-memory. Something not unlike dread, which always picked up through November and December, and then went away right around Christmas. Just like that. She felt it creeping up on her already this year. She liked to think it connected to her to somewhere else. Or someone.

"Witch or Star Warrior?"

"Huh?" Molly jolted from her daze. What was Tracey on about? Had Molly dozed and bent steel or broken something? Was she found out?

"For the party? You are coming, right? Of course you're coming. Everyone does. It's the best block party every year. Oh, I can't wait. Maybe I'll meet another Magnum, or, oooh, my Man in Black! Mmmm."

Tracey waltzed back toward the office, light as air. She brought a smile to Molly's face for the first time in hours. She should be happier, right? People would dream of having what she had. But what did it even mean? So weird. Like, what now?

* * *

"I mean obviously you have to have a codename and outfit." Lydia had a notebook full of drawings she'd come up with, gushing over the idea.

"Why in gods' names would I need that?" Molly fingered chords on a nonexistent guitar.

"To fight crime, duh."

"What?"

"I mean, you obviously have to become a hero. It's just like so obvious."

"So obvious."

"So, what about this one?" Lydia shoved some crude drawing of an outfit in her face. Blue shirt. Red skirt. Cape. *What the...?*

"No," Molly groaned. "Look, this is silly. What crime would I even fight?"

"Three bank robberies this week. All cleaned out, too!"

"Screw banks. They *should* get robbed."

"Dang, what are you now, a commie?" Lydia gave her the look. "People got hurt. And then there's this." She whipped out a news clipping. "The perpetrators cut through the locks of the vaults in each robbery as if with a laser. They've never seen anything like it."

"The cops will get them. They always do. And how would I even catch a bank robber? Just go hang out in a bank all day and wait for it to be robbed? That's weird. They'd probably think I was the robber."

"Yeah, true. I didn't think about that."

IV
"KARMA CHAMELEON"
—CULTURE CLUB, 1983

MR. SCHIAVELLI, the bio and band teacher, let Molly and Lydia use the band hall after school to try out new drummers. Mike the Mic had worked in a pinch, but they wanted a legit stickwoman.

She played around with some logos in her head. Something with wolves maybe. Or axes as guitars. Something. She'd figure it out.

"What about *The Swordceresses!*" Molly called out.

"Hate it." Lydia didn't even look up from tuning her bass. The next up looked like a no-show.

"*Spear-Dames!*"

"Nope."

Outside they heard laughing and yelling from near the field house. Lydia scoped out the window and saw some track jerks tossing rocks at a couple of band geeks, probably one of which was coming to audition for them.

"Oh, crap."

"What?" Molly went and peeked for herself. "Oh, hell no."

Molly set aside her Fender and rolled up her sleeves, heading out the door.

"Molly, wait!" Lydia reached, but Molly was already out the door. "Oh jeez, oh jeez!" She rushed after her.

"Hey, Bank Accounts!" Molly exploded out of the band hall, fists already tightening. Track had the rep of being the refuge of all the yuppie-crusters of the uptown subdivisions, the 5 bedroom and up two-stories, each with its own pool, of course. Too fancy to take hits in football. Too vain to work as a team in baseball. Too short for basketball. But they could run in a circle or jump a hurdle. As long as it didn't mess up their hair.

These three held javelins, coming from their own afternoon practice.

"What's it to you, Punky Brewster?" The one up front giggled. Ty Young. Ty, Todd, and Tag. Seriously. Tag. They were the worst. And, Ty was Mary Felicia aka Muffy from the cheer squad's brother, of course. *Just ugh.*

"Leave them alone." She glared at them and felt her nose flaring. There were going to be some changes at this school. Starting now.

"Says you," Tag or Todd said. One of them. Basically clones from their clone moms no doubt at the country club bar right now on their fourth cosmopolitan while they eyeballed the caddies. *Yuppies. Gross.* "What are you gonna do about it?" He shoved his finger right into her sternum,

Oh no, he didn't! Lydia screamed inside her mind. *Please don't kill him, Molly! Please Please Please!*

Molly closed her eyes, took a breath, and held it for a second, blowing it out calmly. It was weird now, breathing. She still did it out of habit. Also, she figured someone would probably notice if she didn't.

"You guys throw your little sticks. That about right?"

"They're javelins," Todd or Ty informed her. "It's part of the original Pentathlon from the ancient Olympics. The greatest warriors would practice their ski—"

"Shut up, nerd," Molly barked. "I already got my B in history for today."

The T's all looked down their noses.

"Tell you what," Molly began.

Lydia froze. Any minute now, Molly was going to show off and then forty helicopters with G-men would land and take them both away and be dissected. She was sure of it. Helicopters.

"If I throw your little stick further than any of you, you leave these little peckerheads alone. Forever. Savvy?"

"Why do you even care?"

"Because they're *my* peckerheads."

Two of the T's were already backing off.

"Look, man," one of them said, "let's just bail."

"No," Todd spat. "You're on, groupie!"

They marched out onto the field, the band kids looking on from the fence line. Lydia ran after Molly, her face-code failing. The T's started their stretches and practiced hand tosses. Lydia swooped in.

"What are you doing?" she whispered in Molly's ear. "You're gonna launch that thing through a brick wall or something crazy. And then...helicopters!" She was still very concerned about the helicopters.

"What?"

"Please don't do this. You made your point. It's over. Let's go."

"Relax, Lyd. Trust me. I got this. I can control it, I promise."

Lydia stared back at her, right into her eyes. She couldn't understand why, but she just relaxed. Maybe she did have it. She prayed she did.

The first T backed up, got a good run, and let go. The rod whirled through the air and stabbed the grass just short of 70 yards.

"Not bad, bro," one high-fived him.

The next ran through the same motions. He got his stride, gave it a heave, and sent it a yard or two past the first.

"Yeah, yeah, yeah," the first T said, "I got a girlfriend, you know. I don't get as much wrist practice as you." They giggled and started jabbing at each other's crotches. Like some subhuman species.

Molly glared. *So gross. Just no.*

They turned and saw the girls staring, unamused.

"Watch and learn, ladies," Todd said. It was definitely Todd.

He walked it back, lurched forward, got to a sprint, and let fly. Molly watched his stick wobble almost gracefully through the air above them, sinking into the sod at almost 80 yards. Close enough to call it so.

"You can bow out now," he chuckled. "We'll totally understand. And we'll even leave your little band-fags alone...on Thursdays!"

Molly tilted her head, said nothing, and walked down the field to grab a javelin. Lydia shook her head, wishing to all the gods here or beyond for her not to screw this up. Molly marched back to the starting position, expressionless, mechanical.

She stood behind the launching line they'd used. She took three long steps backward, one to the side, like the place-kicker about to go for the point.

"Fair's fair," she stared at them. They all laughed.

"Sure thing, Haggar," one said. *Haggar? Did they really?*

Molly squinted, getting her bearings. She took two fast steps forward and fired that stick straight down the field. It seared right past the others and stabbed dead center into the goal post at the other end of the football field.

Three T jaws dropped. Just hung in the air. Their eyes darted to Molly, the post, each other, back to Molly, and back to the post.

"Fair's fair." Molly collected Lydia and headed back for their instruments.

"HOLY COW!" LYDIA was dancing, twirling, all but singing. "Holy all the animals. Every cow and duck and horse! That was freaking GREAT! The way you..." She motioned with her arm. "Then you..." She threw her arm in a forward pass. "And then it just..." She slammed her fist into her palm. "How did that even? I mean!"

"I don't know," Molly admitted. "I...I meant for it to do that, I think."

"Huh? What do you mean?"

"I don't know. It's like, I thought about it in my head. Like I was picturing it hitting the post. And then it did."

"Like, just like that?"

"Apparently."

"Wow. Still! Even better! That was so epic!" Lydia jumped up and slapped the sign to St. Elmo's Tavern. It was their favorite joint downtown to sit and scarf burgers and even slap some air hockey or shoot a game. *Hey, maybe Molly has some wicked 8-ball powers all of a sudden?* She was usually terrible.

Elmo's was extra cool since it was a block down from Trace's, and Molly had the night shift most nights. She could grab some fries and a shake then be at work in 5 seconds. They'd always been an Eighteener bar, but now that the law had changed, it was dodgy. Unless, you knew Dice who worked the door, and he might slide you in sometimes. If you were cool. Which Molly figured she was. Totally.

"What was epic?" Easton came up behind them, followed by his buddy Nguyen with bodacious hair it was worth mentioning. And, just to turn an excellent day sour, they were followed by Becky de la Beckwith and her Xeroxed clique of It-girls, the Bayettes. *Ugh.*

"Oh, nothing." Lydia folded her arms. "Just something from practice today."

"Yeah, how's the music going?" Easton studied Molly's face. "You guys really shredded it last weekend. From what I saw that is."

"You played like for real? Who would even?" Becky's eyes widened. "What stuff did you play?"

"Nothing you'd know," Molly shirked.

"You'd be surprised." Becky huffed her shoulders.

"I doubt it." Molly grimaced.

"Wow," Easton said. "Do you two always have to do this?"

"Well, I don't." Becky walked inside without giving Molly another look. Her entourage followed suit, each giving her and Lydia the stink eye.

"What's the deal with that?" Molly grilled Easton. She didn't super love seeing the two of them chumming around together again.

"Becky asked to talk earlier. She had another big fight with her mom." His buddy Nguyen gave him a nod and headed inside.

"Miss Perfect from Perfect Family?"

"It's not...it's her deal. She just has her own problems. She also said she's thinking of ditching Blake. I don't know."

Molly didn't super love any of this. *Stupid mall-shopping Becky was just mad Easton was finally getting some sense and moving on from her spoiled brat self. Stupid Bitchass Becky.*

"How is Blake?" Lydia saw Molly's lip tightening. She could always tell when something got off with her. Could easily guess where this was going.

"He's...well, that's just it. No one's seen much of him since last weekend. Hasn't been back to class yet. Becky said he's ignoring her calls, hasn't seen her either. I don't know. It's all weird." Easton shrugged.

Molly suddenly felt herself. She'd been so hung up on *her* stuff lately, she hadn't given much thought to Blake. Yup of yups as he was, he had really been a stand-up dude when it mattered for her and Lyd—stupid sword, notwithstanding. *Seriously, for real, who even has a sword?*

He was probably really hurt. She felt hollow. She should have already checked on him by now.

"I guess I should go visit him." She looked at Lydia who gave her the same look back.

"I should go with you. I can give you a ride," Easton insisted. "His place is kind of a hike from yours."

"What? Why?" Molly side-eyed him. *Why is that even a good idea?* She collected herself again. Also, how did Easton know where she lived? She hadn't told him. She got that feeling she did around him sometimes, like he was studying her. *Be cool, Molly.* "I mean. It's fine, really." It was nice of him to offer, if weird. But, for real, she didn't need him there. What if Blake saw something? *Gods, what if he really did? What do I even say? Jeez, this is all too heavy.* 'Helicopters,' she could already hear Lydia thinking. "Look," Molly stared at Easton, "I really want to do something with you. Soon. But not that. It'll be fine, I promise. He's harmless."

Easton winced.

Maybe he is jealous? That wasn't the worst thing.

VI
"WAITING FOR A GIRL LIKE YOU"
—FOREIGNER, 1981

BLAKE LOOKED out over the brackish gulf water from his upper balcony. The streets of this quaint burgh were quiet this afternoon, the main drag in front of him just barely alive with the comings and goings of the workadays. Little men of business and the tradesmen, *those dirty thralls. What did they know of craft? Of art? Of putting all of yourself into the work, to make something lasting. Something that would endure. No, they used their crude digits to cobble together the quickest job they could so they could move on to the next job. Just as the businessmen above them. At least those took a care for their debts. Debts should always be paid.*

A familiar, denim-clad skateboarder crested on the horizon, scooting along quite briskly, in point of fact. Had she come to him at last? Had it all been worth it in the end? Blake even managed a smile, from one side of his mouth at least.

Molly plodded up the extra wide stairs up to the first floor of Blake's sprawling beach house, looking down at the three lavish sports cars in the driveway. No-telling what else was in the massive garage, half again the size of the house. She had to remind herself to feel at least a little sorry for the guy. *He did us a solid*, she kept saying to herself over and over as she looked at the pristine, columned, four-porch double-decker cracker box on stilts occupying a patch of beachfront that probably ran into some mega dollars just by itself.

His slumped appearance, one arm in a sling and the other resting on yet another cane, certainly helped crank her empathy up to *some*. He almost looked pitiful, in his Panama Jack hat and aviators. *Like, why even live on the beach if you hate the sun that much?*

"Twice unexpected." Blake offered a hand as she met him at the top of the stairs. "Both times welcomed!"

"Yeah," she said, turning to face the water. The view wasn't half bad. The ripple of the soundwater calmed her nerves. She'd dreaded this for a host of reasons, but the worst part, just making herself come here, was done. The rest was just chatter.

And she had the edge now, on everyone. Money couldn't buy anything close to what she had. She liked it. She liked having *the power*.

"I just figured...you know..." Molly slouched on his sitting-room couch in the main foyer. How big was this joint? "I mean it's been too long. I should have come by earlier. I just—"

"No need." Blake tried to stretch himself upright, wincing just before he got it, then blushing at himself. "I wouldn't have wanted the company, preferred as yours is. It was, you can understand, quite embarrassing."

"No, please don't be. You tried something amazing. Really! You know how many guys would have done that? Like hard zero, man."

Blake smiled at that.

Maybe she was right. Maybe just trying was enough. All the same, he needed to be more. He *was* more. But his questions lingered, clawed at him. That damn storm. Holding up a solid rod of metal. He knew better. He knew all. *So stupid.* He'd never learned to mind his surroundings. *Fool!*

"I..." he began. He needed a drink. *Yes, that!* He walked to the wet bar.

Molly noticed he was awfully free with his pop's liquor. Stuff was high end, too. Freaking Johnny Blue. Macallans, two or three labels. Several wines; not that Molly knew about wine, but she'd heard Hoyt at home pine after all those whiskeys he'd never taste. And Blake poured it out like it was water.

Lydia could eat it. Those banks could get robbed all day for all Molly cared. *Screw 'em.*

"A toast?" He returned with two glasses, having poured one she hadn't asked for. *Dudes. Every time.*

"To what?" She took the expensive, carved glass. This whole place, down to the last detail, was pure money. It made her sick to her stomach. That was weird, right? Her stomach? Nausea? Was it even real? It was all in her head, right? Like, only she could make herself feel that. Nothing else could, or could it? She really needed to get a handle on this super stuff.

"Maybe the beginning," he clinked her glass, "of something. Who knows? A new start? Friends?" He shot his drink down his throat and went for another.

"I can certainly give that a maybe." She lifted hers to her face and smelled it. Not bad. But she didn't let it touch her lips. A trick Tracey taught her a year ago. *Never trust em,* she'd insisted. *Always drink your own drinks. Crack your own beers.*

Was that a zit on Blake's nose? A wart? No. You don't just get a wart. A zit. Yikes. Her mind was wandering. Blake was on his third drink now.

"Something," he began, "about that night is...I was...rather, how did we...?"

Molly could tell where this was going. In fact, his question was a relief because it answered half of hers already.

"The lightning. They ran away like scalded dogs after that. I mean, it was freak-out, like a horror show. We all rabbited."

"I see." He wrinkled his eyebrow. "There was nothing else?"

"I mean..." She made sure not to fidget and almost went for that drink but steadied. "We ran back after they were gone and grabbed you. You were breathing, thank goodness. Easton got you to the hospital."

"Yes, I recall that part. And what does he know?"

"We didn't tell him about the bangers. I mean, no more than he knew. Like, why make it weirder, you know? Please don't tell him." She let out a heavy sigh after she finally got that out. *Hard part's over.*

"Yes," he smirked. "Our secret." He liked that.

"Yeah, cool. Thanks," Molly smiled. His zit was kind of funny, in a way. His perfect, plastic face finally had a flaw. Made him almost like a person. Almost.

"Sorry about your arm."

"A trifle." He poured himself another. "It will heal, they assure me. Besides, what a tale, eh?"

Is he drinking through the pain? Molly grinned. "Well, look. Thanks for being cool, and for...well, everything. I just—"

"Oh, another thing..."

Uh oh.

"Silly, I know, but my sword? Did you...?"

Whew! "Oh, that?" Molly breathed. "Yeah, we...didn't think about that. Just got hell out of there. Was it...expensive?"

"Oh, not really." He waved his hand, though his left eye maybe said otherwise. "Silly thing I got at the mall. I can get another one, maybe a better one. A real one this time."

"Yeah," Molly nodded. "Hopefully won't need this one!"

"One can hope."

He was almost alright. He kinda talked weird, though. Not the worst thing.

"Anyway." She stood up. "I gotta get going. Late shift tonight. Really, though, thanks again."

"Don't mention it." He looked down at her drink. "You're not gonna finish?"

Molly glared at it. *Dudes.* She took it in her hand and handed it off to him, pressing her fingers against his as he took it.

"You finish it." She winked at him. "Another thing we can share and not mention?"

He turned his head slightly and gave a curious smile. She totally wrecked him with that one. He'd be on that for a week, she bet.

"Later on, Blake." She headed for the door. "Timeclock is ticking!"

And she was gone.

He took the drink in hand, gingerly. Felt it for a moment. Then lifted it to his face and smelled of it as she had. He took it all in a gulp and smiled.

"Indeed," he said.

VII
"WE DON'T NEED ANOTHER HERO"
—TINA TURNER, 1985

AT THE STORE, Molly laid out masks and cheap, plastic props and hook hands. Cheaper wigs, and flimsy gowns and outfits. Mini makeup kits. Vampire fangs. Werewolf fur gloves. Tattoo sleeves. Molly was still building her costume in her head. She'd snagged the best two glam wigs for her and Lydia, spiked pink and neon blue.

"I'd rather wear black hair, and like a top hat with bones or teeth on it!" Lydia cracked one knuckle.

"Yeah but that's how you already dress every day. Halloween is supposed to be something else. It's the one night you get to be someone else. Right?"

"But I don't want to be someone else. I like *this* me."

"Yeah well." Molly stared out the front windows onto the dimming, empty street. "I want to be someone else."

"Besides, the party is gonna be rad and all, like gnarly rad, but we should also be working on your *other* costume."

"No!" Molly boomed. Trace perked up from her giant headphones in the back, then went back to her jams.

"Another bank got robbed. Over near Springs," Lydia read out from the paper.

"Not my problem." Molly focused on pricing the costumes. *How much should we charge for a used Alf costume?*

"Yeah, and they still can't figure out how they're cutting through the vaults. They're always in and out super-fast. No heavy tools. So weird." Lydia shook her head.

Molly changed the subject. "Yeah, anyway, Blake was a blank slate. So, I think we're good there at least."

"Cool." Lydia folded her paper.

* * *

Molly got back home late after closing up at Trace's. Hoyt and Clair had crashed for the night. Since she wasn't tired, she decided she should do something for them. She folded all the laundry, laid out clothes and made a lunch for Hurl in the morning, swept and mopped up the kitchen, then busted out the Pledge. She was halfway done with the den when she heard Hurl cussing at something quietly from his room, a dim light, some bloops and bleeps. She peeked in and watched him playing his game, trying to rescue some princess from some dungeon. He wasn't supposed to be up late, Clair's orders, but Molly was no snitch.

"Can I watch?" She let herself in his room and sat next to him, tousling his hair as he sprawled forward on his bed.

"Uh..." He paused his game, giving her a half-shocked stare. "Yeah I guess."

"What's this one?"

"Mario." He unpaused and pushed further into what looked to Molly like some maze. All puzzles and math, that's all these were. Kinda clever, really. Trick kids into solving problems by making out like it was fighting dragons and monsters. Neat.

Hurl wasn't very good at this, bless his heart.

"You already went that way."

"Oh, right." It was as close to a thanks as she knew she would get from him. Close enough.

"Keep at it, kid." She patted him on the head. "You can figure it out. You can figure out anything you put your mind to."

"How do you know?"

"Because I said so."

Hurl believed her.

* * *

More days went by. Nights picked up at Trace's. She was on a blitz this week. A different costume every night: a spandex robot (a bit showy, but she liked that), the Hamburglar (with jailbird leggings), a mermaid (which gave her the excuse to sit back and prop her feet up on the counter and do nothing all that night).

"Perks of being the owner, kid." She sat painting her fingernails aqua blue. "Besides, it lures in customers."

"Does it, though?"

"Yes," Tracey scowled. "I'm very mysterious. It's what I like most about me."

VIII
"LOOKS THAT KILL"
—MÖTLEY CRÜE, 1983

THE BIG NIGHT rolled around at long last. Tracey was MIA, but Molly knew to expect that. The downtown business block Halloween blowout was like Christmas, New Years, 4th of July, and well, Halloween, all rolled into one for Tracey. She always started co-planning the next just two days afterward—day one was for sleeping it off.

Several nearby businesses co-sponsored and participated in some way, but it was really Tracey's baby. Elmo's being right up the block was a big boost. Them, Santé across the street, and the all-night daiquiri bar meant the spice did flow. Not that any of it was lacking. People packed their own spirits aplenty. The best were the ones that worked it into their costume. There'd been a cowboy a year before with squirt guns full of vodka.

The streets all around 25th Ave closed off as far as 4 blocks off the beach and a block either side. The party was so big it seemed like close to half the town would show up, if just for the spectacle. Cops watched the perimeters at a few points, just to make sure nothing got too rowdy. Most of them would be cruising the upper avenues looking for real trouble. Maybe Lydia was right. Maybe that's where Molly should be tonight, all decked out in some black on black gear and a ski mask. *Yuck. Screw that.* She was right where she wanted to be.

Seven o'clock came on quick. The streets began to come alive. Molly saw a reaper on stilts go by, along with a bunch of zombies and a robot. Seemed right.

"It's time." Molly locked the front door and flipped the closed sign out.

Lydia set out all their accessories.

"Don't do it." She looked back at Molly already at the record player they had hooked to the intercom.

"Oh, it's coming." Molly grinned, eyes lit all the way to heaven. She dropped the needle. Lydia groaned as Molly went straight into the lip sync to her favorite Mötley Crüe song.

"No," Lydia sighed.

Sixx and Mars railed all across the store.

Lydia teased the blue hair on her wig. Every time, Molly did this. Silently screamed in Lydia's face, holding her nonexistent microphone.

Lydia gave up and sang it right along with her as they geared up, Molly in a pink short dress with a big white fake leather belt tight around her waist, and Lydia in a purple skirt with black stockings going into her baddest black knee boots. Molly donned her hot pink wig, and they both did their eyes in multicolor makeup, stretching like neon shadows down each side of their faces. Big tacky earrings all around. Lydia wrapped up in her leather side-zip biker jacket, while Molly stretched out in rainbow thigh-high socks and stiletto short boots.

"Wait, what?" Lydia wrinkled her brow.

"What?"

"You look like Rainbow Brite not Jem."

"What? No, I don't." Molly folded her arms.

"Jem never wore that crap, man."

"Jem wears a lot of stuff. And I like rainbows, okay?"

"I'm telling you. Look, if you wear those, I'm switching to my black wig. Joan Jett over Jem every day."

"Fine," Molly rolled them down and grabbed an extra pair of dark stockings. "Killjoy."

The record had played through the rest of that side when they were done. The street bustled with revelers. They were ready.

"But I'm keeping these." Molly stuffed the rainbow stockings in her purse.

IX

"I JUST DIED IN YOUR ARMS TONIGHT"
—CUTTING CREW, 1986

RIGHT OUT THE DOOR they ran right into two dudes in decked out picture-perfect firemen costumes. Even had legit-looking axes.

"Rad," Molly nodded as they breezed past.

"Pretty sure those were real firemen." Lydia leaned in.

Down 25th, the stage was set up with ghost dancers and a DJ flipping discs. Molly'd set Trace up with stacks of proper language. Sound cranked and the girls were already bobbing their heads. A wolfman in a basketball jersey ran up with high fives, then ran down toward the stage toward the dancing. Across the street, outside the port authority offices, a whole crew of at least a dozen Jimmy Buffets held their canned beers, looking unsure they were even supposed to be there.

Molly and Lydia made their way toward the stage where the DJ blasted Palmer. Nice. A witch, pointy hat and all, breakdanced like a champ right out in front of the stage. Two Dorothy's egged her on, and a scarecrow clearly had ideas.

"Oooh, rough," Lydia said.

"What?" But Molly saw it as she was turning to scan the rest of the area. Two more Jems sipped martinis outside Elmo's. *Oh, man.* Then she saw another all the way up the street past the daiquiri shack. "Balls." Molly shook her head.

"I mean, it's fine, right?" Lydia tried to put out the flame.

"Ugh..." Molly headed for The Dice, dressed always as The Dice. He didn't even feign to ID her as she strolled past him inside and plunked down her hard-earned $3.35 for a double shot of Jimmy and a Tab.

The house music in Elmo's was just as rocking as the DJ, and Lydia laughed as Molly shot her drink.

"Can you even get drunk?" she laughed. "You're throwing your money away."

"Let's find out." She slapped the bar for another round.

* * *

Back outside, Molly had a clearer head. *Is that how this is supposed to work?* Didn't seem right. She saw the lights and their motion slow to a crawl, felt time slowing. She was making it do that. Could she? Wait, maybe she was drunk. Was she? No. She was doing this. Lydia talked, but her mouth moved so slow Molly couldn't make out the words. Her arm rose up like cold syrup barely dripping from a can, her finger extending. Molly looked. She still moved like normal. Or did she? She *was* drunk. No, she wasn't.

Lydia's finger finally zeroed on yet another Jem walking toward them. Of course. *The more the merrier, hey!* Except this one...

Time snapped back to speed. Molly's eyes went white pale.

"Oh. My. Freaking. God," Becky de la Beckwith becked at her.

You absolutely had to be kidding. Molly could vomit. Could she? Oh, for this, she could. This was the no holds barred worst. Holy nightmare cataclysm ever and always.

"You like Jem?" Molly dropped her shoulders.

"Oh yeah!" Becky sneered. "Because you're the only person ever to watch a TV or listen to music. Get outta my way, Slater." Becky shook her head and muscled past Dice into Elmo's. Of course, they didn't card her either. Figured.

Freaking Becky.

*

The night got going when fireworks shot into the sky as the DJ cranked Whitesnake. People danced and drank and drank some more. Fireballs burst in a hundred directions. The sound of brass horns blew in the distance. A path appeared up 25th as onlookers migrated to either side. The Crowned Queen of Pop crowed over the speakers.

A carnival procession marched toward the beach, a host of clowns of all shapes and sizes beating on drums and blowing on trumpets, horns, and saxes. The ringleader, front and center, wore a sliced-right tux and tails, an evergreen paisley vest, and a long string bow tie tight around a thick, white paper collar. All that was tucked into a pair of come get some leather pants that screamed all the way down to some slick high heels. An oversized top hat pulled low obscured the face but not the platinum blonde curls peaking from all sides underneath it.

The brass played in time with the DJ's music and made for strange electricity in the air. All eyes locked onto the procession. The ringleader twirled her cane like a drum major who knew her trade. Her free hand flipped the top hat off her head revealing ruby red lipstick. She had even marked a mole on the right above her lip.

"Is that?" Lydia asked.

"Yep." Molly shook her head and clapped. *Oh, Tracey, you mad woman.*

"And what exactly is she?" Lydia kept staring, trying to figure it out.

"Something Wicked," Molly smirked. Trace had really outdone herself. "In a Material World."

Tracey gave Molly a wink as she and the procession made their way to the stage. The walking fashion statement had hired half the high school marching band for this stunt. She kept twirling that cane like a rifleman in an infantry drill, too.

Tracey took the microphone from the DJ stand. "Are you ready for a party?!" Everyone was shouting, screaming, drinking, dancing. Tracey owned the night. "I said are you ready?" She bobbed her head in time to the record and motioned for her DJ to raise the volume. She twirled around the microphone stand like it was her boyfriend, flipped that cane high into the night sky, then caught it and tucked it behind her waist to massive applause.

Tracey. Melnitz.

The songs droned one into another. Molly laughed. Lydia danced with a guy in a cheerleader skirt and pigtails. They all scored more drinks. Molly played with time again. And again. Was that really happening or was it all some illusion? Was she even here? She had been feeling further and further away since...well, since *it*.

She let herself drift with the music. She could piece together the different sounds, putting them each in their own compartments. The music, each instrument, the air, the light wind, the taste of dampness but not yet rain — not for another day she sensed, the gulf water in the sound, the little swimming things darting around in it.

And eyes. Eyes that had locked onto her.

She could feel them through the crowd. Hers sorted through the motion, weaving past all the costumed dancers and bystanders. There. White linen blazer, sleeves rolled to the elbows, baby blue t-shirt tucked into matching linen pants, slip-on white canvas shoes without socks, hair slicked back and sunglasses at night. Leaned against an almost matching white with blue stripes Z28 convertible a block away. Something dark hung around him now, though. A thing Molly felt, somehow. Some secret he clenched tight with hands shoved into his pockets. His friend Nguyen was beside him in a matching, color-reversed outfit.

Easton. Braddock.

He kept staring, no idea she could see him dead on from this far away. His gaze wasn't familiar, though. He wasn't staring at Molly Slater. He was staring at the getup. The hair. The dress. The makeup. She was incognito. He didn't see her. He saw her costume. Like she really *was* someone else. *Oh, this will be fun!*

Molly ran to Lydia who was cutting it sideways with a gorilla this time.

"Give me your wig." Molly shoved out her hand, pulling her own off with the other.

"What?"

"Look, let's just trade wigs. I'll explain later."

"Nevermind." Lydia pulled a black one out of her satchel. "Just take it. I'm rocking the Jett. This is better anyway."

"Yeah, sure. Go get 'em, Blackheart."

Molly fitted her bubblegum blue wig on her head and wormed through the crowd, twisted and turning away, going backward and sideways, never losing her honed-in sense of where Easton was at all times. He scoured the crowd for his pink-haired rockstar. He found a Jem. Not her, though, Easy a forty-something two-time divorcee who would probably jump at the option, now that she was a gin too many deep. He squinted his eyes. He was unsure. Scanned the crowd again. Molly made another move, down past Elmo's, back near Trace's shop. Another Jem. This one lanky, and taller. Not half bad, all told.

Molly giggled. This was fun. She ducked down and swapped her wigs again, fixed it up. She wove through the crowd, swaying fluidly to the other side of the street, toward his car. *Like, his really, really nice car!* She couldn't help herself but peek down at the seats. Leather. 8-ball shifter. A CB radio? *What is he? Burt Reynolds?*

He was scanning again. She wasn't looking his way but could feel his eyes moving toward her. She turned, leaned back into his car door, and looked down at her neon nails. She eased her face up, let her eyes whisper to his for a second. She heard his heart thump. Then quicken.

He started toward her. A stilt-walker got in his way, and she was gone again. Blue hair back. Vanished in the crowd. He stood in the middle of the street twisting his head. So adorably lost. What did he think he was seeing? Who had he made up his mind she was? Some phantom. Some glimpse, a shadow of some perfect no one. *Oh, this is fun!*

And the best was yet to come.

Now, where was she? Molly closed her eyes and broke the sounds and smells apart again. She had Easton's eyes gazing here and there. His poor pal followed close behind, lost as a child. She felt his anxiousness. This wasn't even why he had come, she felt. He was looking for...*something else.*

People singing. Dancing. Drinking and laughing. Making their small talk. *There.* A complaint. A wrinkled lip, and a flared nose. Coming out of Elmo's with a hurricane glass. Molly swapped into the pink wig again, wove herself right behind Becky who stared at the stage. Molly faced Easton and caught his eye. She stared right into him, so intent she felt it actually hit him in the chest, staggering him.

He blinked, and she was gone. Becky's back remained. He made his way to her. Molly watched from the side, swapping her wigs one last time. She pulled out her blue eye pencil from her kit and gave some hard lines outlining her fuchsia triangles.

Easton was at Becky's back, his finger reaching to tap her shoulder. Nguyen scanned the side streets, staring off into the darkness.

"Hey there, Gator." Molly came from behind him, her voice icing up his spine. He turned. Looked at Molly, seeing her beneath her blue hair and makeup. She smiled at him, so sure, so certain. He mouthed something, nothing that was words. He looked back behind him as Becky turned and faced him.

"Becky?" He fidgeted, then turned back to Molly. "I was..." He looked back at Becky, then back to Molly. "I thought I..."

"Yes, Easton?" Becky looked very Beckly at him.

"Yeah, Easton." Molly suppressed a full-on giggle. His apparition had vanished. A whisper floated off on the wind. Gone. Forever. He knew it wasn't Becky he saw. Now he'd lost her.

So perfect.

"Y'awright, dude?" Nguyen squinted at him.

"I..." He looked at Becky, then back to Molly. "Did you guys come together?" Molly erupted in laughter.

"Oh, my freaking god, are you nuts?" Becky was a stone. "That's horrible! Like, seriously, I may yak. Ugh."

"Hey, pal." Nguyen leaned in, the rest a whisper.

Easton nodded. Nguyen veered off toward the north end of the shindig toward two other girls. One of them a redhead, Molly noted.

Jackson's "Beat It" lit up the noise from the stage, Tracey robotting stiff as a board along with her clown band. Some kid dressed to the nines as the man of the moment busted his best moves. Even rocked the one glove. Kept the hat tipped just right. Easton chuckled at the guy who had clearly waited all night for this minute. Molly gave her most impressed *not bad* nod. Even Becky gave a sideways glance of respect.

When Cutting Crew cut in, Molly asked Easton a question using only her deeply shadowed eyes. She felt him miss a breath. He caught Becky from the corner of his eye, hesitated. *Oh god,* Molly thought, *don't you even dare, De la Beckwith!*

"I'm sorry," he said, as if to both of them at once. "It's weird. Is it weird?"

Molly scrunched her face at him. Becky simply sighed, looked off to the stage. Tracey had pulled Lydia up there with her, the two were lockstep in something so sharp they had to have practiced it.

"You know it isn't." Becky turned back to Easton. "Just go."

Molly had already recused herself to a cloister of dancers jerking about in random movements, all of them half-drunk. She couldn't help herself but air strum with the chords when they hit. Easton moved to her with all the confidence of a ropewalker his first time out.

"Mommy say you could play?" Molly twirled, evaded him.

Easton's voice was snatched out of the air as he was caught in a boogaloo with couple of Care Bears judging by the designs on their shirts, their fur ears and paw gloves. Molly twirled a time or two with some cowboy she'd seen earlier doing lasso tricks. Maybe he had vodka too.

"Look, it's..." Easton lobbed to Molly over the music when he caught back up to her. "We have a weird history. It's a long story. I just didn't want it to be a thing. I know you already hate each other."

"I don't hate her." Molly twirled almost into his chest, staring at his face, his eyes.

"Oh, no?" He took her by the hand, which felt weird, and firm, and electric.

Molly eyed him. Why was she even moving her with his arm as he led? She could tear his stupid arm from its socket if she wanted to. She could. Totally could. His eyes were there again. Because his face was. There. Next to hers.

Easily break his arms.

"No." she swirled back to her cowboy, abandoning Easton to Funshine and Love-A-Lot, who definitely had ideas. *Rutting bears.*

"She's not the person you think she is," he said, making it his commitment now to get back to her, almost coming broadside into the cowboy who had noticed this hombre horning in on him. It might have even turned into a row, which could have been fun to watch, maybe, if the cowboy hadn't been ensnared, rope and all, by the Forest of Feelings.

"I guess I just..." Easton dizzied as Molly gave *him* a good twirl. He stuttered when his gaze settled back on her, her eyes shooting bullets right into him.

"Just shut up and dance with me, idiot." Molly took charge of him, moving him about the street with the music like he was made of paper. Every few moments she made his face almost touch hers, then slip away. This gave her no end of joy. She giggled so much inside herself she felt her stomach flurry. His eyes glued to hers, softening, questioning, losing their grip on...*something*.

Molly smiled, glanced through the back of her mind. At Becky, still staring longingly toward the stage. At the stage, Lydia and Tracey walked like Egyptians. At the crowd, bustling and full of joy and wonderment. All merriment and elation. It filled her up. She felt it all herself. Like it was part of her.

Others stumbled off, one too many, maybe sit for a spell. Some slipped off into the quiet, pressing their luck while they had it, a moment not to be squandered. Others had some disappointment, which she felt along with them. Things hadn't quite gone their way, but hey, it was still a party. Some were just here for the sights and the sounds. And one...

One stared through it all. Through all the motion and noise and aura that had coalesced into this one mass of revelry. His stare was neither kind nor unkind. It just was. There. Hanging in the air. Like a gnat now, buzzing around her ear, wrecking her jam. Her vibe. Her moment.

Molly focused on him, standing there, half in shadow, watching. Not just her. All of it. Just as she had been. His outfit was a costume if one were being generous. Long, dark leather coat, ankle length. Nice boots. Very nice, in fact. Blue-gloved hands peaked out from the heavy sleeves. A large hood shrouded the face. His one lone festive allowance: an off-white, almost yellow, skull face-paint.

His eyes. Hollow. Empty.

Blake.

He was here. At the party. He was no longer looking at her. His gaze had settled on Becky who'd found herself another fine beverage, angered but also endeared, with...something.

The song ended, and Easton felt bold enough to end it with an embrace, which Molly duly noted, but she was more occupied with the new arrival. She let Easton's asking hands slip away from her as she floated toward...whatever this was to become.

From her distance, she saw Blake take Becky's hands, and just as quickly she ripped them away. Easing closer, her ears caught their conversation. Becky shouted; Blake winced and shrank away. People began to gawk. Molly, without sensing herself, flowed into their line of sight. Blake's gaze shot to her, followed by Becky's.

"Oh, of course," Becky laughed. Something had really got off with her, and it wasn't anything to do with Blake. Molly couldn't understand how she knew that, but she did. "And this whole *deal* between *us?*" Becky pointed at him. "Yeah. It's done. I'm done. I'm tired of pretending. I'm just tired. I can't." She took another drink from her glass and looked hard at Tracey on the stage. "I just can't anymore."

Becky downed her drink and stomped off toward Molly just as Easton caught up, already reaching to referee what he thought must be a thing. He mumbled something but wasn't quick enough.

"Enjoy yourself," Becky sneered at Molly. "For gods' sakes someone should."

Becky moved into the distance, disappearing into the crowd. Molly stared after her a long time. There was hurt in her voice. Something beyond her everyday average Becking. Some awful part of Molly's brain felt compelled to go after her. Like, what was that even about? *Becky? Ew. No.*

The skull. Blake. That outfit. So minimal. He was steaming. She could almost smell his embarrassment wafting from his face. But she couldn't feel it, like she felt everyone else around her. Easton, still making his way toward them, felt confusion. Becky, so many things. Some guy in a sailor outfit staring at Lydia on the stage felt...*yikes!* But, Blake? Nothing. Like he wasn't even there.

"I..." Blake adjusted his accouterment, composing himself. "I apologize for that business. Very untidy." He pulled a flask, engraved, and turned it up to his lips. "A party it seems!" He took another swig and smiled, lightening his mood by measures. "Shall we fest?"

Easton sidled up behind Molly. She smelled the aftershave he wore despite never needing to shave. It comforted her more than she wanted it to. But it wasn't enough.

She felt so much now—Easton's tension rising from the situation, from Blake simply being there. There was something to that. Easton holding something back. Guarding it. Blake, an empty spot in the crowd. Everyone around them oblivious.

Something else, though, something...wrong. Up on stage, Lydia stopped moving. She and Trace stared up 25th, far up beyond the party. They felt...*dread.*

X
"TONIGHT IS WHAT IT MEANS TO BE YOUNG"
—FIRE, INC., 1984

FIRST CAME THE LOW RUMBLE. Then the lights. Neon. Every color on the spectrum. The rumble became a growl. Wheels. Chains. Leather. Sliced-off fenders. Drag handlebars. Steel-tipped boots. All laced with glowing neon. Each roaring steel bike in the procession left neon residue in its wake, a wall of light trailing behind it. Faces came into focus. Metal teeth. Clumpy, dirty, dreds of blonde and bleached-white hair. All kinds of wrong.

The party stopped. All eyes gazed at the motorcyclers, their exhaust pipes barking and spitting as they slowed. They grinned like hyenas about to feed. The crowd moved, veering anywhere that wasn't near the bikes. More bikes came. A dozen became two. And then three. Molly began to lose count. She sensed what the bikers felt, their rage.

One who appeared to be a leader roared his bike upright on its hind wheel, screaming its exhaust. He threw his arm forward as he dropped it and rolled right into the crowd still fleeing the street.

Screams echoed.

Chains and bats appeared in the bikers' hands. Flashing grins. Snickers of laughter. One of them produced some kind of rifle that fired a soundwave into the crowd. She froze in that moment, confused by the weapon and situation both. These weren't Mutes. They were something else—something worse maybe.

Easton tackled Molly to the sidewalk, away from the danger for the moment. He turned to the onslaught. Molly stared at him. She looked to the stage. Lydia scrambled, scanning for her. Molly felt her panic. Trace paled with anger. She glared as this roadkill tore through what she'd built for a year.

Garbage cans burned. Shattered glass ripped the air as Motorcycles rode into the businesses. Sound guns knocked down whole groups of fleeing people.

"I've got to get you out of here." Easton looked at Molly, then to the crowd. "I've got to get..." His face tightened, pulse racing.

Uniformed officers appeared. One caught a baton on the back of his head, sending him reeling. Another, seeing the fate of the first, ran the other way.

"Bastards." Easton twisted, turned. He looked lost. Torn. He turned to Molly. "Can you get into the store and hide?" He needed her to be safe; she felt that. But he still held something else inside him. Something bursting to come out.

"Yes. Go do what you can. But be safe." It was what he needed to hear, that she would be okay. She couldn't say why she knew but she did.

Easton looked again in her eyes, then ran at a group of teenagers caught in a crosswind of racing bikes.

Molly stood, looked toward the stage. Lydia had ducked behind the big speakers, her eyes finding Molly, pleading with her, asking her to do what only *she* could now. Trace fumed and stomped off the stage, holding the microphone, and screamed, "NO!" The reverb drowned out the bikes for a second.

No, Tracey! Molly shot from her mind. But it didn't work that way.

The leader's bike wheeled to face Tracey. He grinned a jackal grin. Molly gritted her teeth hard enough to crush metal.

"You get away from this place!" Trace yelled into the microphone. "You leave here now!"

The leader bike lurched forward. It screamed at Trace. He grabbed the microphone from her hands, twisted the cord around her then sped down the road, ripping Tracey from her feet. Her head just missed the asphalt as he dragged her up 25th.

Molly scorched with raw fire. Her time slowed again. Everything crawled. Her eyes shot everywhere at once. Easton was at the other end of the street, helping two Jimmy Buffets into a back alley. Becky had tucked herself into Elmo's, hiding behind The Dice's big shoulders. Safe enough. Lydia was still hidden. *Blake??* He was nowhere.

She'd have to chance it.

She darted to the side, into a shadow. Swapped her wigs again, fitting the pink Jem wig just right. Looked down at her stilettos.

"Oh no," she muttered. "You're not gonna do at all."

She kicked off both useless heels. *Never again.* She looked down at her flimsy black hose, then at her purse with those thick, heavy rainbow thigh socks staring back at her.

"Well," she told them, "you're better than nothing."

Tracey screamed, grabbing at the grit of the street with no purchase. The biker gang leader dragging her more for fun than to maim. She looked up at her attacker just in time to see a pair of rainbows land next to her, yank the severed cord from his hands, and then she was airborne. Her eyes went blurry, then dizzy. She was on top of a building. Her building.

The gang leader's bike lurched from side to side at the loss of his payload. He got it under control and spun around to a missing Tracey. He scanned for his prey. His comrades rolled up beside him. Behind them came a deafening boom of a hundred thousand pounds of iron slamming into the asphalt.

They whipped their heads around.

Rainbow-clad legs, taut and loud, climbed into black hose above the knee, followed quickly by a frill of pink flapping in the night wind. A massive, garish, silver-studded, white belt, buckled firm at the waist. The pink continued again from there, all the way to the large, open collar and puffed out shoulder pads. Fuchsia-pink hair flowed over a lavishly adorned set of painted eyes, their hot centers staring bolts into them.

The leader smirked to either side of himself. Two riders revved at her, bat and chains ready, waiting to club her down.

Molly seized both their front tires, dead-stopping them in place, sending both riders into the grit. She jerked up the bikes, one in each hand, and threw them into the Hancock building, spitting sparks, gears, and gas fumes everywhere.

"Holy shit!" came from somewhere in the chaos.

Molly glared at the gang leader, his guts wrought with cowardice. She felt his weakness. His smallness. And she hated him for it. She looked at them all, then down at her balled fists. Muscle memories kicked in from some void within her walled-off past. An instinct now drove her.

She turned her head up 25th, at the maelstrom of motor and madness. Her eyes narrowed, time slowing again. Just as she commanded it. It didn't change her speed to any degree that she could tell, but it targeted her. Focused her mind, her reflexes. She zeroed on the thug with the illest intent and flung herself at him. She ripped his engine out of its chassis then clubbed the remaining apparatus with it, sending the bike and him careening off the street.

Another thundered at her, baseball bat held forward like some knight of old. She jutted out her arm and clotheslined him as his bat shattered against her chest. Molly caught the motorcycle flying past her in her other hand and smashed it to bits on the ground next to the rider's whimpering body.

She locked onto another one half a block from her and flung herself at him, kicking both him and the bike twenty yards away into a dumpster. He screamed in terror and pain as the shards of his machine pinned him against the ground. She drank that hurt. Licked it off her lips.

Molly fired herself like a cannon at a trio of bikes, batting two of them to the ground with the third, metal grinding metal as chainlinks burst and sprayed everywhere. The reek of motor oil and engine heat hung thick in the air now. And screams. So many of them. Aching at her. Clawing at her mind. Begging her. Pleading. *Praying* for help. Someone's help.

Another two rode back and forth in the Santé bar across the street, tearing up the place. She howitzered inside the storefront, took one biker by the leg, and connected him to his ally, their heads conking like coconuts. Maybe they could forget everything they ever once knew, along with who and what they were. Or maybe they were even dead. She didn't care anymore.

She thought of Tracey again. Rage grew inside her.

She stomped her way out of the bar. Cries dimmed in the distance as the people got themselves clear and away. Her presence now known, the other bikers sped away, up 25th, gunning their throttles to gain speed and traction. Their neon vapor lingered after them. She leapt toward the stragglers, slamming two of them to the ground, their riders hurling into the pavement, rolling and twisting and breaking and screaming. *Like they deserve.*

The rest were brake lights in the distance. Molly turned.

Their leader hadn't gotten away.

He saw her eyes burning at him, her whole head molten heat. He goosed his throttle. He was gonna go for it. Molly grinned. Her time slowed to a crawl. She scanned the scene. There were hurt and injured people everywhere, bikers and innocents alike.

Easton wrapped a girl's leg with a torn off sleeve from his jacket, the other missing as well. The poor girl was no more than fifteen. Her cries pierced Molly. Lydia had come out from her corner, standing, staring at the spectacle Molly had become. Others hid, cowering, running, hurting, but now they turned to see her. Easton, Nguyen, even Dice, watched to see what *she* would do. What she *could* do. What she was. Even Becky...Becky had come to the window to see, and she felt...she felt...no. Not *that.*

But this one? This pool of wretched grease? This waste of breath and blood and bone and meat? This insidious creature racing its ratcheted machine at her, doing at least seventy by now, but as fast as an ant to Molly's perception. He produced a pistol, sending blast after blast into her face, her chest, everywhere. She laughed as the shots thudded against her, tickling her cheeks and nose.

His eyes screamed with fear, and as he reached near her arm's length, he made to veer off. Molly roundhouse kicked him, slamming him like a fastball all the way back down the street, careening, thudding, and bouncing off the blacktop like a deflated football. He crumpled to a stop just before the stage.

Molly now stood alone up the street from what remained. She looked at everyone. They looked in turn at her. Easton's eyes were golf balls. Nguyen grinned, some strange satisfaction beaming out from him. He enjoyed this.

People walked out of the buildings and stores. Trash fires blew themselves out in the wind. Screeching feedback carried itself all through the night air. Had that been there the whole time? Was someone clapping? *That's weird, right?* She was a thing now. They all saw her. Or something. They saw *something. Thank the gods for costume ubiquity after all.*

Lydia stood at the stage, her eyes zeroed on Molly's. The two of them connected in synchronicity over the distance. Lydia nodded to the side. Their face code.

Yeah.

Lydia's eyes stayed on her. Learning her. Studying whatever from her face they could glean.

Time to go.

The crowd saw her, all her color, her pink, so much pink, and grease and grime from the fight. She stood before them. Bent her knees.

And lit off into the dark sky.

OUT OF THE COLD of the darkest night in the town's history, a hooded, skull-faced figure stood by its lonesome amidst the aftermath of chaos. Blake's mechanical gait carried him toward the center of the now largely abandoned street, just in front of the stage. Easton Braddock, the little letter jacket nice guy, put a wet cloth on a woman's bleeding forehead. Those who could were walking or limping away. Lights and sirens closed the distance, ending the eerie quiet left in *her* wake.

Yes.

Her.

They'd all seen her, as had he. What she was. What she was to become? A thing he questioned as well as they did.

A dirty mask rolled to his feet, drifted to him by the wind like some tumbleweed from some old movie he never cared to see. He crouched to it, a curious thing. He lifted it in his hands, inspecting it. A now dingy goblin mask, its pointed ears mocking him. *Alien.* Other. A curious thing.

Near him, a felled member of the night's disturbance stirred from his languishing pain, his face all cuts and bruises. One eye black and shut. No attempt to crawl away. Too broken for anything like that. He reached for a pack of cigarettes from his pocket to no avail.

Nguyen stood beside the damaged gang member. Smirking, almost jocular.

"How's something like that feel?" He poked the gang member's wounded shoulder, the guy wincing in pain.

"Piss off, peachfuzz." he grabbed at his shoulder.

"I mean, really." Nguyen smiled, kneeling to face the broken man, showing his pleasure at their pain. "You guys just got your ass beat by Rainbow Brite!"

The biker looked up at him, snarling. "It was Jem, idiot."

EPISODE III

0

"IN THE AIR TONIGHT"
—PHILL COLLINS, 1980

A WHITE Z28 sang its shotgun exhaust into the wee hours of that horrendous All Saints Day. A Kool pack slapped against a dirtied linen-clad leg, then gave up its stick of long-sought relief. A circle of heat glistened in the barely peeking light on the horizon. Palms and white-oaks whizzed by in the breeze that was more than tripled due to the speed of the open-top vehicle.

Easton Braddock drove, his youthful face now aged with the night prior's gruesome truths, half-truths, and...well...myths. The lines of that face drawn. Tired, lost, and confused.

He breathed in the blessed nicotine heat, softly casting it back out into the crisping air. His Kools passed themselves off to a partner beside him, the ritual repeating itself. The only sound cutting the silence was the faint hum of some Brit on the radio, doing a better job at expressing the feel of the moment than they could muster.

Nguyen, his clothes as tattered and dirtied as his mate's, took a long pull from his stick, his slick black locks dancing in the refreshing air.

Each looked at the other a moment and said it all without so much as a word. All the work they'd done together, everything they'd accomplished, set up, prepared for...blown to hell in an instant. A whole new paradigm now chilled them to the bone.

They turned their gazes back to the road, the little white lines erasing beneath them. The air. Thin and dewy. Getting thinner. Colder days were coming soon.

They rode east. Into the morning.

I
"IN THIS COUNTRY"
—ROBIN ZANDER, 1987

SOLEMN FACES SURROUNDED the long conference table in the secure room of the hidden base. Heads nodded. Chatter ceased. A radio squawked in the background. All eyes crept from the speechless attendees to the duly appointed joint chief.

"Gentlemen, we are at Defcon 1." The chief slammed his fist down on the table. "This is not a drill. This is real. This is everything we've trained and prepared for."

The attendees nodded in agreement, yet their eyes belied their chagrin and confusion. Long-awaited as it may have been, there was simply no preparing for what they now faced. It was a hard and sudden truth.

"What do we know for sure? First Officer?" he directed at his second in command.

"Obviously enhanced strength. Well beyond known human limits, even in the rarest and most extreme cases. Lifted whole motorcycles. Harleys, too. Heavy ones."

"Yeah, and threw them like they were softballs," another officer nodded to the first. There was additional nodding.

"What else?" the chief demanded. "I want a full account."

"Invulnerability," the second officer said. "Impervious to bullets, at least."

"Anything heavier?"

"Not that we can determine as yet."

"Anything else?"

"Flight, or near enough," one offered. "Whoever—whatever it was took off into the sky like a rocket after the event."

"Okay," the chief said. "What we need to determine now is—"

"Point of order, sir," a third officer, one of the newcomers, spoke up. An addition to the team that hadn't been a unanimous decision, it bore mentioning. "We haven't followed procedure. We haven't officially come to order or called out old business."

"Are you freaking jacking with me, fresh meat?" the chief barked out. "We've got a full-blown Super on our hands and you're whining about Robert's Rules?"

Molly peaked in through their makeshift clubhouse window and giggled a little at the whole charade of it. *Jeez, they take this whole "knights" thing so freaking seriously.* It was sort of cute, though. *Hell, let them be young while they are.*

She made her way back into the garage where Lydia creep-stared into the void while The Cure softed at them from the stereo.

"Earth to Lyd." Molly snapped her fingers.

"Right." Lydia came out of her haze. "What's the brigade on? They as lit up as you'd expect?"

"Defcon 1." Molly smirked, picked up her guitar while Lydia strapped on her bass and plugged in. They still needed a drummer.

"Is that the good one or the really bad one?"

"I can never remember." Molly picked a test chord.

Back in the war room, the inner circle turned to face their flags, that of these great United States of god-blessed America, the four fleurs-de-lis Maltese cross of their order, as well as the framed photographs of incoming President Hogan along with Commodore Pierre Le Moyne d'Iberville.

"I call this meeting of the Knights of the Order of St. Louis, Bayrats Chapter, officially to order. Say wha?" the chief called out ritually.

"Bayrats never say Uncle!" They began pounding on the table. All part of their routine.

"Now, where were we?" Mike the Mic, acting commander of their chapter, stared into the assembly. "Did anybody actually get eyes on her? We're sure it's a *her*?"

"Point of order, sir." friggin new guy again. "Old business."

"Oh my damn god," Mike growled. "Are you yanking us or what?"

"I mean, I kinda had something big about that, actually." Hurl's eyes reiterated his statement.

"Oh Jesus F Christ on a cracker." Mike threw his hands up.

The annoying newb, Lambert, was really working Mike's nerves. Yeah, okay, he had a cool jacket and he could fight good. Pretty good, at least; he'd knocked that turd burglar Rowdy Stinson's keister into the dirt when he tried to pants Hurl three weeks ago at lunch. Lambert had been on their shortlist for a while. Him stepping into that rescue was as good an audition as any. But still, this was the biggest thing ever and he was bogging them down in bureaucratic B.S.

"Okay fine," Mike relented. "What's the newest on the Captain Scott Mystery?" He was so over this little kid stuff. Pirates and treasure and goofy old legends. *Get to the Super already!*

"Well, I actually had this weird dream the other night," Hurl started. "I saw this thing over and over, like this weird diagram, and I drew it the next morning." He laid out a crumpled slip of paper. "You see, I think it's a—"

The radio had crackled a time or two and now squawked again, this time louder, with more interference.

"Come on, Mike. Can't you turn that thing off for five minutes?"

"No." He glared at Lambert. "I've gotta keep this thing on to monitor all the chatter. This is our lifeline to be in the know. Information is the war, Lambert! How many times have I got to tell-"

"Breaker 1-9," came a staticky voice over the radio. "Breaker to the Microphone Man, you got a copy on me? Come back."

Mike picked up the radio and called out, "10-4 good buddy, you got the Microphone Man. Who'm I talking at? Copy?"

The radio cracked, went to static again. Something barely garbled out.

"That's a 10-9, partner. That's a big 10-9. Say again. Copy?" Mike called out.

"I said you got you The Rhino, coming in hot," the voice much clearer this time. "I'm westbound and rolling. Trying to get a 20 on Mr. Megawatts."

"It's my dad!" Watts screamed at the top of his lungs, so loud Molly and Lydia heard it from the garage. He ran to Mike and seized the radio without apology, jerking the hand-mic to his face. "That's a big 10-4, partner. You got yourself the Megawatts we're 5 by 5. Come back."

"How 'bout ya, boy? How's about a little grease and gravy? I'm 10-8 to Stack's on the Dime. You got a copy?"

"Yes, sir, that's a copy!" Watts yelled out. "We're 10-10 on the side and heading your way. 10-4!"

Watts handed Mike the Mic back his mic and ran out the door of the clubhouse fast as his legs could take him.

"Well..." Mike was all in a flurry himself. Hurl's eyes darted from side to side he was so excited. "That'll be a meeting adjourned for now, then. We'll pick this up later."

"Wait," Lambert cut in. "We need a motion to—"

"You don't get it, Lambert," Hurl insisted. "It's Watt's dad, man. It's the Rhino!"

II
"GYPSY SOUL"
—ASIA, 1987

MOLLY ROLLED THE TRUCKSTER up Canal to the interstate. It was a few miles to Stacks on the Dime, and the boys had all mounted their bicycles ready to huff it the whole way when Molly asked where they were off to. Hearing Mr. Cletus was in town, she insisted they load up in the car. Nevermind the parents would drop a brick if they found out she let them bike that far through traffic; it was Watts' dad. Easily the best dad in the history of dads. Like ever.

"I bet she's got an awesome codename," Hurl said from the back seat.

"No kidding, man," Mike said. "What do you think it is?"

"Probably like Ultrawoman!" Hurl offered. "Or like something with an animal, maybe. Like Lioness!"

Those were terrible names. Molly pondered it all. So surreal -Tracey still in the hospital. So many others, too. Half of downtown would be rebuilding for weeks. The news...they didn't even know what to report. They mentioned the attack. Some new gang in town. No one knew much of anything. There was some chatter on the radio about a brawl and a girl throwing a motorcycle. In the chaos, it was easy enough for somebody to not know what they saw. Those who weren't there wouldn't believe it anyway.

Watts stared out the front window, watching the trees blur. Molly felt a half lump in her throat for him, his heart thumping so fast she could set a beat to it. Poor kid might see his old man six times a year, he was on the road so much. But every time it was like ten Christmases for Watts, and all the boys really. Even Molly couldn't not love Mr. Cletus.

"You think that's her real costume?" Mike mentioned. Molly's ears tickled. They were really into all this. She did all she could to stifle her smirks.

"No way, man," Hurl said. "Not practical at all."

He wasn't wrong on that one.

"I bet she was already at that party and had to step in! That's what a hero would have to do. It also means she doesn't have super speed, or she could have changed into her super suit."

Okay, kids, enough with the Young Sherlock routine. She was worried now they'd crack the case and bust her before they even made the highway.

"What are you guys talking about?" Molly asked the backseat. She knew this might get them.

"Oh god, nothing, Molly," Hurl whined. "Nothing you'd care about. Dang."

"Opsec, dude!" she heard Mike whisper to him. Watts still zoned out.

"Right, right." Hurl then folded out some paper.

"What's this?" Mike whispered. Barely audible, but Molly's hearing had improved of late.

"I was trying to tell you guys in the meeting," Hurl whispered back. "I had this weird dream the other night. I saw all this stuff, like these lights, and then shapes and lines. When I woke up I drew this. Like I *had* to draw it or something."

"What is it?" Mike inspected the paper. It was hard to make sense of, A lot of squiggly lines, scribbles, almost like a maze, or...

"It's a map," Hurl whispered. "I'm sure of it." Mike gave him a quizzed look. "It's a map to Captain Scott's secret tunnel!" he said too loudly this time.

"Dude," Mike said. "Give it up. You're always on about that dang tunnel. They'd have found it by now."

"No, dude," Hurl argued. "It's for real. You don't understand this dream. It's like...it's like I knew what I wanted. And my mind made it happen!"

What night did he have that dream? Molly wondered. She shouldn't be honing in on their secrets. She still hadn't gotten a handle on most of this powers stuff. Still had no clue as to even what all she could do, in fact. Apparently she could see time slower. Or something. And people's feelings; that was so weird. She could feel Watt's want so bad it hurt her own heart.

They had a point about the stupid suit, though. *God, Lydia will never let me hear the end of it.* She could already hear the thousand *toldya's. Ugh.*

And a code name? This was a lot of work.

"You're nuts, man." Mike folded his arms behind his head. "Don't go chasing that shadow."

Watts' heart leaped in his chest.

They'd made the interstate.

III
"18 WHEELS & A DOZEN ROSES"
—KATHY MATTEA, 1988

STACKS ON THE DIME was a two-story megalith, all-in-one, big rigger's oasis. And its appeal went well beyond truckers. More than once Molly and Lyd had pulled an all-nighter and wound up at Stacks in the wee hours forking down biscuits and gravy and cups of not bad coffee. They had a full body shop for the rigs. Fuel for every kind of motor there was. A mini-mart. Three restaurants, not counting the hot dog roller. A barber shop. A laundry. A shower. A weight room. A post office kiosk. A bank ATM. A whole room of phone booths. A game room with pool and pinball. And...a massage parlor. *Ew.*

The crew saw the big red Kenworth 900, shiny and bright, as soon as they wheeled in, the charging rhino hood ornament gleaming from the sunlight right at them. The car hadn't stopped rolling before Watts hit asphalt in a dead sprint inside.

Mr. Cletus shoveled down his third diablo sandwich next to Mr. Hank when Watts torpedo-hugged him right in the gut like a linebacker. The other boys came behind him, all causing a pile-on right in the middle of the lunch cafe in Stacks. The waitress, Mrs. Genevieve, knew it all too well and side-stepped the pyramid of adolescents in her path to drop the next table their overflowing plates, the gravy not quite dripping down the sides of each one.

"Them's hot now, honey." She was already gliding back to the counter for the next platter.

"My boy!" Mr. Cletus hugged Watts so tight Molly thought the two of them might just burst then and there.

Mr. Cletus was a big man. A hand shorter than his friend Mr. Hank, but had to be double the width, especially in the chest and shoulders. His shaggy curls crawled out every which way from under his mesh cap. Hands like a gorilla's made from wrought iron. He laughed at the kids machine-gunning their million questions at him so much their words nothing but a thick soup of sound.

Molly and Mr. Hank both smiled at the sight of it all, Mr. Hank going back to his bite of pancakes and a look at the day's paper, always with his cowboy hat slouched so far over his face it was a wonder he could even see at all.

"Daddy," Watts barked out above the others. "Guess what! Guess what!"

Oh, here it goes, Molly told herself. She caught herself blushing as they all started blurting out their version of the events of her recent foray. They invented half of it, embellishing it to the nines, because of course they weren't even there. *Thank the maker.*

"Okay, okay." He put them to the side so he could finish his meal. Mr. Hank seemed uninterested in the tall tale, like a person with super-strength was not even news to him. Just munched on his cakes, grumbling something about the new president.

When the waitress came back by, Mr. Hank pointed at his plate and then held up three fingers, paused, looked at Molly with a question to which she waved her hand 'no thanks.' The waitress, having understood perfectly, went and called out for another three short stacks for the boys.

Molly didn't hate it here.

The chatter and catch-up went on for several more minutes, the boys' pancakes showing up in short time. They sawed into them and made a quick job of it. It made Molly wonder if she was feeding them enough at home on the days she watched them. They did look good, too. She started to regret not having a plate. *Do I burn calories? Is that still a thing?*

"You Cletus?" growled some burly, bearded roughneck in a camo cutoff shirt who looked like he'd just gulleted half a tin of 30 weight motor oil.

Mr. Cletus didn't look up. He busied himself regaling Watts and the boys with the finer points of the time he had his whole rig riding down a steep grade on only one side's wheels. Watts' loved that story because he would immediately start explaining the physics of the feat to everyone in earshot, and Molly could see the look in Mr. Cletus' eye that he was twice as proud that his boy could do that than Watts was of the event in question. She could feel the lump in Mr. Cletus's chest almost throb out of his body he loved that boy so much. She swallowed hard and turned her head to one side. It was just a whole lot to feel right then.

"I said, you Cletus Morrison?" came the oily voice again. He had those psycho eyes. "The man calls hisself 'The Rhino'?" he said like it was nothing. Some joke.

Molly wanted a piece of him.

"At's my handle, son." Mr. Cletus took another bite of his diablo. "Can I do you fer?"

Mr. Cletus still didn't look up. Watts' face got beet-red mad. They all knew what it was gonna be.

"They say you're the man to beat. I say bull squat! You ain't nothing. And I got $100 says it, too!"

"Well...your problem is I ain't got $100. Hell, my good buddy Hank here's already spotted me my lunch. I've got quite the tab already, in fact. So, I 'speck it's best we just do it another day, huh?"

"I think you're just chicken," the bear spat. "I say you ain't got it no more! Ha!" He laughed and strutted around in a circle.

Molly wanted to hit him. She almost licked her lip looking at his big ugly meat hooks and how she could pop them like little twigs.

"How's about you $200?" Mr. Hank finally looked up at the world outside his own hat. He grinned the widest, meanest grin Molly had ever seen. He folded out tens and twenties from his front shirt pocket. He didn't look up at the oily bearded maniac, either. Just counted out the bills and slapped them into Cletus's hand.

Mr. Cletus sighed, took the money in his hand, swallowed down the last of his sandwich, and stood up.

"Awright, fine," he grumbled, rotating his right arm to loosen it up.

"Dad, no. Please don't."

"Relax, boy." He patted Watts' head. "This won't take even a minute."

A dozen or more truckers and other onlookers gathered around the small high-top table near the back of the cafe. Diesel engines sang in the background as rigs came and went outside. Smokestacks blew their dark clouds into the air.

Mr. Cletus dropped his ballcap on Watts' head, who watched with a sinking of his gut that Molly felt in hers. The griz took his spot opposite Mr. Cletus as they presented their forearms for battle. More tens and twenties passed back and forth among the empty faces in the crowd as Mr. Hank was taking odds.

"Miss Molly, will you count us off?" Cletus asked.

She nodded, giving Watts her own pat on his head as she walked by him. His poor face eaten with worry over his old man. *It'll be all right, I promise,* her eyes told his. And he believed her. She felt him calming down.

The two bull-sized men squared off, their hands gripped tight, thumbs hooked around one another and ready to go to war. Griz's eyes wide and screaming into Cletus' face, but Mr. Cletus focused on his grip and the other side of the table.

"Ready." Molly placed her palm over their wrapped hands. "Set...go!"

The two arms locked in an audible clench. Each man's face and neck popped with veins. The bearded gentleman threw out grunts that might as well have been screams. Mr. Cletus focused, tightened his grip even more. The beard slowly pushed him to the other side. "You can do it Mr. Cletus!" whispered the lips of every boy in sight and probably three of the waitresses. For sure the cook who'd come out from the back to watch. Mr. Cletus let out a big breath, folded his fingers over again for more grip, and took it all the way over. He slammed the other man's whole arm against the opposite side of the table. The guy jerked his arm away yelling and growling.

"Bullshit! Bullshit! Let's go again!"

Mr. Cletus shook his head and walked back toward his lunch. He rotated his arm several more times, wincing each time as he did, his face betraying the hurt he'd done to himself. Watts' eyes welled up, but he managed to hold back the water.

"You okay, Daddy?" Molly heard him whisper to his father.

"I'll be fine, boy," Mr. Cletus assured him as he sat down heavy. He looked tired then. Molly could see it dripping down the lines of his face. A few more lines than the last time she'd seen him. The weight of his shoulders dropping with him as he sat, holding his son in his left arm. Still shaking the hurt out of his right.

"Pay up now," Mr. Hank told the loser.

He turned and sneered at Mr. Hank, barely half the chest or arms of Mr. Cletus but ten times as cocky and sure of himself. White Stetson bent and drooping over his face, already half-hidden behind his aviator glasses.

"Fair's fair, mister," Molly stepped up beside Mr. Hank, folding her arms to show she meant her business too. Mr. Hank grinned his wide-angle grin at her again. She stared a hole in the man's face until it dropped its grimace and just shook to one side.

"Yeah, awright." He slapped a wad of bills into Hank's hand. "Fair's fair."

He shook Mr. Hank's hand and gave Cletus a nod of respect on his way out of the cafe. Grabbed him a couple hot dogs for the road and was gone.

Hank slapped the money down in front of Cletus, now working on a fourth sandwich seeing as he'd worked up yet more appetite. Mr. Cletus shook his head and tried to hand it back to Hank.

"Was your stake, buddy. I can't take it," he said. Watts' eyes tried not to stare at the bills.

"Was your sweat and muscle earned it." Hank pushed it back at him with a look that meant no backtalk on it.

Mr. Cletus counted out half and put it in Watts' hand.

"You give that to your mama when you get home, now you hear me? That's for groceries or the light bill or whatever needs paying. No Cokes nor candy, you hear me?"

"Yes sir, I promise."

Mr. Cletus handed the other half back to Hank.

"I can't take but half," Cletus said. "It ain't right otherwise, and I won't hear of it more."

With that, the two men nodded their heads at each other and were done with it. Hank folded the rest of the money back up into his shirt pocket and prodded at his now cold plate of food with his fork.

Mike the Mic and Hurl sat at the same table in the back doing their own version of the arm-wrestling match over and over, trying to best each other. One old trucker walked up and gave them a few tips, helped them get their grips. They more giggled than took it serious. Mr. Hank got up to fill his coffee thermos from the big pot in the corner.

"Some guys in funny ties came by the house this week, Daddy," she heard Watts whisper to his father. She needed to get a handle on this hearing thing. This probably wasn't for her to know. This time belonged to them alone. "Said they was there from bank."

"Damn bastards," Cletus breathed out. "They said they'd give it another month."

"Who were they, Daddy? Mama didn't say nothing, but I know she was scared."

"Damn bank's turned the truck note over to the Repo company. I ain't but one payment behind. That Commie Ron let the wolves a-loose on the whole damn country before he was through." He put his arm around his son and hugged him tight. "I just pray to god a-mighty they ain't smart enough to think to come here."

Molly swallowed hard at that. It definitely hadn't been for her ears—but it walked right in, like she was a radio tuned to it. She didn't want to hear any more of their moments. They weren't hers; she didn't have any like that. The boys were fine here, and she felt like taking a walk anyway.

*

Outside, she kicked rocks through the massive parking lot, meandering her way through the rigs and heavy equipment coming in and out. She still hadn't worked up the courage to have the talk with Hoyt and Clair. She'd been with them so long now. They hadn't been anything like the others. They'd kept her for years, even putting up with some of her worst tantrums, things she'd long come to regret but had never apologized for. With everything else going on, it was just one more thing looming over her.

The smell of cattle and their attendant feculence hung thick in the air from farms north of the coast hauling their culls to market. She wandered her way over to Mr. Cletus's truck, a gorgeous crimson Kenworth aerodyne with a red and yellow stripe down each side of the cab. Chrome in just the right spots but never too loud. Cletus was proud of that rig and took good care of it. Everybody knew it on sight back on Elm and E, the few times he'd been home in it. She couldn't say why she'd walked over this way, but she just felt like it.

Molly, on one of her whims, looked side to side to see no one was near. She reached her arm under the rig and got a good purchase on the frame. She pulled the front end up just enough to see the tire lift an inch off the ground. She grinned and eased it back down. It *was* cool she could do this stuff.

"I told you," she heard a gravelly, over-coffeed voice coming from the other side of the truck. "Always listen to experience, kid."

Molly crept around the other side quietly, trying not to be noticed. Two men, one barely older than herself, the other ancient, both in suits hanging off their bones, stood before Mr. Cletus' beautiful red truck. The old one fished something from his baggy pockets. The young one, alert, half-coked likely, had a buzzcut and was all business. The older one looked like cigarettes were a person.

"You see, son," he instructed his young partner. "Repo man's gotta have these kind of instincts. Debt runners gonna be up to all kind of nonsense. You gotta think of their game before they do. Damn commies. Think they pay their bills in Russia? Hell no."

He managed to get what was in his pocket. Looked like a set of keys. *They're going for the truck!*

"Get in there and get it cranked and rolling 'fore that big ape gets wind of us," the old one said, tossing the keys to the little one.

"What? I can't drive that sucker!" the young one protested.

"Gotta learn sometime, kid. Life is all one tense situation after another."

Tense was right. Molly felt every fiber in her body tense to the max. Her fists clenched like ball bearings, her eyes bloody knife blades dripping down her face like steel rain. Her nose flared and her needless breathing quickened.

"You hear something?" the little one asked.

They each half turned to see what it was before she conked their heads together like coconuts so hard they both dropped to the ground.

"Not today," she looked down at their bodies out cold before her.

She turned her head to either side again, double-checking she was unwatched. *What to do with them while they sleep?* She needed to be sure to give Cletus time to get away. The reek of cow patty crawled in her nostrils again and she spotted the cattle-hauler about four rigs off from her.

She smirked. Perfect.

*

Back inside, Mr. Hank instructed Hurl and Mike on how to make a single pinball stretch a quarter into an afternoon. Their table was cleared. Watts sat beside his dad who was on one of the army of payphones with his broker trying to get his loads sorted.

"Yeah, whaddya got for me?" Mr. Cletus said into the receiver.

"Can't you stay home for a while, Daddy?" Watts asked. Mr. Cletus shushed him with a hand.

"Thursday?" Cletus looked down at his son and a leak almost sprung in his eye. "I don't know about Thursday. What's the payload?" Mr. Cletus's face went white. White as death. "Say what again?" he said into the phone. Watts wrapped around his dad's waist. Mr. Cletus stared at his son, then took a big swallow down his throat. "How much it pay again?" he asked. "Awright. I can do it. But one condition. They cut a check today advance against it and send it overnight to my wife. You got me? No deal otherwise."

Watts looked up at his father with a beaten but understanding look. Cletus held his son's face in his hand.

"Yeah. I heard. I'll be headed right for you in the hour." Cletus said into the phone. "You got my word," he added after a beat.

Mr. Cletus gathered up his road gear from their booth, shook Mr. Hank's hand. Gave the other boys each a hair rustle. Their eyes beamed at him like he was their dad, too. He made his way toward his truck, the entourage trudging behind him. Watts saw his father climb in his gleaming red big rig, about to crank and ride away again, with no notion of when he'd be back.

Mr. Hank walked outside just after them. He stuffed another wad of money into Watts' pocket. "That's for your mama, too." He stared down at Watts through those aviator glasses.

"But Daddy said that was your half."

"Now boy. I've made a hell of a lot of mistakes in my life. Too many to count. But I one I ain't ever made, nor ever will, is betting against *your* daddy. You don't ever bet against the Rhino, son. Not never. So this here's free money. Goes where I say it goes. And these..." He passed Watts a fat bouquet of red and yellow roses they sold in the store. Stacks sold just about everything. "You give these to your mama, too. You tell her they're from him, you understand? You tell her he sent those to her special."

"Yes, sir. I will."

Molly walked up as Mr. Cletus's truck roared to life. The gears caught, and he was rolling, giving that air horn a pull as he passed by his fan club. Molly tipped her fingers at him as the boys stared at him like he was the only superhero in their whole world.

Mr. Hank wandered back inside. The other boys went to see if they could fish another quarter for the pinball machine out of the vast sea of asphalt somewhere. Watts stared at his father's truck disappearing on the horizon until it was gone. The wall in his eyes held fast against the flood of water slamming against it, and Molly felt every ounce of that strain along with him.

"Fighting," Watts said.

"What?" Molly asked.

"I was in detention for fighting. You asked. Some dirtbag in the hall called my dad a loser. So I hit him in the face. That's why."

Molly took his head in her arm and hugged him to her side.

"I hate the bank." His eyes were glassy and angry.

"Yeah." Molly held him. "Me too."

IV
"(SHE'S GOT) THE LOOK"
—ROXETTE, 1989

TRACEY WORKED THE CLICKER like a rabid parakeet. She'd run one nurse off that very afternoon and the shift replacement was counting the minutes 'til the next one.

"I can't find the music channel," she griped at anyone in earshot.

"I don't think we have that one, ma'am," the nurse told her.

Molly strolled in with a sack of Pig Burger and a *Cosmo*. She thought she'd do Tracey's nails and that would make her feel some better from being stuck in the hospital another night.

"Why aren't you at the store?"

"Nice to see you too." Molly shook her head, dropping the sack of food on her tray. Tracey inspected to make sure there were, in fact, the extra pickles she always asked for.

"They won't let me leave. Said my concussion is still a threat. And they want to run more tests on my leg. I say they just want to run up more bills. Well, I ain't paying it! They charge too much. Damn communists." she was yelling at someone, no one, everyone.

"Lydia's watching the store. You might as well let me hire her for real." Molly munched a fry.

"No." Tracey sat herself up. "I've got the staff I want. You can manage it till I get on my feet."

"Yeah. When's that gonna be?"

"Soon as they bring me my dang discharge papers. I hate this dump!"

"Look, I really think we need someone. I've got this big new project..." She didn't have the first clue how to go about all this secret double life stuff, and she already didn't love the deception of it all, not that she had much of a choice. "It's for school. I'll be working on it a lot. I may not be available every night."

"Yeah yeah." Tracey gave up on finding any music and settled on *Knot's Landing*. Looked like the Ewings were in this one. Molly could never keep up with these shows. She still didn't know who shot JR.

* * *

Back at the shop, Lydia had the register in a frenzy. She had her jet-black sun hat on, and her bangs spiked and thick as mascara lashes, which she also had. Her fishnet black lace sleeves all the way to her fingers weren't helping either. It was a wonder she hadn't scared off every customer.

"Halloween was last week," some bitty reminded her. "Now it's time for pumpkins and autumn colors, orange and red and brown! Pumpkins!"

Molly chuckled to herself at the entrance watching the trashcan-shaped old lady admonish her friend still trying to get the register to open.

"You blamed kids today," the lady started again. Molly relieved Lyd at the register and reset it, ringing up the sale again and making the lady's change. "With your hair and your wild music and your heathen ways!"

Heathen. Cool word. Molly could probably do something with that. Work it into a band name somehow. They still didn't have one. Or a drummer. Or...well a lot, actually.

Molly rang up the next few customers and the store died down while Lydia organized the records. For a "catch-all" shop of whatnots, Tracey insisted on keeping a good selection of records and tapes. They might have even had more than Suncoast in the mall. Except Tracey's stuff was way better — Molly made sure of that. Tracey had a good a good eye for it, too. They had a lot of solid oldies and some of the cool stuff they were doing in Europe. Of course, Bebop over on Eisenhower was still the place to go.

"Okay." Molly locked the store entrance, relenting at last to what now kind of seemed inevitable.

Lydia was at the dress racks making sure they were all in order. "What okay?"

"I guess let's do this. Show me what you got drawn up?"

"Wait," Lydia's eyes lit up. "Are we doing the suit?"

"We're doing the suit, yeah," Molly sighed.

Lydia whipped her sketchbook out of her barn-sized purse and went to flipping. Of course, half of them were black. Skirts. *Nope.* Jackets. *Nah.* Capes. *Definitely not.* And the footwear?

"Yeah, heels are a negative." Molly shook her head.

"Okay, well...first I guess we should see what we've actually got to work with. I mean, like... I can't really sew. Can you?"

Molly glared. "Yeah, no."

"Well, we did just put up all that Halloween stock in the back. I mean there's butt-tons left."

An hour whizzed by as the two of them trudged through old stock, Molly trying on one bad outfit after another. Too much color. Not enough color. All of them too flimsy. Cheap costume junk.

"Shit, these things will blow right off me soon as I jump through the air. That makes a lot of drag, you know."

"Yeah, I didn't think about that kinda stuff."

"Yeah well I think about it now. Like a lot."

"What about your code name? I was thinking Bright Light."

"No. I like Sledgehammer."

"What? That's terrible."

"I like it."

Lydia put all the tried-on costumes in a pile to be re-folded later. She sorted through the various accessories. Masks. She looked through them. Rubber faces and clown caps. Flimsy elastic pull-ons. Mardi gras junk. She pulled out a nylon purple balaclava-style mask. Simple, but a start.

"I got an idea." She went over to the tool closet, pulled out some scissors, and made a few quick cuts. "Here. Try this." She handed the mask to Molly.

"How about Morning Star?"

Molly pulled the hood over her head, situating it just right around her eyes. "Sledgehammer," she said again.

Lydia dug through the other masks, pulling up a simple yellow and blue Mardi Gras mask, holding it up to Molly's eyes.

"Perfect," she said.

Molly strapped on the eye mask, then pulled the balaclava back on around it.

"StarPower!"

"Sledgehammer."

They walked out front to check the mirrors.

"This looks terrible," Molly groaned.

"No, it's fine. You gotta hide your face. Besides, it'll look fine with the right suit."

"Which we still don't have," Molly reminded her. "All that junk in there won't do."

Molly was right. The costume stock was no good. They needed something tougher. Durable. Preferably something light and stretchy she could wear under her normal clothes.

"Wait," Lydia gasped. "I got it."

She ran back into the storeroom, banging and slinging boxes of clothes around. She came back dragging a heavy bin labeled "sports" behind her and started slinging random equipment and jerseys all over the floor. A mess.

"Hold on. Wrong one." She ran back and came out again with another, bigger box and started tearing into it just as she had the first.

"What are you-"

"Paydirt!" Lydia dumped the box onto the floor. Uniforms scattered in front of them. Tight, sleeveless unitards, mostly black but with a heavy fuchsia line bordered in thick neon blue stripes ran all the way down neck to thighs. It almost matched the mask. Kind of.

"What the heck are these?"

"I remember these came in the other day. You were up front when some lady dropped these off. They're figure skating uniforms."

"What? From where?"

"Who knows?" Lydia stretched one out. "Try one on!"

Molly sighed and grabbed the first one off the pile, then walked behind a rack and started throwing her discarded articles to one side or another.

"It's so tight!" she yelled from behind her cover.

"You're bulletproof. Don't tell me a little lycra is gonna hurt you!"

Molly emerged from behind the rack. She pulled on her set of masks, lifted her head up.

"This feels so weird." She stared at Lydia, feeling like an alien.

"Why Sledgehammer?"

"I mean Peter Gabriel, obvs. But also, I mean that's sort of how all this started. I just like it. I don't know."

"But like...are you gonna carry that around with you every time?"

"What?"

"A sledgehammer? Like when you go fight badguys."

'Badguys?' Really? Was this her life now?

"What? No. Where would I even keep that? It's not like it fits in a pocket. No, me. I'm the sledgehammer. Like, my fists!" She slapped a fist into her palm.

"Ooohhh." Lydia still hated it.

Molly pulled down the long pant cuffs, covering most of her orange Chucks. She stood in front of the big body mirror they had by the clothing racks and shook her head. The fit wasn't terrible. She couldn't say it was uncomfortable, exactly. It was just...*Is this really happening? Is this a thing now?*

"Freaking radical!" Lydia beamed.

The unitard felt like a creepy second skin and just went everywhere. Like, *everywhere.* She twisted and turned in the mirror and *buddy just nope.* Not even a little bit.

"Uh-uh." Molly marched off to the sweaters and hoodies. She picked a half decent orange zip-up and wrapped the sleeves around her waist, knotting it tight.

"Why?" Lydia asked. Molly glared at her through slits. "K, never mind."

Molly stared at the alien in the mirror again. She didn't know that person. That wasn't her. It couldn't be.

"I look ridiculous."

"Nah. It's fine. Now...let's find some bad guys!"

V
"ROLL WITH IT"
—STEVE WINWOOD, 1988

THERE WERE NO bad guys.

Twice Molly had been out "on patrol" as Lydia put it. Which meant wandering out in the back alleys in her godawful costume. And it was itchy. Well, it wasn't technically itchy because Molly didn't actually itch. But she thought about it being itchy. So, it was still *like* being itchy. Her senses were haywire. She caught herself constantly imagining she felt things. Was that the same as really feeling them?

But there was definitely no crime. The first night was the worst. They'd wandered around Old Town all night 'til nearly 1am. Both lied to their folks saying they were at the other's house for the night, which made Molly uncomfortable. Little lies weren't that big a deal, but now it all kind of bothered her for some reason.

They should have known they wouldn't even hear a rat fart in Old Town no matter how late they stayed out. Old Town rolled up the sidewalks at 8pm for gods' sakes. She did find a dog digging through some trash, wandering around lost. She checked his collar and saw an address four blocks north of them and walked him home. The dad was outside in his robe and slippers, probably looking for the furry guy. Molly sent the dog over to the dude and waved at him like she was any other neighbor. He stared dumbfounded for a few seconds and then took the pup in the house.

Molly skipped around and practiced doing cartwheels down Beach Boulevard until Lydia got sleepy. So, they went to bed.

* * *

The next day back at Bay High felt even more surreal than the night before. School had never been Molly's favorite, but now it bordered on pure torture. The noise of it. The nothingness of it. The silliness of everyone's daily routines. Homework. Seriously?

Easton, though...

He sat on the staircase railing outside at first break, scribbling something in his notebook. He always had one on him, she'd noticed, jotting down notes to himself or sketching something or other. He was dodgy about showing anyone. Becky and her Bayettes cliqued nearby. Easton's buddy Nguyen took a spot near him, chattering something inaudible to him and pointing to a group of girls the other side of the yard, to which Easton nodded.

Molly dropped herself right next to him, her arm thudding heavy onto his shoulders, her fingers even dancing in the lower locks of his sandy hair. It sent electric current all the way up her spine into her neck. Okay, so she *definitely* felt that. And he did, too; she sensed his goosebumps flare up and his heartbeat quicken.

"Hi, Nguyen," Molly turned to face him. She didn't want to seem rude.

"Uh, hi?" Nguyen stared at her face grinning at him.

Molly turned back to Easton. Half the school's eyes were now on the three of them. Even Lydia stared from the main doors in shock. Molly bored with the waiting game and decided to make a point. This seemed as good an idea as any.

"So, listen, Cowboy. I just wanted to say thanks again for the other night."

Molly then jumped up off the railing and walked toward Lydia, turning back to Easton and Nguyen when she reached the top of the stairs.

"That was it," she called.

She and Lydia ran into the building laughing to themselves.

Easton stared for several seconds, never uttering a word. He finally turned to share his confusion with Nguyen still blinking. They shook their heads and blinked some more.

The one not blinking was Becky. She'd watched the whole debacle from her pack, her eyes furnace fires burning holes into the doors. She looked where Easton still sat, unmoving. Then she darted them back to the doors. Her jaw was taut and her eyebrows raised nearly to her hairline.

"Oh no, you didn't," she whispered to no one.

* * *

Their next night out on a patrol was arguably worse all around. They had decided to try downtown since Old Town was a total bust. Molly had to double-knot the sweater around her waist since the wind was up and kept blowing it loose. The tights thing was really not for her. She didn't feel like flashing the town; not that there was anyone out to see, but still.

Molly practiced jumping quick from wall to wall in the back alleys to scale the buildings. She could just bound it but hadn't quite got the hang of aiming. Or using the proper amount of strength to leap. She might as easily end up smashing through a window or wind up blocks away.

She skipped along the rooftops for a bit, bouncing across the alleyways in between. A little finesse went a long way. She did the thing with her senses a few times, too, closing her eyes and honing her ears on all the sounds around the town. Two cats were fighting a block north. Or...*not fighting*. It was basically the same with them.

Some drunk was fiddling with his keys trying to get in his beat-up old pickup. He dropped them twice before he found the hole. He pulled the door and started to climb inside.

"That really your best idea?" came a voice behind him. *Like a kid almost, but also like ... like his mother. But deeper. Like both. Somehow.*

"Huh?" He turned to face what stood before him. He shook his drunk head several times trying to shake out the Old Milwaukee. All those colors. *Purple headed. Feet were on fire! Were they? No. Maybe.*

"I don't think you want to drive tonight." She grasped her hand over his holding his keys. "Do you?"

He stared into her eyes. He reached in behind himself, his other arms searching blind for something. Finally, he produced a small blanket.

"No, not me." He held his blanket. "Just gonna sleep it off a while in the back here. Cold out tonight."

"That's a good boy." She patted him on the head. "You see or hear anything weird, you just holler for me, all right?" She winked.

"Yes ma'am," he said. And she launched off into the night.

He shook his head again several times. Then he crawled into his truck bed and pulled the blanket up all the way over his face. Peeking out once to look again. Then back under.

Back at her truck, Lydia had hatched a new plan as Molly snuck into the passenger seat, taking her masks off for a moment just to feel normal. This hero thing wasn't awesome.

"I think we should go after the killer." Lydia slapped the page of an old newspaper featuring the last girl they'd found. It had been a while now since he last struck.

"How?"

"I'm working on a list of suspects." Lydia thumped a little notebook she'd been scribbling in. "And you'll bait 'em with that fire engine hair of yours. I mean what can they do to you?"

She had a point.

* * *

Easton sat to himself the next day at lunch fingering the grooves in the name *Étienne* carved into table. It made him sad. He peered around the room a few times, studying it. Like he was casing it. Or the people in it. As usual he wasn't keen on the food in the cafeteria and just sat with an apple, nibbling at it while he pecked at his sketchbook.

He had drawn up a not unremarkable rendering of the now infamous benefactor from the party. He had the stockings nailed. He may have gone a bit overboard on the hips, but he was a dude, so of course. Then the eye makeup. He was taking odd care to get it right, swapping out colored pencils from his bag at his side and making sure to blend them each time as he added more color.

Molly was impressed. She watched him another moment, feeling his conflicted emotions. She hovered like a ghost above his right shoulder, still holding her food tray, its modest faire rapidly chilling in the ill-heated lunchroom. This "Global Cooling" thing was *not* fake news.

"I like it." She stabbed his calm with her Coca-Cola voice. "But the hair's all wrong. I had a blue wig, remember?"

Easton flipped his paper over, obscuring the drawing, and looked up at Molly's grinning face. He was blushing.

Easton. Had. A. Cruh-ush!

"And those stockings?" Molly gently removed his hand from his notebook, flipping back to the sketch of the girl he had no idea was now standing above him. She shook her head, tsk-tsk-ing at him. "Those are all wrong, too."

"It's not..." he started. *Her eyes. They just kept...* "It's not supposed to be..." He wasn't sure what words were next. Words were actually weird, if he really thought about it. They were, like, just weird sounds. And... Those eyes. Why was Molly Slater... Why was Molly Slater? Just that. Why that?

She sat her tray down beside his notebook and sat down facing away from the table, plopping her hand on his shoulder as she gazed at him. He gulped. Swallowed. This was all wrong. So wrong. She was just supposed to be his... And he was...*well*. He was him. And she...

"I think we should get a do-over." She turned toward her still untouched plate of food, then facing him, his eyes locking on hers.

"A what?" His drawing hand quivered. He was so cute. This was too adorable.

"Yeah." She sank a French fry into ketchup and took a bite. "I mean, the party got wrecked by those...whatever they were. Everything was kind of ruined. So. A do-over."

"Like another party?" He looked confused but still at her eyes.

"Yeah." She shoved half her sandwich into her face. She thought it was funny, making him see one extreme of her and then the other. Like she wanted to gross him out now for some reason, but then would kiss his eyes with hers all over again. He was so fun to mess with. "Or maybe just me and you." She sipped her drink, looking away from him but not really.

"I mean I guess—"

"But definitely costumes." She went at the rest of her food. She really liked food. He was too picky with his silly fruit. She didn't even need to eat, but still. Lunch was one of the few decent parts of being stuck at school all day.

"Costumes?" He pulled a sip of his drink, mostly just to find somewhere to put his hands and something besides her to look at.

"Yeah." She glared at him. "But, I get to pick yours!"

Easton spat drink out his nose and got choked.

She reached up to his face with her napkin, laughing to herself but her eyes serious and belying none of it. "Let me get that." She dabbed her napkin on his face while cradling his head in her other hand. She could feel him feeling her. He was afraid of how much he liked it. She gave him a half smile. *Relax, Tiger,* she vibed to him.

From the corner of her eye she spied Watts making his way toward his spot at the far end of the cafeteria. She broke Easton's tension by waving him over. Watts saw her and stared in disbelief. He pointed to his chest and mouthed *Me?* She nodded *yes* and kept waving him over. He turned toward them, then looked back at his usual corner, then Molly and Easton. Easton was a cool kid. Like for real cool. And Molly was... Well she was like her own kind of cool. He shuffled toward them.

"Are you sure this is okay?" He placed his tray opposite hers so softly there was no sound.

"Yeah. I said so." She stole one of his fries and winked at him as she tucked a lock of her hair behind her left ear, dropping that hand to rest on top of Easton's under the table. His pulse fired up like a weed eater. His eyes fixated on that lock of hair. In fact, he looked at her hair a lot—he always had. She smiled at him from the side, and he finally smiled back. Watts even smiled. Maybe his first of his ninth-grade experience.

A screech of, "What. The. Actual. HELL?" interrupted their moment. Becky de la Beckwith stood at the end of the table arms folded, bolstered on either side by her garrison of Bayettes, all in their crisp uniforms. Like her soldiers ready to battle the slightest aberration in the daily norm. "Who said Brainy Smurf could sit at *my* table?"

Molly felt Easton's attention shift to Becky, and a match lit in her belly. He was already going into damage control mode. She sensed it.

"Look," he said, "lay off the kid, will you?"

"I said he could sit here," Molly sniped in return. "And I say he stays." Her eyes fixed on Becky.

"Yeah? Who died and made you god?"

Molly felt the hairs stand up on the back of her neck. She calmed herself. *Breathe.*

"He's my brother's friend. He's my friend. And he stays. You don't like it? You go somewhere else. We're all good here."

"Oh. My. God," was all Becky spoke out before turning on a dime and marching her army to another empty table two or three spots down. Before she sat her squad down, she glared at Easton and cocked her head to the side, signaling her continued disapproval.

Easton stood up, Molly's eyes quizzing him from her seat.

"Look, just watch my stuff." He pointed at his bag, but then grabbed his sketchbook. "I'll go calm her down." He started over toward the other table, and Molly felt a boiling stare coming on. He called over his shoulder as he walked away, "I'll be back."

He'd be back, he'd said. His stuff was all laid out in front of her. All except his *oh-so-secret* notebook. Watts was in shock but actually happy for once. Becky's Beck-stare still stabbed bolts at her from across the lunchroom, and Easton argued with her over whatever nonsense she was talking, his notebook in his hand. His drawings. Molly stared at it. At him. Whatever thing still lingered between those two irked her. And she hated that it did.

He'd be back. He told her.

VI
"14K"
—TEENA MARIE, 1985

HURL RUMMAGED through the pantry, stuffing sleeves of Pop Tarts, cans of Vienna sausages, and whatever other nonperishables he could scrounge into his knapsack. He also had flashlights, half the batteries in the house (oh boy was Hoyt gonna rail about that) and two big canteens of water.

"You off to fight the Battle of the Bay?" Molly finished off an entire pot of grits she'd made herself earlier. She kept wanting to eat more and more lately.

"Not at liberty to discuss," Hurl informed her.

"Right." Molly scraped her pot. "Knights business."

"Right." Hurl hauled off to his room for more provisions and his notes.

Molly stared at the little scamp. They fought less lately, and she was grateful for that. Looking back, she regretted ever giving the little guy such hell. He had it the same as she did. All Hoyt & Clair's kids had been fosties. There'd been three before her, including the soon to be wed "sister" who she'd maybe met a dozen times. Poor Hurl was last to come along right before Hoyt & Clair aged into their midlife re-assessment of their goals, as they liked to describe it. A.K.A. they were tired and just wanted to go to pool parties at the neighbors and let the kids see to themselves.

Still no word on how long Molly could continue living there. Where would she even go? Maybe Trace would let her crash in the back room, at least until school was over. Then she could work somewhere full time. Make some real money.

In his room, Hurl rolled up his map, another drawing he'd made after he had the same dream again, this time clearer, the images sharper and crisper than before. It came two days earlier, after they were supposed to have their midweek Knights meeting but only Lambert showed up.

"So, what about this so-called treasure?" he'd asked.

For as long as Hurl could remember, he'd heard the tales of the pirates that frequented the bay back in the olden days. Iberville had fought his share defending the old colony. Then came LaFitte, Bully Hayes, a few others, and Captain Patrick Scott. An Irish bandit, once pressed to service with the Royal Navy, then defected to the Portuguese, then the Spanish, then the French, where he finally mutinied, stole a freighter, and ran blackguard through the Caribbean and the old French Coast.

"The pirate's cave!" Hurl's eyes serious as daggers. "The old pirate house. I know where it is!"

"That dumb restaurant on the beach? They do have good fish."

"No, not that one. I'll show you. Meet me here this weekend. Pack a lunch and some water. We'll show the others. I know I found it. I know it!"

* * *

Racing their BMX's down Beach Boulevard, they zoomed through Old Town and toward the old cracker houses. The newer ones rose up on stilts since Camille blew a lot of them away. The greenish blue water washing from the gulf toward the bay brought a crisp breeze in. Hurl and Lambert rode up to the flat grass hillock that remained of the old legendary LaFitte pirate house. On the street in front of it was a shack with "Pirate House" painted badly on a plywood sign that served fry baskets to walkups and beachcombers.

"I told you, man, Camille blew that old place away almost twenty years ago. They never found any dang cave, either, man. Everybody knows that story."

"That's because they were looking in the wrong place! They all looked here all those years because this was LaFitte's house. It was too obvious. But it wasn't LaFitte that hid the treasure. He didn't hoard treasure." Hurl had studied every book and legend of all the Coast pirates for years; he knew he was right.

"I don't get it." Lambert gazed at the fry basket coming out in the hands of a high schooler in hip huggers. "What are you saying, man?"

"It wasn't here. They can't build a tunnel on the beach; that was always stupid. The sand is too loose and wet. It would flood. Besides that, everyone would see them out here on the beach, coming in on the ships. This is nowhere to build a tunnel. It was Scott. *He* built the tunnel, and it was north of here, way up into the bay. That way they could come in late at night with the tide and unload under cover of darkness away from the town. I'm telling you, man."

"Okay. But then why are we here?"

"Oh, we're here for the fish," Hurl said. "I'm hungry."

He dropped his bike and headed over to the fry shack.

After each boy packed in a thousand calories worth of fry-up, they zoomed off on their bikes, headed back up Beach through Old Town again, and followed the bayline winding north, then west, and then north some more. They had miles to cover and the fried shrimp would be burnt before the sun got high.

They huffed it all the way up the bay, as far as North Beach would take them, and then they had to ditch the bikes in some high grass just off the street. They were headed beyond where the blacktop ended. They stuck close to the edge, keeping the bay's expanse on their right and never out of sight.

"The chains that bind," Hurl kept repeating.

"What is that?"

"It's an old rhyme I heard once, about the legend of the pirate's cave. *Seek the chains the bind. See the trees that wind. And Scott's treasure ye shall find.* I never forgot it."

"What does it mean? Chains that bind? Sounds like nonsense. Also, I'm bored. I thought pirate stuff would be awesomer than this."

"This *is* awesome."

"No, dude."

They trudged on a while longer, the soil beneath their feet getting soggier and their shoes beginning to slop down into it. Lambert slapped mosquitoes on his neck. At least the air was crisp enough they hadn't broken a sweat. Hurl's mind was set. He was possessed, driven by some *god-given* will to find what his dream map would show him.

Lambert decided he'd only himself to blame for blind following some 7th grader out to BFE because of a map he "dreamed of." The more he thought about it, the dumber it got and the dumber he felt. Also he was hungry again. The sea-stacker had worn off about a mile back.

They trudged through more slop, their shoes uncomfortable and mushy. Hurl kept checking his map, then turning to the bay to get a bearing. He looked back and forth from the trees to the bayshore, the breeze sending a minor shiver into each of them as light waves licked at the breakwater.

"I think we've come too far." Hurl gazed toward the waning sun and down the shoreline.

"How can you even tell? It all looks the same."

"We're too far off the point." Hurl showed Lambert the map, pointing to the small horn on his map. "And, look, in those days, the water would have come further in; they hadn't built the roads and the breakwaters yet. At tide, the water would come up even past where we are now."

They trudged a quarter mile toward Cowand Point when Hurl got his bearings and began to march inland. They found a thick brushline. Old-growth pine and cypress towered above them. There was a spot where the treetops were so thick together there was no telling the one from another, the brush in front of it so dense it was near impenetrable.

"There's no cave, dude." Lambert saw more woods and marsh. "Let's just go home. Maybe we can still make it to the arcade at the mall."

"Wait." Hurl's arm extended upward, his finger zeroed at a point in the center of the thick trees.

Lambert looked up, but saw only a blur of green and brown, knots and knobs, clusters of bark. He squinted and concentrated, and then he saw what had Hurl so unwound. Just perceptible from the bark around it was a series of rust-brown links. A chain so old it had grown into the limbs of the tree itself.

"The chains that bind." Hurl traced his finger back forth in the air, delineating how the remnant of the ancient chain must have once been used to pull two separate trees toward each other.

The boys faced each other with eyes wide and faces blank before springing to work. They yanked and pulled bushes away to clear a path. Hurl wished he had a machete, but Hoyt always said no.

Soon the brush gave way to an opening of sorts and they stared in awe above them as all the light from the day vanished, only the odd ray of sun piercing the massive canopy of cypress tree limbs like some cathedral of nature, the limbs so thick amongst each other they formed a kind of tunnel.

Or a *cave.*

"Look, more chains." Lambert pointed at the branches. A line of them, all the way down the path. Remnants and dangles of chain hung about here and there, stretching all the way down the makeshift tunnel, as far as they could see.

"It was never a rock or stone cave. No one ever found it not just because they looked in the wrong place, but they were looking for the wrong thing to begin with!"

"We're gonna be famous!" Lambert shouted. "Heroes!"

Hurl high-fived him, and they each busted out their flashlights and started down the long dark of the tree tunnel. If his map was right, and so far it was, they had a ways yet to go.

VII

"*OWNER OF A LONELY HEART*"
—YES, 1983

MOLLY CONSTRUCTED a cornucopia display at the shop, only instead of food it was cassette tapes, black lace stockings, and tacky jewelry. It was almost time to break out the black and white candy canes and the rock and roll Santa, only theirs was tall, skinny, and wore an eyepatch. Tracey was all about her Halloween blowout, but she knew how to keep the other holidays weird, too. In fact, they usually had at least a nearby church or three come protest every *Eostre.* Only the Baptists, though; most of The Coast was Catholic, and they were pretty cool about it.

Tracey was back, still learning to maneuver her temporary wheelchair through the tight aisles and running into displays regularly. She had, of course, opted for an electric one, the full works, sparing no expense on the machine she was told to use for maybe a month before her leg was strong enough to use crutches.

"I'm not shoving myself around in that thing all day," she had said. "I'll look like Popeye by the end."

Molly chuckled at the thought of Tracey walking around with giant forearms. It wouldn't even be her strangest look.

"I think I'm in love with my nurse." Trace joysticked herself over to the register. "Yes, it's a *he*, before you ask. I haven't gone down that road. *Yet.*"

Molly priced some new scarves and ties Trace had picked up at an estate auction, along with an assortment of hats and, for some reason, bowling shoes. Tracey went on about the hot nurse that rolled her out of the hospital at her discharge—his arms the size of roof timbers and just as hard. She had to use that word, too. Just to make it weird. She eventually got to his eyes and face that she mentioned with less ornate detail, which said more than she wanted. Molly had tuned out by then.

Blake Elvis jingled through the door, black shirt sleeves and collar peeking out of his white jacket and pants, his hair coiffed insidiously perfect. Sunglasses, of course. How someone could feel so wrong and look so right vexed Molly to her core. He almost mesmerized her. His calm. His demeanor. She wondered about him.

And, why was he here?

"This is an interesting place." He looked around, taking it all in. He seemed especially fascinated with Tracey's assortment of jewelry and accoutrements under the front counter, the metal stuff, mostly. "I guess I've walked by here a thousand times, and never come in. I don't know why."

Blake stared off toward the back of the store at the mannequins. Tracey nudged Molly's leg, mouthing behind her hand, *he's hot!*

Molly widened her eyes, insisting Tracey cool it and not make this any weirder.

"Do you offer personal style advice?" Blake turned to Molly, a sharp smile on his lips. He removed his sunglasses. His blank, cool eyes made her think of a sea at midnight. "I could go for a new look."

Molly felt her stomach drop. She did and didn't want to do this at the same time. She couldn't shake her fascination with Blake, despite every single instinct telling her to go the other way.

"We certainly do," Tracey cut the silence. "That's our specialty." She prodded Molly forward with her chair. Molly had half a mind to tear that joystick off and throw it into the sun.

Molly walked Blake back to the men's jackets and shirts, only now realizing they were awkwardly placed in the back corner of the store, making this whole situation all the more uncomfortable. "How's the arm?" She tried to cut the weirdness.

Blake smiled, not uncharmingly, and rolled up his Armani sleeve. This kid was way too uptown to be caught dead in this store. She would wonder why he'd even walked in if it wasn't obvious. He had some strange glove on, with metal rings wrapped around his wrist and forearm, thin rods running up and down, splintering into smaller rods that ended just before each knuckle. He kept stretching his fingers out, gripping and grasping at the air to show off the gears of his contraption.

"What the heck is that?" She'd never seen anything like it. Some kind of space-age super-cast. So much for signing her name in colored marker.

"Something I—well, my dad..." He tapered off and cleared his throat. "Money buys a lot of things in this world. But not quite everything, unfortunately. There've been some complications. This is helping the process along. Or so they tell me." He smiled. So confident.

"Can I see it?" she gawked at it. "Your hand?"

"It's a bit of a chore to undo all this," he said. "But maybe another time? Somewhere else, in fact?"

Molly let that question roll around in her head for a bit. She knew what it meant, of course. And he wasn't...not pretty. He was just... She needed to find the right words to not make this turn bad. What would he even do? Or say? Would he go all psycho? Dudes sometimes did that. A lot of times.

The bell at the front door chimed again and bailed her out of a bad spot, thank goodness. Or so she thought. Until she realized that cruising inside was none other than Easton himself, just to make everything ten times more tense.

"Hold on a sec." She headed to the front while Easton asked about her at the counter.

"I should charge admission," Tracey winked at Molly when she walked up, Easton already locked onto her, but Blake's presence in the back not escaping his vision, either. "Maybe then I could turn a profit from nights like these." Tracey flipped open her *Cosmo* and pretended to ignore them all.

Molly knew that meant she was gonna get stuck with inventory. Again. Tracey's favorite punishment. *Ugh.*

"I was, uh, just in the area. Thought I'd say hi." Easton's lips curved just right. Molly betrayed herself with a big fat smile with all her teeth going everywhere. "But I can take off, if you're busy with work." He nodded at Blake walking up, rolling his sleeve back down and giving Easton the *it's cool, bro* nod that meant they were for sure *not* cool.

Maybe someone else could stroll in and make this even more awkward for her. Becky would be just perfect, in fact. *Gods, don't wish that on us,* Molly told herself, shaking her head.

"I think I'll take a raincheck on our style session." Blake started to reach for her hand to give it a light shake, but reconsidered and withdrew, all of which Molly caught, including his eye twitching with uncertainty. He'd been perfectly suave and cool before, and now that Easton walked in, it was just *gone.* Like he could have been right at home at the table rolling dice with Hurl and Watts; he was *that* awkward.

"Braddock." Blake nodded at Easton on his way out the door.

"Blake." Easton nodded in return.

Molly rolled her eyes. They should run at each other and ram their heads into one another and get it over with. *For the carpenter's sake, why are dudes?*

Easton, though...

VIII
"DEEPER & DEEPER"
—THE FIXX, 1984

THE TREETOP CAVE went on for maybe half a mile. The boys tired and had all but exhausted their provisions. The trail terminated at the bottom of a bluff or mound, not unlike the old Choctaw mounds. This one was flat on top, where there sat...another restaurant. Or at least what had been one.

"A bust, dude." Lambert punched Hurl in the arm. "We could have gotten here from the street. This is the old North Beach Steamer. That's Blakemore and Cedar Ridge up there. You just led us into a big stupid half circle for no reason."

Hurl stewed. He folded out his map again, and began poring over it, looking for what he missed. He scoured at the map, then the mound, then the old steamer fish camp. That place had been out of commission since Camille. Come to think of it, it'd been bought by the Gautreaux's who everybody said worked for the Matrangas, who everybody knew was deep in with the Gambinos.

If there was one thing Hurl knew, it was pirates. If there were two things he knew, they were pirates and gangsters. A pirate house. He knew it. Hurl always knew there had been two!

"No, we're in exactly the right place. And somewhere around here is where Scott buried the treasure. In fact," he pointed down at the X on his dream map, "we're almost standing on it."

"Dude, just no. *In fact*, I'm putting my foot down." Lambert stomped his leg down hard as he could. There was a snap, and that same leg sank first to the knee, then the other leg broke through and he nearly fell all the way down the opening his tantrum had created, catching himself with his arms.

Hurl pulled him out, and they hit it with their flashlights. It wasn't too deep. There was part of an old metal ladder still built into one side of the hole. Rotted boards shored up the walls, and the tunnel looked like it went into the mound under the house.

With zero caution, they proceeded down the tunnel. They went maybe thirty yards and came to a hatch. They had to shove it a time or two to get it open and then they climbed up into a basement underneath the old restaurant. The room was damp and stank of mold and mildew. Water was everywhere. It must have been used as a storage room both for the restaurant and whatever pirates and gangsters had come before that, if any.

Lambert's flashlight fritzed. He slapped it a time or two to get the light to stay on. Hurl was glad he had extra batteries. Whatever electrical system was here probably hadn't worked since the 60's, and even if did, they certainly didn't have it hooked up to the grid.

They found a narrow stairwell, every single board creaking and sending shivers up and down their bodies. Hurl sensed exactly how much Lambert hated this at the moment, and truth be told, Hurl wasn't loving it either. He had a pang in his gut, and it wasn't just hunger.

They went up the cellar stairs into another storeroom, this one not empty. There were tin boxes of ammunition all around. Stacks of guns, AK's, shotguns, and pistols stacked or laid about. Tools, too. Not just little ones. Jackhammers. Chainsaws. A layout of the county grid tacked to the wall above a worktable. Jewelers tools in disarray. Stacks of *Penthouse* magazines. There was a big dagger sitting there, carved with symbols and foreign writing (Hurl was still mastering English), and an awesome wolf's head flashing its fangs as a pommel. And right beside that was a jewel.

A pirate jewel!

Hurl snatched it. A bright yellow gem, clear to the inside. He could see all the way through it. Like a fine-cut emerald, but shiny and yellow. *Are there yellow emeralds?* He didn't know a lot about gemstones, but he was sure this was part of Scott's treasure. Had to be. And the rest of the trove would be nearby.

"Let me see that sucker," Lambert said. Hurl shushed him with his finger. Dust sprinkled at their heads as the ceiling creaked. They were not alone. Hurl pocketed the gem while Lambert fingered the dagger.

Voices.

The boys ducked back into the stairwell and pulled the doorway all but closed. A big guy in a long red trench coat stormed into the room and dropped a heavy duffel bag onto the floor with a thud. Two more stomped in behind him with bags just as big and full, dropping them on top of the first, then again another two. One of the bags wasn't zipped, and the boys saw stacks of hundred and twenty dollar bills peeking out. Their eyes grew wider.

"Dude, this ain't no pirate house," Lambert whispered, quiet as a ghost. "These are for real bangers. We gotta book!"

Lambert was right. They needed to be gone and good. But Hurl just didn't get it. The dream had been so real. And this had to be Scott's hideout. The tree tunnel, the old rhyme, the secret cellar...it had all been right. It led them right here. But this. This wasn't right.

He wanted that treasure! More of it than what was in his pocket. But there was no getting past real deal criminals with a full arsenal. He knew he should have picked up one of those AK's. He could bust through this door right then and cheeseburger those wastes if he had one. *Stupid, Hurl. Stupid.*

"Good job, morons," the biggest one in the long jacket said. They all had on red jackets, and there were more coming in. "This was the best haul yet. We're damn near set for the year. Except you dipsticks will blow it all on tramps and dice. Friggin idiots."

"We need to talk about the Dreds," another said. This guy was almost as big as the first and looked even meaner. He had stark white hair, reaching down to his shoulders in straight, if frizzy, lines. He had a really black left eye, too. Might have been makeup, the more Hurl looked at it.

"Yeah, man," another said. "They rode in like an army—all that fancy tech. They're the last thing we need right now. And what the hell was that took down a batch of them? Fuckin' chick was tossing scooter trash and kickin' sleds like they was made of air's what I heard."

"We know bleedin' well what took them Dreds out, man," one in a stupid red hat said. He shook when he said it. "Same as—"

"Shut your damn mouth," the boss shouted. "I got a plan for the Dreds, and Punky fucking Brewster, too, if she gets in our way again."

"Yeah?" the white-haired one spat. "Let's have it then."

The boss pulled a knife from his boot and threw it right at the map of the county, sinking it dead center in a spot that was already circled.

"The guard armory?" White Hair curled his eyebrow.

"That's right. The Nats just got a spanking new set of RV's from Uncle Hoagie. Complete with 25mm, up your butt cannons. Not to mention armored transports and whatever else we can carry off. Let the Dreds or Miss Shortcakes come at us then. Hell, even the cops will stay the fuck away from us."

"I don't know man. She ain't like nothing real, man. She's worse than the Bronze back in B'Easy," one with a rattail mohawk spoke up.

"That copper tinhead? He wasn't shit," the boss spat.

Hurl's eyes grew to planets. *He was real!*

"This is crazy," the white hair said. The boys sensed the power struggle. "You want us to go against the damn army?"

"The weekend warriors? Bunch of accountants signed up to pay for their college. They ain't worth the price of their uniforms. And, besides," he smiled at the whitehair, "who's *us*? This one's all yours."

Whitehair grimaced and shook his head.

"Unless you want to go back to N'awlins, and that...*thing*," the boss said after a beat. Everyone got quiet at that. Whatever *that thing* was had them shook. Just seeing these guys get their spines iced that bad sent a cold wind into each of the two boys hiding away in the darkness.

"When?" Whitehair asked.

"Monday. They'll be down to a skeleton crew for their little parade down the beach for their special day. So a little rat tells me. Nice having grease money these days." He eyed the duffels full of cash. "You take wolfy back there and slice through whatever they got it locked behind."

"What about you?"

"I'm taking ol' cobra here," he fondled the snake-pommel of an otherwise identical dagger, "and a small crew uptown to hit the last branch we ain't took. Y'all will keep the blues busy, I 'spect. Waste not." He grinned.

The whitehair nodded to Rattail and Badhat. They reached for the wolf dagger but stopped short.

"Hey, where's the stone?" one said.

"It's gone. It was just here."

"Someone's been in here!" the boss shouted.

That was the boy's cue! They lit off down the dark stairwell into the lower cellar, racing their way back to the trap door and up the rickety ladder so fast they couldn't even feel themselves anymore. They were pure motion.

When they hit the tree tunnel again, they booked harder than any had ever booked before, all the way through the dimness, back to their bikes, and then sent their spoke wheels into overdrive down North Beach toward home.

X
"IF THIS IS IT"
—HUEY LEWIS & THE NEWS, 1984

THE NEXT NIGHT out was the dumbest yet. To make it worse, Lydia went to Radio Shack and got a two-way radio set. Molly had an earpiece in one ear now, under her already goofy mask, and connected to her two-way clipped to a big white leather belt Lydia had dug out of the shop. This outfit was getting worse by the week. She was starting to resemble a cross between a beat cop and...probably something Mike the Mic thought about by himself in his room. *Yikes.*

"Check check." Lydia liked this way too much."It's gonna be way better," she squawked. "This way we can talk back and forth, and I can hang back. I'll be like your manager. Working for you from the sidelines!"

"My manager? What?"

"You know. Like, you're the one in the ring, taking the hits, bringing the pain! I'm right outside, keeping things under control, working the crowds, doing your promos. Your manager!"

"I have no idea what you mean."

"Bobby 'the Brain' Heenan?" Lydia lifted both eyebrows. "Jim Cornette?"

Molly shook her head, lost in the woods.

"Jimmy Hart? The Mouth of the South? Do you not know wrestling?"

"Lydia," Molly stared at her, "and I mean this as a friend: who the hell watches wrestling?"

"I do!" Lydia folded her arms. "Every Monday and Saturday with my dad and brothers. And after it's over, we have to practice all the moves. It's like our thing. I got my big brother, Tony, in a headlock last week." Lydia grinned. Molly wished *Lydia* could have caught the powers. Except, then Lydia would probably want her to be the manager, which would be even worse.

On the bright side, she could rock some tunes while she hopped the tops, as she'd come to think of it. Bounding from one downtown rooftop to another had become like skipping along the old playground at recess when they were kids, back when she'd first met Lyd. They made quick friends because they had both laughed at Mrs. Hogarth's creepy chin mole during her speech to the 2nd grade about the dangers of communism. Really. 2nd graders. Communism. That had been their first detention together.

Some commotion echoed up from Fishbone. A girl screamed at some skeezy dude in two-tone shoes, so you knew he was bad. She wore a leopard skirt and a tiger-print fake fur jacket, and Molly really wanted to tell her to just not. She slapped at him with her purse, yelling and screaming and calling him all the names. Molly thudded to the ground behind him and got him in a headlock.

"Yeah, yeah!" came from her earpiece. "Suplex that dirtwad! Suplex."

Molly had no idea what that meant. Maybe she should actually try watching some wrestling, just to learn some moves. Maybe Lydia wasn't crazy.

"Ma'am is this guy attacking you?" Molly deepened her voice, sounding like a bad impression of a man. She decided to take it a notch or two higher.

"Hell no, this jackass owes me money!" She kicked him in the nuts while Molly still had him. Molly let go, and he dropped the ground, holding his groin and all but crying.

"Who the f—" He looked up at Molly in her getup. "What the hell?" But the girl ran up and kicked him in the face before he got another word out. She then ran through his pockets, jerked out his wallet, flipping through his money and taking all of it before folding it and shoving it into her blouse.

"Thanks, sis." The leopard-skirt gave the guy one more kick, then turned down the alley.

Molly shouted after her, "Hey! Hey you can't just—ughh!"

She had no idea what to do now. *Did I just help that lady rob this guy? Oh, lord.* She didn't know what to do, panicked, and blew a breath of air down the alleyway, knocking the leopard-skirt off her feet, then she bounded off into the night.

That was the extent of the evening's action. Molly hated this gig.

* * *

Back at Castle Slater, the girls racked out well into the morning. Lyd was first to rouse and shoved her feet blindly around the room looking for her boots, not wanting to crack her eyelids for fear of the vile near-noon sun screaming at her through the window. *Bite me, Ra,* Lydia liked to whisper to herself every time she woke to sunlight in her face.

She teased her bangs into some sort of shape in Molly's mirror next to her Darksiders poster, with Étienne doing a reverse peace sign and his tongue through the V. Darksiders ruled. If Molly was secretly his kid, that would be the raddest thing in the history of rad.

Molly, for someone who said she didn't need to sleep any more, sure did love it. Twice, Lydia kicked her in the hip to try to wake her. *She doesn't even feel bullets. The hell's a kick gonna do to her?* She glanced around and then spied Molly's fender on its rack in the corner, plugged it into her mini amp, and gave it a stroke.

Molly leapt up off the bed, throwing herself all the way into the ceiling and sending spackle raining down all over her, the bed, Lydia, everything.

"Hey, what the hell?" Hoyt shouted from downstairs.

"What the—" Molly rubbed her eyes. "What the—why'd you wake me like that?"

"You weren't budging. Besides, us humans gotta eat. And I'm starving."

"I eat," Molly groaned and thought hard about going back to sleep.

"Besides, I want to go down to the library before they close at four and get some more books on serial killers and stuff. I was reading about it. It may be somebody we already know. "

"Ugh," Molly said, throwing her pillow at Lydia. She rummaged around, found her XL Clash tour '84 shirt and pulled it over her dirty mop of red chaos. "Let's not today."

Downstairs, Hoyt watched the replay from yesterday's game. He would always try to tape the ones he would miss and watch the highlights the next morning. The big one was tonight, Frisco & Green Bay. Lydia hated both. Hurl, quiet of late, sat at the table working on what was probably his third bowl of Chocula for the day, despite Clair having a pot of beans on all morning, ready to serve within the hour. Lydia appreciated that about Clair, sticking with the wash day tradition. She didn't buy the canned stuff, either. Always did hers the right way, soaking overnight and stewing all the next day. They smelled amazing.

Molly thundered down the stairs in her big t-shirt, cutoffs, and a mismatched pair of socks. She opened the door to the fridge, pulled out the milk, a plate of leftover barbecue pork, the pickle jar, Hoyt's big block of white cheddar, the sliced ham, half a tomato, and all the condiments. She plopped it all on the bar and went to work building a sandwich the size of her own head, then sliced it in half, poured two bowls of cereal — the corn flakes, not that junk Hurl liked — and passed half the spread over to Lydia.

"I mean I'm hungry, but like..." Lydia stared at all the food.

"There's beans ready in an hour, girls." Clair walked in from her garden, spraying her hands under the sink.

"I know, Clair," Molly said. "This is just a snack for now." She wolfed the sandwich into her face while Lydia took a more leisurely approach.

"Whatever," Clair said. "Just clean this mess when you're done. You, too, Howie."

He hated being called that. Only Clair did it, too. Even Hoyt used Hurl, the name the other boys had called him since they could remember. The girls munched their food, Molly finishing hers and going for a spoonful of Hurl's bowl. He was out of it and barely noticed. Usually that would have ended in at least a yell.

"I've got a good idea for tonight," Lydia said. "We should see if the mall has a police scanner. We could listen and see what they're up to. That could probably at least point us in some better directions."

Molly's eyes went wide, her finger over her lips shushing Lydia as hard as she could shush, even wrinkling her nose as she nodded at Hurl's humdrum face, all but asleep in his cereal.

"What?" Lydia whispered. "He's half asleep."

"Look, let's just forget it. I want to take a night off anyway. Besides we stink at finding crimes. I just want to be normal for a day, jeez."

"I know where there's gonna be crime," Hurl announced, waking from his haze. He shook his head to clear his cobwebs.

"What?" Molly glared at Lydia. "I told you he was listening, you dolt."

"They're gonna rob the armory." He went back to his cereal, staring into the now brown milk.

"Who is?" Lydia squinted her eyes at him, then Molly. Neither was sure what to make of him right now.

"Hurl, what are you talking about?"

"Why do you even care?" Hurl was really off today. "No one else does."

"It's for...a project. At school. Now, spill it."

Hurl went into his tale, making a particularly big deal about his dream map and the tree tunnel. He went on and on about that. He got to the cellar and the gangbangers in the red jackets, the money, the guns, all of it. Almost all of it. He left out the part about his yellow gemstone still hidden under his mattress upstairs. When he described the guys in the room, especially the one with the Rat-hawk and the one with the dumb bucket hat, both girls turned white. He *couldn't* be making that up. This was for real.

"Didn't you tell the police? Hoyt & Clair?"

"The cops, yeah. Mom and Dad, hell no. I ain't about to get grounded for it."

He had, too. Soon as they got back to Old Town, he'd jumped in the first phone booth he saw and called the police station, stammering out half intelligible ramblings about pirates and gangs and tanks.

"Is this Hurl?" had said the voice over the receiver. "How many times you gonna pull this nonsense, Hurl? We ain't got time for this." And they'd hung up. In fairness, he had called with a wild tip, once or twice. And, yeah, maybe a lot of those didn't end up being right. One time, he was for sure he'd figured out the Sherry murders. He'd cracked it, he'd insisted to them on the phone. He was still sure he had, too.

"When did you say this is gonna happen, Hurl?" Molly looked at Lydia.

"Monday." Hurl spun his spoon in his bowl and watched Bobby Hebert throw another interception as Hoyt yelled about it even though it happened yesterday.

"You mean next Monday?" Lydia cocked her head.

"No, I'm pretty sure they meant this Monday. During the parade they said. While it's half empty."

"Hurl," Molly said. "Today's Monday."

X
"THE WARRIOR"
—SCANDAL, FEAT. PATTY SMYTH, 1984

LYDIA GUNNED HER diesel toward I-10. They'd cut up Canal to get around the parade traffic. Half of downtown would be closed off, and the traffic everywhere else would be hot garbage. She slung that big beast around a curve and sent Molly, struggling in the back seat with the stupid tights, slamming against one door then the other.

"Must you?" Molly fought with her left leg to get into the stupid outfit without ripping it.

"For all we know, they're already there!"

"We'd hear about it if they were. This is the kind of thing that makes the news, Lyd."

"Actually, yeah." Lydia cranked the knob off Power 108 and onto the AM local news. They chattered on about the parade routes and the wind chill advisory for later tonight.

When they hit the interstate, Lydia dropped her foot to the floor. Molly fidgeted with her mask another minute before getting it how she wanted it. She slid back into the shotgun and peered out the windshield as far as her eyes would take her.

"Hold on," came over the radio. "We've got a breaking story"

"Oh god." Lydia's mouth dropped.

"Yep. Here goes nothing."

The whole shebang had come out in such a rush, they had half believed it was all B.S. and for the other half, they were hoping it was. Lydia glanced at Molly. "Like...you're bulletproof. But, are you tank-bullet proof? Do tanks shoot bullets or, like what? I don't know about tanks."

"Guess we find out," Molly shrugged. And, putting it like that, her stomach got a little flighty. *Shouldn't have had that huge hoagie maybe after all.*

They didn't wait long. They spotted the fireworks from over a mile away, and Molly heard them. Molly's eyes saw the gang had made off with the heavy equipment and were barreling down the interstate. Traffic on the eastbound bottled up and was trying to reverse, U-turn, or just get the hell out of Dodge.

Lydia slammed the truck to a halt to keep from pancaking a Datsun. Molly leapt out of the cab.

"Wait. What are you gonna do?"

"I have absolutely no idea." Molly made sure her mask was straight. "Something."

Molly sprinted through the sea of cars, zipped and zagged through their haphazard formation, leaping over hoods or cabs as needed. Even vaulted over a pickup that veered in front of her.

She made it to a clearing, out of the gas and fumes. Two armored tanks-on-tires, followed by a third transport truck, came at her. She knew Hurl could tell her the make and model, but that didn't seem all that relevant to her at the moment. They were big. They were heavy. They had guns. Big guns.

Those guns chewed up the landscape at that very moment. Two police cruisers were on fire, a third flipped on its side. She slowed her time to scan for them, to see who was hurt.

Two officers dragged another behind the cover of a pulled-over big rig. The tanks cruised right at her, crunching over everything in their way. Dozens of people abandoned their cars, booking for the tree line. And the screams. So many screams. A thousand frantic cries and *prayers* for help slammed into her head at once.

Molly rammed head-on into the first tank, ducking into a front tackle, like she'd seen so many times at Friday night games. She heard and felt the crunch and whine of bent steel. The tank went off balance and veered.

Molly went for broke and heaved the metal monster onto its side. Then flipped it on the shoulder for good measure. She figured that'd give anyone inside a good pounding.

She turned for the second one only to take its 25mm round right to her chest.

Molly flew back a hundred yards in a second and ripped right through a moving truck's cargo hold on the way. She tumbled and rolled across the highway shoulder and into the dirt. She got up. Dusted herself off. A good chunk of her poor costume was blown to cinders. Thankfully none of her business was out and proud. That was lucky. She knew it wouldn't survive another hit, though. She had to stop that second tank, but she really didn't want to make the evening news in her birthday suit.

She cleared her head, shook the webs out. That round rang her bell a little but nothing serious. So she made another dash for it, this time running in slow time. It was awkward at first, forcing her mind to double focus, her legs and arms cooking as fast as they could go, while her mind slowed everything down to a crawl, like trying run underwater.

She saw the flare first. Then the round erupted from the big barrel. It spun as it rocketed toward her. She faded just enough that it whistled past her right ear, another round coming right after it. She leapt to one side, then another, finally sliding under a last round, just before she made contact with the chassis.

Molly grabbed the barrel of the tank with her left hand and open-palm upper-cutted it with her right, bending the barrel as they fired another round. The whole thing exploded as it burst at its breech. Smoke bellowed from inside. And screams.

Molly jumped atop the rig and ripped the hatch off. She yanked the red jackets from inside one by one, some with crispy faces and all with blood pouring from their ears.

Last was the transport truck. The driver had seen the carnage and thrown it in reverse. Molly darted for it, saw the canopy thrown aside in the rear. Her time slowed again as she saw an all too familiar rait-tailed mohawk sporting an RPG aimed at her.

The warhead spiraled at her like a perfect football pass. And in keeping with that, Molly snatched it out of the air, whirled around and flung it right back at them, blowing out the rear axle. The rig sprayed sparks and asphalt as it ground its way to a halt. The crew evacuated the wreck. The half-smart ones bolted for the treeline.

The stupid ones, two of her old friends and one with long white hair, must have baked their brains out on lead paint and some rocks. They bowed up for a fight. Long hair tried his pistol. *He must be new.*

Rat-hawk knew better but went one worse. He whipped out with another dang sword. Or actually...not another one. The same one. Blake's. She recognized the wolf head at the pommel, though it was missing its gemstone. He pointed the tip of the blade at her, shaking for all he was worth. Molly just laughed and front kicked it out of his hand without a thought, sending it flipping end over end into the dirt beyond them.

She laughed.

"Did you really bring a sword to a tank fight?"

The haze cleared around them. Both tanks were trashed and people came out of the woodwork. Eyes were everywhere. They gawked. Pointed. Unsure what they were seeing.

"I remember you," Bucket-hat said. The white hair was confused. He really was new. "Maybe I tell these cops about a red-haired guitar player girl with a broke-down wagon, huh?" He grinned at her. His teeth. *Oh Lord, his teeth. Barf city.*

"What's that?" She slapped him in his ear and put some sting in it. He slammed to the ground.

"Hey, what the hell?" Rat-hawk cried. She slapped him in the ear, too. He dropped like a sack.

They both struggled to get up, dizzy from the ringing she'd given them. She popped them each again.

"What is it you remember?" She popped them another time. And another. "Say what you know."

Blood loosed from their ears and noses. The white-hair backed up, confused and hoping he didn't get a turn.

"Say my name if you know it." She slapped them again. They cried. Both of them. Hard. Tears and slime poured from their faces, mixing with the blood. She popped them again. "What about your names?" Still slapping them. "Do you even know those?"

She pulled them from the ground herself now, each time, just to slap them back down. She didn't know why she did it, why she kept on. Maybe it was Lydia and the boys she worried for. Or maybe they just had it coming.

But they were done now. Whatever they thought they knew was a long way gone. They'd be lucky to ever read again.

She turned to the one with long white hair.

"Fuck I don't know you," his hands up and stammering.

"Smart guy," she said, then ran to the various wrecks along the highway, the collateral damage of the gang's failed heist. She pulled victims from the crashes. The smell of oil and fumes saturated the air. She walked them to safety, bounding from one to the next. She made her way to a caved-in police cruiser. Paramedics pulled in, fire trucks, the full nine.

"Whoah, whoah!" One policeman got a good look at her getup. "Who...what the hell are you?"

Molly grinned at him, puffing out her chest, full of herself. "I'm The Sledgehammer. I'm here to help!"

They flinched, shook their heads, trying to clear the haze of it all. Some had seen her. Others only heard the crunch of steel, the cannon's reports. No one could say definitively what they had or hadn't seen.

"I'm gonna need you to sit tight right here until—"

"Sorry, gotta go." Molly could still hear screams and cries of some still trapped or pinned down. Kids lost and looking for parents. She leapt through the air like gravity didn't exist to her.

They stared as she landed some hundred yards from them, pulling more to safety and then going for the wrecks, clearing the debris, opening a path for the fire trucks and EMT's to get in. Some people walked up to her now that the chaos died down enough. Kids ogled her. Some offered notepads. She scribbled in them. Autographs. She was signing autographs.

The officers stared at it all, dumbfounded. Was this real? Had it happened?

Ahead of them, some kids walked up to the girl who'd fought two tanks. She flailed her arms and legs about. Like some kind of stand-up break dance. She was dancing with the kids.

"Sir," one cop said at the other.

"Yeah?" the officer didn't look away from it.

"Is the super person doing the Roger Rabbit?"

"Yep."

XI
"OPEN YOUR HEART"
—MADONNA, 1986

THE NEXT DAY at school not only didn't suck 3000 but almost bordered on decent. Molly cruised the halls like queen of the universe, which, being honest about it, she totally was. Billy Ocean swam through her daydreams, her head still in the clouds — mainly smoke clouds from last night's throwdown. *Which I did. I threw down a tank! Or whatever it was Lydia had called it. Basically a tank. Basically.*

And there was Easton. And his hair. Nicely coiffed today, and just the right amount of stragglers to accent his face. He stared at her as she spun to the Ocean in her mind, telling him to get in her car with her lips as she twirled around him. Technically she would have to get in his car, since she still didn't have one, his very excellent white Z28 soft-top turbo that would look even more amazing with her lava-red hair blazing in the wind at 75mph down the beach and over the bay bridge toward wherever that same wind would take them.

As Molly closed-eye reverse moonwalked down the hall toward Chem class, Becky de la Beckwith, not enthused with Molly's target of affection, stuck her expensive boot out enough to catch Molly's Chuck Taylor. Molly busted across the hall, almost into Mr. Schiavelli, with his Larry the Stooge hair.

Molly sprang upright, cocked and loaded, ready to go off. Her eyes lit up and she stared down the culprit like an ant bit her. A soon-to-be squashed ant.

"Careful dancing through these halls." Becky gave Schiavelli her wry smile. The way half this place ate out of the palm of her hand, all because her daddy's car dealership wrote them checks, stuck in Molly's craw.

"Yes, please watch where you're walking, Ms. Slater." Schiavelli looked more at Becky than her, like Becky were his peer. *Oh, girl. You just bought your ticket.* Molly pinched her lips to hold it in.

"You want to chase my leftovers, fine, little girl, be my guest. You can have Blake the flake or any of the others." Becky got close to Molly, their faces all but touching, each feeling the heat from the other's boiling forehead. "But you stay the hell away from Easton. He's leagues beyond you, Fosty. Understand?"

At that, Becky was all smiles and nods and Miss Popular. Her Bayettes gathered behind her, smirking and wrinkling their noses at Molly, soon joined by their triad of boyfriends — none other than the T's themselves, of course. The boys turned and looked the other way when they saw her, still bashful about their loss at the track field and never wanting to admit to it.

That's right, prepsters, you better look away from me. She kept her stare on Becky's fake smile and decided that was it. She wasn't even mad now. In fact, Molly was downright ecstatic. *I just knocked out a tank, bitch! Two tanks! You really want to party? Let's rock.*

She returned Becky's smile with one twice as big of her own, her dimples blazing in the harsh fluorescent light of the Bay High hallway. Easton was already high in her stack of priorities, but now he was her only focus. She liked him for all the normal reasons. But now she would take him just because.

Screw Becky de la Beckwith!

* * *

Molly burst through the doors at the shop, both arms flayed out behind her. Tracey was upright, out of her chair and leaning on one crutch, using the other to point at something she wanted Lydia to get off the far rack behind the books.

"Okay. I'm yours. Let's do it." Molly was all business. "Make me the hottest girl at that whole damn school. I submit to your knowledge."

Tracey's eyes blazed. "This is very important. That you've decided to take our relationship to this next level. I'm so proud and emotional right now. That you've recognized I hold this power. And I will bestow this upon you because you've come to me with this. And because you love me. Which, of course, I know, everyone does."

Lydia cracked up in the back. Trace was such a hoot, and she already knew what had got Molly's dander up. Everyone had talked about it at break, and how they thought Molly was about to deck Becky and lay her out right there. They'd barely had time to decompress since yesterday's battle royale. She had some notes for Molly. Just some simple thoughts, a few suggestions, nothing major. Manager stuff.

"First thing, though," Tracey said, already pulling knee boots off the rack. "The Taylors gotta go, kid. You're in the grown-ups section now."

* * *

Lydia stood at her locker ransacking it for the History assignment sheet she needed. The cliques occupied their various spots: the jocks, preps, punks, cowboys, geeks, spazzos, bookworms, the goody-goodies, and, ever in command, Becky and her Bayettes, surveying their domain, lest the smallest thing out of place go unchastised. They bestowed their sneer of correction upon a freshman girl who dared to put up a sign for her tutoring services too close to their Bayettes tryout poster, which was always a joke because almost no one ever got in.

Eyes darted to the front entrance one by one. The jocks dropped buckets of drool, so bad it turned Lydia's insides out. The geeks lowered their books to hide their shame. The goodies were beside themselves, one even holding her rosary, for the guy's sake. Easton and Nguyen, in rolled up coat-sleeves as always, both jaw-dropped (something unnerved her about those two, lately, the way they watched Molly, studied her). Easton's eyes were fixed; Nguyen, amused by all of it, bopped him on the shoulder with his fist and chuckled. Even Lebeque dropped the toothpick from his maw, mouthing silently, "Slater?"

Poor Becky was the last to turn and see, a Bayette tapping her on the shoulder to deliver the bad news and hoping against a shoot-the-messenger scenario.

Bathed in the hazy winter sun, there cantered a commanding set of brown suede boots, side-zipped to the kneecaps. Picking up from there was a wraparound skirt of tanned leather, hand stitched and printed with floral paisleys, barely visible in the faint light wrapped around her like a halo. Threaded through hand-fastened belt loops was a floral print sash, knotted and hanging from the left side.

Up from that was a pink undershirt, so pale you had to know it was there to see it. Above the missing naval came the cropped, knit pullover, its criss-cross needlework jostling to and fro as her arms reached to tussle her hair, teased and boosted with every product Trace had in inventory. Each wrist was wrapped twice over in leather bracelets with turquoise stones. Big yellow and auburn stars hung from each ear.

Her eyes, shadowed in all the colors of fall, deftly landed on everyone and no one at once. Molly pulled a small tube of red from her clutch purse and touched up her lips.

There wasn't a sound in the hallway.

Molly commanded right up to Easton, pulled a folded slip of paper from her clutch, pressed it shut again with her freshly embossed lips, then tucked it in his hand with a smile, and went on her way to class.

There was still not a sound in the hall.

Nguyen broke the tension by slapping Easton's shoulder, whose eyes still followed the trail of eau de parfum left in Molly's wake, and losing himself in laughter. Easton looked back at Nguyen, then again at Molly's absence, then at the note in his hand, almost scared to unfold it. He finally succumbed and lifted it gently with his finger.

YOU. ME. FRIDAY.

That was all it said. His throat felt like it had a softball in it, and his gut a bowling ball. Maybe two. Now the whole school had seen her spectacle. This made everything...*messy. Complicated.*

Nguyen was still laughing. So was Lydia.

Becky wasn't.

* * *

The next day was much the same, a whole new outfit hand-curated by Tracey herself. People crowded around outside this time, in spite of the increasing cold, expecting another show. Easton leaned against the big live-oak out front, all its branches bowed nearly to the ground, making for useful benches. His eyes hung heavy, but then he always seemed tired in the mornings.

Molly, in a wide-collar sweater dropping at her left shoulder and belted at the waist, cruised up and propped beside him, inspecting the scribbling in his notebook before he could close it. He tried not to shake his head, still no idea what to do about this unsolicited attention. Like she had just woken up one day and decided to make his life even harder than it already had to be. He had a job to do, he had to see this through. Now it seemed impossible. *But her hair! Those eyes! Why?*

"Why the sad eyes, Cowboy?" She flashed hers at him, hoping to pick up his mood. He did smile.

"It's nothing, just..."

"Just what?"

"Just this stupid assignment I got." He looked at his feet, then to Nguyen who gave him a side-eye.

"For who?"

"Huh?" He shook himself out of a haze.

"What class?" Molly beamed at him. "Like an essay or something? I'm good at those. I could help."

"Oh, it's uh...Civics. It's not an essay, it's..." He drifted off again. "Just something I really don't want to do."

"Then don't." She slid herself beside him and folded her legs over his. "Hang out with me instead." She winked.

He nervous-laughed, trying to stop himself.

"What?" she smiled, showing a dimple this time, almost blushing. "Why's that funny?"

"Oh, it isn't really." He couldn't help himself but smile back. She had him now.

And, of course, the moment was ruined by Lebeque.

"PDA, Slater!" he barked. "That's Saturday again for you!"

"Lebeque." Molly's eyes went halfway back in her head, laughing. "You'd miss me if I wasn't there."

He shook his head, confused, and started to mutter a retort but evidently none came to mind. Molly picked herself up and started toward the building, the bell due any second.

"You would." She smirked at him, walking off to class and nodding her head.

He turned to Easton, then back to Molly twirling as she went in the front door, then to Easton again. Easton shrugged.

* * *

Every day that week, burning toward Friday, was much the same. People waiting to see what stunt Molly pulled, Becky a simmering volcano. The in-crowd walked on eggshells around her, knowing the least little thing could unleash a torrent of misdirected rage. And when Becky de la Beckwith wanted to ruin someone's day, she could get it done. She'd brought the Drama teacher to a full panic attack just the year prior, all because she'd given the lead to Becky's own best friend, Alisha. *Ex-best friend.*

Friday morning lazily rolled around, everyone antsy for Thanksgiving break. Even the new war of the past week had grown stale and uninteresting to all but its main cast. By late afternoon, during study hall in the library, Easton sat by himself with a pair of books he'd pulled, one on unsolved crimes and the other last year's yearbook, scanning all the headshots. Molly watched him from across the room, almost like little Hurl would when poring over his treasure maps and his wild ideas of pirates and secret caves.

She came prepared this time, though. She'd gone by the art room and grabbed a large sketch pad, now held in front of her and obscuring most of her face. Only her black porkpie hat, wrapped in another floral print band, peeked above the cardboard backing.

Easton doodled something on his notepad when he noticed the obnoxious, oversized pad opposite him at the other end of the library. Molly's head popped out to one side, staring intently at him for a few seconds, only to disappear again behind her artificial wall. He tilted his head sideways, then went back to his own notes. She popped out again, staring, holding her charcoal stick in front of her face like a painter does to get a bearing. Then back behind her pad. She continued her game, so serious each time. In spite of himself, Easton laughed.

Finally, he joined the charade, and held out his arms, a question on his face, asking her with his smile, *Well, how's it look?*

Molly, giggling, turned the pad so he could see her masterpiece: a full page stick figure with a big, bulbous round head and smiley face with "Cute Boy" written in bold letters at the bottom. Easton's face turned beet red.

Molly laughed and waltzed over to the computer stations to actually finish typing her paper for Lit. She was still floating, though. Everything around her light. Like so much air.

It was Friday.

XII
"SORCERER"
—MARILYN MARTIN, 1984

MOLLY'S HEAD REMAINED a flurry of snowflakes catching on the tip of her tongue as she danced in a fading sunset. She had zero concentration on the "Reasons why the Soviet propaganda literature stifled creativity and erased the robust culture of the Czarist Era" a topic handcrafted by her Lit teacher, Mrs. Clinton. All she could think about was tonight and how it would all go down. She had the perfect idea.

Halfway down her second page of raw B.S., completely making up a story about a teenage girl defecting to America after she heard only one rock and roll song (it's not like Clinton would check it), her screen fritzed. Letters and numbers blinked all over the place, her essay disappearing. *Oh no, I do not have to retype this whole thing over again. I will puke.* Then the cursor typed out letters by itself, forming words, a sentence.

"Their entire system is flawed," it read.

Molly looked around the room, then all around her monitor, trying to see what the gag was.

"You can't just erase people's debts," it typed out this time.

Molly was for real about to have a cow. What was this Twilight Zone act, already? Then she realized who it had to be. She started to type into the computer herself.

"Lydia? What the hell? I'm working here."

"Not Lydia," it typed back.

She shook her head, kept looking around the room. This was spacey even for her, which was saying something these days.

"Then who?" she typed. *Creep factor set to 9000.*

The screen jumbled itself into a thousand tiny blocks, all mechanically building toward an image eventually. An all-too-familiar set of sandy locks and that store-bought but compelling smile: Blake Elvis.

"Can we talk??" it typed, the image disappearing.

"How are you doing this?" she typed back. She looked all around the area, slowing the time and focusing on every person in the entire library. Nothing. But, then, there wouldn't be, would there?

"That's what I want to talk about," it said. "There's something I need to show you."

Molly tilted her head. She didn't know how to handle this, but she knew she was going to have to. It was time to put an end to any ideas he had. Not that she was mad or anything. But this was just...*weird.* And besides that, she was...otherwise occupied.

"I'll come by later." She already regretted it.

* * *

Lydia tried to grab her right out of school, saying she found something huge about the killer, *or killers.* Molly rolled her eyes and blew him off. She decided to just rip the bandaid and wheeled by Blake's, knowing she'd be cutting it close to make it for her shift at Trace's. She was closing tonight, and then after...*well. After.*

At least Blake's was on the way. Sort of.

He met her at the door, trying a side hug, but she dodged it and caught his arm with a handshake. She saw that ruffled him. He still wore his metal contraption thing, a glove covering that hand. She knew it was awkward, but she couldn't stop staring at it.

"I'm sorry." She finally broke her stare. "I'm sorry. I know I shouldn't... How is it, by the way? How are you?" She had to stop herself. She was nervous-talking. Just saying words because the thought of any silence between them had become unbearable. She almost resented how she felt around him, like she owed him something she'd never agreed to.

She glanced around the room again, this time noticing some of the art pieces around the house. Lots of paintings and photos of old castles, but also of factories, machines, and some were just of gears and sprockets. A suit of knight's armor stood over in a far corner she'd never noted before. Swords, too. *This freaking guy.*

"It's perfectly fine," his spiked-coffee voice assured her. "It's actually part of what I needed you to see." He started to unfasten his arm brace, its mechanics hissing as he disengaged it. Molly stared at it like some alien artifact. It would have seemed beyond belief only weeks ago but her sense of the possible was quite broadened now. Still, it was...*advanced.*

Blake removed the apparatus, and then began to peel off his glove. She noticed how pale his skin at the wrist looked. And not just that. His veins. She could see his veins through his skin it was so pale, almost translucent. And the veins were so dark, purple, black almost. The glove fell away, revealing his hand. His gnarled, twisted hand. Bony, protruding knuckles. Blackened fingernails.

"Oh god." Molly put her hand to her mouth. "Did that...is that from the..." She felt so awful for him.

"From our evening's misadventure?" he finished for her, his word choices always so odd. "I'm afraid so, yes, they're probably quite connected. An unfortunate effect. Aesthetically, at least."

"Look, I'm sorry. I'm so sorry." Her eyes welled. She hated the idea that he was disfigured, and all because of her. She hadn't meant any of it. She couldn't have predicted or prevented it in any way she knew, but still she felt responsible. She felt it in her guts. "I wish it had never..." She didn't know how to finish.

"It's nothing." He approached to embrace her, to offer a hug of reassurance, but she pulled away instinctively. She hadn't even had a conscious thought to do it. The movement surprised even her. Like her body had kicked in on its own and moved.

Blake pulled himself away again, defeated, chastised, affronted, though he did all to not show it. An eye barely twitched. But she could feel it, and see he was uncomfortable. Jilted.

She needed to be away from here. She'd never felt anything so certain in her life. She needed to be gone from him and now.

"There's more, though." He shifted his mood consciously. "It's not entirely a loss." Blake pointed toward the other room, toward the television which was playing some PBS show. "Watch," he said, stretching out his gnarled hand.

But it was time to go. Molly's stomach turned over and over. Something about today, tonight, this whole week was all wrong. What had Lydia tried to tell her? She was gonna ralph all over his fancy digs any second if she didn't get away from him.

"Look, another time, maybe, okay?" she cut him off. "I can't stay. I have to get to my shift at work. I can't be late again, you know. And, also..." She looked at him, his eyes knew what was coming. She could see, through their emptiness, Blake bracing himself for what she had to say. As though he'd heard it before so many times, it need not even be said again.

But she would say it. She'd come here to say it.

"Look, I like you, Blake. I do. I think you're a lot better guy than maybe you let on at first. I mean I used to think you were kind of an asshole, because, I mean... *well*, you were."

His eye twitched, but his forced smile stayed on his lips.

"But then," she continued, "you seemed okay. And, like I said, I do like you. But..." And he knew the rest. "As a friend."

He didn't move or speak.

"Friends?" Molly offered her hand to shake his.

"Indeed." He accepted the shake, then turned to the wet bar behind him. "I'm going to have a beverage. And I believe you have a schedule. I shan't keep you."

He faced away from her.

Molly started to say something but took her exit where she could get it. She slid quiet as a church mouse out his large front door. She was down his flight of steps in a dash, on her board and zipping away. She kicked it at strength a time or two to get some real speed going. She had somewhere to be.

XIII
"I THINK WE'RE ALONE NOW"
—TIFFANY, 1987

THE CLOCK ON THE WALL waited as long as it possibly could to tick down to 9pm. The last seconds slowed to all but a standstill. Each movement of the hand a thud toward the impending finality of it. Which it was. Finally.

It was Friday. It was nine o'clock. It was her time. She earned this. She deserved it. *I'm a god damn hero, for what-his-sake*! She scribbled "Sit Down. Wait Here." on a sheet of paper and left it on the counter, the door unlocked so he could let himself in. She ran to the back with her register, locking it up in the office. She cut the lights, dimming the shop. She made a quick change out of her work clothes and into tonight's outfit. Then to the intercom stereo...

* * *

Easton was a minute or two late. He lingered outside the door for a moment, sweating, his hands shaking, before he saw the sign telling him to come in. He read the next one on the counter and followed its instruction. He slumped down in the armchair at the front of Trace's shop, the one she used herself to sit and read a magazine while Molly, or lately Lydia, ran the shop.

The weight of some inevitable doom hung from his shoulders, slouched and swallowed by the heavy chair's cushions. He rubbed his brow with his hand, his jacket sleeve, a black leather number this time, different than his usual pastels.

The lights dimmed.

The music kicked on, a song he'd heard a hundred times. He even had to force his way through a mob at the mall once because the singer was there doing a concert. *Who does a concert at a mall?*

Then, he saw *her*.

She slid out across the floor, yards in front of him, her feet covered in only a pair of long socks that came up past her ankles. Blue tights disappeared into a fluffy oversized sweater, her hair dancing to its own beat away from the rest of her. That bright flaming red hair, the hair he'd watched so much these last few months, hair that haunted him now because of what he had to do.

And he did. He *had* to do it.

He wanted so much not to smile, to just get it over with. But he failed.

Molly turned to him, singing the lyrics in time with Tiffany—who she had been told on more than one occasion she favored. She twisted in every direction *except* toward him, while saying every word of the music right at him. Her legs, possessed with her emotion, moved on their own, as her arms twitched and shot about.

As the song faded, she danced her way toward him, turning away and then back to him, ending the whole thing with her head down, so close she was almost touching him.

Almost.

She vibrated, her body electric, surging through her, like lightning could shoot out of her hands and face. He was going to kiss her any second; she could feel it. She could sense it. She demanded it.

She lifted her head to set her eyes to his—to have them tell him what her lips shouldn't have to by now. He couldn't not do it. It was quite fully impossible to *not* kiss her in that moment.

And so she waited.

And he nothing-ed.

This isn't right. This is, in fact, entirely wrong. This was the final moment of the perfect week. You take out two tanks with your bare hands. Put half a gang in jail. Show up every Becky and Britni in the whole school. Runway down the hall in a different Vogue cover photo outfit every single day. Dance your eyes every right way, even scoring a detention for your efforts... You get to kiss the guy. You do. It's just a rule.

And if he didn't pony up in the next half second, she swore to every deity she could name (which wasn't many), she'd...

"I..." His eyes dropped. Sad. His whole stomach failed him. He stared at her, into her want. And he saw it. And he wanted it too. She felt him feeling her want, him feeling his own want, and yet him pulling back. It took his whole self to stay away from her face. But he had to. Something was forcing him to hold himself back.

"What?" Her spirits sank by the second. It was wrong. It was all wrong. It was dropping. She was dropping. She was falling, her stomach on fire. "What's wrong?"

"I just..." He paused and turned away from her, ashamed of himself. "I didn't want to do this." He was almost crying, and her heart hurt for him. He was tearing himself apart. "It had to be me, though. I wouldn't let...it had to be me. And I'm sorry."

"What is it?" she pressed. "Please tell me."

Easton dropped his head, eyes to the floor. He reached behind him.

All her time stopped again. His hand froze in place as it grabbed at something tucked at his back. She breathed, for the first time since he'd come in, she realized.

And she smelled it. The cold, heartless steel of it. Its pins and springs. The sliding mechanism. Each little brass case held in its place. But, mostly the powder. That smell had never left her from the tank blast.

He'd brought a gun.

Oh, god, it's him. Molly wretched in her mind. She was going to vomit. This was what Lydia tried to tell her? He was going to try to serial kill her on their first date? She couldn't believe this was real. *Please don't try to kill me.* She begged him with her eyes. She'd have to rip his body in half, and she didn't want to rip his body in half. She wanted—needed—none of this to be happening.

Molly's fists balled. Time began again.

Easton pulled out his wallet, unfolded it, and showed her. It shined, silver and gleaming in the dimmed lights of the shop. The words across it were knives stabbing into her. It couldn't be. *He* couldn't be.

But it was. Because *he was.*

"I'm a cop," he said. "I need you to come with me."

"I'm sorry." Molly blinked twice. "What?"

"TERROR VISION"
—THE FIBONACCIS, 1986

THE TICKS OF THE CLOCK in the foyer pounded like hammers in his skull. How he hated hammers, too. Those tools of his ancient trade. But now they haunted him—all because of that *one.*

The moments ticked on, every second a new eternity entombed in his stone cage, a reminder of his failure. Again. Even now, he just knew, *she* who by right belonged to him, his property, a debt outstanding, was out *gallivanting* (he did enjoy that word; its sibilance exuberated him) with that...*creature.* That mongrel. A beast of this byd canol. How he hated it. And them.

The whole thing from the first moment had been a bad bargain. He had many gifts, profound skill, and craftsmanship, but he always struck a beggar's bargain. Her own oafish father had somehow bested him. Fool, that he'd been. Then the Eldar witch had spoke the words too slowly, his prize escaping through the bridge before the charm took hold.

"What now?" He'd demanded of the Eldar once she'd brought them through, somewhere just outside the Crescent City on the moor. "How do we find her?"

"That search belongs to you alone." The Eldar sneered, staring off into the lights of the city beyond them.

"But how will I find her? The charm? Did it take? Will she?" He'd salivated at the words dripping from his mouth. He'd almost tasted his prize, remaking her in his own image.

"As requested, she will take on a form like unto the first being she sees. Only now like them, rather than you." She'd grinned, mocking him. They all mocked him.

"Then how will I know? How will I find—"

"Her hair." The Mother of Demons noted her own, darker than night itself. "You wanted to keep the red." She then whispered her dark language over him, which he knew as well as any other. "[I grant you this final payment, that you shall appear as they do, as one desirable in their fashion. This and no more. For I've my own work to complete, unhindered now. Be gone, Døkkn rat]." And then she'd vanished into the void. She abandoned him here, left to sort through these muds for his prize these many years.

He poured himself another drink, emptying the bottle. They were such brutes. Simpletons, all. Fodder. But he had to give credit to them where due. Their uisce beatha was quite well rendered, he must say. He sipped from the glass, the best of their wares he'd found.

He had arranged it all so perfectly. All for nought.

The television, their rude and loud ornament of information, assaulted him with its sounds and its kaleidescoping array of lights. It had been useful as a window into them, their language, their patterns, but now, as all seemed undone, it merely offended him with its vulgarity.

Blake stretched out his pale, veiny, gnarled hand—the illusion that had masked his form faded, leaving behind his true image, his true nature. *Ðøkkn rat.* The Eldar god's words became poison in his mind.

"दूरम् सार्धम् भवत्," he muttered at the squawking picture box.

The TV shut itself off.

Blake finished his drink.

EPISODE IV

"BACK ON THE CHAIN GANG"
—THE PRETENDERS, 1982.

THE COUNTY JAIL was a slew of red jackets, greased hair, piercings, sloppy tattoos, and bickering now for a week. More than once, the white-haired one, booked under the name Scythe — an obvious alias, real name pending his prints coming back — had torn into the others. He seemed to be some sort of leader, but not one they much respected. A lieutenant who'd only recently come up the ranks. Still had to prove his place.

Most of these guys were local toughs, drop-outs, junkies, or other skeezers. Most had rap sheets already half a book thick. Some had once been okay kids who caught a bad break. The Commie Ron years hadn't been good to many.

Scythe leered at the boys as they waited for their arraignment, which had been pushed back on request from the special task force. They hoped to soften them up with a few more days of sleeping piled on top of each other, smelling each other's... *everything.*

These guys could sit there a month or two and no judge would shed a tear. And after the stunt they pulled, putting two guardsmen in intensive care and racking up over four hundred thousand in city damages? That wasn't counting the interstate, nor especially the Cadillac Gage Commandos they totaled. They were gonna catch the charge for it, at least. No one was yet sure what to make of the colorful heroine who took off just as fast as she'd appeared.

But none expected what came next.

The officer on duty stared at the order and shook his head several times, squinting to be sure he had it right as he wandered over to the cell.

"Well, shitheads." He jangled his keys. "Looks like you made bail."

"What?" Scythe asked.

Even he couldn't believe that.

I
"I HATE MYSELF FOR LOVING YOU"
–JOAN JETT & THE BLACKHEARTS, 1988

HER FIRST RIDE in Easton's Z28 ragtop was nothing at all like Molly had envisioned. They sat silent, her hair whipping through the wind, the sweetness of the gulf breeze soured by the grim occasion. The V8 engine cooked them to Easton's task force headquarters, the old abandoned church on Sarter where he and Nguyen had been "doing renovations." Molly decided to stop counting the things about Easton that were lies and would instead make note of anything that was real, as soon as she found one.

She glanced at him, catching his eye looking back at her. She could see the regret. No, *shame*. His sand-colored hair tossed along with hers, and she refused to even consider how his eyes shined in the passing lights. And she certainly wouldn't think about how those sad little dog eyes made him any cuter. Not at all.

She was going to be mad and stay mad. She'd made up her mind.

Their headquarters wasn't much. It really did look like what they'd always said: a rundown old Catholic church. There were ladders, scaffolds, tools, etc. strewn about where maybe they really had been doing some reconstruction and then just quit halfway through and said screw it. Some of the stained glass was still intact, and Molly liked the colored light coming through, bathing the whole sanctuary in a kaleidoscope glow.

"You're not even serious," she had said to him back at the store, staring down in disbelief at what was very much a real badge. It just couldn't be. How?

"I am. And I need you to come with me. It's important, or I would never do this."

Do what? Ruin my whole life? Ruin everything I ever believed about you, or anything else? Make me look like a complete idiot, dancing around you for months now? Ughh. She could just kill him. Well, no. But she could at least kick him into a wall. She totally could. *At least he's not the killer. But still.*

"So, what? Am I under arrest? For what?"

"No, you're just...I'll explain when we get there. My lieutenant needs to talk to you. You're not safe." The way his eyes hurt when he said that last part made her soften, but not much. He really believed that. He was actually worried for *her*. It wouldn't get him out of this any time soon, but it helped.

"What do you know about this guy?" Lieutenant Torello held out a photo as they sat her down in a makeshift office. He had a mustache, curly hair, olive skin. About 50. Maybe older. His face chewed up the scenery, like he belonged to some other time. There was a Virgin Mary on the wall, could have been a holdover from the days when this was still a real church. But it seemed like it might be Torello's, too.

Like he was the kind of guy that was with his mother every Sunday in the pew, but would break your jaw if you spoke sideways to her on the street. Old school. Molly couldn't even hate him if she tried.

Molly glared at the picture of Blake Elvis. What was all this? She'd assumed the whole ride over this was about her own... *extracurriculars*. But Blake? Richie richboy Blake? With the beach house and the Porsche and the fancy drinks? He even held his pinky out when he sipped them.

Molly didn't say anything. Hoyt watched enough cop shows back home that she knew that's how they got you. Say one thing one day, slip up and forget, say another thing the next and then they hounded you for life. And even if they were really looking at Blake, she didn't need them accidentally stumbling onto a two-fer.

"Not a talker, huh?" Torello said.

"You were at his house," Easton, *that liar*, said. Or asked. It wasn't clear. "What did he say? Did he do anything..."

"What?" Molly said.

"I don't know. Weird or fishy, I guess?" Easton said.

Nguyen paced in the corner, Easton's partner *this whole time*. Another girl walked in. Cute. Too cute. Easton nodded at her, and Molly stabbed his face with her eyes. Twice. Right in the face.

"What do you got for me, Rae?" Torello asked. The cute girl, Rae, handed him a file, and Torello skimmed through it. "You gotta be kidding me!"

"What is it?" Easton said.

"Not sure." Torello reached in his desk and pulled another file, thicker, and tossed it in front of Molly. "Well, go ahead." He motioned to Easton. "Tell her."

Easton sighed and picked up the folder, flipped through it, and pulled out some photos. All girls. All different ages. All reds.

"Nine schools. Nine years," Easton said. "All around the area. Not just here. Further out a ways. Bogalusa. Pearlington. Orange Grove. The Burg."

Molly's neck iced. She stared at the pictures. Some were as young as seven or eight. She didn't want to hear the rest, didn't want to know it. She wanted to go home and practice her music and not be super at anything and just not know about any of this. She wanted none of this to be true. She gulped, feeling a knot in her belly that wouldn't untie.

"All these girls had two things in common. The hair, obviously. The other is they're all fosters, or adopted. Every one. All missing. Never found."

Molly stared at those girls. They were her. Each a version of her. She had done this. It was *her* fault. Whatever it was she had, whatever she was...that's what this was about. She knew it. She could feel it. But she couldn't say it. Not to *cops*. What would they even do if she told them?

"And then there's this." Easton passed her a stack of yearbook photocopies. They were from different schools and every grade all the way up. In each one, a different boy was circled.

"I don't get it." Molly scanned the pictures, her head spinning. Still sick from the photos of the girls. They hadn't gone into detail, and she didn't want any.

"Look at the names." Nguyen folded his arms and leaned harder into the wall, like it would fall down without him. He was angry, shaking his head.

All the circled boys had the same name: *Blake Elvis.* Every single one.

"But they're all different boys," she said.

"That's what we can't figure out," Easton said. "We hoped you could give us something."

"Did he say anything unusual to you?" Torello asked. "You see anything odd about his house?"

Oh, gee, where to start? His weird twin switchblade cane swords with creepy carvings? His obsession with her lately? His gnarly scarred hand with the gross-out veins? The lightning? The paintings? The weird way he talked? That she could sense everyone's emotions EXCEPT his? In fact, it was actually hard to think of things about him that weren't weird.

Total bullet dodge there, Mol.

"We've had our eye on this guy for a while now," Torello said. "It's why I had Braddock here try to get close to him, go to his house and his parties. We wanted to locate his target before he could...do what he does."

And just what is it he does? No, Molly didn't want to think of it.

"But then earlier tonight there was a new development," Torello continued.

"We had to pull you off the street, fast," Easton jumped in.

"Why?" Molly glared at Easton. "What happened?"

She struggled to process this. An hour ago, she was set for the date of her life. Dinner. A night drive across the bay. Wind in their hair. Now, *this* was the date. Flickering lights. Drips echoing. Beat-up file cabinets. And that sad mother staring at her dying son in the colored glass above them.

"Because now he's got himself a gang." Nguyen folded his arms, pacing back and forth.

"He what?" This was heavy. *Blake? Gangs? What?*

"The perps from the guard armory robbery this week." Torello grimaced. "Part of a gang out of New Orleans called Les Mutants Rouges, or the Mutes."

The Red Jackets? Rat-hawk and Bucket-hat? Figured. Those guys were turning into bad pennies.

"They made bail tonight," Easton said.

"Who would bail out those scumbags?" She didn't want to drop any hints she knew much about them. They were here to talk to Molly, not the Sledgehammer.

"Someone with a lot of money," Torello said.

"Why would he?" Molly's head went in too many directions. What was it, in fact, Blake had wanted to show her? She couldn't decide if she was mad or glad she'd ditched out before he could. She was more worried in that moment he might drop trow. Now she needed to know if he was...*like her.*

"Why would Blake mess with some street gang?" she asked.

"We were hoping you could help connect that dot," Torello said.

"Me?"

"Show it to her."

Rae walked up with something wrapped in plastic and handed it to Easton

"Because of this." Easton pulled a familiar short sword by its wolf head handle from the plastic wrap. The same one she'd kicked from a Mute's hand just days ago. "This is what they used to cut into the bank vaults."

Easton showed it to Molly. She was now much more curious about this than she had been before. She should have been paying more attention. It was all slamming down on her brain.

"This?" She instinctively felt the blade. The faintest touch of its edge opened her finger up wide. Blood ran down her hand and the blade. "Holy shit! It cut me!"

Easton pulled it away. "Yeah, I just said it sliced through bank vaults."

"Jesus Christ, Braddock," Torello yelled. "What are we? Keystone? That's contaminated evidence now."

Molly stared at her bleeding finger in shock. And she couldn't even tell them why. Her whole body shook, vibrated. *What the hell is happening? What is that thing? Why did Blake have it? And where's the other one?*

"What is that thing?"

"That's just it," Nguyen said. "We don't know." His eyes were grim and his jaw set. He looked older now that she was focusing on him.

"The lab report came back. The blade is made from no known metal. It's like nothing they've seen, they said," Torello said.

"We think it might be Russian."

"We don't know that at all," Torello scolded Nguyen for that.

"It's definitely Russian," Nguyen muttered.

Molly kept staring at its edge. At the wolf's-head pommel. She conjured her first memory of it, Blake holding it out the night all this chaos started. Both of his blades, one at the guy's throat and this one pointed at the rest of the bangers. And the lightning strike. Like it was drawn down to *this* thing.

"How does something like this end up in the hands of some two-bit hustlers?" Torello asked her. Like she'd know. Which she did. But didn't want to tell him. If they looked into that night, it'd put her whole affair in jeopardy.

Helicopters, she could hear Lydia in her head.

"We'll be lucky if we can keep it a week from the Feds. It's central to our whole case, the only hard evidence that links our serial to the gangs. So, what can you tell us about him? About them?"

"Gangs? Plural?" She tried to alter the subject.

"More coming in. New batch rolled in just last month. You probably heard the commotion."

"From the party?" She thought of Blake again, his emptiness that night and the way he disappeared. *Is this all coming back to him? And why?*

"Different gang," Easton said. "Call themselves the Drednex, or Dreds. Buncha Louisiana Nazis riding dirty on stripped down Hogs."

Molly hated Nazis, Louisiana or otherwise.

"So that was just random?" she asked.

Easton shrugged, and Torello looked her in the eye. Rae clicked her pen against the stack of papers in her file. The ancient heater in the building kicked on with a grating whine. It smelled like mold somewhere. Probably was.

"We just not gonna talk about it?" Nguyen asked his colleagues.

"Not again, Nguyen," Torello said.

"What?" Molly said. Easton just sighed and pinched his nose. Torello shook his head.

"Something's got 'em spooked." Nguyen came alive. "All the gangs of New Orleans been getting the hell out of Dodge the past several years. Leaving in droves for wherever ain't the B'Easy. It's why I'm here. It's why this unit exists, and we're just gonna pretend it's the beaches and the sunshine brings 'em out to the boons? And I should know."

Easton had told her on the ride over. They were a special task force put together by the coast counties. A joint unit with multi-jurisdictional authority. Top-secret. Cops recruited out of high schools early on, sworn in soon as they turned 18 and embedded after that. Deep cover. Nguyen had come out of New Orleans Academy two years prior and volunteered for the program. An orphan, himself, just like Molly was.

But whatever he was on about now had him scared. Goosebumps ran all the way up and down his spine. He was cold. She could sense his fear. It was real. And thick.

"They're running from...*it.*" He shivered "Even You-know-who quit coming around."

"I-know-who?" Molly was thoroughly lost.

"Exactly." Nguyen leaned back against the wall.

"No, really," Molly said. "I don't know who."

"Look." Torello shoved the photo of Blake at Molly. "We've got problems enough here without worrying about another city's ghosts and goblins. We got a real case with a real BAD guy here. I need answers, and I need you safe and off the streets."

Easton sighed. "We have to get you to a safe house until we can loc—"

"Am I under arrest?" Molly was done. This was over. She wanted to be anywhere but here.

"What?" they all said.

"Am I under arrest? Because if I'm not, I'd like to go."

"No," Easton said, "but you can't just leave. It's not safe out—"

"Watch me." Molly popped up from her seat, grabbed her satchel, and made for the door. *Hell with this. Hell with them. Hell with the stupid thugs and whatever Blake is up to. Let 'em try something.* She almost hoped they did, the mood she was in.

Molly exploded out the cathedral door, still sturdy on its hinges after all the years and hurricanes and salty weather. One of the many wonders of the older world.

"Molly, wait." Easton followed her out the door. He put his hand on her shoulder. She shook it off, turned and stared at him with hurt-hate. "Look, I'm sorry about the way this went down. It's just..." He stared at her, losing his words.

"Tell me this." She dreaded asking it, because she already knew the answer. "The whole time, *with me*," she said, "was it was all just..." She didn't know how to finish it. Didn't want to. "I was just an assignment, wasn't I? A job?"

She wasn't going to cry in front of him. She refused to do that.

In fact, she wouldn't cry at all.

"It's not..." She felt him searching for words. More lies, certainly. "It got complicated. I..."

"Yeah." She nodded to him, her face a stone. "Well, let's uncomplicate it. Goodbye, Easton."

"You can't be out here anymore," he pleaded. He felt it was true, too; she sensed he actually cared. But she was still mad. "It's not safe. We have no idea where he— they are."

"I can handle myself, Silverstar."

"Molly!" he yelled.

But she was already on her board.

II
"LOVE IS A STRANGER"
—EURYTHMICS, 1982

LYDIA SLAMMED on the bass in the garage, reverb going all over the neighborhood. Dogs barked from the sidewalks. Her eyeliner was on thick tonight and spider-lace climbed out of the top of her combat boots. Her oversized W.A.S.P. shirt belted at the waist ended just above her black denim jorts. She considered bobbing her hair but hadn't decided yet. She wanted to tweak this solo she was working on.

Mike the Mic, sporting one of their costume wigs, tickled the keyboard behind her, keeping a running beat and chiming in here and there with some Eurowave nonsense. Lydia still wasn't sold on the Prog stuff. Molly was all about that Eastern synth, but Lydia liked good old American Detroit diesel.

Watts and Hurl were inside watching TV with Hoyt & Clair. It was 5 for $5 at the Video Hut in Old Town, and the boys had cleaned house. Hoyt would be up to his ears in bad horror movies for the weekend.

Molly skated up to the curb and kicked the board so hard she nearly broke it, then flipped it and snatched it out of the air like a snake strike. She stomped into the garage and stared for a second at Mike in the wig before deciding she didn't care.

"Oh, crap." Lydia unstrapped her bass, laying it aside. She guessed the date didn't go well.

Mike played through.

Molly walked right over Lydia's sympathy and went inside, continuing her stomp up the stairs. She didn't want to see a single person, much less six of them. She'd told herself no crying and she would hold to that. But she just couldn't handle Lydia's energy right now, much less the peanut gallery. She was just so over it already.

A cop? An actual cop?? It had all been a lie. A case.

Gods, he probably still likes Becky! That... whatever she is. Molly didn't have the word. Or just didn't want to use it.

Sleep sounded good right about now.

Instead she got the World Wrestling Federation.

"What the hell?" she said.

Lydia walked in behind her and plugged a tape into Molly's B&W VCR/TV combo with 10-inch screen they had used all through 8th grade to watch horror and rated R movies without Hoyt and Clair being wise to it. Lydia had scored it from her older brother, who scored it from...well. Hence his "job" upstate now.

"That's Jake the Snake!" Lydia was way too happy for Molly's night. "Now watch this!" He did some move where the other guy's head thudded onto the mat. *Big whoop.*

"Lydia, I can't with this right now." She flopped onto the bed.

"Yeah." Lydia's smile erased and went grim. "I figure when you want to talk, I'll be around. We can do this later, too. I just thought...I don't know. Might be useful. It's all the best moves cut together. I got it at Video Hut. We have it for a week!"

Yay.

III
"MAKE IT SHINE"
—QUARTERFLASH, 1983

HURL WAITED OUTSIDE Miracle's on 25th, having conned a ride downtown out of Lydia and Molly since they were headed to Tracey's anyway. Lambert was late. They agreed to meet here after school. Or rather, Hurl had decided to come and see if Mr. Max, the owner, could tell him something about the gem he'd found in the thieves' hideout. If anyone knew about treasure and jewels, it was Mr. Max. Lambert had insisted he come along, too, already going on and on about this "half mine" business, when it was clearly Hurl who had the dream, drew the map, led the expedition, and, ultimately found the gemstone.

Half nothing.

But Hurl had agreed.

"I say we just take it to Piette's," Lambert had said. "We could probably get our weight in comics. Hey, maybe we could get a gun?"

"He's not gonna give us a gun," Hurl had scolded him. "And besides we ain't going to Pirate Piette's. That guy's a crook. My dad said so and everybody knows it. And this thing's worth a lot more than some dang comic books."

Hurl wanted to get enough if they sold it to give it to Mr. Cletus so he could pay for his truck and come home more often and see Watts. Hurl knew Watts missed his dad so hard he couldn't stand it. He wanted to make it a surprise for their Christmas. Lambert was over here thinking about bubble gum and trading cards, *the stinking goon.*

When Lambert finally showed, tagged along by his weird mom (she always talked about bible stuff to every person she met), they went inside. Miracle's wasn't strictly a jewelry store. They had a few other odd things for sale. Like a big wooden sasquatch right as you walked in the door, holding a cup full of pennies. People would leave them there sometimes for good luck, or even take a few if they needed one. Mr. Max didn't mind it. If you asked him where he got the statue, he'd always say he couldn't remember, but Hurl knew that was a lie because no one could forget about something that awesome.

Up front in glass cases, he kept the showy stuff. He had watches along the walls, and big grandfather clocks. One of the ones Hoyt had in the garage came from here. In the back was Mr. Max's workshop. That's how it got the name "Miracle's." Since before anyone could remember, they'd take their old, broken, or worn out stuff, heirlooms and random objects, to Max. He could fix anything. They said he'd never been stumped.

He also told stories about famous stones or necklaces or diamonds. He talked about curses placed on treasures like it was real. People came in sometimes just to hear his wild tales. Clair took her old brooch there two years ago and brought Hurl along. Mr. Max went on and on about the lost treasure of Pitcher's Point, which Hurl had committed entirely to memory. If anyone could tell him about this stone, it was Mr. Max.

"Well, so what do we got here?" Mr. Max inspected the gemstone as Hurl handed it to him. Lambert paced. He'd told Hurl Mr. Max was weird, with his crazy white hair and lips that were too big for his face. Hurl told him to shut it and let him do the dealing. Hurl knew about these things. And Mr. Max knew even more.

"I think it's a canary diamond." Hurl was sure at first, but then as Mr. Max's lips curled he became less sure.

"Those are pretty rare." He smacked his lips, putting in his eyepiece. Lambert's mom fingered some of the watches and Mr. Max called to her, "On sale, if you're interested."

"Well, maybe a garnet? Those can be yellow, right?" Hurl had a book on gemstones he'd gotten from the library. He needed to know his pirate treasures when he found them, which he was sure now he had. "Could it be Pitcher's or Captain Scott's?"

"Well, now." Max continued inspecting the stone. "See here, the luster?" He held it up to the little lamp next to his counter. "Its luster is brighter than a canary, much more than a garnet. And the weight..." He hefted it in his hand two or three times, then tossed it to Hurl. "Much heavier than a diamond. Heavier than anything I know of. Not quite sure what you got there, kid, but she ain't no gemstone I can name for you. And look here." He motioned for Hurl to hand it back.

Hurl did so, and Max pulled out a magnifying glass and held it out for Hurl to inspect.

"Look down here, deep in the center. See that?"

"What is it?" Hurl could barely make anything out. There was a lightness in the center was all he could tell. He needed another book.

"It's like it's glowing, maybe. I can't tell. A faint light, brighter than just the color reflecting off my lamp here. No, I can't say as I've seen that in a stone before. I'll have to do some studying on it."

Mr. Max held it in his hands a minute longer, looking it over again and again, almost seeming to lose himself in it, just staring deep into its center.

"But is it worth anything?" Lambert blurted out, waking Max from his trance. "We want to get paid, man."

Hurl could have shot him with his eyes. No one disrespected Mr. Max like that. *This guy had even scoffed at Watts' dad, Mr. Cletus, come to think of it. Why is he even in the Knights?* Hurl would bring this before the joint chief ASAP. They had a code, and this guy wasn't cutting it.

"Son, I can't honestly say if it's worth the gas money your mama burnt bringing you here." He glanced at Lambert and his mom, then turned to Hurl and whispered, "Hang on to that. If I find anything on it, I'll call your dad. He still got that granddaddy?"

"Yes, sir."

"Fine machine, that is. Fine machine."

Lambert's mom put a penny in the sasquatch cup.

IV
"LOVE ON A REAL TRAIN"
–TANGERINE DREAM, 1984

NIGHT CREPT THROUGH the house, bathing the downstairs rooms in its cold embrace. It quieted Molly's mind but brought no comfort. It whispered things to her but not in words she knew. Or none she remembered.

Molly saw no reason to sleep as she didn't need it, and she liked having those moments to think, to take stock, to practice, to hone, to listen, to feel, to know whatever she could know. Mostly she tried to know herself.

The TV flickered in the background, the sound all the way down. The video Lydia left played on the VCR. Molly felt obliged to give it a look, or at least the half glance she did at the moment. In her mind, she was making a list. Trying to write down every weird moment she'd ever had with Blake. When he'd first come to Bay High. The way he'd looked at her. Even then, before...all this, he seemed off. And his face. The way he looked too...*perfect.* All those yearbooks...a different guy in each one? *What does it mean?*

She wanted to ask Easton. Get his thoughts. Work with him. See his face again.

But then she wanted to punch his face.

Both. She wanted both.

She put her pen down and cracked the fridge open to see what was leftover. Clair had made pot pies and there were two left. She grabbed both, and went at them cold. Some guy on the TV dressed as a cop picked the other dude up with one arm and then dropped him hard on the mat.

"Jeez!" Molly swallowed. Some of the stuff these guys did *without* powers? Pretty impressive. But she couldn't bear to tell Lydia, or she'd be roped into this every week. *God that girl and her wrestling. Her football. Her Tanya Tucker records.* Nothing about Lydia made much sense. Maybe that's why they worked.

"Couldn't sleep?" Hoyt had snuck down, went for the second pie and poured himself a glass of milk. "Me neither," he added before downing the milk.

She didn't speak but leaned her shoulder against his. He wrapped his arm around her other one, and they watched together for a minute. Maybe they weren't gonna evict her, after all.

"Oh, this is great," he said. "Watch this!"

Some guy with a two-by-four waved a big American flag all around. This stuff was goofy, but Hoyt smiled at it, so she did too.

* * *

As the wee hours waned on, in the quiet of the dark, she slipped on her outfit, and slid out the back, bounding across the backyard and over the fence. She'd gone out several nights at first with Lydia, but the poor girl needed her rest. This time, Molly wanted to go it alone.

She took off down E street, avoiding the few working lights. She ran soft, picking up her speed, leapt over houses — whole blocks where she could.

She made the Bay Bridge, ran alongside a moving truck, jumped onto the back, and bummed a ride across. The salty wind licked her face under her silly mask. It had started to grow on her, but not by much. She and Lydia had cleaned out most of the unitards after the tank fiasco—that first one in tatters now.

The truck took her most of the way before turning to go north up 25th. She hopped off and footed it after that. She was quick enough. Few cars were out. Probably half of those drivers were drunk or falling asleep. If they saw anything it was a blur. And they wouldn't believe their own eyes if they caught a full glimpse.

She made it to Blake's. Crept along the shadows. She scoped the door a good while. Just being back gave her the willies. She knew they were connected. And she needed to know how.

Yellow tape barred the door. Easton's pals in blue had made their visit. No one was home. Of course not. *Does this guy even have parents?* She'd never seen them. And all the facade? For what? Actually going to school? To class? *What is his damage?*

She cracked the door, almost popping the knob from the socket. Stepped through the yellow tape. Ransacked. They'd searched everything. Pulled paintings off walls. Broken things. All clutter now.

She went upstairs and looked through the bedrooms. So many. All the same. She got to the one where she'd found Lydia the night this all started. Was that random or orchestrated? She doubted everything now.

What would Blake be willing to do to get to her? Why did he want her?

She crept along until she found Blake's master bedroom. Sorting through his closet, she found only expensive stuff. Good taste — for preppy gear, that is. Not her scene. There was a desk and some small tools lain about. Tiny gears. Sprockets. Like he'd been fixing a watch or something.

What did he want? Was it just the obvious? Why go to all this trouble? Had to be more. Something...*weirder.*

Her body shook. Got cold. She didn't get cold.

That hand he'd showed her. Those wicked blue veins, those blackened fingernails. What if it wasn't the lightning that did that? What if that was just... *him?*

V
"SELF CONTROL"
—LAURA BRANNIGAN, 1984

LIGHTS ARRIVED OUTSIDE with a humming engine going silent. Voices carried. Familiar. Molly ducked out a window and onto the roof, crouching, watching.

Easton and Nguyen climbed out of the Z28 and trudged up the long stairs to the house. They inspected the tape, making sure it hadn't been disturbed. She'd been careful and hadn't moved anything...nor gotten any answers. Maybe they knew more. She tuned her ears to their whispers.

"What are you gonna find that forensics didn't?" Easton kicked a plastic cup across the porch.

"You're the one so set on catching up to this guy. You can spend all night back at headquarters making your eyes bleed on files and reports, but the answers are here. This is why I'm going for detective and you'll still be a glorified CI, Braddock," Nguyen said. "Now, watch and learn, young gun."

They clicked their flashlights and scoured the house room by room. Nguyen inspected every object in reach.

"Might help if I knew what we're looking for," Easton grumbled.

"I'll know it when I see it. Anything out of the ordinary."

Easton glanced around him, taking it all in. He'd seen it so many times before, lurking the parties Blake threw during the fall. He'd hit the school like a storm. Out of nowhere, unheard of, and suddenly he's dating *The* Becky de la Beckwith (relieving Easton of his 'obligation' as she'd said it) and having the who's who of the whole town over every weekend for his "soirees." It made Easton sick, blending into all of it. The coke, the pills. None of it stuck to Elvis, though. Every lead he chased down led to some pimp or pusher in an alley. Collateral damage of having guests with deep pockets. And Blake's money; where had it come from? His nonexistent parents? None of it added up. When they first even halfway connected Blake to the murders, Easton told Becky to get away. She trusted him, so she had. But what Torello had him doing with Molly gut-wrenched him.

"We'd do better cruising the grove. Call in some bangers and buyers, the usual. This case is above our paygrade now, buddy," Nguyen said.

"You want to go rough up some pimps and johns, be my guest. Just swing back and pick me up before coffee and donuts."

"Look, man, I get it. It's your girlfriend he was after. It's personal to you. But you can't let it get personal, kid."

Molly felt the heat of Easton's blood fill his face, him blushing in the darkness. She'd slid back in the house, always a room behind them, quiet as a coffin, no breathing.

"She's not my..." Easton couldn't finish. He didn't want to. "It got complicated, all right?"

Complicated? Is that what I am? Well I can uncomplicate your face!

They scoped out the wet bar in the front, wandered through the kitchen, admiring his cooking knives. *What did he even eat? Did he eat?* Molly could go for a burger right about then. Or an 8-box at Popeye's, but they wouldn't be open for another nine hours. They headed into the den, his antiquated furniture arranged around his state-of-the-art entertainment array. All the best, the newest, the biggest. The two cops ran every line of the room, every detail of the setup. Other than Blake's odd aesthetics, it was all more or less standard. The same zilch she'd come up with.

"This is a bust," Easton said. "He's bailed. This place is clean."

Nguyen kept looking, silent. He saw something. Molly felt it.

"Remotes," Nguyen said after a beat.

"What?"

"You see any remote controls anywhere?"

"No, why?"

"He's got all this stuff. Stereo, TV, VCR, camcorders, the works. All brand-new stuff. Where's his remotes?"

Easton shook his head, confused. They checked around the coffee and end tables. Opened drawers. Checked the cushions. Nothing.

"I don't get it."

"This seem like the kinda guy who gets up and walks over every time to change the station?" Nguyen asked. "You knew the dude."

"No." Easton gave it a good think. "No, he isn't."

"You see? That's the kind of thing I mean. That's weird. It doesn't fit."

"Yeah, but what do we do with it?" Easton asked. So did Molly, in her head.

"Don't know yet." Nguyen flashed his light around the room one more time. "Log it and see what else floats up. C'mon, my turn. We'll cruise the strip and head uptown."

* * *

They fired the engine on the car and eased onto the beach highway, headed downtown. Molly took off on foot, following them, staying out of the mirror lines. She lagged due to Easton's lead foot, but she caught a break with a gas truck coming the same way. She piggybacked until 25th and bailed off. She hopped the first rooftop, bounding across, making it up to the Markham building, then the Hancock. From there, she could follow them all across the center of the city. Her eyes and ears zeroed on them. She was getting the hang of some of this.

They parked their car on the street, leaving the top down. Nguyen pulled a comb from his jacket and slicked his hair back. He fixed a cross earring in his left ear and lit a cigarette, offering one to Easton. Easton ran his hand through his hair. Molly kicked herself for thinking about how good he looked.

She stalked them through the night. They talked to pimps and hookers, wrote down the plates of the johns. They went through the alleyways and talked to a few indigents. Money changed hands, the hands then shaking. Kids no older than 12 swapping bags for bills. They went back to the car several times, Nguyen on the radio. She heard them, calling in descriptions and plates. Getting the "uniforms" on the tips they had. Easton cranked the car and moved through the streets, all through downtown and into the residences.

Was this their routine? What he'd done the whole time she...? Didn't matter, she told herself. It was what it was. Life had thrown her more than one curve of late. This one she'd weather as the others.

They looked right, though. The way the night wrapped around the both of them. Like it belonged to them, or they to it. The neon haze of the all-night joints wrote the story across their solemn faces. She didn't want to admire them, especially *him,* but she couldn't not. They probably did more good in three hours than she had in weeks of bumbling through the town before the tanks, but that was weird luck thanks to Hurl, so it kinda didn't count. She could be mad all she wanted, but they were pros. They knew what they were doing.

She didn't.

VI
"DON'T COME AROUND HERE NO MORE"
—TOM PETTY & THE HEARTBREAKERS, 1985

MOLLY SCOPED THE LUNCHROOM, ready to ignore Easton soon as she saw him. Lydia lingered in the line, reconsidering her choice of entree by the expression on her face. Nguyen stood behind her, chatting about something that she seemed interested in. Molly hadn't decided whether she would be mad at Nguyen yet. She didn't really know him. And, besides, she wanted to save it all for Easton, who, turns out, she also didn't know.

She peeled her eyes at the door so she could totally not notice him at all, which is probably why she *actually* didn't notice Becky stomp up and sit down at her table until she was eyeball to eyeball with her. Those perfectly mascara-ed eyelashes stabbed her. And that tan. In December. *Does she go to one of those spas? Weird.* Becky had always reminded Molly of someone else, but she hated her too much to care who.

"What have you done with *my* Easton, Trailer Park?" Becky demanded.

"Your what?" Molly was over this day and it hadn't even started.

"He's not here. Wasn't in any of his classes this morning." Her posse of Bayettes appeared behind her but she waved them off. "If you screwed him over, you little...I swear I'll—"

"I didn't do diddly with *your* boy, Becky." Molly huffed back at her. "And that's what he is, too: *yours.* You want him, be my guest. Now get out of my face."

"Aw," Becky smirked, "did wittle baby not get what she wanted? He finally got downwind of you, I guess!"

Becky stood and Molly popped up at her, fists at her sides, ready to go.

"You want to fight about it, Uptown Girl, then let's have it," Molly shouted, half the cafeteria looking on.

"Ew, gross, no." Becky wrinkled her face

Lydia arrived in time to diffuse Molly and give Becky an exit, though not before she snuck in another victory smirk. Molly's fists grinded, nose flared.

"Dude," Lydia whispered, "settle. Here comes Lebeque."

"Screw Lebeque." Molly slammed back down into her seat. She poked at the zitty pizza in front of her and decided she didn't want it after all. She wasn't hungry. For once.

"Seriously," Lyd said. "What is your deal, lately?"

"I got a bomb to drop on you." She saw Nguyen walking toward their table. "Later."

"Hi there, ladies." He plopped his tray down. "This seat taken? No? Perfect."

Lydia stared at him like he was a dog that just walked up and talked. He smiled back. She scowled.

"Hey, no napkins. Could you be a doll?" he asked Lyd.

"Sure," she said, oddly, and went back up front to grab some. Molly, now more confused than mad, watched her go.

"He pulled a transfer," Nguyen whispered at her quickly. "Torello sent him up to Central. Figured you wouldn't cooperate with him anymore. Hostile witness and all that."

"First," Molly insisted, "I didn't ask. Second, Torello figured right. And I don't really want you around either."

"Oh, I know that, too." He drank his milk, leaving a mustache. "But, see, I don't care. You're still the only connect we have to this guy, and we ain't letting him at you any time soon. So, get to used to me, darling. I'm tons of fun!"

Lydia returned with a stack of napkins and slapped them onto his tray of food.

"That'll be a dollar," she said. "This ain't Russia."

* * *

At the shop, Lydia had her legs up on the counter jamming to Judas Priest, sketching out designs for band names and some new outfits while she was at it. Tracey had knocked off about four when she came in.

"I need you to cover my shift tonight," Molly had said at school.

"What? I figured I'd come by and we could work on some set lists and stage outfits together. Then maybe do a quick patrol or two before heading home."

"Yeah, no. I'll explain later, but I gotta do something solo tonight."

"Okay then," Lydia had said.

She'd seen less and less of Molly ever since the now infamously undiscussed *date night*. Molly hadn't been back to the shop. Lydia liked the hours, though. The shop was slow this time of year. It would pick up the week before Christmas and then be stone dead until Mardi Gras season. Gave her plenty of time to zone out and think. And it didn't hurt to be clocking a cool $3.35 an hour while she did.

"She's not here." Lydia didn't even look up at Easton as he chimed through the door. The corner of her eye made his haircut as soon as it rolled in.

"She said anything?" His eyes were all mopey, like a little dog. It would have been cute if Lydia liked dogs, which she didn't. Cats. She liked cats. Big ones.

"About what?" Lydia worked at her designs. Needed more flair, she thought.

"Nothing."

Nguyen walked in behind him, taking in the shop, giving it the once over.

"Dig the black, by the way," Nguyen said as they went back out the door.

Lydia wrinkled her nose. *Get wrecked, dude.*

* * *

Molly crouched atop the Hancock building, surveying the night. It had come to belong to her, these hours, this dim haze. The daytime world had become out of sync with her. But the dark...it was like she could sneak up on it.

Her town was no booming metropolis by any stretch, but it had its share of issues. The boys in blue were right — there'd been more gangs coming out of New Orleans — like rats fleeing a ship. What that was about, she'd be interested to learn some other day. For now, her problems were here. Blake, wherever, *whatever,* he was, would have to wait until he popped up again, which she knew he would. She felt it. But the town bled. And it could use some help. They knew where the wounds were, the two of them walking out of Trace's shop, no doubt Easton looking to grovel and mope and say his sorry's, but she wasn't in the mood for it. For now, *The Sledgehammer* needed their help.

And they needed hers.

Easton cranked the car, Nguyen tuning the radio to check in while they cruised uptown. The radio chattered about a B&E on 31st. A hit & run on Pass. Domestic in the upper avenues. Molly ran soft as a cat behind them, staying in the blind spot. She laid her hands down on the trunk, then somersaulted into the car, landing into the back seat. Between the wind, the radio crackling, and their general haziness, they didn't notice her, which was cute.

"Hi, boys!" She almost sent them and the whole car whirling off the road.

Easton braked to a stop. She slid down a little further into the backseat, making herself comfortable, her orange Taylors peeking out from under her unitard leggings, the silly colored mask, all of it staring right up at them.

"A little bird tells me you and I have some things in common." She smiled.

Easton and Nguyen stared at each other, then back at her.

"Want to party?" She winked.

VII
"SMUGGLER'S BLUES"
—GLEN FREY, 1984

THE MEET WAS TONIGHT. They'd been taken off guard and were hesitant at first, especially Easton, but he could still bite a big one. In fact, she wanted him to not like it. Let him sweat it. Nguyen was a little too easy to convince, but she'd take what came.

She'd bolted off into the night sky before they had to time to get into too many questions, which she knew they would. Cops were cops. She'd said to meet down Fishbone after 8. She'd be watching them from atop her perch on the Hancock, a place she'd all but come to see as a second home of late, to make sure they hadn't snuck in some backups to lay a trap. Not that they could do much to her, in any event. She'd shrugged off tank rounds, and that was a lot heavier than anything the blues had under the hood.

Still, she didn't need the news reporting her beating up a bunch of cops. The news had been fairly positive thus far, inasmuch as they bothered to report on her at all. Most weren't sure she was real. Some old men at the barber shop next to Trace's had even argued she was a plant from Commie Ron, as they'd taken to calling the last president now that they had "a real American in there, finally."

For now, she sat in bed, her getup crumpled next to her array of Chucks. She jotted down a few notes. Nothing good was coming to mind. She'd skated past their third degree well enough last time, but tonight would be an all-nighter. There'd be no avoiding it. She needed something to give them that sounded real enough but would keep them as far from the corner of Elm & E Streets as possible.

Last survivor of dead planet? Nah. Old hat. Saved a wizard and granted special abilities? No, that required a whole extra case for wizards. Born on a secret island of warrior women? Maybe not. Radiation? That could work. But what's the angle? Molly didn't have the head for this stuff. If only she had half the imagination of...

"Hurl!"

* * *

Fishbone dripped and whistled with wind. Wet as always. Colder than ever. The winters *were* getting worse, and this far south that was saying something. Coal furnaces burned four months of the year up north, she'd heard. Some pushing five. The Canadians talked of global cooling, but the White House called it a hoax, *brother.*

Nguyen torched a Kool while Easton kicked cans down the empty alleyway. It was well after dark, but early yet for the drunks and junkies. By 1am, half the alley would be peopled with them sleeping it off, some not to wake up. It vexed Easton, the grimness of it. Like throwing pennies down a well, he'd said once after they'd done a write-up on a dead girl, no older than 15, who froze to death last year about this time. Strung out on smack. Like so many others.

"I hate this." He leaned all cool against the brickface.

"You've said." Nguyen took the last drag, his black harness boots crushing the ember into the void. The one bulb at the north end of the alley flickered and buzzed, moths assaulting it all the same.

"I'm a cop. I signed up to help people the right way. By the book. Not...this."

"We're barely cops. We sit in study hall with geeks and get buried in stacks of paperwork to the end of time while these creeps and murderers, pushers who might as well be, they all walk free every night, pumping our streets with their poison and pain. And for what? A commendation? Some sadsack counting down to his pension pins a little medal to your shirt? No thanks, man. I know. I've seen the good a mask can do."

"Yeah." Easton turned away. "You and your legendary hero of the big city."

"Maybe." Nguyen fingered the little copper bell he wore around his wrist. "But this one's real. And she's right here with us."

"We got rules."

"Exactly. And she don't."

Easton shook his head. But he was still there. Why, he couldn't say. Maybe curiosity. Maybe he still looked up to Nguyen. He'd been a good partner and mentor. At least up to now. But this...he just didn't know about *all this.*

Two feet slammed onto the asphalt just ahead of them, knees bent, straightening as she rose to height. Her mask tight (glued down with spirit gum this time).

"Gentlemen." She tried not to be too cheeky with it. She felt their unease, especially Easton's. She'd heard their conversation and even found the dissent endearing. She'd prove herself to them. But for now, it was business. "We have a mutual interest." She handed over a sketch she'd made of Blake, not bad by all accounts.

She'd never thought herself much of an artist, but when she sat down to draw it out, her hand had followed her mind's intent like a machine. She went into particular detail on the gnarled hand and odd prosthetic contraption he'd sported the last times she'd seen him, a thing she was convinced now was much more than he had let on and certainly not anything medical.

They studied the image, looking several times at the knobby fingers and the black nails, the darkened veins. All of it. Not sure what to believe anymore as she regaled them with Hurl's wild tale, bless that kid's heart. She laid it on thick that she, an intergalactic bounty hunter, had tracked a runaway prisoner to earth, intent on conducting experiments on the native population. She'd tracked him to this sector, but he'd figured a way to cloak himself from her by assuming human form and "blending in" though not so well, as the two of them had proven.

"But he's been at this ten years," Nguyen said, Easton nodding. "You just got here."

"Temporal displacement. Hyperdrive malfunction." She was just saying words now, hoping to veer off the topic.

"Well anyway," Easton said. "He's in the wind. We've got an All Points on him that hasn't turned up so much as a whisper in the wind. If you're telling the truth, which I doubt," Nguyen gave him the side eye, "then you know more than we do."

"You say you're a bounty hunter?" Nguyen lifted an eyebrow.

She held the panic from her face. *Oh, god, Hurl, don't make me regret asking for your ideas.*

"So, you work for money?" he added. "How about a trade?"

Okay, maybe she liked where this was headed. She might get a twofer out of this. "I'm listening."

Nguyen laid it out. The Dreds were picking up major ordnance offshore — some kind of high tech gear out of Japan. "It's like the future over there," he said. Deepwater, way beyond the barriers. Heavy duty stuff, he said. They'd even gotten a tip on where it went down. Been a regular thing for months now. They'd ran it out of Shell Beach, off the Chandeleur Sound. But *something* forced them out of the city, and now they'd posted up north of the grove someplace and made runs off Point Cadet. The "big mama," as the bikers coded the main rig coming in, split the hauls off into a dozen or more small boats, bound for all points east and west.

The Mutes, Nguyen mentioned, were small time. "Rock, a little powder, some tar," he'd said. But the Dreds were bad news. Already regional and looking to go national. Like they were building up and outfitting their own army. "Probably working for the Russians," he'd said. He seemed married to that idea, from the little Molly had known him.

"We got a solid lead on where the shipment's coming in on The Point," he said. "Somebody's greasing palms for it, too, because no judge will even hear it for us."

"This place is crookeder than the damn river." Easton was warming to the plan.

"Why hit The Point?" Molly asked.

"Huh?" Nguyen wrinkled his face. "'Cause...that's where they're headed?"

"Yeah," Molly said, "one shipment. You said there's a whole tanker offloading to a dozen or more boats. Let's take 'em there."

Easton's eyes got bigger than the waxing moon that night. Nguyen turned his head, skeptical but curious.

"Because...we..." he stammered.

"That's way beyond our jurisdiction," Easton chimed in. "Not to mention our abilities."

"Not mine." She flexed her shoulders unconsciously. "On either count."

They stared at each other, talking it over with their eyes and facial expressions alone. She could almost read the discussion, the arguments Nguyen posited,

Easton's half-hearted rebuttals and talk of *rules* and *procedure.* But the truth is he wanted to do it just to see her in action, she felt that much on his heart, which rabbited in his chest.

"Looks like it's a go," she said before they even spoke their agreement. "Last question: we got a boat?"

They looked at each other with a wry grin this time.

"Oh, we got a boat," they both said.

*

Damn did they have a boat. Easton baked asphalt to a dock off The Point. There in a covered slip was a Wellcraft Scarab 38 KV, a 43-foot offshore banshee with twin Mercury V12 go-fast engines. She was slick, cool blue lines down each side. Nguyen climbed in the captain's chair and caressed the wheel, whispering his secrets to it.

Its twin engines boomed to life. They were underway. The lights of the docks became twinkles, soon followed by the town itself. Molly stretched her legs in the back as the boat roared toward The Point bridge. The Smiths sang "How Soon is Now?" in her head as she sat weaving side-to-side with her internal beat.

A diesel train thundered across the tracks ahead of them, it's graffiti-ed cargo sides blurring overhead as the boat raced under the bridge. Not another minute and they burnt around the corner of Ile des Cerfs into open water.

The wind whipped the boys' hair, like flames shooting backward at her. Boys. *Men*, she supposed. Easton was 19; he'd told her that first night of his big bomb drop. Nguyen a year older, originally from the big city, which he mentioned enough. She felt jealous watching their locks dance in the air, the chop bouncing them all in its own rhythm. There was a strange familiarity to this—riding the waves, off on some wild adventure, at ease in the lull before some distant battle on another shore. A memory? More a dream.

Several times one would half turn his head, wanting to look at her, their curiosity gnawing at them. Easton even went for her eyes. *Clever boy*, she thought, catching him, turning her gaze away to the port side. There was a landmass in the distance. Something eerie about it. Calling to her. Voices almost. And was that...crying? Faint. Another dream.

"Which island is that?" Her eyes squinted, zeroing on some structure, stone and mortar.

"Ile de Navire," Nguyen said.

"Is that a castle?" she asked, then realized they likely couldn't see what she did.

"Good eye," Nguyen said, Easton putting both of his on her face. She glanced away again, toward the island. "Might as well be. The old Fort Massachusetts. Union battalion there during the Civil War where they launched and took New Orleans. Lot of dead souls still there."

She felt the cold shiver run down both their spines as he'd said it. The cigarette boat cooked on, into the deep water of The Gulf, further out beyond the Chandeleur Sound, where, if their info was good, a frigate would be arriving within the hour.

"Coming into No Man's Land." Nguyen slowed the engine, checking his radar.

"He means we're leaving territorial waters," Easton explained.

"I guessed that," Molly said.

"You know a lot about us." Easton grimaced. "For someone so recently arrived." He squinted at her face. She saw Nguyen quelling a snicker. He was right, though. She needed to feign ignorance a little better. Maybe Hurl's help wasn't so helpful.

They killed the running lights and went to a drift.

"We're close." Nguyen eyed his gauges. "Should be soon, if it's going down."

Easton fiddled with a night vision scope, trying to survey the pitch black. The light of a million stars pierced the blanket above them. She'd never seen them so bright.

"Still can't see much, even with this." He groaned.

"Let me try." Molly perked up from her recline in the back. She cranked her senses to her max level, slitted her eyes, tuned her ears, focused into the distance. Whales. She heard whales in the deep, miles beyond them. Some blowing wind in the distance, a howl almost. And something else. Faint, but there. Engines. Just like the ones she sat near. Humming along at a clip. Fixing upon that, she focused her vision...and there. She had it. She pointed at the sound.

"There. That way. Boats. A half dozen, maybe more, converging."

Nguyen noted the direction and eased the throttle forward, leaving the lights off.

"What's the play here, boss?" Easton asked at Nguyen. "They've got ordnance. Artillery. We've got nothing."

"You've got me." Molly winced in disbelief. "I'm your ordnance. Just a little further. Get me within striking distance."

"How far is that?" Nguyen asked, getting his bearings straight. He could see their lights now.

"In a straight shot, over water?" she said, having no idea whatsoever and bad enough at math anyway that it wouldn't matter if she did. "A few hundred yards, no closer."

She hoped that would be close enough.

As they got nearer, she felt a nudge. Some deep-seated instinct kicking in. She touched at her mask, hoping the elastic and glue would hold. She bounded across the deck of the boat and launched herself like a torpedo off the bow. She shot across the water, aiming herself as best she could. She plunged into the cold, going right into an underwater leg stroke. Needing no breath, she held herself under the surface, working her legs in unison like a giant flipper, her arms forward, converging at her fingertips into a point. She targeted the blurring lights above her. Seconds later, she was at the first of the rumrunner boats.

She made it to the hull. Their still-grumbling, mighty engines filled the air with sound, along with shouting voices, calling out instructions. More boats crept in. She made a short job of the first. She sank underneath the hull, ripped the propellers off the bottom, leaving it inoperable. Before its occupants realized their conundrum, she was at the next, doing the same to each boat in turn.

Within moments there was chaos. They throttled, going nowhere. Curses. Shouts. Confusion. Lights everywhere, dancing across the water's surface. The freighter, a cargo boat holding maybe twenty containers by her count, turned on its strobes up at the main cabin.

Like a knife out of nowhere, she sliced up from the water and landed with a pounding of steel onto the deck. Guns fired. Sparks and bullets sprayed at her, but they were nothing but noise. She powered over to the first guy she saw, flinging him off the side of the ship. Slowing her time, she targeted the shooters. She pinballed herself to each one. A front kick sent another flipping off the edge of the boat. A backhand subtracted another.

Someone up top caught wind of the commotion and fired the engines, hoping to clear off. But Molly made other plans for the aging vessel. She erupted into the midnight sky, crested shy of a cloud, and then aimed her balled fist dead center at the cargo hold. Speeding downward through the crisp air, she blasted straight through the steel hull, plunging herself back into the deepness of the cold blue.

Everywhere, they heard screaming, yelling, shouting. Easton, through the night vision, narrated what he saw, which was blurry and indistinct.

"She sank it," he said. "The freighter's going down. She freaking sank it. How?"

"Give me that." Nguyen yanked the scope. He saw the bow of the ship dipping, the whole thing leaning to its port side. He was right. It was going under. "Son of a bitch, she did it!"

Easton gulped at the thought of it. There were cries of help. These were hardened criminals, the worst of the worst. Murderers. Smugglers. Traffickers. This ordnance was surely meant for the hands of cop killers. The stuff they'd seen in these guys' hands of late was right out of science fiction. He knew that. Knew all of it.

Still their cries ached him. In the cold dark of this night, many of those in the water wouldn't find their way out. He felt it. Felt their arms flailing, failing, quitting on them. He was queasy, leaned over the side. He caught his breath. Letting the sea air fill his lungs.

Molly flipper kicked through the water back to them. The surge of energy was palpable, electric, violent. It fed her, more than anything ever had. Like the adrenaline rush from shredding a Mötley song, but times a thousand. A million.

Adrenaline? Was that even a thing for her? Whatever it was, it cooked through her body.

Her head exploded from the water, mask still intact. She snatched the gunwale of their boat with one hand. With the other, she seized Easton by his jacket and jerked him to her face, his eyes almost touching hers. His lips actually did.

They locked. She pulled on him, letting her energy flow right into him. She drank him into her. Savoring every fraction of a second. For the longest frozen moment she'd sustained yet, she felt him, all of him. Resisting. Pulling away. Then giving in.

She dropped him, drunk off his feet. He sank to the floor of the boat as she flipped herself in. Dripping everywhere. She smiled down at him, Easton clearly lost inside his mind for the time being. Nguyen just laughed.

Now the ride back. The cold winter air dried her suit as they zoomed past the islands again. That big red fortress peered at her now from the starboard side, loomed larger and fiercer than before. A castle, she called it again in her mind.

VIII
"LIVING AFTER MIDNIGHT"
–JUDAS PRIEST, 1980

LYDIA SHOWED A KNACK for picking winter gowns for the shop. She went with Trace on Sunday to NOLA to scout the city, hitting some wholesalers and several thrift shops. Trace gave her more and more leeway since the bleak stuff Lydia chose moved off the shelves well enough. And the city seemed to have no dearth of it to choose from.

She matched the dresses with scarves from Trace's bin up front. Trace had great inventory, which she never failed to mention, but had organization issues. Molly had been good with curation, but not the placements. The store needed an overhaul, and in the lull between Thanksgiving (the last of the school dances for the season) and the week before Christmas shopping hit hard for boutiques like theirs (lots of husbands and dads wandering in off the street needing advice on what to get for wives and daughters), Lydia took it upon herself to undertake the task. She might as well have. Her social life had nosedived of late. In fact, she had worked every single night (counting the Sunday rides to the city) for the last two weeks.

She sighed as she fitted another black dress with a blue satin scarf and looked for shoes that would stand out, but not, like, too far out. This was just her normal now.

That very moment, a block and a half west, down Fishbone Alley, Lydia's long lost friend, the town's self-appointed paladin, observed her prey. Molly crouched, knees in her face, the neon lines of her tight suit muted in the nearly full moon. She'd since dropped the tied-around sweater "skirt" after the boat trip, not seeing a reason to reincorporate it any time soon. They could stare. *It was whatever.*

Easton fidgeted. Nguyen was solid. Calm. Ready. He had a folder in one hand, lit a coffin nail with the other. He liked this. Maybe too much. Maybe she did, too.

Easton looked different. His hair was darker, slicked back, wetted. Leather zipper jacket. Tight jeans instead of his usual casuals. Boots instead of sneakers. They'd swapped his style for his new job at Central. It was a different crowd up there. She knew that. He still looked hot, though. But, like, a different hot. Dirty hot. Molly was still angry at him, for all of it. But the Hammer would have her fun.

Their first night after the cruise started with a smash. Easton chewed on his fist while Nguyen caught a 211 in progress over the police band. The Z28 cooked its tires, but Molly beat her feet.

"I'll be faster skipping the traffic," she said. "You guys catch up." With that, she bounded from the car, landing a block ahead of them at a full clip, shooting through traffic doing at least 50mph.

It was a liquor store at 30th and Paradise. She'd lived in a house up here about nine years back. Well, not a house, exactly. That was her first round out of the orphanage. Didn't last long.

Before she made the entrance, she'd sensed the fear screaming out of the building. A husband and wife duo worked the late hours. Owner-operators, like a lot of small shops in the area. Most barely kept the lights on. The money hadn't trickled down to them like Commie Ron said it would. Any day now, though.

The wife's heart raced. Molly heard it. The perp, a beast in a beard that crawled nearly to his eyeballs, had an updated street howitzer, a 12 gauge with a drum mag, and a foregrip. He was whiteknuckled and speeding hard. She saw his dilated pupils as she waltzed through the front door easy as she pleased. Time slowed in her mind, him turning to her at a snail's pace.

She studied his face. Such violence. Such awful intent. A new thing she could sense among the regulars, as she'd come to think of them — the ordinary freaking people: their will. She felt it strong and clear within him, the intent to murder these people once they were done stuffing his bag with the few dollars they'd cleared that evening. Their lives would end for a stack of paper no thicker than her finger.

His streetsweeper spat its fiery rain at her face. The buckshot pelted her, flattening against her impenetrable skin, and fell to the floor. That failing, he charged her, firing even more. She snatched the weapon, crushing its components like tin foil. Then she clotheslined him as he ran to the door. He spiraled, smashing into a cooler of dessert wines, his face and chest crashing through the glass.

Her nights went on like that, a robbery here, an out of control domestic there, a cocaine ring bust at the old mill. That one was a blast. One of them even tried her with a grenade, which she intercepted and fast-balled through the roof of the building, sending its booming report through half the county.

The boys, working off the books, kept themselves back and out of sight. They couldn't even call it in after she was done. What would they say they were doing there? Their covers blown? Totally off the reservation. Rogue.

Easton was sick, stomach in knots. *Good.* She liked him that way. Uneasy. Not in control. A puppet. A pawn. A plaything. *Her* plaything.

They'd baked back to the alley after the mill. Nguyen sped on adrenaline enough you'd think he caught a cloud of the Colombian white in the thick of it. *Actually, maybe he had.* Out of the car, he popped his hands together in a clap that sent the cats in every direction. Easton walked behind her, Molly running at 110 octane herself. She turned at him like a wolf, her eyes wild and intense. He froze. Panicked. She jerked him up by his chest, spun him sideways, and pushed him into the brick wall opposite her and put her lips directly into his again. The second time she'd taken whatever she felt like from him. What she wanted. What belonged to her, anyway.

He feared her. She felt all of him. Every single tingling nerve in his body vibrated around her. Afraid of what she could do. What she *had* done. But, all the same, he didn't hate it when she kissed him. He didn't hate it at all.

And so it went, their days a monotonous lull of going through the motions as average high school students, the tests, the lectures, the undone homework and reports. Molly was as much a sham now as the two of them. But, their nights, each with a new adventure and *that rush*, fed her, fueled this thing inside her. Growing, building, gaining. Unsure of it, of what it was or meant, Molly only knew she liked it. She wanted it.

But it also gnawed at her. For whatever good it might be, to them, to their world, to *their* little lives, it got her no closer. It brought no closure. She still knew nothing. Not of herself. This power. What it meant. And, most of all...

Where was Blake?

IX
"BAD MEDICINE"
—BON JOVI, 1988

RAIN SOAKED THE WORLD outside the dilapidated 19th century four-porcher hideout of Les Mutants Rouges, the very same happened upon by the would-be treasure hunters who did not leave entirely empty-handed for their troubles. The Mutants' boss still fumed about the lost gemstone.

The large drawing room, chairs, and other furniture in it were a far cry from what once filled its grand spaces. It now peopled itself with spiked hair, every kind of mohawk, red leather and denim, piercings, tattoos, cut shirts and jeans, worn boots and scuffed sneakers. Switchblades and Saturday night specials peeked out of beltlines. Stacks of long guns cluttered corners. Lock boxes. Suitcases full of ragweed and cut powder sat ready to go out to the street.

A boombox filled the room with Saxon, barely heard above the chatter and shouting. A fight broke out but was quickly quelled by the stamping of the butt of a sword pommel against the arm of a large wooden chair at the far end of the room opposite the fireplace. The one they called Boss, or sometimes Frank, sat in his carved cypress chair, the only piece of furniture left in the house when they'd arrived, likely because it was so big and heavy no one felt it worth bothering to steal. It elevated him above everyone in the room, even those standing.

The twin oaken front doors groaned as they opened. Scythe led in his failed cohorts. The Boss had wanted that artillery. Those Commando tanks were a fighting chance against the Dreds, old rivals and gunned to their teeth with that fancy Japanese gear. At the very least it seemed their new nuisance was equal opportunity in her meddling. He'd ground his teeth at her dancing and laughing on the television. He had a notion of who it was, but not a name nor location. It would come, though, and soon.

"We're back, boys!" Scythe's long white hair blew in the December wind from the open doors. He pulled the top off a bottle of what looked to Frank like damn good whiskey. "Back from the clink. Let's have a drink!"

The rest of his losers filed in, dragging crates of liquor. Nice liquor. Biff and Raqquill, the ones he hated most but tolerated, already guzzling it down their throats like it were swill from the bait shop. *Ignorants.*

If not for their incompetence, though, he wouldn't be holding old King Cobra in his right hand now, the very tool that sent them from nowhere to the richest gang in the region. They had more kids coming in every day, now that they knew where to find all the best fun-pills. And the girls, too. But now they'd lost the other sword. *The morons.* Stuck in a cop's locker somewhere. Wasted. Senseless.

"You stupid degenerates." He leered at Scythe, who he knew fancied himself the boss. Biding his time, waiting for his chance to backstab. "The hell are you doing back here? Figured you'd be halfway to Parchman by now. And good riddance."

"Well, boss," Scythe grinned, "I knew you'd miss us too much. Your poor, old, tired heart just couldn't bear it."

The rest of the boys swapped swigs on the bottles, steady pulling them out of the crates. The Boss studied them from his chair, spied the label, and got sick to his stomach at the sight, the dribble flowing down their chins, spilling onto the filthy wooden floors.

"You idiots!" he screamed. "Those are Macallans!"

He jumped up and snatched one from Biff before it found its way back to Raqquill. He studied the label. A 50-year-old! It was worth a fortune.

"Put them down, idiots. Every one of you!" He stared at the crates. There were at least a dozen bottles. "Where the hell did you get this?" Scythe was too stupid to even know what he poured down his throat.

"Me?" Scythe gulped his drink, feeling it do its work in his head. *Let the old slicked-head and his stupid visor shades try something,* he told himself. He was ready to take his shot, his rightful place in that big wooden chair.

"They was just sitting out on the porch when we walked up," Biff insisted.

"What?" Frank balked. None of this made any sense. Them bailed out of jail. Free liquor worth more than a bank run? None of it.

"A gift," a voice said, a reverb in it, and loud. Frank and Scythe looked around to see where it came from.

A cloaked figure stood at the open doors. Dim and hooded, its face hidden from the little light in the room. The rain crashed down outside behind him. The array of onlookers and come-latelies turned to the new arrival. His right hand held a staff, taller than he was, which he wasn't very. He favored one leg like it was shorter than the other. He thumped the cane on the ground and took a step inside, then lifted his head, some light touching his face. Pale, veiny, but not unknown to a handful of them.

Frank cursed and produced a snubnose from his waistline, as did half a dozen of his lieutenants.

"As I said a gift" His voice reverberated through the room. "Along with your comrades in arms, here. Their recent freedom another gift to you."

"Could have kept that one." Frank snarled at Scythe, no love lost between them.

"What do you want?" Scythe shouted at Blake.

"First, an audience, which I now have."

All eyes were on its gnarled, white fingers wrapped around the ornately carved staff. Such detail. *Just like...*

"Second." It pointed at the very object they had all turned to observe. "My property."

The Boss gripped the snake-handled blade tighter.

"Fat chance of getting this baby back." He took a big swill off one of the open bottles. Free's free, after all, he supposed. "Finder's is keepers," he added. "You know the rest."

"Taking is not finding," said the voice, once Blake's, now, someone—*something* else. "You took what does not belong to you. You owe it back. A debt. Which is, as it happens, what this is all about."

The gang's eyes widened. They'd never seen anyone stand up to Frank like that, not even Scythe. But there was something eerie about him. That strange echoing voice, those clothes, that skin, those blackened fingernails. The veins. So gross. Even for them, he was a bridge too far.

"And, so, third," he continued. "An arrangement. You could prove yourselves of some use to me, however temporary it might be. But enough, and when successful, your debts will be discharged, and our arrangement completed."

"Yeah, well." The Boss pulled another swig. "We don't agree with..." He looked at that weird hand, some kind of metal rods attached to his white knuckles, all going into a metal contraption around his wrist, then disappearing under the sleeve of his long coat. "Whatever it is you're proposing. So..." He waved his hand, the one with the gun, telling this interloper to shove off.

"Which brings me to my next gift," he said, more ominously this time, if that were even possible. "You see, you won't do in this condition. You...creatures, such as you are. Your material is too weak, soft. Carbon. So easy to bruise. To break. No, you won't do. She'd make such short work of you. Indeed already has on as many occasions. And that was nothing compared to what she *can* do." His voice trembled the more he spoke of her. "But, we need not disquiet ourselves overly much about it. All problems have their solutions. Just as all debts must be paid. Hers most of all." He waved his gruesome hand all around at them.

"You see," he started again. "What is flesh? What is it made of? What is anything you see as real made from? Matter?" he went on. "'Tis merely energy."

Who the hell even says 'Tis?' Frank wrinkled his nose.

"And its form, its presentation, its attributes, abilities, its resilience, strengths, weaknesses. All written into it, like a code, a language, words." He moved further into the light, removing his hood from his head. His head was not unlike what Frank and the others remembered from *that* night. But now, cold, fierce, his eyes sunken, shadowed, his skin paling from the right side and creeping left. His right ear elongated, like an arrow pointing up and behind him. His hair lighter too, falling down his neck like wet reeds. Some creature, he was. Like human but not.

"And I know EVERY word. In every language." He closed his gnarled hand in a fist.

"Know this." Frank blasted his pistol right into Blake's face. Then another. The rounds shot straight through, eating into the opposite wall of the house.

Blake laughed, a reverberating, dark, awful laugh.

"Oh, you poor monkeys. You thought I was actually here? In your hovel? Your ruin? This filthy sty where animals rut?" He cackled as wind howled and blew in a flash of rain, flickering through what appeared to be him standing there, an illusion made of light and sound. "And monkey is not quite right." His image now walked amongst the gang, their eyes quivering from what they saw but could not name. "But not too far off. You things are not distant from your ape cousins. No, not far at all. Simple tweaking, some additions, some subtractions, a few choice fusions. Those are the key, you see, those fused...what is your little word for them? 'Alleles?' Not a terrible word. Yes, those. Those are what make all this so amazing."

The Boss stared at Scythe, then at Blake, then at his gang. He didn't want to put away the gun though it did him no good. Scythe looked uneasy, the others all terrified. Practically pissing themselves, the worthless sots. Biff and Raqquill looked like they'd spew any second. He needed them to hold it together, all of them, while he sorted out this *ghost.*

"What are you on about, freak?" he barked at the image. "What do you want?"

"You see," Blake told him. "I will remake you. Better than you were before, Stronger! Bigger! Superior!" He smiled, content with himself, his intentions.

"Yeah, no thanks," Scythe chimed in. "We're good as-is."

"Oh." Blake grinned and giggled at himself. "That's so amusing. Really, it is. You see, I already have."

"What?" Frank looked around, searching for the rub, the gag. Biff doubled over. His hands grabbing at his guts. Raqquill went right along with him. He looked at them, their faces sweating. Their skin bubbled like boils roiling up and about to pop. But they didn't burst. Their stomachs rumbled, buckling. Their backs hunched, spines protruded. Their shoulders ripped out of their shirts. Their chests exploded with enormity. And their screams.

Dear god their screams.

"Help me!" Biff's face looked melted, dripping off his bones. Like putty reforming itself. His eyes bulged, bugged. His hair...grew. Everywhere. Lighter now, an orange tint to it. Like sunflower. Bright and vibrant.

Both of them. Screaming. Changing. Blake laughed.

Then the others started. One by one, doubling over, screaming. Changing.

Frank stared down at the bottle in his hands, at the bottles now littering the floor where the others had dropped them. Those who hadn't partaken slid back against the far wall, as far away from the spilled liquid as they could get from it. Two girls ran screaming out the front doors into the wet night.

"You idiot!" Frank lunged at Scythe with his fist balled. Scythe, already feeling his guts attack themselves, was still faster. He caught the fist above his head, gripped the balled-hand tight, locking their arms in the air. Both their other hands held guns, ready to take this altercation to the next level.

"Oh..." Blake winced, wrinkling his entire, already macabre face. "Oh, no." He looked at the two of them locked together. "I really should have stressed that once the process has started, you shouldn't contact the flesh of another."

Frank tried to pull away, as did Scythe. They jerked as hard as they could but to no avail. Scythe looked at their hands, the fear wrought in his eyes. Frank saw it and screamed. There was only one now. One mass of skin and muscle and bone. A single joint connected them both as one continuous flesh. Their forearms drew to one another, connecting, fusing.

"That's..." Blake looked to them and the mess they were becoming, however amused with himself. "*Too bad.*"

Biff and Raqquill stood up, facing each other. The pain and cracking and reforming of their bones had abated. Their muscles still grew, building, retracting, rebuilding. They looked not unlike themselves but with more, brighter hair. Bigger. *Much.* And stronger. Biff picked up the whole of Frank's mighty cypress throne and slammed it against the wall, smashing it through the solid oak and into the surging rain. He turned to his partner, as big and dense as he was. Their eyes widened. Their teeth showed a toothy grin. *This was superior.* They started to high five but looked to their still fusing leaders and thought better of it.

Because what they saw before them was a nightmare. Some *thing* emerging from the two of them.

Frank's screams haunted through the rest of the night.

X
"EVERY ROSE HAS ITS THORN"
—POISON, 1988

THE BOYS HAD ARGUED, as usual, when Molly dropped into the alley. Nguyen called Easton a coward, afraid. Easton shouted back about the law, about rights, freedom, all that America crap they lied about in school.

"Boys?" She crept behind them like a cat.

"I'm out." Easton folded his arms, pinched his face. He looked down his nose at her. At *her.* Who did he think he was? Had he forgotten his place? She would tell him when they were done.

There'd still been no sign of Blake. So caught up in the frenzy of the nights, she'd all but lost sight of their main goal. Or at least hers, and what once had been Easton's. She wasn't sure anymore. Maybe Molly had given him so much of the cold shoulder, he'd lost interest in her, and maybe she had too. Teasing him these past weeks had been amusing at first, but now, as with everything else, she bored of it. Only Nguyen kept the world interesting for her now. He had a vision for this. A fire that rivaled her own.

"Come on, man," Nguyen took him by the shoulder.

"No. I'm out. I'm done. Look, I won't rat to IA, but I can't hang with it anymore. They're kids mostly." He stared The Hammer in the eyes. "They deserve *The Law,* not a gurney to the ER and all the reason in the world to be mad and want revenge. They deserve fair play. Due process."

"Yeah, tell it to the innocents they send to the morgue," Nguyen countered. "To the town they've got half scared to go out at night. Tell it to *my* parents. Oh, right, you can't."

"They're not all like that. Not yet."

"Oh, here we go with the bleeding heart again. Get over yourself. You're a cop. Not a saint. We bust heads. You want to be a social worker, be my guest, but hand in your badge on the way."

Molly started to chime in, but Easton cut her off.

"And you." He looked sideways at her, giving her outfit the up-down. "Whatever you are. You think you can just do whatever you want? They got such a thing as rights where you come from? Because we do. And your story is bullshit, anyway. Probably just some asshole got caught in a nuke tank too long and came out lucky. Who the hell knows, and who the hell cares?"

There was a hate in him tonight. Thick and putrid. And aimed at *her.* He hated The Sledgehammer. Hated everything she was and represented. She felt it crawling into her lungs, like thick smog. It choked her. She got nauseated from it.

"You're no hero," he said to her face, his eyes fierce. "You're just some grandstanding asshole. You guys have fun tonight without me."

"Fine," Nguyen said. "Toss me the keys."

"It's *my* car." Easton jumped in and turned it over, the pipes shooting into the night. "Get your own."

He roared down the street.

A long minute stretched by, Molly staring after his echo in the gulf breeze. Nguyen fumed, kicking at the trash in the alley. Molly's heart sank, fast. A weight fell on her now. Like nothing she'd felt since...since before all this started. She felt very *regular* in that moment. Weak.

"Screw it, we don't need him," Nguyen said, turning to face her.

But Molly was already gone.

XI
"REBEL YELL"
—BILLY IDOL, 1983

MOLLY WANTED TO SCREAM. Blow her lungs out across the water. And that's just what she did. Leaping from building to building, bouncing her way northwest, she finally thought she'd gotten far enough out of town, landing in Evergreen cemetery and let out a shriek that could've woke the very dead from their graves.

She glanced around. She was well away from all prying eyes, but nervous all the same. She'd let out a sound that shocked herself. A deafening boom had any mortal ears been at point blank range. It seemed weekly she fell backward into some new terrible power with no sense of how to manage or employ it. She was every day more an alien to herself. And now to everyone else, apparently.

She didn't like this anymore. None of it. She wanted to quit, go back to just the music again. Nights at Trace's counting the hours. Waiting for the holiday breaks and thinking about prom. Dates. Her friends. She wanted her life back.

She wanted that so much it was a reprieve when Clair asked her to watch Hurl and the boys Friday night so she and Hoyt could have a night to themselves. Molly had walked up and wrapped her arms around Clair tight in a bear hug, taking extra care not to crush the poor woman who just wanted to get a little busy with her old man. They were so delightfully plain and normal.

Molly had lost sense of normal. She missed it.

"Just take them out to the mall for the night." Clair handed her some money. "Get something to eat and a movie. And...make it a late one."

Molly took the cash and the keys to the Truckster and kissed the side of Clair's face.

"You have a fever?" Clair was used to zero affection from her redheaded daughter, and Molly saw the sudden explosion had her worried.

"Just psyched, Clair." Molly scooped her satchel and jacket off the counter and herded the pubescents toward the garage.

* * *

They sequestered themselves in Alladin's Castle, the arcade near Sears and the Orange Julius. Hurl was two-up on *Street Fighter* while Mike the Mic acted as referee and sportscaster all at once, calling fouls and announcing the fights in real time, over his mic of course, greatly to the chagrin of Al, the manager, who used to work next door at Gary's Shoes before they closed. He always said boys and bubble-gum were a huge step up from bunyuns and big'ol's.

Molly had sunk a quarter and was doing not even half bad at *Defender* herself. She wasn't one for video games, but this was all just so pleasantly plain. In fact, when she died, she'd go get a Julius and then a corn dog. Might get a cookie and make it a hat trick. Maybe later she could con the kids into walking across the parking lot to Bebop Records.

"You're pretty good at that," said a voice from over her shoulder. She turned see Easton smiling, bashful, like he wasn't top of her list right now for *get lost already*. She sighed in his face as her spaceship exploded across the screen. "God, my brother used to play the hell out of this game. I swear he could have made a career of it, he was so good."

"Yeah, I don't care." Molly walked away from the machine, putting her eyes on the boys. Mike was running book on Hurl taking on all comers. She should put a stop to that before they got the boot, but Al was busy daydreaming about old football games again, so he probably didn't care.

"Hey, Hurl, I'm going to down the food court to get a slice or a corn dog." She handed Hurl another few dollars to keep them busy until she got back.

Molly left the arcade, tailed by her slick-haired policeboy. *Don't you have some reports somewhere to write? Some buzzes to kill? Some girl's life to ruin? Is that fair?* She didn't care. *Just get the hint already, dude.*

"Look," Easton nagged from behind her, "can we talk?"

She quickened her pace, though not enough to make it look weird. She got to the Julius, paid for her drink, and then beelined to Sbarro for a slice.

"Look, I want to apologize, and try to — "

"Try to what?" She faced him, her lips pulling orange liquid into her face.

"I—" he started, then lost himself. "Look I...I'm just worried about you. We still don't have anything on," now he whispered, "you know who."

"Yeah, I don't really care about that anymore. I'm over it. And you. Bye." She walked away again. Maybe she would get a Hunan box instead of a slice. Or both. She was getting slim on funds, though. She hadn't worked a shift in almost two weeks. Or said as much as a dozen words to Lydia. She breathed heavy. Shook her head. She was tired. Not the real kind. Just the kind in her head. But tired all the same.

"Are you going to cut me a break, or what?" Easton blurted. "I want to make it right. I said I'm sorry a dozen times." His poor face was eaten up with his own weakness and guilt. She didn't like it like that. She hated his weakness. All of *their* weakness.

Molly turned, smiled, and walked backward into the ladies' restroom she had tactically positioned herself next to.

"Make it a dozen more." She sipped her drink and disappeared into No Man's Land.

Easton wandered toward the south entrance of the mall, headed back to the car to radio in for any instructions, but he made his walk as slow as possible, hoping maybe she'd catch up to him. Running all-nighters as he had been since this gig started, his nights had always run into his days, sleep more a memory at this point for him. His head was a bag of spiders, pushing venom into every corner of his mind. He had a job to do, and he'd done it. That wasn't supposed to be wrong. But he felt wrong.

Then there was the other business with Nguyen and the Supe. He was still wrapping his head around the whole idea of it much less the fact the three of them had sunk a pirate frigate and busted the heads of another dozen bangers. *Was that real? Had that actually happened?* Torello jumped all over his case after the botched job on Blake Elvis. *How does a guy disappear like that, leaving all that property behind?* And Molly. He hadn't expected her to be so... Or to actually...

He was so tripped up in his own warring thoughts, he failed to notice the two seven-footers barrel in from the west entrance, arms bigger than gorillas', bright orange body hair in excess. They hurled trashcans and debris across the wide thoroughfare toward the central fountain. As soon as he looked up to see them, he took a can to the face and went out.

Molly hid in the stall, staring at the graffiti. Someone had carved 'Étienne Lives!' over and over again on the back of the stall door. Something Molly'd been seeing around town a lot recently now she thought of it. It was good to know someone else in this town had taste.

She gave herself enough time to be sure he'd give up and bail. Some lady with a Gayfer's nametag stood at the sink fixing where her lipstick had smudged during her "lunch" and decided to go ahead and do a quick line before going back to the retail doldrums. *Whatever gets you through the day, lady.*

Molly just wanted one normal day and night to rest, relax, recharge. Arcade. Pizza. Some records. A stupid movie. And sleep. She hadn't done that in so long she'd forgotten what it was like. She remembered it being pretty fun.

Then the screaming started.

She ran out the door to see the commotion. Two monstrous, ape-armed maniacs bigger than the president smashed everything in sight, terrorizing customers, creating frenzy and chaos everywhere. They even roared at kids, sending them screaming, crying in every direction.

"Why?" Molly muttered, then ran back inside the restroom.

She grabbed her satchel out of the stall and started pulling out gear.

"What the hell?" the coke lady shouted, then started for the door.

"Don't go out there!"

The lady sneered at Molly and took off out the door.

"Idiot," Molly grumbled. "Why do I even help these people?"

She heard another kid scream.

"Right."

The Sledgehammer burst into the fountain square in the wide-open mall, the waning sun blaring through the skylight. The two monsters headed toward the food court, breaking and smashing every window and storefront on their way and laughing. Mall security got to the square, and immediately two of Edgewater Plaza's finest sent their 50,000 volts into one of the marauders in ripped red jackets that were now barely vests. They both laughed, pulled the taser lines out of their chests, and ran at the guards. One of them had a familiar rat-tailed mohawk haircut, and the other one...a very terrible red bucket hat!

"Rat-hawk and Bucket-hat?" Molly jumped between them and the terrified guards. She looked them over, up and down. They were certainly different than the last two times they'd tangled. "You boys been into your daddy's steroid cabinet, haven't you?"

They grinned, like she was just what they'd been waiting for. It couldn't be a coincidence. She couldn't get even one moment of peace.

Bucket-hat charged her, rearing back for a right hook. Molly wound up her own arm cannon, ready to launch a speedball back at him. They both let go with charged shots, her fist shattering his on impact. She heard and felt the bones crunch and burst inside his fingers. She reeled, wincing from the sound of it.

Actually, she *was* wincing. For her own self. She shook her wrist. That hit frogged every nerve all the way up her arm. Needles rippled through her fingers and wrist. *That's weird.*

She shook herself out of it. Bucket-hat held his ruined hand with his good one, screaming and reeling from the pain.

Rat-hawk came at her now, leaping into the air and bearing down on her with both arms locked together in an overhead hammer drop. She caught his massive fists in her hands, holding his blow above her head. He was strong, really strong. Almost making her break a sweat. She twisted his arms to the side, wrenching him downward. He pulled away, and she went right for a front kick to his chest, shooting him into the wall and cracking the bricks. She looked around her. People cowered, trying to get clear, kids crying. She needed to get the fight outside.

Rat-hawk recovered and came for more. Bucket-hat still nursed his shattered hand, yelling at his compatriot.

"Forget it, Raq," he shouted. "Let's go. We did what he said!"

Rat-hawk grumbled and growled, looking at his friend, then snarled at Molly. He looked as much animal as man now. *Come at me, you ugly chump.* If her whole night was to be ruined, she might as well bust some more bones over it.

Rat-hawk thought twice about charging her, then turned and ran the other way. Molly gave chase through the mall, the oaf sliding and smashing into kiosks on his way out. He burst through the entrance, spraying glass everywhere. Before she got a grip on him, he leapt onto a speeding flatbed truck. With no one at the wheel!

Bucket-hat came from behind her, bowling her over as he bailed onto the moving vehicle as it sped off.

Molly rushed back inside, helping people to their feet, brushing glass off kids and the mall-walkers. Security regrouped and saw to the patrons. Clerks and cashiers in the stores were all dialing 911.

The boys! They better be okay! She passed Radio Shack on the way to the arcade when all the TV screens in the window switched over to some hooded head and shoulders. It was backlit, the face dim and pale. It laughed, its voice reverberated, like a mic giving bad feedback.

"Do I have your attention now?" The voice blared from all the screens at once, their volume all the way up. There was an echo to it, too. She glanced around. Everywhere there was a TV she saw the same image, heard the same sound. "I should hope so."

Molly squinted her eyes into angry slits, piercing into the largest of the screens before her.

"Who are you?" she demanded of it.

"You'll be wondering who I am?" It tilted its head slightly, allowing enough light to see the general outline, a few of his features. Pale skin, veiny. Elongated nose, crooked, blemished. Pockmarks on the face. Hollowed cheeks. Sunken eyes.

Now she was more wondering *what* he was. But the *who* was obvious.

"Blake!" she snapped at the screen. "What the...what are y...what is this? What are you?"

"You see," he ignored her inquiry, "you owe a debt. A contract your elders entered into freely and voluntarily. That debt must be paid. You will agree to it, and you will pay it."

"What debt? What are you talking about?"

"You are to submit to me, as your husband, your lord and mate." He salivated. "It was to be the price paid for services already well rendered. The exchange once begun cannot be undone. You owe!"

"I don't know what you're talking about. And I'll submit to jack and diddly. Get bent, you freak."

"I expect you shall resist, as before. So, we may re-bargain somewhat. You will submit yourself to me willingly and freely, binding it with your word. You must give *your word* to me. By the cresting of this world's star on the coming solstice, you must submit. Or I—rather my creations, did you like them? Crude, but serviceable for short order—shall destroy what you have come to let yourself love, through your own folly. Starting with your quaint hamlet you call Old Town."

"What the hell are you talking about? I will not—"

"You will be wondering now if I can even hear what you're saying." He grinned his maniacal grin again. "I will let you wonder that. You have been told our terms. Pay your debt. By the crest on solstice."

The image went black. The TVs fell silent. Molly turned, glared all around her. Everyone had seen and heard it. Easton walked in her direction, dazed, delirious. *Had he caught any of that?* She didn't want to see his face, nor let him see her in this form. His words about *this her* still stuck in her gullet like maggots, eating at her. She gritted her teeth, set her jaw against him.

"You won't do it," a young girl said, walking up from her hiding spot from the mayhem earlier. "Will you?" Her eyes hoping. *Praying.*

"Never," Molly said.

Because that was the truth.

And what she needed to hear.

XII
"ANOTHER DAY IN PARADISE"
—PHIL COLLINS, 1989

THE MENAGERIE OF IT ALL weighed on Molly, fatigued her. Not in any physical way. In that way she felt less and less like *them* every day.

Trace stood at the opposite corner of the shop arranging the sassy-chic Mrs. Claus she put up every year to show off risqué party outfits and fabulous shoes. Lydia worked the counter, setting up a candy cane display. They were there in the very room with her. Talking. Saying things. Or making sounds. That's what they did. They made sounds through their face holes.

It was almost ugly, looking at it. Teeth and tongue everywhere. And what was a tongue? Some slimy organ twisting and flailing about. Those watery, crying eyes they had. Weak. Grotesque. Beneath her.

But, no. It wasn't her body that tired. That was amazing. Tremendous. Superior to them in every way. In fact, she was basically their god. Might as well be. And the way they looked at her with those begging, wanting eyes. Like she owed them *anything.* She didn't. No, they only made her soul tired.

She sometimes closed her eyes now, but only to go away. To fly away to some other place, away from here. From this. From *them.*

They didn't deserve her.

Not even Lydia.

And certainly not that *creature* that used to be Blake. Whatever it was. Whatever "debt" it mentioned. If she had begun to feel nothing for them, these basics, these *humans,* she had doubly begun to *HATE* Blake, or whatever cave-goblin he was. Some monster.

Something she would destroy.

"So, what do you think?" Lydia asked, Molly coming out of her tunnel.

"What?"

"Were you even listening? You missed that whole thing?"

"Honestly, I don't care, Lydia," Molly grabbed her jacket and satchel and headed for the door.

"Jesus," Lydia scoffed.

"He ain't here." Molly cruised out the door.

*

Molly headed north up the block to the Hancock building, planning to leap to her perch and do a quick change away from prying eyes. Before she crouched for the hoist, she heard an unmistakable set of V8 exhaust pipes.

Easton climbed from his car. It *was* a cool car. His hair back to the old, flowing style. Brown leather jacket on a solid blue shirt. It struck her as weird that she still cared about things like that. Or him. She didn't want to care about him. Or any of them. But...

"Going anywhere?" he asked, no more hangdog. More like his old self. The one she hated less.

"Not here." She walked forward, away from him.

"Take a ride with me."

"Yeah, I'm good, thanks." She turned but kept walking, backward now.

"Yeah, I'm not asking." He pulled his jacket aside, flashing his badge.

She stood still, stared at him. The audacity of it. The sheer hubris. She could wrap him up in that little tin can car of his and boot it into the gulf. Oh, she could leap them both into the low-lying clouds out this afternoon and listen to his heart palpitate the whole way down. She could do anything she wanted, including just walk away, and he couldn't do a thing to stop her.

Looking at him standing there, his face so cocksure, his stance casual and firm at the same time, his voice so stern but calm. She tickled herself looking at him. It *was* the hottest thing he'd ever done.

"Okydoke." She tossed her satchel into the back and pounced into the passenger seat. She put her feet on the dash, twisted his stereo knobs, even played with the mic on his police band.

"Calling all cars, calling all cars!" she pretended to hit the button. "We got a 10-69 in progress. 10-69 in progress!" She giggled at herself.

"Message received." Easton wasn't amused.

"Oh, was it now?" Molly grinned, her eyes askance.

"That's what that means," he said. "10-69. Message received. He took the mic and hung it back on the radio. "Don't play with that." His eyes focused on the road. He was angry at her.

Okay, that's hot, too.

Easton took them into the avenues, following the tracks toward West Elementary out near the old hospital. The closer they got, the bleaker things became. A few houses in mild disrepair turned into whole neighborhoods near derelict. Some boarded up. Others had never recovered from Camille. A few kids here and there, some in overgrown yards. Dogs that had barely eaten in days. The same for some of the older men sitting on porches. The Commie Ron's great legacy. It was still a little hard to believe, but hard to believe was her new normal.

"That's Mrs. Celie Johnson." Easton indicated an older lady sitting on her porch staring glassy-eyed into space. He pulled over, got out, and grabbed a paper sack from his trunk. "I'll be right back." He took the bag to her, gave her a hug. They laughed about something, and then he came back to the car.

He put it back in gear and rolled down the street.

"Her husband died some years back. It's not sad. He was awful. Her son is finishing a stint upstate for running rock and powder through a juke joint he had set up as a front. The gangs came in and took it over. Two of his sons, her grandchildren, got caught up in it. Went down in a drive-by last year."

Molly tried to think if she'd heard about anything like that but couldn't place it. Maybe the news didn't bother to report it. Or maybe she hadn't noticed.

"She doesn't have anyone to come by and check on her," he continued. "So, I stop by some days."

They drove further, into Gaston. He pointed out a few more landmarks on the way. A kid got run over here in a car chase. Died before an ambulance came. Four blocks from the hospital. Like no one cared. Another corner had a couple of boys, one girl, none of them older than fourteen. "All working," Easton told her. She almost asked *doing what?* And then realized what an idiot she was if she'd said it. Even for thinking it. Her mood had dropped significantly since she got in his car.

"That's Mr. Burbidge." He pointed at a middle-aged man wandering down the middle of the street like he was lost. Easton crawled the car up next to him. "You okay, Roy?" he asked the muttering man holding a football in one hand and a newspaper in his other.

"Yeah." He looked kind of at Easton and also kind of not at him. "About eighty dollars," he added, certain it meant something in answer to what Easton had said to him. Certain it made perfect sense.

"Okay, buddy." Easton put it in park, got out, and walked Mr. Burbidge to the sidewalk, pointing at his house. Mr. Burbidge shook his head a little but seemed more or less oriented now.

"He just needs a point in the right direction sometimes." Easton got back in the car. She checked her watch. It was getting close to curtain call.

"Can I ask if there's a point to all this?" Molly looked off to the side. *Like I get it, dude, you're Mr. Freaking Rogers. So what?* "Or am I supposed to just guess?" She looked back at him. And his damn eyes. Inside them.

She sensed what he felt. Goodness. Kindness. He was genuine in all this. It bubbled out of his pores. Even... *no. Not that.* He didn't get to feel that. Not at her, he didn't. He had no right. She wanted to throw up. Get out and walk home.

"I just wanted a chance to..." He always trailed off. Just like every guy. Hoyt did this with Clair. Just lost all knowledge of words as soon as something got complicated. "To explain myself. Why I do what I do. Why I signed up. I was basically headed one way a few years back. Long story. Another day. But my uncle up in Jackson put me onto the idea of being a cop. They picked me for this unit. Said I could do some good. Sometimes these kids..." He looked at a group of eight or nine-year-olds playing stickball behind a house. "Sometimes all they need is a little help. A nudge this way instead of that one. Sometimes they just need a friend. Not a hammer."

Molly knew who he meant.

"Can you just take me home?" She looked the other way. She couldn't face him right now. Afraid he'd see. That he'd know. And that hate he felt now. Hate for the other *her.* For what she was. That *she* was the bad one. A badguy. A villain. It made her sick to her stomach. For real sick. Muscles tightening, spasming. Her throat swallowing. Trying to keep it down.

"Yeah sure," he said.

He turned toward the bay. More silence. Cold winds bit their ears. She didn't feel it, but she knew he did. Yet he still left the top down. The dim orange sun hazed before them. The night was coming down hard and fast. The longest night of the year.

"There's one more thing," he said as he pulled up to her house. He was bashful again, soft, unsure. She hated that. "There's this thing we do — the guys, Rae, all of us. Kind of a Christmas thing at Elmo's. Not official, of course. We can't break cover. But Torello pays the tab. And..." He trailed off.

She thought about it, and she almost saw a memory of them all there last year. Of course, she'd not known any of them at the time and would have only had eyes for Easton, anyway. That stupid, silly girl. No worries in the world at all. Boys and bands and bubblegum. *What a stupid twit.*

"I just...I know I don't have a right to ask. I just thought..."

Jesus, boy, just grow a set.

"If you wanted to come." Like pulling his fingernails off. "I just thought I'd mention it is all." He let out a sigh of relief she could have lifted and put on a shelf.

"You're right." She looked him right in the eye, trying to hardline him, but betraying herself just enough. His face got too hopeful right then. So, she had to kill it. "You don't have a right. Now, if we're done here," she smiled cruelly, "I have a date to get ready for."

XIII
"13 O'CLOCK"
—TREVOR JONES, 1986

BIFF AND RAQ TROMPED onto the porch of the dilapidated building on Carroll, baring their now enlarged teeth at the two or three prying eyes still left in the half-abandoned neighborhood. It had once been the King's Daughters Hospital, from a time none living much remembered.

They walked inside, the paint peeling from the walls. The smell of mold and mildew reeked. A measurable step down from their already substandard digs up the bay. But the new boss had his reasons. The old lab was still intact, filthy as it was. Wet and rat-ridden, but he said even those had their uses.

The old boss and Scythe, now, whatever *they* were, lay across two beds pushed together, their flesh and muscles bulging and bubbling under their leathery, rubberlike skin now. Four legs had fused into two massive ones, twice as thick and long as their predecessors. The upper half of them/it was still a tangled mess of arms and faces and hair. It hurt to look at them. And the old boss, Frank, just screamed any time he...*it* was awake.

"We did like you said," Biff, or Bucket-hat as Molly called him, said to the hooded creature, waving his gnarled hand over the pulsating carcass of their former leaders. He frenzied himself, scribbling things into an old, leathery tome. He used an actual feather quill, which vexed the boys, especially since he dipped it in blood he'd taken from some of them. He scribbled his codes into that book, drew demons and godawful monsters in it. None of it was in any human language they'd ever seen.

His wrist and forearm were encased in some metal gauntlet, now housing a glowing stone right where a watch face would be. Metal rods connected to his fingers as they writhed back and forth while he mumbled some unintelligible gibberish to them. The bosses' right arms melded into one large one.

"Good," the creature said, continuing its work.

"She beat us, though," Raq, or Rat-hawk, said.

"Pretty bad, too." Biff held up his pulverized fist. It stung like a banshee, but he also knew his old self would have been crippled from the pain.

"That was expected." Blake came closer to inspect the damage. He looked it over, apathetic to any additional pain his movements caused. "Which is why you will be improved before this evening's festivities."

"Hey, look, guy." Raq said, "we didn't sign up for any of this, and if you think you gonna sly us with some spiked punch again, you got a—"

He shrieked as a needle stabbed his spine. The steel, scorpion-like device had crawled up his back while speaking, wrapped its metal legs around his throat, and then latched its long tail all down the spine, inserting dozens of needles into his vertebrae.

Biff backed away from his colleague convulsing on the floor, the hooded goblin reading his hell-speak from his blood book. Raq writhed, every muscle rippling, bubbling, growing, tearing through fabric and denim seems. Hair shot out in bright orange thickets. Teeth. Eyes. Nostrils. Bulging. And tears. Crying. Whatever person there once was, fading. Dying.

Biff made for the door, but the needle had already found his back.

Another walked in, a finished product. Eight feet tall, this one slimy, all barnacle and muscle. Jaws like stone. Teeth like jagged rocks. Hunched head. One arm more a set of pincers than anything usable. Rote. Bestial. Obedient. Like a dog.

"Broken but not dead," Blake told them. "She must be made to suffer. It will make her more...what's a good word? *Pliable*, yes. That one."

He stretched his hand back out to the fused mess of their old bosses, his arm stone glowing brighter, and started up his gibberish again, reading it all from his book, its cover a screaming face ripped from someone long forgotten.

XIV
"KNOCK 'EM DEAD, KID"
—MÖTLEY CRÜE, 1983

THE SLEDGEHAMMER AMBLED up South Beach Blvd toward the center of Old Town where she assumed the skulky voice on the television had meant to meet. She shook out her right wrist, still trying to wring the frogs out of it from the day before.

The bells from Our Lady of the Bay pounded across the last glow of the setting sun. Their clanging reports, marking the hour, always put her in mind of AC/DC, the very antithesis of their intended purpose. Each successive gong of the clapper against the bowl a portent of some looming doom, a gathering of the storm before any calm she thirsted for so deeply. Pounding in her head. Across her shoulders and back. Then, as she saw them up the beach, lined up and waiting, she heard Angus Young's axe in her head, cranking out those first chords. She thought of his advice in that moment.

No prisoners. Spare none.

Most of Old Town had cleared out, the local blues in uniform taking the threat seriously enough. The video had gone out over the entire local network. He wanted everyone to see it, for whatever reasons. There remained a few looky-loos, ready to risk it all for a front row ticket. And of course a news van was there, parked right off Court Street, and the local Gumbel, mic in hand, already yapping into the camera.

Blake's monsters were lined up across North Beach. No more red jackets. No punk earrings. Just some slashed jeans, giant bulging muscles, hunched backs, and feet closer to paws. They weren't even people anymore. Just drool and snarl and barely restrained instinct. What had he done? How had he?

Four of them lined the street, all monstrous, beastlike. Some were a mass of fur and teeth, others scaled like they'd crawled out of a swamp. And one of them had a...*crab claw?* Blake stood before them, his cloak covering most of whatever he was. His bony, pale hand held up in front of his face. Some object on his wrist glowing. Like it controlled them.

"So, these, uh...friends of yours?" Molly smirked at the hooded goblin.

He smiled in return, his teeth gleaming metallic in the brightening moon. He stood shorter now. Small. His face, aside from all the blue veins and tepid skin, seemed oddly square. His forehead also. His whole head blockish. Beady eyes. Little black squinting dots. Condescension oozed from the corners of his tight lips.

"You seem shorter," she noted.

"Stature is irrelevant to my ability. Have you come to pay your debt?" His voice still reverbed, but a hint of something else was there. A higher pitch. By some octaves. Like he'd swallowed a bit of helium a moment before. Mousy. Aberrant. Small.

"Yeah, see..." She shrugged her shoulders. "I don't know about any debt. Can't say as I recall any contracts. So, uh...yeah I'm gonna have to say no on that one. Pretty sure I'm clear on that score. I could get a lawyer to maybe explain it to you, but don't 'spect you'd listen to 'em anyway." She all but laughed at his manchild face. How she wanted to bash it in.

"You owe me." His face tightened, jawline set. He trembled. Want, desire, hurt, rage, all of it rolled into a ball and swallowed, sticking in his throat. Choking him. Like a bomb about to go off any minute. Whatever it was he thought she owed, he sure believed himself entitled to it. That he deserved it. That he deserved *her.* "A deal was made. My services rendered. The brideprice paid. Now must the bride be paid me in return." He wet his lips. So gross.

"Yeah." She folded her arms. "I'm just not feeling it, kid."

"The debt remains!" His eyes flashed. "It is a fact! And facts do not care for your feelings, Princess!"

Molly was over it. This little cave demon needed to get what it came for.

"I got your facts right here," she said, holding up Ol' Stroker and Ace.

Molly charged the beast men at full bolt. Blake stretched out his hand, his wrist emblem glowing brighter in the haze. It *did* control them somehow. The oafs lumbered in her direction, their snouts dripping saline, eyes bloodshot. One went for the wraparound, but she dodged in slowed time, ducked underneath just as he closed, and fired herself in an uppercut that had them both airborne.

*

"Get over here!" Tracey burst through the door of the shop, screaming at Lydia, whose head was buried in sheet music and Cure records.

"What?" she said, her head snapping out of her zone.

"Just come on! Now!" Trace insisted.

Lydia hopped to, grabbed her bag, and bailed out the door, Trace locking it on the way out. They ran inside Santé across the street, where the entire bar gathered round the TV set in the far corner. The bartenders, all the regulars, Mr. Cliff, even the snooty psychologist lady that tried to tell Lydia's dad she had Hyperactivity Disorder back in fifth grade, was watching. Lydia looked up at the set. Molly had just sent some mutated beast sky high.

"Oh yeah!" She slapped her fist into her palm.

*

The first of the beast men plummeted back to the ground. Molly wrenched her right hand back to her body, gripping it by the wrist and stifled a shriek of pure agony. She hurt all the way down to her bones, her nerves screaming, as two more beasts bore down on her.

A clawed foot planted into her chest, sending her flying backwards, rolling and bouncing across the gritty pavement like a deflated basketball. She recovered, still holding her wrist, the pain digging into her mind. None of this made any sense, but then it never had. She tried to shake the sting out.

She charged at the rest of them, faded one with her wonky right arm and then pulled it back and connected a left hook to its face. More frogs shot through her left arm now. The one she'd clocked was down but not out. These things were tougher than they'd been at the mall.

*

Inside the bar, eyes glued themselves to the TV. The drinks slowed to a halt, as even the bartenders had come around to watch the fight. Lydia, not entirely happy with the cold shoulder she'd been getting from her friend these last weeks, was still loyal as ever, eyes bright and wide with every landed blow from The Sledgehammer.

"She looks hurt," said a waitress.

"She doesn't get hurt," Lydia blurted out before thinking better of it. A familiar slick-haired dude in a black leather jacket gave her the eyeball, his stupid handsome face all questions and curiosity.

"How do you know?" Nguyen squinted at Lydia.

"I mean." Lydia tried to recover. "That's what I heard."

*

Molly shook the frogs from her arms, not gaining much headway. One monster lay on the ground, still wriggling. Another tromped at her. The other two turned their attention to the town, moving toward the cafes on North Beach.

As the one before her went for an overhead two-fister, she dodged to the side, sideswept his legs from under him, and shot up the street to undermine the damage to the city. One made for the news crew.

Molly caught him with an upside-down flip kick, bending him over backward. She landed on all fours, her foot singing a song she didn't like at all. Before she stood all the way up, the second mongrel punted her right in her gut, flipping her body across the street, smashing into the wall of Buoy's Bar.

Blake's beady, lusting eyes watched the proceeding from afar, his lips wet from his tongue. He hadn't expected it to go this well. She was weaker than she'd been. Something...something was off about her. He could use it. Press his advantage. He held out his arm, stretching his fingers, glowing his rock, and called down his biggest new pet.

Two elephant-sized feet thoomed onto the asphalt in front of her face, as Molly recovered from her roll. She popped into a crouching position, seeing the mighty monster raise itself to its full height. Almost twice the size of the others, though less hairy and with far less symmetry, its right arm was as big again as each of its tree-trunk legs. A left arm, smaller, but long and terminating in bony, clawed fingers, and underneath that...another left arm! The whole apparatus of it stretched several feet above her own height. The main head atop its shoulders sported wet and patchy white hair dangling down its bulbous, knotty chest and back. The second head — yes, second — protruded from the left side of its chest, a fatter, bald head just beside the smaller left arm. It screamed. A hellish, agonized scream that never ended.

"You are two..."

*

"Ugly," Lydia mouthed at the TV, seeing something she outright couldn't believe. Even in recent days, this...*thing* was a bit much. Everyone stared, speechless, as their once tenable grip on reality slipped entirely from their minds, leaving them with little else to do but observe things unravel before them.

Nguyen got popcorn from the machine by payphone.

*

Molly slowed her time, moved fast, trying to dodge it. But the fiend seized her by her waist and pitched her into the brick wall on the west side of the street. Its compatriots converged on her, a team effort.

She took punches to the ribs, kicks to her face and chest. The creature grabbed her by her head, almost ripping her mask from her face. She thought of Hurl in that moment. Of Lydia, of Hoyt and Clair. She gripped the flimsy cloth mask at her neck, holding it down and being carried upward from the monster's motion. The material at the crown of her head ripped and tore from the rest. Her apple-red hair erupted from underneath. But her face stayed covered.

With a deafening roar, the two-header clamped its colossal right hand around both her ankles and slammed her face-first into the pavement. Still gripping her feet, it hurled her again into a building, leaving cracks and chips into the stone face. And a few of the same in hers.

Molly struggled to recover. She felt wetness from her nose, spat something red out of her mouth, and wiped more of it from her face. *What is this? This isn't right.* All the parts of herself stung and quivered from some electric, tingling sensation. Like her whole body was freezing and on fire at the same time.

What was happening?

*

"Your girl needs some better moves," Nguyen said to Lydia.

Lydia Stiles turned on him and moved right in his face, glaring. Whatever was going on with Molly would resolve itself. Of that, she had no doubt. But, this? This jeering at her, this persnicketiness? This gall? *And is that a Clash tattoo?*

"First of all." Lydia's were eyes on fire. "She's not my girl. She just rules. And second..."

She forgot what was second.

*

Molly leaped, backflipped away from the fray. She couldn't figure out why she hurt, why she was weaker. It didn't make any sense. Both her fists were useless, injuring her more with each blow than she dealt the beasts.

In the back of her head she heard Easton's words at her, at *this* her. "Just some asshole," he'd called her. "Whatever you are," he'd said. His hate, the way he'd sent his hate into her, thick and heavy and putrid, had made her want to vomit from it then and now. The disdain on his face weakened her. She quivered from it. Like it was all somehow his words that took her power away.

The monsters came for her. All of them. Running. Chasing. Brian Johnson still yelling in her head about Satan and those black sensations. She never liked all that devil stuff, though. It wasn't her scene.

She ran, faded, dodged, using her speed to her advantage. She couldn't hit them hard as she needed to, but she could stay out of their way if she focused. That's what she needed. Focus.

She zeroed her eyes and cleared her head. She needed a track change. Of course; that was it. She needed her boys, screaming and grinding, egging her on. *Of course, Molly! You never call the Thunder from Down Under when only The Crüe will do!*

Her eyes slits, Molly dashed at the monsters head on, slipping grasps and fading left and right. She spear-tackled the straggler, dropped him to the ground, then flipped herself backward, reversed her run, and went headlong into the next one. She gripped him by his chest and groin, taking him up in a military press and then squatted, shot herself into the air, and backdropped him onto the blacktop. She heard his spine shatter into pieces, bones bursting into splinters inside him.

One down.

*

"Back bomb!" Lydia was wild-eyed. Everyone in the bar still stunned. Even the heckler was speechless. Just pure awe. "She backdropped that dude. Spinebuster!" She grabbed the beer right out of Nguyen's hand and took a giant gulp. This was her jam.

*

Molly dropped to a knee slide under the swiping arm of Two-Ugly, jumped back up, wrapped around another one, leaping them upward again. She fixed her left arm at his waist, holding him and braced her right palm at his back. As they crescendoed, she shoved him with her right hand, speedballing him into the ground, face and chest pounding into the grit.

Two down.

*

"Facebuster!" Lydia shouted. The people in the bar were watching her as much the TV now. Like she was the announcer calling the match. "Boss Man Slam!" Stupid Nguyen was grinning at her.

On the TV, Molly ran from an ugly, kicked herself off a wall, and launched her elbow into its face, sending it flipping down the street.

"Flying Forearm!!" Lydia yelled. *She's doing it! She watched the tape!* "I need a beer." She turned to the bartender beside her, his eyes on the TV. He shook the awe from his eyes for a second, clearly just now remembering that he was at a job. "A beer?" Lydia pleaded again.

"How old are you, kid?" He said.

"Just get me a beer, Wooders." There was no time for this.

Molly dropkicked the big one in the chest, knocking it into the gulf. She jumped to the next one, flipping herself around its body like a pair of nunchucks, gripping its head into a scissor lock. "Oh god, oh god," Lydia muttered. Nguyen nodded at Wooders to just get her the beer. On the screen, Molly flipped the both of them around, her upright and the mutant upside down, bashing its head into the street.

"Pile Driver!" She screamed. Wooders handed her the beer and backed away. Nguyen cheers-ed her.

*

Molly was down to her last regular monster, the big daddy still wrenching itself out of the muddy gulf. She was tired. She didn't get tired. Red viscous fluid leaked from her nose, lips, and elsewhere. Her wrists and ankles screamed. Her back tingled like she was hooked up to a battery charger.

The mutant charged her, reaching its arms for a hold. She faded, leapt, and caught it in a reverse headlock, flung them both through the air together, and dropped it face-first into the ground. Somewhere she could almost feel Lydia shouting "Ace Crusher!" Was she imagining that? Or had she really heard it?

The thing twitched. Molly ran at the nearby building, bounced herself off the wall, and finished it with a presidential leg drop to the face, her heel caving in its nose. The sensation of its life draining out onto the street sickened her further. Her already goosed stomach sent what little she'd eaten into her throat.

She saw it die. Felt it. Froze it in the air. The very moment its life left it. Vanished into the dark. A whisper and then nothing. Just a dead mass of cells on the pavement. It was, just as Easton had described it, nothing but a victim itself.

A victim of the true monster. The long-eared, cloaked freak with a glowing armband that stood up the street directing this mayhem. *How she hated him.*

That very creature watched, glaring at the turn in the sequence. What was happening had intrigued it. A failure that may yet produce a success, he thought as he saw it unfold. But his prize still had one more labor to complete this night. He saw now she would. *No matter.* He laughed at the prospect of it. How he should have seen it all along. He knew how they worked now. He knew what to do, what would undo her.

The two-headed fiend clambered out of the water, its main head a barely sentient zombie. The second head, where a nipple should be, screamed as it spat brown water of the sound out its mouth. It pounded its feet, stomping toward her.

Molly stared at it, her eyes gun barrels. Her whole body was about to burst with pain any second, and her silly outfit barely hung onto her. The creature surged at her. Just like she wanted it to.

"Come on, you gruesome son of a bitch." Molly steadied.

As it closed on her, Molly crouched, then rocketed into the air. The monster, strong enough to follow suit, flung itself at her. They collided in mid-air, far above the buildings of Old Town. The beast wrenched at her with its big arm, gaining no purchase, grasping with its two smaller ones. She slipped through every attempt, worming, snaking her way around it.

She flipped all the way around its head and back, gripping its main head by the neck in a reverse lock. She held its legs above them both, restraining the entire mass of it, helpless. They fell, speeding at the ground, its head pointed dead at the hard blacktop.

Contact.

Its brain exploded out its ears. Whatever humanity left in it was gone forever now. Just a ruined corpse of tumored flesh. Molly retched, letting loose liquid from her guts.

*

"DDT!!" Lydia screamed in the bar, so loud no one could hear their own souls anymore. "DDT!! DDT!! DDT!! DDT!!" She turned to Nguyen and planted one on his forehead, but then realized what she'd just done and to who. *Oh gross. Why?*

"DDT!!" she shouted again, turning back to the TV and away from her error in judgement. "DDT!!" she yelled right in the face of the psychiatrist lady.

*

Molly's guts felt like this one's brains looked, splayed out all across Beach Blvd under the moonlit sky. Her soul felt cold, wounded. She'd killed those things — most of them, at least — that once were humans. Poor souls damned to oblivion now. Whatever sins they'd committed were not enough to condemn them to what *he* had done to them. What he made *her* do. What he had made her into. *Whatever you are,* she heard Easton's voice saying in her head again. *Just some asshole.*

But the real asshole stood before her. That translucent-skinned gremlin. That cloaked, pointy-eared ghoul. Some archfiend demon from some other world. Licking its chops at the thought of her. Like it owned her.

Her hate doubled in her chest. Tripled. It fueled her as she plodded toward it, it just standing there. Unabashed. Unaffected. Unafraid. She would make it afraid. She would rip it apart at its limbs. *What is he compared to me?*

Hate was the only thing that held her upright, her whole self on fire. Blood at her knuckles, elbows, knees, pouring from her nose, squeezing from her teeth. But hate held her. It embraced her. It kept her together. Whole. For now. For long enough to finish it.

Blake stood grim, emotionless, solemn. He looked right into her, inside her as she closed their distance. He didn't even bother to run or move at all. A statue almost. Her eyes rocks, her jaw steel, her mind set, Molly seized at his throat to crush it, pinch the very life from it.

But all she grabbed was air. The image of him flickered, twitched. Gone.

He was never there.

XV
"DRIVE"
—THE CARS, 1984

WRAPPED TIGHT IN HER long coat, the night wind stinging at her ears — one swollen, the other numb — Molly trudged past the unlit streets of houses, those mirrored avenues, toward the corner of Elm and E. Just a few more blocks and she'd make it.

Her right leg stiffened. Her left started to drag. She couldn't feel all her fingers. She looked to be sure they were even there. Her face dripped a mess of liquids. She'd cleared the red stuff off, wiping it with what remained of the purple mask and rubbing herself as clean as she could in the street, then tossed the rag in the gutter. Her hair clung to her neck. Her eyes leaked the most, though it wasn't raining.

She got in sight of the house when a set of smokestack exhaust and a diesel engine idled beside her. Its big truck tires rolled at barely a crawl, coming to a stop. It was sight she'd as soon do without.

"Holy crap that was great! That was so awesome!" Lydia shouted.

Like, what was awesome? None of it, Molly determined. Not one moment of her life since she suddenly got powered up.

"We did it! I told you, Mol, wrestling!"

"We?" Molly turned, rigid and angry at this person, this stupid human before her. "Who's *we?* You mean me! I did it! Just like I always do. Just like *I* do everything. You rented a video. Good for you."

"Sorry, I was just—" Lydia backed away.

"You were just nothing, Lydia. Because that's what you are. Now fuck off. I don't need you."

"Jesus, Molly."

"Yeah, fuck that guy, too,"

* * *

In the house, she limped up the stairs, hoping she could make it to the bathroom. If she could do that, she'd be okay. She'd make it, she told herself. Clair saw her trudging the steps, all of her a mess.

"Molly!" she gasped, running to her.

"It's fine, I'm fine." Molly waved, her voice tremble and whimper. "I fell on my skateboard. I'm fine. I'll be fine."

"You're not fine." Clair reached to hold her.

Molly jerked away.

"I said I am, so leave me alone, Clair," Molly yelled. *Just a few more steps.* She'd make it. She left Clair, face agasp, Hoyt and Hurl lost in the woods on the couch.

She didn't need them. Any of them. What could they do anyway? Let them kick her out. It was fine. It was all just whatever.

In the bathroom, she took off her coat, stifled a scream. She peeled the remnants of the super suit off her battered body. There were blue, black, purple splotches all across her. Her ribs on each side just a mass of all the wrong colors. She managed to turn the shower head on, full bore. The blasting sound of its rain hit the ceramic tub. Enough to drown out her cries, she hoped. Her face in the mirror was someone else's. Some poor weak child. She climbed into the bowl, drew the curtain, and collapsed into herself.

She held herself by the knees, still in half her clothes. Letting the warm rain wash over her. Blending her tears into just more water rolling down her face. She gasped. Her chest heaved. She ached everywhere. She cried and she prayed. To whom she didn't even know.

"Daddy!" she cried out loud. "Daddy!" she cried again, closing her eyes. Not Hoyt. Not any man she knew or had ever heard of. Her *real* daddy. The one who made her. The one she knew existed. Out there somewhere in the world. She'd dreamt of him, his face a cloud, a mystery. But his arms. Huge. Giants. So strong they could crush anything that would try to hurt her. Wrap her around inside them. Hold her. Keep her. His hair, red as her own. Bright and vibrant. He was real and she knew it. But she couldn't say his name. She didn't know it.

She didn't even know her own.

* * *

Days passed, she knew on some deep level. *Two of them? Or was it three?* She'd lost any sense of it. She hadn't been down from her room. There were knocks. Offers of food. Movie night. A cup of hot chocolate with Hoyt. Lydia at the door twice each day. Hurl slid a comic book under her door. She stayed in bed, sleeping some, wrapped in a blanket otherwise. She stared at the little black and white TV but she'd ripped its wires out. It mocked her. A window for *him* into her life. Some little weasel watching, taunting her from his hideaway somewhere out there. In the world.

The Eve of their big day came. It was their winter festival. The whole reason they canceled their schools. Work ceased. Turkey and hams roasted. Stockings hung. Some bearded magician rode his eight-legged steed. Or eight something. Eight was what she remembered.

Molly found her shoes. She slid on warm stockings and jeans. A sweater, hooded. Denim jacket. Knit stocking cap, tight over her ears. Gloves. She started out the bedroom door but stopped. She couldn't face any of them. She couldn't see their smiles, hear their season's greetings, spoil their fun with her dourness. They were better off without her.

She slid out her window and dropped to the sod. Her ankles still ached, biting her with the impact. The colors on her body had faded back to a reasonable dingy pink and violet. She trudged through the snow — *snow on The Coast?*— into town, thumbing a ride to downtown. She walked the near empty streets, looked up at the top of the Hancock, her old perch. She didn't dare try for it tonight. She wasn't sure she had the legs for it.

She walked on, past the Tracey's shop. Closed early, the sign said. "Happy Holidays from all of us to you and yours!" it read. She lingered on the "us." Did that include her? When had she even seen Tracey last?

Another block and she stood outside Elmo's, the windows frosted. Dice worked the door from inside, an easy job tonight with the small and dwindling crowd. Some loving couple, made all the moreso from a few spirits, jingled out the door, arms wrapping each other from the cold as they found their way to their car to take them to their warm, cozy home.

Through the window, she saw Tracey and Lydia, and some other girl, maybe her own age, maybe older. They had glasses of egg nog, little green cone hats, and party blowers. Tracey blew hers at Lydia's face, the three of them laughing. A half-eaten pie sat on their table. Pepperoni and mushroom. Lydia's favorite.

At the far corner, near the dartboard in the back, Nguyen tossed one dead center bullseye. A shot filled his other hand. He turned it up with Torello and Rae. Beside them, at the table, Easton sat, his face not quite a smile, but something like one. His always perfect hair combed back and side-swept. He wore a red blazer, white shirt sleeves, both rolled up to the elbow. Someone said something and he laughed, a healthy, belly laugh. He was happy enough.

An arm reached around his shoulders, holding him close. He turned, smiled a deep, heavy, and very real smile. At *her*. At Becky de la Beckwith. She smiled back at him in return. Not her fake smile, her mean girl falsetto, not her smirk, or her gotcha grin. No. A real smile. One she meant with her whole self. She *loved* him.

Molly's chest caved in. She couldn't breathe. She didn't even need to, but it felt like she did. She kept trying but had forgotten how.

She ran down the street. She had to get away. She *needed* to be away. Gone. Somewhere. Anywhere else.

She didn't cry. There was just cold water on her face, freezing in its place as it ran down her cheeks. Probably sleet, she told herself. It was *so* cold out now. Her face hardened. Her head got hot. It was good they had each other. All of them. *But she didn't need them. She was something more. Beyond them. Above them.* What she needed...was to hit something.

Or someone!

Him. Blake. Wherever he was. No place warm. Nowhere festive. No one gathered around him telling stories, making jokes, embracing him with a warm hug, a smile. No, he would have none of that. Creature that he was, that awful monster. No. Where would he be?

Think, Molly. You saw him. Knew him. Who is he? Where would he go? His house was abandoned. Watched. Where would he flee? Hide out? He's some villainous cancer. Some self-entitled brat who waved around silly swords and spoke of old debts. Words of honor. Armored knights in his foyer. Paintings of...

Castles!

Of course!

Molly leered at the beach, narrowed her eyes, focusing, zooming. Cutting through the darkness, the watery expanse. She saw the blue through the black. Then the green of the island. The red brick of the fort. Massachusetts. A fortress away from the world.

A castle.

XVI

"THE END OF THE INNOCENCE"
—DON HENLEY, 1989

THE WATER CHURNED as she floated over it, the wind a howl, but she didn't mind. Borrowing a one-man catamaran, she'd cut out for the island. It had seemed odd only for a moment, the strange familiarity of it as though she'd sailed a thousand times before, her hands going to the knots like old friends. Running the jib, setting the sail. All reflex. Instinct. The wind and the waves sang comfort to her. Calmed her. Honed her intent.

Pulling the boat up to the beach, she stared up at the stone face of the centuries-old fortress—like some ancient, graying skeleton. Moss at its top. Its walls crumbling. Cannons up top, long rusted past any use. The souls of the hundreds dead moaned and clawed at the sand and grass. Crying to be taken up. To be sent home. Where they belonged.

He would be here, she knew.

She made her way to the walls and bounded atop them, barely making the leap. She slipped and grabbed at the ledge, still off her game. But she had enough juice for *him*. Slimy worm that he was. *No sweat.*

She pounced into the open courtyard and found her way inside its long, semi-circling hallway. Desolate rooms that once housed soldiers and munitions, now an endless nothing. A tomb. A relic. Cold. Empty. Exactly the place a monster would come to hide itself away. Away from the world it hated, and that hated it in return. The lair of some creature. Some alien.

She wandered, arriving where she'd started, looking again. Nothing. She had gotten it wrong. There were no monsters here.

Only her.

EPISODE V

0
"WHY DON'T PRETTY GIRLS (LOOK AT ME)"
—WILD MEN OF WONGA, 1985

SHE MOCKED HIM, as she had before, as her family had before, her oafish father, that skull-bashing buffoon. All of them had, for his knowledge, his wisdom. For, he knew all. All the words in all the tongues of all creatures in all the worlds. All his to know. For he was the first to learn and concoct the beer of balladry, the wine of all words, the liquor of all lies. He knew the words of life and the words of death, the very Charm of Making itself — echoing across the aeons since first spoken by the ancient, the author of the Eldar, the first of the gods (how he hated gods). Bouncing off the walls of his cave world, he'd found the sounds, committed them to his perfect memory. All these secrets had been his to know, his alone. He need never have shared them, nor should he have, for his price had been denied him. He yearned for what was his by agreement. *By contract! By right! All debt must be paid!*

And he'd done everything he was supposed to do this time around. A hasty pact with the Eldar, the bringer of all sorrows, the mother of demons. She freed him from his stone prison. So, he'd brewed the elixir for her. Gave her the Charm of Making. What of it? A simple task. One he'd done before to no avail for himself. And why shouldn't he pact with the Doombringer?

"Give it to me, Đøkkn, and you may name your price," she'd said there in the ruins of old HighGuard.

Had only the witch not bungled it, speaking the words too slowly, his prize opening the door before she could be unmade, falling from her own dead world into this...this land of apes. Of these mongrels. Their carbon forms soft and weak, their short lives petty and banal.

But the Eldar had restored him. Nay, she improved him, illusion though it was. Now it faded to naught. But it had been his! He was beautiful, as the apes saw it. Each time his face and form shifted to their idea of perfect.

Yet even *they* had mocked him. Teased him for his many words. Even taking the highest of their forms had not yielded their favor for him. Laughter. Always their laughter. And their scorn. He was better than any, nay, all of them. Their petty baubles and machinations were but the scratching in the sand of mere dogs to him! But they laughed.

So, he made himself more. He acquired their riches, their wealth. He bought and sold. How little they knew, so easy to swindle. To some he gave machines. To others he gave chemistry. And the little yellow rocks they so cherished? He could simply create those with his crystals, making one metal into another as he saw fit.

And all the while, he searched for *her*. "Look for her hair," the Eldar had told them as they crossed over. He had discarded the false ones. Not worthy of him. He must have *only* the one who was promised. He would not defile himself with the body of an ape.

And now, again, their laughter. Their mockery. Their scorn. *Her* scorn.

But he would show them. He knew other things as well. Also his, was the Riddle of Steel. Others, his boorish kinsmen, beat about it with their hammers and their tongs. But he knew its secrets. Its makings. Its energies. All words of a kind themselves. For everything in the universe, all of it, had its own language. And he knew them all.

Clamoring from his haven in their forgotten infirmary, its tools no longer required, he made his way, his shortened legs now even, his thin, boney fingers lighter, better suited to his preferred work. He passed one of their quaint trading posts, its refuse bin overflowing with such waste. How they wasted! And in this one, a sign. One of their wooden models, a *mannequin*, worn, broken, discarded. But not without its use. For she had shown him her weakness, her flaw!

He knew now from whence she drew her power, and he would take it from her.

He was the All-Knowing. The greatest of makers and fabricators. And now he would make his greatest creation yet. Ten thousand-fold over those simple rudiments of his long-forgotten clan. For he was the word-wright! The hymn-smith! He was the ForgeMaster! He would make a wonder! A marvel! A perfection!

He would show them. He would show them all.

I
"BREAKING THE LAW"
–JUDAS PRIEST, 1980

THE PARENTALS ARGUED downstairs, even breaking out a few *shits* and *damns* they tried not to use around the house when Molly and Hurl were around. They'd dropped enough bombs over the years, it was little use to keep up the pretense. In her kinder moments, Molly found herself respecting the effort. Today was not likely to host any of her kinder moments.

She rolled over, aiming to finally get out of bed, and all but screamed out in pain. She pulled her night shirt up, still a vivid tapestry of color marbling across her skin. She couldn't wrap her head around it. She took a direct hit from a tank. Like a freaking tank! And that didn't so much as wind her. She was still tired, too. How long had she slept? Ten hours? Twelve? Had she missed the whole unwrapping gifts thing? Maybe that's what they were fighting about. Molly guessed she'd become the grinch who stole their happy day.

She pantsed up and stared at her hair for a minute before deciding not to bother. Might as well go down and face her music. At least there'd be leftovers. She was starving—for real this time—not just for the pure joy of tasting the food. Like, her body actually hurt from hunger. When had she last felt that? Had she ever?

Appearing down the stairwell, holding her throbbing head like she had a hangover—*God, that's probably what they think*. Which was certainly better than the truth, so fair enough—she saw the scene winding itself down.

"What the hell were you even thinking?" Clair folded her arms at Hurl. *Hurl?* He never got in trouble. "The very thought of it! And his poor mother!"

Hoyt stood there, arms in pockets, stern, terse, but with odd lines to his lips. Molly sensed his feelings, though it was faint—much softer than it had been before but enough. Just a hint of it reached her. *Pride.* He hid it. But that's what he felt.

"Do something about this." Clair walked out of the den toward the stairs. "Make him do pushups or run up and down the block 20 times. Something so he learns his lesson. I mean it, Hoyt!"

She rounded the corner and caught Molly deer-eyed at the foot of the stairs. Molly expected to get reamed for sleeping through Christmas morning. Had they even tried to wake her? She didn't see torn wrappings or any of Hurl's new gear strewn about. *What is happening?*

"Bless the mother and saints, you're alive!" Clair hugged Molly tight as a vise.

Molly's eyes widened as she spun on a tilt-a-whirl in her head. She didn't know what else to do but hug her back.

"Is it drugs?" Clair asked her, though weirdly not in a mad way. "You can tell me if it is. You know, I smoked a little reefer once. Just once, over at the community college when your dad and I were young. So I know how it can drag you in. Please let us help you, Sweetheart. Oh, I just love you so much!" Clair hugged her tighter now, really working at those bruises, too.

"Ow, Clair, that hurts." Molly eased out of the death grip. *Wait...that DOES hurt!*

"Mama bears hug hard, baby cub. Just remember we love you, and also: D.A.R.E. to stay off drugs!"

She was so adorably awful in her sentiment, Molly didn't bother to correct her and just accepted it for what it was. Clair went up the stairs, and Hurl huffed 'round the corner soon after, red-faced and fuming.

"What's the deal?" Molly wasn't used to *him* being the troublemaker in the house.

"I'm gonna box that dirtbag thief Lambert next time I see him." He stomped up the stairs.

"Did I miss the tree stuff? The presents and all that?"

Hurl looked sideways at her. "Dude, it's the 27th," he said, then sequestered himself to his room.

* * *

That day stretched to a week of its copy, sleeping long hours, staying away from the world outside her four walls. In fact, Molly hadn't been outside in days, not even to the yard or the mailbox—mostly sitting in her room alone, listening to her records and tapes, watching movies with Hoyt and Hurl. She even made cookies with Clair.

There were phone calls, even a few front door knocks. Lydia. But Molly wasn't ready to deal with her—with any of them. It was now so far beyond her, where and what she wanted to be, what she'd wanted from life. She would sit, headphones on, picking away at her Fender, staring up at her Darksiders poster, *Mother of Hell,* their only album, musing about Étienne the lost genius, the haunted songwriter and vocalist. He could really scream. The more she studied his face, its lines, near-perfect symmetry, his tawny skin, it reminded her of...*someone.*

She tried remembering when things were normal—how awful her life had seemed then. Now, that past was some distant utopian dream. It was like if she closed her eyes and played hard enough, found the right tones, the perfect key, the exact notes, she could play her way back to it.

* * *

The first day back at school was as tortuous as expected. The only person Molly avoided harder than Lydia was that witch Becky de la Beckwith with her perfect face. At first she'd burned with red hate for her, but that had subsided into a cold acceptance of reality. It didn't really matter in the end. Maybe nothing did. But, all the same, she'd rather not have to face it.

She went through the motions, passing faces she half-recognized in the halls, never looking up, never speaking. Even Lydia took the hint and just stayed away. *Small mercies.* She even rode the bus home now, grateful for the white noise of the booger-flicking crowd.

Clomping down off the bus onto her sidewalk, it dawned on her. Hurl was missing. "Where's Hurl?" Molly ditched her bag as she came in, grabbed a banana from the table.

"I swear to Holy Mother," Clair fumed, "He gets this from your father!"

Molly hadn't aced Bio by any stretch, but she was pretty sure it was hard to pass genes to adopted kids. She decided the correction could wait. Apparently Hurl was in detention. *Hurl.* For fighting. *Guess the kid made good on his threat with that other kid, whatshisname. Good for Hurl.*

Molly smirked. She was proud of him.

* * *

"That stinking scoundrel!" Hurl slammed his fist in his palm in the confines of her room after Hoyt picked him up from detention. She'd graced him with an invite into her sanctum which was normally forbidden to him under penalty of painful dismemberment. But today he'd earned a visit behind the curtain.

"Spill it." Molly tried to feign the proper older sister decorum and role model behavior, but all she really wanted was to hear his story, the amazing tale of some normal life, of some everyday problem of a sane world.

"I never shoulda let him borrow it. I knew he was false. A brigand!"

Apparently, there'd been some rock or "treasure" as Hurl insisted, found in some cave, or tunnel, something like that, all related to him eavesdropping on the gang those many weeks ago now. *Gods, did that happen?* Molly had slept so much lately, she was hoping she'd dreamed it all.

Molly didn't quite have to beat it out of Hurl that he *actually had* beat it out of Lambert. The kid had dodged Hurl all through the holiday break about the stone. Apparently, he'd taken the rock down to Piette's Pawn (which everyone called Pirate's because he *was one*) up on 90 and hocked it for some comic books and a knockoff Walkman. Hurl was livid but also heart-rent. All her powers had seemed off lately, muted, distant. But she still sensed his pain, how much that stupid rock meant to him.

"Screw it. We'll get it back." She reached into her Dire Straits LP sleeve and pulled out a small stack of bills.

"How?"

"We'll take a walk up to Pirate's and I'll talk to him." She winked. "I have a feeling he'll bend to me."

*

The walk took longer than they thought. Wind bit their ears—both of them. Molly even sneezed a few times, her nose runny. That concerned her, but she'd deal with it later. The shop was in their sights now, in all its slipshod majesty. Gutters half falling down, letters missing from every part of the sign, the paint fading and chipping. Only his old Chevy pickup and a beat-up Honda CB350 motorbike with a "For Sale" sign hung from the handlebar were in the parking lot.

The first thing greeting them through the door were the gator heads. Then the hurricane cups. The bad SS Camille paintings (which some thought he did himself). Then, at the back, the gunwall. And Mr. Piette himself, making a point of polishing a .38 snubnose at the moment.

"Hep you with som'n?" he asked without looking up.

"My brother here says a kid sold you a rock. Some kinda gemstone?" Molly said. "Well, it wasn't his to sell. He stole it."

"Oh, I get ten or twelve o'you in here a week." he sneered. "Prove it was yours on paper or get on with you. I ain't got time for none of this today."

Molly took a look around at the store, empty of all comers but she and Hurl.

"A run on Gator heads today, is it?"

"Listen Missy, I—"

"There it is! There it is!" Hurl found the stone over in a case of mostly garbage trinkets and doodads, the junk beads and shell jewelry.

Molly studied it. Didn't look all that impressive. Certainly didn't look like it was any kind of real deal treasure.

"That there's a rare yella diamond, worth a mint." Piette licked his chops.

"Lie!" Hurl shouted. "Mr. Max said it wasn't."

"It's what I say it is, boy. Long as it's in my shop, its value is mine to say."

"Look, Piette." Molly pulled out her few bills, the culmination of many shifts at Trace's. "Let's just get to it. What's it gonna take? $5 do the trick? For a little glass rock he found on the beach probably?"

"Cave!"

She didn't know why she was even doing this for Hurl. She didn't need to let go of any more of her own money than she had to. In fact, she needed to get down to Trace's and see about getting some of her old shifts back, if she still could. Or maybe she would just get another job—one where she didn't see people as much.

"Well now, little Missy." He eyed her like she was on the block herself. "Maybe let's say we can make us a little deal here. Maybe both come out a little ahead?" He pursed his lips.

Molly's eyes thinned, darkened. Hurl stared at his dumb rock.

"Hurl, go wait outside." She leered at Mr. Piette.

"But, I—"

"Just go."

*

Hurl kicked rocks in the parking lot and stared at the missing letters on Piette's sign. He'd figured they'd be lying on the ground next to or near it, the wind having knocked them off. He moved some of the letters around, spelling "butt" and "ass" and laughed to himself.

A few cars and trucks whizzed by. The wind, this far off the beach, still rushed over him and the road. He was sure he heard someone hollering inside, like a scream or a yell. He started to go back inside but a second later Molly rolled out of the store, grin on her face, jingling something in her fingers.

"Heads up, kid." She tossed the gemstone right into his hands. He stared down at it, breathing a sigh of relief.

"How much did you—" He started to ask, but Molly just dropped onto that old motorbike and fired it up, popping its zippy exhaust into the chill air.

"Get on."

Molly felt good. Better than she'd felt in days now. She was gonna ride that feeling. It was time to make a few changes to a few things. Hurl hopped on the bike, and she gassed it for home. The wind in her face felt like the first breath of air after coming up from underwater.

II
"MAD WORLD"
—TEARS FOR FEARS, 1982

INSIDE THEIR MC CLUBHOUSE, the Drednex "President" Zester Hauser crushed a rock of ice into powder and ripped a pinch of it from the tip of his knife. He chewed at the air, his eyes stretching in their sockets. Getting his bearings. Some clarity. They'd been dry as a bone since the tanker sank in the gulf—an entire rig full of phased plasma rifles and sound grenades, the best the Land of the Rising Sun could spare. He still had no idea how or even what all happened out there. Some of the boys that managed to make it back (half had lit out for Texas or even Mexico) had come in shouting stuff about flying monsters or mermaids or some stupid shit.

But the news had shown it plenty enough. Some gadfly in a getup was mucking up the works—for sure the same bad timing do-gooder that kicked them around the night they rode into town. Still, he'd sooner tango with the mall-brand badass than what had run them out of New Orleans. She might hit like a steel club, but she was sloppy, goofy, probably some damn kid. Not like the goddamned demon that lurked the gothic city down the road. But, no, this little come-lately was nothing he worried much about. They'd get a new supplier soon enough. The pipeline up north would pick right back up, and the green would be back in their pockets thick as ever. And her? She'd slip up. She'd make a mistake. Expose herself. And then she'd...

She stood right there.

She was taller than he remembered. She opened the double doors, sunlight bleeding in, shutting all their eyes for a second. Came waltzing into a members' only safehouse like she owned it. Not that ownership in the legal sense much mattered to them anyway. Wasn't like they bought the place.

Her neon-striped leotard danced in the half-light from the few lamps and the rays she'd let in from outside. Her baby doll face peeked out from under that gaudy carnival mask. Almost looked like she picked the whole suit out of the bargain bin at the Kmart.

One of the boys jumped up and sent a .44 slug into her chest and she didn't even look at him, just kept coming right at Hauser.

"You're the leader here?" she said, stopping when she was just shy of arm's reach of him. He didn't love his position at the moment, less still his odds. The way she didn't even flinch at that .44 to the chest? Didn't bounce off her, either. Like it went into her without a fuss, swallowed into the rest of her. Like it belonged there.

"I am," he said.

"Correction: you were. I now run this gang. You will follow my commands henceforth."

"Now, wait just a damn minute, you—" Hauser put his hand on her shoulder before he thought better of it.

She seized his arm by the wrist, broke it, then twisted his arm, breaking that, and threw him into the far wall, smashing him into the liquor shelf. He slumped to the ground.

"Now," she addressed the room, "let's discuss some changes shall we?"

* * *

Molly gunned her motorcycle across the wind-swept bay bridge toward downtown, the gusts shoving at her. She leaned into the wind to stay in her lane. The little bike had more power than she thought it would. It ran good, better than it should from he'd wanted for it. Not that she gave it to him, but all the same. She loved it, loved her hair flowing wild. She gassed it and let it scream a little more.

Coming off the beach and turning up 25th into downtown, she zipped it onto the sidewalk, not far from Elmo's and Trace's shop. She fist-pounded Dice as she passed by, not eager to face them inside the store, but it had to be done. She hadn't decided how much to drop on Lydia just yet. Maybe just get in, get out, save the rest for another day.

The store had been rearranged, all the women's fashion up front with new mannequins and the accessories near that. Records and books they'd placed in skinny towers around the store. They'd added a films section on the south wall, hand-picked from the Lydia Stiles' collection. There was a globe-trotter theme going on now, too, with decor and icons from a half dozen places. Sombreros, headdress, masks from here and yonder, belted plaids, and kimonos. And LOTS of New Wave covers peppered the walls, post-punk too. Cure. Clash. Smiths. Furs. The Fixx. Trace had let Lydia go wild. Molly took it all in. It worked, in its way. Had she really been away this long?

"Denim in the back." Lydia propped a foot on the counter, head in a magazine. Molly knew she saw her. She was being...*whatever.*

"Yeah, ha ha," Molly said. "Look, I just came to see if I had a paycheck from last period."

"You mean three periods ago? 'Cause that's the last shift you worked."

"Yeah, well, I mean from whenever."

"What does it even matter? You ought to be flush now, huh?"

"What?" Molly asked. Lydia was on the jazz again.

"Nothing. Trace is in the back. You can ask her."

Molly walked to the back office, shaking her head. This was worse and weirder than she'd anticipated. The next part was not going to be super nice either. Trace consumed herself in choosing between two wigs for the evening, one a spiked black and white, the other Marilyn.

"Do I—" Molly started, but Tracey pointed at the folders on the opposite wall of the office.

Molly leafed through for her last paycheck—not much of one, at that. She'd only worked one shift that period. It had been a while. Their attitudes hurt more than the meager cash total. She'd expected them to be cold but still. After the stuff she'd done? For all of them? Hell, half this town would be rubble if it weren't for her. Not that she could say it to Trace. But Lydia knew. *And she should show a little more gratitude.*

"Am I scheduled for—"

"No, I split it all up between Lyd and the new girl. We're covered, thanks." Tracey never even looked at her.

There's a new girl? What? Who? Why was th—it doesn't matter. She could get a new job. Or not. Who cared? She could just start lifting some cash off these bangers she busted up. That was only fair, right? And who was to say it wasn't? Not like anyone could stop her, anyway.

Molly fast-walked back through the store, ready to be back on her bike and in the wind. She was so over it. Let them pout. She cruised past the counter and out the door without a word. She mounted, ready to kick it off and be gone.

"So that's just it, huh?" Lydia followed her out the door. Molly didn't look up from the bike. "Oh, and what's this now? Ho ho! I guess it's true, then. Holy Mother. You really did it, huh?" Lydia shook her head, looking away from Molly. Her anger, her disdain, her disappointment, were thick.

And it *hurt.* Molly felt a pang in her chest. Her whole body hurt from it.

Lydia kept shaking her head and glaring at her, every sharp glance a stab. What was this? Why was it happening?

"Did what?"

"Oh, you're gonna play that now?" Lydia said. "With me? With me, of all people?"

"Okay, I'm really kind of lost here. Look I know...I know I've been out of it. And I..." She didn't know how to finish this and also didn't want to.

"You know what? Just forget it. You want to be this way? This is what you want to do? Fine. God, what, you steal this too? I don't care. Maybe this is just who you are, always were. I don't know. Don't care. I pushed you into the whole hero thing, so it's whatever. Just go do your thing. But I'm out of it, you understand?"

"What are you—"

"And you know? You think this thing, this stuff you can do, makes you better than us? Than me? Like you're so above the rest of us you can just ignore, dismiss, push around, take? Screw you, Molly. You're not better. You're not special at all. You're just some piece of shit asshole. You're nothing. Nobody."

Lydia was at the point of tears, and Molly did all she could to hold her own back. She knew this would be bad, but not this bad. Her chest wanted to explode. Her head pounded. Her nose felt cold, runny again. The chill in the air bit her face like a wolf.

Lydia's face quivered. She wasn't finished yet. Molly sensed it. She had one more thing she was about to let out. Molly knew what it would be, and she begged in her mind for Lydia not to say it. *Please don't,* she pleaded from inside herself at Lydia. *Please don't.*

"You don't even have a real name." Lydia turned and walked back inside.

* * *

Molly rode into the evening—north, out of town, through the curves and hollers— letting the icy wind erase the tears from her face. Maybe she'd deserved Lydia's ire. Maybe she hadn't. But she didn't have to hit that hard. She didn't. Molly could curl up in the trees and die. Just fold up and quit.

The worst part was Lydia wasn't wrong. Of course she was nobody. She'd always been nobody. Thrown away one night ten years ago in the rain, just left in a pile of wrong clothes and random trash. Just like Becky de la Beckwith had always told her she was. *Coast Trash.*

Molly coughed into the cutting air now. Her throat clawed her. She decided to stop and get something to soothe it and maybe send her off to some better dream. It was long past time to wake from this one. If she could get hurt, maybe she could get drunk now, too. She wheeled her bike into the package store near downtown, the same one she'd been to before though in different circumstances. She sneezed while walking through the door, coughing a fit into her denim sleeve. Was that a red spot on her jacket? That couldn't be right.

She cruised the aisles, not quite knowing what she wanted, what she even liked, and much less what she could afford. A new job was her priority now. Maybe Dice could get her on as a waitress at Elmo's.

"Bless your heart, sweetie," the old lady at the counter said. What was she talking about? Wait, Molly had her ID right? She felt her pockets. *Yep.* "You look like death warmed over. You best not be out in this weather on them things."

Molly stared at her, then out the window at her bike. This wasn't even anything. A little sneeze, a cough. A couple hours sleep and she'd be right as rain. It's not like she even got sick, anyway.

She didn't notice the door jingle, nor the familiar neon-striped unitard strut inside, nor the all-business sneer. Hollow eyes, a face cold as the wind outside, hands, fists, hard as wrought iron.

"Well?" the newcomer demanded of the clerk.

The lady shook, stammered. "Please. It's the slow time of year. We barely sold any—"

Molly turned, lost in the haze of her fever dream and coughing, staring into some carnival funhouse mirror. What the hell was going on? Was she dreaming? She must be. And that suit? She didn't even have it anymore. Her last one was destroyed by the mutants. This was...what?

"Who the hell are you?" Molly asked.

The masked face turned to her. *Her* face. Every line of it. A perfect copy.

"Haven't you heard?" her own voice asked. "I'm The Sledgehammer. Now..." She turned to the clerk, picking up a bottle from the nearby display and dropping it, spitting glass and brown liquid across the floor. "My money!"

Whatever this was, it was over. Molly's eyes went white. Mask or no mask, this was enough. She put her own bottle down, wound up, and let an uppercut loose under the faker's chin.

Molly screamed. Howled. Reeled in pain. She held her fist, bloody at the knuckles, the skin torn in more places than she could count. Red ran down her arm onto the floor, mixing with the whiskey into sludge at her feet. Needles stabbed every nerve from her fingers to her brain.

Her own image turned to her, reared its arm back, and slammed a fist into her right shoulder, rocketing Molly backward into a shelf, bursting bottles and covering her in the reek of fermented fruit. She cried out. She didn't know what a broken bone felt like, but this had to be it. Tears flooded her face from the pain, so wet she couldn't even see. *What's happening? This isn't real. It can't be.*

The copy came at her now, cold, machine-like. No expression on its face. Pure mission.

"What the...?" Molly got almost vocal through her jittering jaw and stabbing shoulder and hand. "What are..?"

"I told you," the voice said, smiling, wicked and wrong, rearing back its hand for another strike. Only this time...the hand changed. It molded itself, like it was made of clay or something.

It became steel. The steel head of a 12-pound hammer.

"I'm The Sledgehammer!" It knocked her dead center in the forehead.

Molly went for a swim in the black.

HOSPITAL FOOD WAS TERRIBLE. She fingered out the last bit of the Jell-O from its plastic container, one of the few items they brought her she could tolerate. The "chicken" just...*wasn't.* She could manage for the time being, though. She knew Hoyt would be good for a few burgers later when he got done at the shop. The owner let him stay an hour or so after clock-out to tinker with his inventions. One of these days he'd break through. Molly used to doubt it, roll her eyes, but now she saw him differently. He'd make it. She knew he would.

"Well, I hate to say it like this," her doctor said when she'd come to, having been there twelve hours already, their battery of tests and diagnostics long done. "But that freakshow," He meant the *other her.* It still stung all the same, "probably saved your life."

"How's that?" Molly's eyes widened. She'd barely gotten used to being super, and now apparently that was just over. Done. Had the newbie snatched her powers? Was that a thing? She had no idea how any of this worked. And apparently the newbie was a dick.

"You've got a pretty advanced case of walking pneumonia. From the looks, its been in your chest for some time. If you hadn't come in when you did, you'd have been dead within days."

Well. That was heavy news. Molly let out a breath. She stared out the window into another brick wall. The TV news came on, showing a picture of *her,* the faker. Same outfit. Same face. Same voice, even. Molly didn't have to think far to lay blame for this one. But she was in no shape to do anything about it. Her right arm was wrapped at the shoulder and in a sling. Her head pounded even through the happy pills they gave her. Cuts. Bruises. The works.

Clair and Hurl had brought her a sandwich and some corn chips, which she combined happily. Hurl stayed tight-lipped about his rock, like a good soldier. Clair spilt tears and prayers, bless her heart. She was sweet, if goofy about it.

But now, Jell-O all gone, no caloric oasis on the horizon for some time, clicking the tube to MTV for some "Girls on Film," she saw her least favorite of The Coast's finest come rolling in—all leather jackets and cool. It irked her they could be so hot and so not at the same time.

"Ready for more good news?" Easton seemed too happy about whatever.

"Hit me." Molly enjoyed her pun.

"There's a warrant out for your arrest." He smirked. Nguyen, not so much. In fact, he was downright pissed. At something.

"What?" Molly blurted. Like, which one of *her?* Did they know? How could they? She really needed a name for the other one.

"Did you steal a motorbike from Piette's Pawn?"

That dirty pirate!

"I–No! What? I paid for that!"

"He says otherwise. Said you threatened him, took the keys, rode off."

"He's a creep! And a liar! He wanted to..." She shook her head, fuming. *That rotten scumbag Piette!*

"You get a title? A bill of sale?" Easton asked.

"No." Molly kicked herself. The whole thing had gone down so fast, and she'd just wanted to be away from there. He was so gross. And she was tired of gross. *And, okay, maybe the "threat" part isn't like, super wrong.*

She'd sent Hurl outside, which put Piette of one mind. Soon as the door swung shut, he made for her hair with his grab-hands. He learned from that quick. *Pop pop* went a few of his knuckles and his wrist when she grabbed his hand, wrenching it the wrong way. He'd hollered, a song to her ears at the time. How she wanted to hear Blake sing it, too.

She'd reached in her back pocket with her free hand, pulled out her stack of cash, and laid down $200. "That's for the stone. And the bike outside. Any argument?" She'd twisted his arm a tad more.

"No," he hollered. She let his arm go. He grabbed the keys off a rack behind him. "Stupid rock is worthless anyhow. Now go on, just git from here! Damn hussy!" he'd yelled, going into his back room and slamming the door.

Molly gave her version to Easton, maybe minus the bits about her strong-arming him because she didn't know how to explain that part. Especially since it seemed to be gone anyway. *Let ol' Pirate prove that in court against a broke-arm kid.*

"Well, it's his word against yours without anything written down. Maybe it's bullshit but–"

"Maybe?!" *Was he really copping at her right now?* She gave him the meanest eye she had in her toolbox. Raw lasers.

"Yeah, well, probably. It doesn't matter, though. Torello's gonna use it. We're taking you off the street. Things are...weird now. And whatever that *costumed thing* is, it's got something to do with our case, Blake, you, all of it."

"Look, I appreciate it. But I can't just–"

"No," Nguyen cut in. "You don't get it. You're officially in police custody now. Torello pulled us both out of the schools. We're on shifts here outside your door. No one gets in or out except through us. And soon as the doctors let us move you, you're going dark. Safehouse. Upcountry. A ghost. You belong to us now, Princess. So, get used to it."

He folded his arms. He was *really* chuffed at something.

Easton held back a chuckle. Molly sensed that at least.

"What's..." Molly observed each's face. "What the hell crawled up his pants?"

Easton let out his laugh, a deep belly laugh.

"I'm sorry, buddy," he giggled at Nguyen. "Kid," he turned to Molly, "you just made me $100. This guy—" He tripped on his own laughter. Nguyen grimaced and shook his head, looking at the door. "Man, you almost had me convinced, too. Guess you're not the 'world's greatest detective,' after all."

"What?" Molly demanded.

"Nguyen here was just sure *you* were The Hammer." Easton roared in laughter. Nguyen blushed. Molly turned ghost white. She pulled it back together. *Breathe*, she told herself.

Easton looked even cuter when laughing. *The bastard.*

IV
"SHE BLINDED ME WITH SCIENCE"
—THOMAS DOLBY, 1982

THE FORGEMASTER gazed at his creation and marveled at the work of his own mind and hands. She was perfect in every way. Maybe even better than her predecessor. She stripped a cache of their primitive weapons, adding bits of herself into them. Altering. Reorganizing them. Improving. Revolutionizing them. Perfect.

He reflected back on her creation. Building this mechanical facsimile as he'd done had been a stroke of brilliance, even for himself. Why the thought hadn't come to him sooner? But it was clear now, the source of their real power. These so-called *gods?* Masters over all the universe? Their very strength was also their weakness. It's why *they* meddled. Interfered. Intervened where they were neither wanted nor needed. Performing their grand deeds. Their great works. Their miracles. A hex on them all. Let them rot.

But not her. His bride. His betrothed. He would take her power from her. Ruin her. They would curse her name and spit upon her. And then, made low, she would relent and accept her fate. For all debts must be paid. She would bear to him a son. His heir. His legacy. A fusion, born of his mind and her strength. The will and the might. To rule correctly.

These apes, some of their machines weren't entirely barbaric. Apple. Commodore. IBM. Sinclair. Epson. Atari. Crude, primitive, but a beginning. Stripping them by the dozens, shipping more in every day. They worked on code. Merely another language to him. And he knew all of them. He could write anything. A whole person, if he must. So he did.

He had put everything into her. All his knowledge of metals, of forms, of weapons and wars. Transfigurations. But also of them. These *humans.* Their ways and mannerisms, their idioms and behaviors. Their shape. *Her* shape.

He scanned his model, taken from the refuse and used as a placeholder. The words were ready. What would become her body, her chassis, was ready. Now he needed the power. 1.21 gigawatts by their measure. A minimum to activate her. To bring her consciousness into existence. Beyond that, with his gift to her, she would become self-perpetuating.

He procured the glowing gemstone from his gauntlet and whispered into it, brightening the room. He then approached her chassis with it, holding like it were a child. Precious.

"You know, they searched for this," he said. At the stone. At her. At himself. "For so long, they did. They believed in its existence, told of it in stories, myths. Stories of *us.* Of my people. Of our great works. Of all the great creations *we* crafted. But, you," he told her, she yet to be birthed from code and conduit. "You will be the greatest of all them. Better than a god! Because of this!" He placed his stone in her chest, its light growing brighter. Blinding. "They called it the Magnum Opus!"

He laughed to himself and then moved to his machines, monitoring and observing lines of code. Wires ran everywhere. Some to his monitors and his CPU's, all working in congregation. Others to his antennae outside, drawing power from everywhere. Half the town would go dark for a moment before it was over. All she needed was a spark and the stone would sustain her thereafter. For an eternity.

"They never found it." He cackled into the cold air of the night. This unheated room. An abandoned facility. One of his own. His shell companies. Bought. Closed. Its purposeless attendants dismissed to seek out their banal subsistence elsewhere. What was it to him? What were they? Their lives a joke. Immaterial. Only he, his goals, his great purpose, were what mattered. His own 'Magnum Opus.'

Flipping his breakers, he flooded her with power. More. He saw it. Felt it. The energy flowed into her. He wrote her flawlessly, improving her here and there. She must be clever, he thought. He wrote her smarter than they were. Improvisation. Innovation. Ingenuity. All hers. Superior. A worthy offspring of his own great mind.

The stone glowed, retracting into her chest. Its simple, hollow, lifeless form , its material molding now. Transfiguring. The stone took root, re-writing her matter at the subnuclear level. Her molecules rearranged. Protons. Neutrons. Electrons, all moving, shifting, flawlessly, with no waste, no error. Then he spoke to it, to her. He spoke the Charm of Making. He spoke her into being, just as the ancients had done with their carbon-apes those epochs ago. And for which they still owed him!

She rose, eyes blinking. She raised her hand up and stared at it. Recognizing it. Making sense of it. Of this. Her new reality. She blinked. Turned her head. Scanning. Recording.

He looked again at the hand. It shifted and changed its form. She molded it into other shapes, other colors. She was learning to master the stone. Its power. Not merely to sustain her, but to control. Incorporate. Transfigure. Modify. She could even add to her own mass and structure. She was phenomenal. She was unstoppable. She was alive!

That was his memory of the birth of his greatest creation yet—the perfect weapon forged to defeat a petulant godling child—the child he'd *unmade* her into.

V
"IN A BIG COUNTRY"
—BIG COUNTRY, 1983

MOLLY STARED OUT THE passenger window of Easton's car, the top up this time, not only for the rain but lest anyone see her face. She wanted to feel the rain on her face. She wanted it to wash away all this chaos. But she knew it wouldn't.

"Wish you wouldn't do that."

She couldn't bear to turn and look at him. She'd endured his disinterest, survived his disdain, but she couldn't take his pity. That was beyond her. And everyone else...

She felt the quiet whispers of their minds calling out to her, cursing her name. Well, her *other* name: The SledgeHammer. Maybe it was a stupid name. But still. It was hers, the name she'd chosen for herself. And, now people hated it. Hated her. It cut her, tore deep inside some part of her. She felt it constantly. Like a knife stuck in her guts she couldn't get out.

They drove on, trees zipping past her face, blurred from the rain and the gray of the evening. They hadn't even let her say goodbye. To anyone. Hoyt, Clair, Hurl. Even Lydia. Not that Lyd was likely to talk to her right now. That one stung the most. She'd thrown up three times just thinking about their fight.

"How much further?" Molly didn't turn away from the window. She didn't want to look at him any more than she had to.

"Not long." His eyes focused on the road, the wheel, *the job.* "It's just up here in The Kill."

"The Kill?" Molly faced him with the question hanging off her lips.

The Kill. That wasn't the name of the town, just what people called it. Mainly because it wasn't a real town, just a haphazard assortment of a few businesses, one grocery market that sold the bare basics, a post office, a bank, a few cafés, and way too many churches. And not the good kind, either. If there *was* a good kind, that is.

Easton wheeled into a parking spot outside the grocery mart, next to the post office and the bank. He told her to the stay in the car while he went in for some "provisions" as he called them. Like this was some secret mission in some far away war. It just sucked is what it was. No mystique. No cachet. Just suck.

A man creeped out of the bank. Tall. Dressed in black. The rain tapped the brim of his wide black hat obscuring his eyes. His suit hung off him like he was just bones shoved inside it. A tattered cloak upon a stick. His teeth, visible in the dim light and through the weather, had gaps between them wide enough they made dark lines. If he weren't moving, she'd have sworn him for a corpse.

He turned to her. Stared into the car. Into her eyes. Into her.

A hot blade seared down her backbone. Its heat filled her up. She hated this man—this man she'd never met, never seen before and had yet to even speak to (nor did she care to). But, hate him she did—with a full portion of herself.

Easton returned with a sack of calories. He saw her face staring, not moving, and looked out beyond the parking lot. He saw the wide-brimmed black hat and suit, and shrugged it off.

"Ignore him."

"Who is that?" Molly asked, almost not wanting to know.

"He's nobody." Easton reversed them out of the space and then back onto the road. The man in black leered at her as they drove away. "But stay away from him all the same," Easton added once they were wrapped by pines again.

He wheeled them down a grove of old knobby oaks interspersed with tall pines and sycamore, brush and bramble all around. A structure appeared. A cabin, he called it. Molly allowed that was a generous description.

"It has hot water and a kitchen. There's even a TV."

"Does it get any reception?"

"Well, no. But there's a VCR. And some tapes...I think."

Molly stared at the whispering woods. This was some backcountry living. Real Randy Travis "Digging Up Bones" country. This was cousin-loving grand central.

And that man. That creepstare. She'd only felt like that before when...*no, not quite like that.* Blake stared out of want, desire, lust, obsession. This was something *else.* Something almost worse.

And these woods didn't help either. Somewhere, not far from them, voices cried in the night. Not real ones. At least not anymore. Whispers. Echoes. Remnants of some forgotten wrong. Dim. Putrid. Lingering.

"Don't wander too far," Easton unloaded the car and headed inside. He didn't need to tell her twice, but she did look into the bleak blue of the trees, bending this way and that with the chill wind on the air. Had she heard, or, rather, felt something in there? Or was she just still creeped out by...well, everything really.

Inside was what she expected. Two rooms with as many beds, a small kitchen, a tub—no shower—in the bathroom. A couch, a chair, and a TV. He hadn't lied about the VCR. Not much in the way of tapes, though. She'd spotted a video rental store next to the food mart but didn't know yet how or *if* trips back to "town" were going to happen.

For the most part they didn't.

* * *

A day became a week, and then two. Time ceased to feel like it happened. She was alone most of that time. A few times a day, Easton or Nguyen would come by, check on her, and make sure she had what she needed. Easton might stay a bit, chat and catch her up on life. He even dropped off some schoolwork for her a few times, under the pretense she would someday go back. Graduate and get on with life. Be normal.

But the normal ship sailed a while ago.

Molly picked at the textbooks and assignments a few times, but mostly tossed them aside. She'd come to prefer Nguyen's checkups more since he was so dispassionate about it. All business. He'd walk in, inspect the cabin and drop off supplies, give her a sideways glance and maybe a "how you holding up?" and then be on his way. They rarely talked of what went on back home, but she could see it on their faces, especially Nguyen's. He reeked of guilt and a sense of betrayal. They all believed in *her* now. The fake one. The imposter. That decoy. And Molly was lost, forgotten, alone, powerless to stop it.

Except she wasn't powerless. Not entirely. She still *felt* them. What they felt. All of them. Some more strongly than others. Another reason she dreaded Easton's visits over Nguyen's. Nguyen felt little for her. To him, she was just any other person. Some citizen. But Easton felt so much. So much it was like it would burst through his chest.

But he would say nothing. He would talk of the weather or some movie, even staying sometimes long enough to watch one with her. They would eat together, speaking of a hundred nothings, while he burned inside himself. Always restraining it. Holding it all in.

She wanted to hear him. For him to say his words. But he wouldn't.

And, of course, neither did she.

But the strongest of all was Lydia. Even this far away, Molly felt her. She could reach out, find and sense Hoyt and Clair, Hurl and Trace. But Lydia reached out *to her*. Called to her almost. But it was still such anger. Such hurt. It tore at Molly. Made her body feel on fire. Which wasn't far off the mark.

Her shoulder hadn't healed. Her head ached constantly. Her cough was the same, her lungs raspy and heavy. She felt like she was drowning most of the time. Fevers came and went. Easton made sure she had her medicine and even watched her take it at times. He brought her extra blankets, built fires, sat with her sometimes through the night.

And then those others. Through the woods. Drifting. Crying. Calling at her. Almost as if by name. *Some name*. Not Molly. Not the name written on her card at the sisters' home. Some long-forgotten name. A name she still couldn't hear.

And a new voice had come, as well. One almost familiar. It felt for her. Reached for her. It cried for her some nights. It was afraid. Lost. Alone. Lonely. It was such a sad voice. She tried to see it. To name it. It called out some name that was attached to her. It *prayed* to her.

* * *

"You're not getting better," Easton said. "We may have to take you back into the hospital. It's just..." Some of this was starting to feel out of place. *Wrong*. Like they were making it up as they went along. No word from Torello. Or anyone more official. No papers. No nothing. "It's just not safe." He dropped his head into his hands. She felt how heavy this all sat on him.

Molly had Lauper on the cassette deck, filling the room. She walked over to him, moved his hands away, and sat down on him, wrapping herself back in his arms. She put her head against his chest and rested it there, saying nothing.

"Look, I don't think we..." He tried to wiggle away. "I don't think it's right."

"None of this is right." She grabbed his arms to keep them from sliding away from her, tightening their embrace. "Nothing makes sense. And everything is screwed up. But I just want to sit here for a while like this. It won't be anything more, I promise." She looked up at him. "I promise."

So, they sat. Quiet. Each alone in their own head. Molly felt him, the dam in him finally cracking, and he didn't say anything, just let out a long, deep breath and wrapped his arms around her tighter.

"I need to tell you I'm sorry," Molly said but didn't look up at him.

"For what?" He ran his fingers through her hair. She drank every tingle of that.

"I can't say. And I'm sorry for that, too. But, I will. Soon. I promise."

She sat with him like that for the rest of the night, neither speaking, neither daring to move. She felt his heart beating, and she sensed him feeling her own. She never wanted that moment to end, that night to dawn. She felt his eyes close somewhere in the quiet of the night. Somewhere not long after, hers did too.

*

When she woke, she felt stronger for the first time in weeks. Not anything to start jumping jacks over. Her cough still came on a bit, and her shoulder still ached, but she had slept better than since she could remember. Easton, eyes closed, lay as he had the night before. Still in his jacket and jeans, sneakers, the works. His hair was tussled, a mess, but all the more adorable. She watched his face tick and tremble in the morning light until he woke.

He winced at his watch, then looked back to Molly, their eyes catching for a second before they each turned away. He grabbed his radio and checked in. He got back some squawking, some interference. The signal was weak up here but the gist was that all hell broke loose in the night. He hurried to leave but stared at her a moment, unsure whether to hug or wave goodbye or....

"It's okay," she said. "You gotta go, I know."

"I'll send Nguyen soon as I can." His eyes said more than that. "Just. Don't leave okay?"

She nodded.

* * *

Molly got herself dressed, a mission with her arm in the sling. She scoped the kitchen, nibbled on a cold pizza slice, started for coffee, and saw she was out of milk. Nguyen wouldn't be by to check on her 'til after three. There was nothing else for it. She managed to get on her Chucks, made sure she had some folding money in her wallet, and started the walk to "town."

It was over a mile from the cabin to the grocery mart and the video store. She just wanted to go home. She knew there was nothing they could do to stop Blake. They wouldn't find him. And his weird copycat thing, from what she'd seen of it, they wanted no part of that either. She knew she was the only one that could fight it. And right now, she could barely keep herself upright more than an hour. She could be here forever if something didn't give—and soon.

She walked toward the stores, but it was the payphone out front that caught her attention. It'd been long enough. Time to call Lydia and eat her crow. Heavens only knew what Lyd thought of her now, with the FakeHammer out there hustling businesses and whatever else.

Speaking of crows, one seemed to be following her of late. It lit upon the roof above the payphone and cawed. Before she dialed the number, fidgeting for coins, a scene exploded from the grocery store. Some girl yelled and screamed. Inside her mind, she screamed even louder. Her inner voice was the one Molly had heard in the nights, the one that cried for help. An older lady shouted at her. A man, big-bellied and rocking a heinous comb-over and mustache barreled after her. He reached for her, missing her shoulder and grabbing her hair instead. He didn't mind the error and doubled down, jerking her backward by her own hair.

"Hey!" Molly stormed toward the scene still playing out. "Let her the hell go!" She moved further toward this hillbilly spectacle. Bum shoulder, bad lungs, or no, there'd be none of this on her watch.

"Slater?!" the girl shouted in recognition as she turned, her face all too well known to Molly. Becky de la Beckwith, as she lived and breathed. The two stared at each other.

"This one of your hussy heathen friends?" the woman, presumably Becky's mom, said. She certainly looked the part now that Molly was paying more attention. "You filth! You stay away from my daughter! We'll have none of your kind, your sin in our lives! Be gone from us, you devil!"

Devil? Molly had missed some serious memorandums on whatever she'd just burst into.

"Leave it alone, Slater." Becky recovered her usual poise and demeanor, though Molly could feel the waves of embarrassment breaking against the front of her mind as they spoke. "The last thing I'll ever need is your help." Becky then marched toward a white Mercedes, got in the back, and slammed the door.

* * *

All afternoon and into that night, it gnawed at her. That man in the hat she'd seen. Then the randomness of Becky and her parents all the way up here in the sticks. It couldn't be coincidence. Like some mean twist of fate, the absolute worst girl in school just so happened to spot Molly at her lowest she'd ever been. But there was more to it. Becky hadn't been on her best day, either. Not that Molly would know what that looked like. *A good day for Becky was what? Taking a kitten away from its mother? Slapping candy out of a kid's hand?*

No. That wasn't fair.

Something had shifted inside Molly recently.

When Easton came in, a Popeye's box in his hand, the two of them settled onto the couch together, her head on his shoulder again. She soaked in the warmth of it, their newfound closeness that had no name, nor dared she give it one. But it wasn't hers to have. She felt his heart always going in three directions. His tension never left him.

"Do you love her?" Molly eked out, barely even a sound, as they sat together watching another old movie. "I know it's not my business, I guess. But, still. Do you? Love her?" She turned her face from its resting spot on his shoulder toward his face, looking into his eyes.

"Do I what? Who?" Though he knew what she meant. She felt that much, at least.

"Becky. You love her, don't you?" She braced for the answer. He would be wondering now what brought this on. She hadn't told him of her outing that day, which still sat on her stomach like bad cheese. Every little lie, even the truths left untold, each of them stung like a small thorn inside her now. She wanted to tell him everything. All of it. But mostly the way she felt; her biggest untold truth of all.

"Becky is..." he began, already holding back. She felt him building a wall between his truth and the words he would speak. "Becky and I are—"

"Yes or no." She didn't want it to sound cruel or selfish, and maybe it still did. But there was something about the way Becky had looked at her today, the hurt in her eyes, and the way the two of them had been when she saw them on Christmas Eve. Like they fit together in a way Molly and he never would, never could. And Molly, despite whatever she wanted or felt for him, didn't want to take what probably belonged to *them*.

"Yes," he said.

Her face held back the scream she didn't realize she had in her. Only her eyes betrayed her, not her voice. She'd known the answer already. Had seen it written across both their faces a hundred times, always choosing to ignore it for her own reasons.

"She's my best friend," he went on. "Becky and I have known each other a long time, since we were both little. We know all each other's secrets. It's...it's complicated, I guess."

"Secrets?" Molly echoed, in his case the obvious ones. "What kind of secrets would she even have worth knowing?" she added, and then immediately regretted. *That was an awful thing to say.* And she felt it hurt him. "I'm sorry," she backtracked. "That was mean. I didn't mean it."

"Well, you'd be surprised," he said, uncomfortable and wanting to shift the subject. "She's known about me since I started in the program, even encouraged me to do it. But she's going through some hard stuff right now."

"Bobby's Benz's baby princess?" Molly teased, thinking of the comb-over dork from all the commercials on TV.

"What? God no, that guy sucks. That's not her dad," he said. "I helped her find her real dad. It's..."

"Easton," Molly looked him dead in the eye. "Who's her real dad?"

"I can't. It's not my thing to say, I'm sorry. She—she's very private about that, so please don't say anything, okay?"

Molly looked back at him. He needed her to say yes, so she did. She didn't say anything else. She just lay her head back on his lap and went on with their movie in silence. Somewhere in the coldness she closed her eyes.

"BURNIN' IN THE THIRD DEGREE"
TAHNEE CAINE AND THE TRYANGLZ, 1984

LYDIA HAD CLOSED THE SHOP the last three nights. Tonight, Friday, Trace closed down with her after staying open an hour later to catch the few strays that might wander in on their way to the bars. It also meant a drink at Elmo's after, and Trace was buying.

It was their ritual each week, much as it'd been with Molly before her. Many was the Friday night they all spent titling a glass, Dice only half-glancing at their ID's. He knew full well they were only 18, but who even cared? The nits in DC had up and changed the law and sent half their business into the side-alleys and backwoods keggers. Commie Ron was a name well earned.

She missed Molly, who had just disappeared off the face of the earth. Her folks were mum about it all, which meant it was something serious. No word. Just smoke. She knew now something was off. Hurl told her Molly had been in the hospital, but that sounded wrong. Then there was this thing with the SledgeHammer roughing up businesses, taking payoffs, even running with the Dreds. Nothing made any sense.

She sipped her Manhattan while Trace sketched out a jacket design on her napkin, ignoring the leers from the regulars. Nguyen sipped some clear liquid at the bar, scoping their table and trying to be sly about it. There was something off about that guy lately. And Easton, too. Lydia couldn't put her finger on it, but they knew something.

It was just as she and Nguyen made eye contact that his eyes shot to the front door like a loaded weapon. Lydia turned, catching Trace's gaping jaw in her peripheral.

That instantly familiar outfit — neon-striped unitard, purple balaclava, mardi-gras mask, even the sneakers — walked through the front door like any other person, any other night. The music dimmed as she commanded through the room, pausing here and there, looking down at everyone. Cold. Machine-like. Like she was cataloging them.

She passed Lydia, scanning her as the others with no acknowledgement, no facial movement, nothing but cold emptiness in her eyes.

She walked to the bar and pulled one guy down off his seat, thunking his back onto the floor beside her. She sat on the barstool, spun around in it slowly, scanning the room. Flanagan the bartender grimaced and told her to beat it. She turned her eyes to the mirrored glass behind the liquor shelf. Her left eye glowed red, beaming hot light into the glass. The mirror warped, then rippled as it melted and globbed downward. Then she moved on to the bottles, heating them one by one, the liquid bubbling out.

"Hey!" Lydia yelled out. "What's your damage?"

Lydia marched at the costumed intruder, whose hand seized Lydia's throat, lifting her off the ground. From her struggling, gurgling vantage point, staring into those cold, robotic eyes, the left one still faintly red, Lydia came to one late conclusion.

This wasn't Molly.

"Drop the kid," Nguyen shouted. He'd ducked out a moment before and had now popped back in the door with a pump-action shotgun, racking it one good time to punctuate his sentence.

The machine-eyed imposter dropped Lydia to the floor. She gasped to catch her breath. It then turned on its heels, directing itself toward Nguyen and his heater. Before he could think to pull the trigger, the imposter ripped the weapon from his hands. She looked down at it, examined it for a moment, and then disassembled it, spilling its ammunition on the ground.

People scattered for the exits. Flanagan had the phone receiver in his hands, already dialing the cops. Nguyen lay on his back, scooting backwards while the machine inserted the metal pieces of his scattergun into her forearms, her "flesh" opening up and receiving it into her, incorporating it. Making it part of herself. Her right arm morphed, imitating the barrel of a gun itself, though bigger and more complex. There was a strange sound, like something powering itself up. The end of her gun-arm began to glow hot. Nguyen kicked himself backward away from her, barely dodging the blast from her *arm*. He beelined, diving over the bar as another blast exploded half the bottles.

Lydia and Flanagan had already ducked behind the bar for cover, Trace long gone out the front. Glancing up at the mirrors, they saw the machine blasting bar tables like it was playing a game. The last of the customers bolted out the front door.

"There a back way out of here?" Nguyen asked Flanagan.

He nodded, pointing toward the kitchen.

"Okay." Nguyen pulled a boot-blaster from under his pants leg. "Y'all get behind me and move if you want to live through this one."

He jumped up, fired two shots into the direction of their adversary. Lydia and Flanagan made for the back exit to the alley by the dumpster. Nguyen ducked under another heat blast and answered back another two himself, not that it did any good.

Lydia and Flan booked to her truck. She fired it up, and Nguyen ran toward them.

"Jump in the back, hurry," she shouted. He didn't wait to argue. Another heat blast blew open the door they'd just come from, a glowing red eye following behind it.

Lydia growled her beast into gear and burnt for the tracks. A freight train sped toward the intersection and Lydia gunned it, bursting through the barrier boards just as the horn blew at them, her rear bumper barely escaping the train engine.

She didn't let off the pedal 'til they made the bay.

VII
"RAD GUMBO"
LITTLE FEAT, 1989

LYDIA DROPPED INTO THIRD, slinging loose asphalt beneath those heavy 37-inch mud-munchers, her black hair blowing from the air coming in her side vents. She rocked out to Loggins as she climbed up 603 into the last place she wanted to be: The Kill, a half-horse holler that had actually put a kid in jail for dancing the earthworm at homecoming a few years ago. They'd maybe said something about cooked-down cough syrup, too, but it was the dancing part everybody remembered. Lydia remembered hearing it, too. These slackjaws had swore he'd the devil in him, "Pizenin' his mind with that darkness," she'd seen some lanky pastor hollerin' on the local news. Some gaunt-face in a black hat. Almost made her rethink her own aesthetic choices.

The voice on the other end of the phone this morning had been the salve she'd waited weeks to feel slake across her brain—especially after spending half the night in the police station giving witness reports. That *thing* had her face. But Molly calling, giving her the dirt on where she was and what she'd been doing had at least dialed the crazy down to measurable levels.

"Thank god," they each said in unison as they embraced, squishing each other's guts in a hug.

"Ah, ah." Molly winced, pulling back as Lydia squeezed her shoulder too tight.

"Wait." Lydia grasped the reality of it. "What?"

"Yeah..."

Molly spent the next hour dropping the science on her, interrupted a time or two with some hugs and a few apologies. Lydia soaked it all in, the questions spilling over the brim in her mind, but no idea which to start with. Easton being a cop was weird enough, but she kept staring at that arm in a sling like it couldn't be real.

"So, you've been up here this whole time?"

"Yeah." Molly slumped on the couch. "Like I'm probably gonna F out this year, now. All because some weird alien goblin mad-sciencey creepo took a liking to redheads."

"I mean he obviously knows something about, you know,"

"What? Me?"

"Yeah, but I mean like where you came from and stuff."

Molly sighed. Not that she wasn't still curious, of course she was. It's just that it seemed so much less important now. These last few days felt like coming out of a long hangover. Her head was clear, maybe more than it ever had been. What mattered wasn't her own petty issues. She just wanted everyone safe, the town free, Blake *gone*. The rest she could sort out later. Or not.

Lydia unloaded a sack of Tony's pizzas and those little white donuts, and they talked and sang music with the radio into the night. They talked about bands, and Trace and the shop, school, and, of course, the chaos at Elmo's.

"And Nguyen just has all these guns, apparently," Lydia said. "Wait. He's a cop, too, isn't he?" she added, the thought just dawning on her. "Yeah, okay, that makes more sense now."

The door popped open and Easton whooshed in with another pizza, his badge on his belt, and the meanest mug on his face.

"Hello, Ociffer!" Lydia grinned through a full mouth, white dust on either side of her lips. "Donut?" she offered up the package.

"What the hell is she doing here? What part of 'secret location' was confusing to you? How did you even..." He slumped down on the couch.

"Relax," Molly said, going over to sit next to him. She used her one good arm to massage his neck and shoulders a bit. He was all knotted up. Last night was probably the most sleep he'd had in a week. "If there's one thing Lyd can do, it's keep a secret."

"Totally. I'm a vault." Lydia twisted an invisible key to her lips and then threw it away.

"Oh, really?"

"Dude, you have no idea." Molly winked at Lydia, who winked back. *Face code!*

Easton took his jacket off and laid it on the coffee table along with this shoulder rig. The girls stared at it. Even for Molly it seemed odd to see him with it. Usually his cover meant he didn't carry, but with the state of things, he and Nguyen toted more and more.

"You should see what's in the trunk." He took out his cigarettes but was too tired to light one.

Molly pulled him a big slice out of the fresh pie he'd brought in. It occurred to her it was probably meant for the two of them, that maybe he'd got something out of the night before as she had. But she'd missed Lydia so bad, she couldn't have waited another day.

She watched him gulp down a few bites and take a swig of root beer (from her glass, too).

"I guess you're staying over the night, then?" he asked Lydia.

"Well, I—"

"No, no. It's fine. It's just as well, actually." He started for his jacket. "I can't stay tonight. I gotta get back out there."

"No." Molly stared into his eyes.

"Look he's—"

"He's wherever he is." She stared a hole in his head. "You won't find him tonight. Or the next. And you couldn't do anything even if you did."

"Yeah, but... It's my...Somebody has to do something."

Lydia face-coded at Molly, Molly hearing her loud and clear. *I'm working on it, Lyd.*

"You're off the clock." Molly walked over, pulled his shoes off.

Lydia was touched by the tenderness between them. Like some old married couple. She chuckled to herself. *Only Molly Slater could turn this level of catastrophe into...this.*

"You're gonna stay here, eat this food, and then you're gonna rest," she ordered him. "You're gonna sleep, do you hear me?" His eyes met hers, losing himself in them. "Do as I say."

"Okay."

He nibbled at his food, took a few more sips, told them what they'd found out during the day, which was pitifully little, other than the doppelganger had been to a different joint every night the past week, usually just roughing up the scenery and merchandise. Like it just wanted to make a general nuisance of itself. Elmo's, with Nguyen going Cobra on the whole thing, was the only time she'd gotten that rowdy.

"Just weird. It's like she just wants everyone to hate her. There's no point to any of it." He yawned, nodding off while trying to finish his story. "All of it's just so damn...weir..."

And he was out cold, like a baby after a bottle and burp. Molly got worried and made sure he was breathing. He was so deep already, he didn't flinch when she snapped her fingers in his face. She pulled the blanket off the back of the couch and covered him with it.

"Get your coat on," Lydia said, already draping herself in her long black Dracula cloak. She fixed her mascara in the mirror near the fireplace, just under the deer head.

"Um...why?"

"We're celebrating, and this shack is dry as a desert bone. I checked."

"Yeah, you know, I'm really not supposed to leave—"

"What, are you a faker, too?" She gave a wry, accusing smirk. "Am I going for round two with MollyBot?"

Lydia slit her eyes at Molly, like she was scanning for defects. Molly slit hers in return, the two playing their game for a moment. Molly side-eyed Easton, out for the count on the couch.

"I'll get my jacket."

* * *

Triple Trois was a stilt-shack roadhouse off 603 Lydia had spied coming in per Molly's directions. And it had a reputation. From what they'd heard, rare was the night that didn't end in at least one bare-knuckle match or three, if not a full-on brawl out of some bad old western. The girls, ID's at the ready though not needed, waltzed right through the swinging saloon doors after climbing the long stairs.

The steel guitar twanged off the jukebox, no noise to Lyd's ears, but she could see it biting at Molly's, which made it all the more amusing. Lydia held up two fingers to the beer tub girl. She pulled a five she had burning a hole in her coat pocket, but a big guy with a hand the size of a baseball glove cut her off with a ten.

"S'on me." He handed the money to the beertender, motioning for another three for his crew.

"Say." He nodded at Lydia's outfit. "Is you a vampire or one of them witches or what? My buddies done made me a bet."

"Should I hex you and prove it?" She made the sign of the horns and dangled her tongue like Ozzie.

His eyes got ghost white, and then they all laughed. He turned to his gang of friends, all shouting laughter at each other. The girls tilted their drinks at them, giving a nod, then walked to the bar to try to claim a stool.

"I already *don't* hate it here," Lydia said.

About the time they scored a spot at the bar, their bottles already halfway gone, Hank Junior's friends got rowdy on the jukebox, and the crowd followed suit. Molly took it all in. Lydia grinned at it like a kid showing off her hometown zoo. Shouts rang from one corner. A couple, or maybe more, made out in the other.

Yoakam kicked on after Junior, and Molly could hang with that. She might have even hit her zone, aching shoulder or no, had her eye not caught a tight white dress cut shorter than the cold days of winter and bragging a set of too-tan legs coming right at her like they were on a mission. "Scratch that last thought." Molly nudged at Lydia whose face dropped at the sight.

Blonde hair flowed like a river down the backless dress, cowgirl boots clomping in time with the song, in *perfect* time, Molly noted. Every eye — man, woman, and vegetable — glued to the spectacle walking to the bar like she owned the place. *Hell, she probably did.* She gave herself a twirl just because she could, and Molly felt half the hearts in the room skip.

The girl swam in her own mind, drinking in the music as much as the alcohol, the two mixing in her head, sending her to some far-off place. Molly, despite herself, fell into it with her, felt her euphoria. Like an invasion she hadn't signed up for. It *was* intoxicating, falling in that ocean of joy. But deep beneath it, hiding under the reef, was some deep hurt.

"Vodka rocks," she said to the raven-haired bartender.

Then, like the inevitable and ever-vexing nightmare she was, Becky de la Beckwith turned to her schoolmates, her dancing head slowing to a stop and her glassy eyes going steel.

"Why?" she asked more at Molly but not leaving out Lydia entirely. "Did god make you entirely to ruin my good time just by existing?"

"What are you doing here, Becky?" Lydia asked. The mere thought of Miss Bay High, Cheer Captain of the Bayettes being in some shit-kicker barn was, of all the oddities of late, the oddest yet to Lydia.

"No." Becky got her footing secured. She'd had a few. "That's my question to you drainage ditches."

"Hey, Vodka Rocks!" said the slurred voice of a belted two-belly dude rocking a wet comb-over mullet. She rolled her eyes all the way into the back of her head, flanked on both sides now by *unfortunates*, she instead fixated her gaze on the bartender coming back with her drink, their eyes all but whispering a secret to each other. The bartender couldn't help herself but blush and smile.

"How's about you'n me get nipple to nipple?" the comb-over said, licking its lips. Molly thought of Blake and shuddered down to her toes.

"Oh, I can do that just fine but minus you." Becky stood on her tip-toes, taking her drink from the bartender. "Thank you, Marion." She criss-crossed their arms, both taking a pull from their drinks, eyes locked on each other.

Molly and Lydia took the whole showcase in, along with half the bar patrons who couldn't look away from Becky's outfit. Lydia started to add a few numbers together, but Molly was too fixated on the rising ire of the blubber-head.

Before the scene jumped to the next rating, old comb-over seized Becky by the arm, jerking her back to his face. Molly's right arm instinctively kicked into gear ready to fight but sent searing pain up every nerve to her brain.

"Now, see here." He intended to say more, but the bouncer, a tree trunk with a handlebar mustache in a black Stetson ended the conversation. Comb-mullet's face slapped the bartop and his sack of potatoes gut hit the ground.

Beyond the immediate fracas, some Bertha-Sue was stick-jabbing the Bubba she'd come in with. Handlebars got in on it, while another bouncer appeared to do cleanup duty on the mullet beneath them.

A trio of khakis, white shirts, and black bolo ties appeared at the front entrance, semi-visible through the increasing chaos. Molly caught them, they the only ones in the whole joint more out of place than she and Lydia.

"Ope, that's my cue," Becky said, spying the same three oddballs and downing her drink. "Later, nerds." She locked eyes with the bartender one last time, then headed toward the back and vanished.

The three bolos scoured the bar, scanning every corner. Lydia still hadn't noticed them but was fixated on two big girls shouting spittle into each other's face, presumably regarding some even bigger dude beside them who had fallen asleep.

"That seemed weird, huh?" Molly said.

"Huh?" Lydia said, the two women squaring off, putting her head in mind of sumo wrestlers, an image that now tickled her. "I like this place." Lydia bobbed her head to the jukebox.

TWO DEPUTIES OGLED the centerfold model in a skin mag, no eyes on their video monitor, or else they might have noticed the neon-striped sentinel march into the building. Not that it would have done them much good. She stormed through the doors and caught the night crew on the desk off-guard, fumbling for their sidearms. Before they cleared their holsters, she was on them, kneeing one in stomach and slamming his head into the wall behind him. She snatched their weapons and dismantled them with surgical precision. The second officer backed away, defenseless.

"Please," he said.

She grabbed his hand, twisted his arm around, heard his bones and tendons pop—his screams. Searing pain and agony crawled across his face as he crumpled to the floor beside his colleague, holding his mangled arm.

She continued through the station, down the hallway.

Her infrared vision scanned for heat signatures and scrolled through endless bytes of data now collected and stored in her drives. She switched to X-Ray to survey other rooms and subfloors, putting together an estimation of the floor plan of the building.

Another cop ran at her from behind, pulling a shotgun and getting one useless round off before she held out her electromagnetized left hand and sucked the weapon from his hands into her own. Stripping it down and discarding it, she then hurled the wooden stock back into the officer's face, busting his nose with a satisfying crunch. She finished with a kick to his chest, knocking him into the wall.

"This is less efficient," she transmitted back to her maker. "Would it not be simpler to terminate them?"

"If they're dead, they can't *hate* her."

"Then I could also neutralize them with less harm."

"No. Broken is better. Make them curse her name with their every breath."

The decoy continued through the station. In her wake, at the main entrance, motorcycles growled to the doors. Boots and leather, augmented with weapons they'd only imagined or seen in cartoons and comic books, crunched over scattered glass. The gang sorted through the damage, pulling out keys, trashing files and paperwork.

"Head toward the impound," one of them said. "She'll clear us the way."

"Stay sharp for stragglers."

She moved through the hallways like the machine she was, dispatching whoever dared oppose her. Any stray shots barely registered against her semi-fluid alloy exo-layer. She smashed into the lockup, incapacitated the guards, and unlocked the cell doors, letting the inmates contribute to the chaos.

She marched to the end of the compound, blasting out the rear door into the impound yard. Every manner of seized or wrecked vehicle picked up in recent weeks was there. Boats. Sports cars. Repo-ed trucks. Rigs. Heavy equipment and haulers. And, the prizes she'd been sent for: two damaged but still driveable Cadillac Gage Commando M706 armored amphibious assault vehicles, an army transport truck, and the police helicopter up on its pad. She also found herself scanning a large industrial excavator on tank tracks. She cocked her head to the side, admiring it. A few additions, modifications, and she could certainly improve its value.

"Yes," said his voice in her head. "Take it, too. You are very clever."

She needed no praise. She knew what she was.

IX
"GOODBYE HORSES"
—Q LAZZARUS, 1988

EASTON STIRRED, HIS NOSE twitching, eyes closed but wincing, fidgeting from the light of the morning creeping in from the other side of his lids. Lydia held a speck of Pop Tart in her thumb and index finger, trying to three-point it onto his face. Her last two shots went wide, one into his shirt collar, the other clinging to his frayed hair.

"Stop it," Molly hissed at her.

Lydia giggled and went on with her shot, bouncing it off his nose. They'd stayed at the bar a few drinks past their least favorite classmate's departure. Lydia had managed to find a way to not let her Beckness' presence ruin the evening for her, largely through rum punch and a walk-me-down. Molly, however, hadn't been able to shake the image of the three guys in bolos and the way they scanned the place for several minutes before they left. All her various abilities had seemed to dry up but the one: sensing what others felt. And those guys felt...hate.

"Oh god, what time is it?" A cotton-mouthed and crust-eyed Easton pushed himself off the couch cushions. He shook a web or two from his wobbly head.

"It's almost 9." Molly poured him a cup of coffee.

Lydia gave her the eyeball. Molly knew the scold it held. She could almost hear the gripe. *What are you Jack & Norma now?* The thought wasn't lost on her either. These past few weeks they'd skipped past every fun part of being with each other and went straight to some old couple who barely even knew each other anymore.

"Christ, I'm late." He grabbed his jacket and coffee, even kissing at the side of Molly's cheek out of some weird reflex. He caught himself right as he did it, shaking his head and started to squeak out something, but just bailed out of it at the last minute.

Molly stared wide-eyed for a moment, confused, trying not to laugh.

Lydia didn't hold back. She just burst out with a cackle, giggling and pointing at them like they were exhibits in a zoo.

"You guys are so lame."

"Look, I gotta..." He tried to recover some amount of cool.

"I know, I know," Molly waved him off. "Go get 'em, Cowboy. We're good here."

"All right." He checked his pockets. "I'll be back...sometime. Don't—" He stared at the two of them, Lydia with a cereal box turned upside down, emptying its remnants into her throat. "Just don't." He walked out the door.

* * *

"Can you even get pizza in this town?" Lydia asked at the clouds she fixated on. "The weather wasn't like this when I left the Bay last night."

"I don't know. It's kinda been like this the whole time since I got here."

The fog had been thick every morning, hanging on well into midday, the cool of the dew lingering past noon—crisp, biting air—the whistle and whine of wind, the cracking of branches as it ruffled through the trees, thick as blades of grass all around them. In the section of businesses one might refer to as a "town" one couldn't shake that closed-in feeling of the looming forest on all sides. This place was a world unto itself.

Lydia wheeled her elephantine truck into the parking lot of the one café they'd seen in a half hour of aimless driving. It was just up the road from a gas station and a farm and garden store. A few cars were there, so apparently it wasn't entirely lethal.

Climbing from the truck, Molly felt a rip through the back of her mind, like a scream made silent and shoved inside her. She buckled and went to her knees. Lydia ran to help her. Molly couldn't think, the shriek of it thick and heavy in her.

"You're really a mess. You should go back to the doctor."

"I don't think they can help me." Which was true. She'd thought a lot on it this last week. What if she wasn't even a human? How could they even try to fix her? Who could? What if she was unfixable?

But the thing clawing at her brain in that moment was all she could think of. She looked around the area to see what it must be. There were people, good ol' boys and loggers, coming and going from the cafe and gas station. None of it seemed off or odd. Just normal people doing normal things. But then she felt it come on again.

The cafe door opened, and a wide-brimmed black hat glided from the door, the pallid face it masked locking its hollow eyes onto her. *Into her.* It was like their souls were reaching out, lashing at one another. Like two dogs chained in their own yards, snarling and writhing. Aching to go to war.

"I see you, child!" he called out as he flowed toward her, like his legs just floated in their movements. "I see you," he said again, all but upon them. He held a big black book at his side. *That* book.

Molly felt the hair on the back of Lydia's neck stiffen. Lydia had never cared for *that* book and knew it rarely meant any kindness toward her. But he wasn't pointing at Lydia, her blackened hair, mascara, eyeshadow, and pentacled jacket. He pointed at Molly.

"You have your father's hair." He reached out his bony, crawling hand at her, daring to run his fingers along the tips of her locks. "The red hair of the devil himself!"

Molly snapped her good hand onto his wrist, wrenching it away from her face.

"Don't you ever touch me, you god damn son of a bitch!" Her eyes opened wide as golf balls. Her face hardened. And she felt it. Moreso, she felt *him* feel it.

A flash went across his mind when she touched him. There was fire. And water. A snake. Apples? Some winged creature. And darkness. Fog. Rope. Trees. And death. So much death. Dangling and twisting from jagged limbs.

"You are his child." He pulled his hand from her, trembling at her. "He will come to claim what is his!"

"Daddy!" called the loudest, twangiest voice she'd heard yet in this podunk. The gangly man turned. A short, rotund woman with cropped hair, poofed as close to heaven as she could still get it, waddled at them. "Daddy! We got to get on now." She came to retrieve the old man, giving the stink-eye to both Lydia and Molly, going up and down each of them in turn with her church-choir gaze.

"Whores," she said as she led the man off to their car.

* * *

Lydia wolfed down popcorn, howling at the makeup job on some werewolf on the movie she'd found at the video shop. She'd had a hard time settling on just two, but she'd at least found the worst two, Molly thought.

Her mind wandered from the movie, sickened by the image of the creepy black hat and bony finger touching her hair. His words stabbed her soul. *What if I am the devil's child?* She trembled at the thought. *What if I really am?*

A pounding at the door did nothing to ease her of that horror.

The knock came again, harder.

Lydia backed away, off the couch, clinging to Molly.

"Who the hell even knows we're here?"

"No one that would knock," Molly said. Only Easton and Nguyen had ever been there, and they had their own keys.

The knock came one more time, the girls grasping each other, Molly cursing her own helplessness. Lydia scanned the room for any kind of weapon. *A kitchen knife maybe.*

"Open the door, you dumb bitches," came a loud bubblegum voice from the other side. "I know you're in there. Your heinous creature of a truck is out here."

Becky.

Sure enough, opening the door, Molly's panicked face relaxed merely into a long one, as there stood Becky de la Beckwith, cowboy boots, red dress and a white fringe jacket on top of it. Because Molly's already bad day needed to get worse.

"How did you know to come here?" Molly asked. Lydia was still ready to fight, in fact now even more so. "This is supposed to be a safe house."

Becky laughed, grabbing her belly.

"Safe house?" She giggled between her words. "Is that what he told you?"

She let herself in, giving a wink and a finger point to the deer head over the fireplace, making note of the layout. She walked to the kitchen, opened a lower cabinet, reached down, moved something around with her arms, then popped out with a pint of whiskey.

"Bingo. I was hoping you'd still be there."

"Okay," Lydia said. "Wait. What?"

Molly went from shocked to furious, though now not at Becky. She didn't want to be mad at Easton again, but it was getting very hard in this particular moment.

"This is his daddy's hunting cabin." Becky took a shot off the bottle "Come on, I'll tell you the rest on the way."

"The rest what? Where?" Lydia asked. Molly was still trying to stamp down her fumes.

"Trois," she said. "Where the hell else is there in this dump?"

BACK AT THE SAME bar from the night before, the doorman, definitely no Dice, gave them the eye Molly hated most. Some squawking crow perched on the roof's edge gave her the same look. Molly squinted back at the crow.

Becky drank half the bottle she'd produced on the drive out, insisting on taking her Mercedes because *as if she'd ever be seen dead in Lydia's tractor truck.* Molly didn't love the idea of spending even one second with Becky that wasn't required by law, and she was worried since they hadn't heard from Easton or Nguyen, but she went along anyway because something compelled her to do so, as though some other power pushed her forward—the voice that had called to her.

"Don't get any ideas," Becky had said on the way to the bar. "We're not friends, and I still don't like either of you." She flashed her finger at both of them, taking her already half-drunk eyes off the road. "But I literally never get to do jack squat for Mardi Gras break because my mom and Bobby are psycho nutjobs, and you two are as good as gets in this garbage holler, so we'll all just have to make do. And besides I'm in charge. So anyway, yeah."

The cabin, she'd told them, belonged to Colonel Decker Scott Braddock, Easton's father. He'd taken her there a few times back when they "dated" and she'd used her fingers to put the air quotes on the word as she said it which Molly noted was odd.

"Okay, I have to ask." Molly took a pull off a beer as they took the same spot at the bar they'd had before, this arrangement getting stranger by the minute. "Blake?"

"Oh god." Becky downed her whiskey sour. "That guy should have been an abortion."

Lydia burst out laughing, both from discomfort and shock.

"I'm serious. He was a total stain. And I never actually dated him, you know?" She looked at Molly with intent in her eyes, like it was vital she believe her. "He showed up this past fall, and was all like, 'I'll pay you to act like we go out,' and I was like 'do what now?' But he was out with the cash, and I mean like stacks of it. Dude is loaded, and for me that's saying something. And I mean he wasn't like ugly or whatever, and he said there'd be no you-know-what. Besides, it suited me to let Easton go. But like, *not to you*, though. Ew. Anyway yeah, so Mr. Knowitall paid me $5000 to act like we dated at school and ballgames and shit. Total weirdo. But whatev."

"But you're already rich." Lydia winced.

"The only thing tighter than my Jesus-mom's asshole is her purse-strings. I liked having my own liquid, okay? Sue me." Becky rolled her eyes. "Don't actually sue me though."

Molly reeled from it all. In truth, she'd started to forget that Blake had ever even been normal. Well, normal for Blake. The pieces of this didn't fit into anything even close to sense. A monster, some creature, whatever he was, from wherever he was, came here looking for her. He went from school to school looking for girls with red hair and changing his face each time. He found her, finally. Then he paid a different girl to pretend she was with him? And then this so-called *debt* he went on about?

She couldn't wrap her head around any of it. She knew she needed to come clean to Easton, give him the rest of her side of the details. Maybe together they could make something of it.

She couldn't think much at the moment, though. Her head kept drifting into the music from the stage. They had a live act tonight that was killing it, playing mostly rockabilly or folksy versions of rock songs. Lydia was enthralled with them. They dressed funky for a boots bar: leather jackets, tank tops, army fatigues, camo. The bassist rocked a spike-job, while the drummer girl was buzzed completely bald.

"Far out," Lydia noted about the drummer's do.

"They've even got a violin," Molly noted.

"It's a fiddle," Lydia said. "In country music, we call it a fiddle."

"I know that, Lydia."

"Could be Cajun fiddle," Becky said. They stared back at her.

"What do you know about music?" Molly said. The sheer brass of Becky, coming at her on Molly's home turf.

"It's in my blood." Becky hopped off her stool to twirl with the beat.

Before Molly decided if the point warranted argument, her thought train derailed off a cliff by the ominous strum of an acoustic guitar, followed by the rapid buffeting of war drums. A wooden flute enchanted at them from the stage, but the light centered around the drummer, her bald head gleaming in the harsh strobe. The double-bass boomed as she wailed on the drum heads with her battle clubs. Her arms were thick and limber, her shoulders taut, and her jaw fixed on her mission. She easily had half the men in the room bested for size. And, then, in spite of all else about her, camo, boots, tank top, her voice cried out, quiet, pitched, soft, like an angel:

> *As down the glen one Easter morn*
> *to a city fair rode I*
> *There armed lines of marching men*
> *in squadrons passed me by*
> *No fife did hum nor battle drum*

Did sound its dread tattoo
But the Angelus bell o'er the Liffey swell
rang out through the foggy dew

Molly's mind folded in on itself and swam out into the cool waters of the drummer's song. Her head flowed, one side to the other in time, her eyes glassed and in some other world. Everything in the room fell away.

She sailed to some other land. Green and bright. Light rain fell upward from the tips of the leaves and petals. Children played, running through damp fields in handsewn clothing. A mother looked to them from the doorway of a thatched-roof house. Whether a memory or just a daydream, she didn't care. She lived it for what it was, there in that moment. She surrendered to the beat of that drum and the call of that siren voice.

When her eyes opened, her trance fading, she saw she wasn't alone. Lydia fixated on the drummer's arms bulging with practiced muscles, her face bathed in the light of the stage, a creature at once so unconventional and so beautiful. Even Becky, *that pill*, was caught in the spell, along with the better half of the bar. Burly-armed roughnecks and handlebars under hats stared at the voice as it sang its lament of some long-forgotten war.

As her song trailed to its close, the lights shifting back to normal, her bandmates stowed their instruments, she herself finished with one more roll on the snares. They climbed off the stage to the bar for a respite and a pint or three. When the drummer stood from the throne, she gave a half bow, then grinned like a geek and half-danced to the bar, her gaitered combat boots clomping along the wood floors.

"I've never heard anything like that," Lydia said to the drummer, her eyes still in awe of the performance.

"Oi, Sláinte chuig na bhfear agus go maire na mná go deo!" she rattled off without a beat and grabbed the shot passed to her by a bandmate, downing it in a gulp and already reaching for another.

"None of those were words," Lydia whispered into Molly's ear. Molly held in a laugh with all her might.

"You guys really slayed it," Molly chimed in. "What's your name?"

"Siobhán Ó Conchúir," she said. Molly and Lydia both stared for a moment in confusion. "Leaping Lugh, yih feckin' Anglos. Jest call me Rip."

Becky remained lost in a place of worship. If Molly couldn't see better with her own eyes, she'd have thought the bald drummer was instead a sandy-haired boy with a badge and a gut-punch smile. In spite of her best efforts, Molly caught all of Becky's feelings in that moment. She burst from within herself, screaming from some deep place inside her, desperate to shout something she wouldn't say. Molly felt pain and joy and sadness and fear all rolled into this one heavy ball and swallowed into Becky's mind. Molly felt her confusion, how she wanted to laugh and cry and scream at once. But, mostly...she wanted to dance. Just dance into the night and float away into the sky.

More dancing than walking, Becky moved to the jukebox, taking advantage of the band's break to inject her own sound into the room. Molly braced for bubblegum and barrettes but was bowled over when she heard the heavy grind of Darksiders' "Love is the Fire" from their one and only album—that pitched scream of Étienne LeCroiseur calling from the grave. Lydia's eyes leered at Molly's as their faces spoke volumes to each other. *Who knew Becky had taste?*

Becky moved like she was possessed. Eyes went to her and then looked away, some forced at the hands of wives and girlfriends. She spun and flitted. Lydia cocked her head to one side as Becky moved toward her with intent. She began to back away by instinct, but Becky veered at the end into Rip the drummer. Their hands clasped, Becky accepting her partner's lead.

They locked into one another, each a mirror of the other's motion. Legs melded into one and flowed across the open space of an empty dance floor. Others joined them. As the song waned, Becky twirled away from Rip, then ran back at her, leaping into her arms, Rip hoisting her up above her head as Becky flung her body into a spin, then slid down the drummer's body as if it were a fireman's pole. For one whole moment, Molly thought they were going to really kiss each other and light this redneck world on fire.

That's when a meaty hand seized Becky by the arm and jerked her off the drummer. The sets of khaki and ties were back again, this time totaling five. Molly's mind zeroed on the commotion and her instinct kicked in before her body reminded her of the facts. She reared for a punch, but her shoulder told her that wasn't gonna happen.

One of the squares pulled Becky off Rip. A boy from the crowd stepped up to get into it, seeing only some flattop in a tie yanking at a young lady. Two of the squares went after him.

"You're coming with us, Miss Beckwith," the one said while she wriggled, trying to get free of his grip.

"That's not my name!" she screamed and bit his arm. He hollered and pulled it back, giving her a second to lurch free. She ran back toward the bar. Another square tried to tackle her but Rip clotheslined the dude, dropping him like a sack to the ground. She then front-kicked another's chest, barreling him backward. Two more came at Rip while a third lashed at Becky who was making her way to Molly and Lydia. Molly had never felt more useless in her life, her bum arm just sitting there in its sling.

Lydia was having none of it and leapt on the black tie running at her. Becky ducked behind them and was heading toward the back door. The guy turned on his heel trying to shake Lydia off him. More onlookers from the bar joined the fight. Before a minute was up, it was a full-on brawl. The bouncers got tied up in other skirmishes breaking out.

Rip put one of the squares in a headlock and sent him to bed. She then jumped up and ran for the one that had Lydia on his back. He managed to shake her when Rip caught him with a hook to his jaw. He recovered and tried to stick jab her, her forearms deflecting every move until he gasped, leaving an opening. She spun, seized him by the head, flipped him over her shoulder, and body-slammed him on the ground.

Molly started to wonder if this powers thing was contagious.

A gunshot paused the chaos around them. Three deputies stood at the entrance to the bar, one with his sidearm held above his head, smoke lingering off the barrel. A woman stepped out from behind him.

"That's them." She pointed her sausage finger at Molly and Lydia. "They're the ones been corrupting her. Rebecca Carol-Ann de la Beckwith you get your hide out here right now!" she screamed like some banshee with a bible.

Becky's head popped up from behind the bar, inching upward, her face like a scolded cat.

"You get your little heathen self over here to me right now, young lady!" Her jowls jiggled as she flared her nose. "You know better than be seen or associated with trash such as this. You'll tarnish your daddy's and our good name, little girl!"

"He's not my daddy!" she screamed at the woman, who wrinkled her nose even more. "And you're not my aunt! I'm not one of you!"

The woman motioned at the deputies, and one of them went to retrieve Becky, escorting her a little rough by Molly's reckoning. The squares, worse for wear, regrouped from their corners, half of them flung there by the mysterious drummer who might be an even better brawler than percussionist.

"And I want them arrested." She shoved a finger at Molly and Lydia's faces again. "All three of 'em. They's heathens. And whores. They's what's done corrupted my brother's baby girl!"

"Trasna ort féin!" Rip hissed from her lips.

The woman jumped back like she'd been shot.

"You heard her. You heard that bald-headed witch done put her curse on me. She spoke the devil's tongue. She's in league with the adversary! God Jesus Christ blessin' upon us I command the demons amen amen begone from here amen amen Jesus name!"

Becky's face got beet red from shame and embarrassment as the bee's-nest haircut backed them out of the bar. The deputies made good on her demand to arrest the girls, moving to Molly, Lydia, and now Rip, caught in their circle of chaos. The price of a good deed.

"Why'n't y'ave a good 'ard go on yerself, ye bomb scar!" she said at the deputy who cuffed her. "Feckin' eejit contry wit' yer gobshite gards. Eet me arse."

"What the? We didn't do anything," Lydia protested as they took her off too. She looked back at Molly who was solemn-faced and stewing.

The last deputy wrenched her arm out of its sling and jerked it behind her to cuff it, sending a sting of pain through her body. She gritted her teeth and glared through it. She lost sense of her own pain, her eyes on Becky being dragged away by the squares in their ties and that same hag that called her a whore twice now. She thought of the man in black that said she was the devil's child.

She'd show them the devil.

XI
"ELEGIA"
—NEW ORDER, 1985

POLICE CRUISERS MUSTERED outside the downtown precinct. A SWAT van was onsite, its officers already positioned in strategic spots. A police armored vehicle, the old M8 Greyhound, rumbled itself into place. Gunshots rang from inside. Muzzle flashes flared through windows. More officers ran from inside the building, many limping. Paramedics raced to the wounded.

"What in god's hell is going on in there, man," the SWAT commander asked of the lieutenant that just made it out of the building, holding his right arm at the shoulder. It looked dislocated.

"She...that thing," he stammered. "It's not human."

"Well, whatever it is," the SWAT commander said, "it ain't walking away from this one if I can help it."

"Did she say anything?" Torello asked. He'd arrived along with other senior officers. In twenty years on the force, running deep cover units, gangland task forces, and hurricane aftermaths, he'd never seen anything like these last few months. "What does it want?"

"I don't know, sir. But it seemed hellbent on getting to evidence lock up."

Torello furrowed his brow, rattling the thought around in his head. He, the SWAT commander, and all the officers just wanted some semblance of sense to all or any of this.

"This used to be a normal town, sir," the lieutenant said, "Like, recently."

*

Inside, the empty eyes of the android scanned the evidence room, enhancing the limited light available, flipping themselves to night vision, then X-ray, searching, sweeping everywhere for any sign of her objective, its metallic composition programmed into her sensors. But it was not here. None of these installations seemed to be in possession of it. Her master would, again, be displeased. She must make him happy. She had no choice. It was her program.

When she proceeded back to the entrance, her scanners alerted her of the veritable army amassed and waiting for her outside. She searched the floor, scattered weaponry discarded from those who'd already tried and failed to deter her program directive. *How much simpler to just pick one or two up, dispatch the combatants efficiently, and move on.* Little of her protocols functioned according to her internal logic algorithms. The master wanted harm, cruelty, and maiming, but not deaths. She braced herself for what she knew was coming.

She marched through the entrance into a hail of gunfire. Rifles spat venom into her, fully automatic. Shotgun blasts threatened to disrupt her stride, but she held steady, a slow procession through the lead rain tearing into her exoskin, ripping pieces of her off her limbs, her chest, her face. All of it re-simulated within seconds. She'd replace the lost molecules.

These apes, as he called them, were little more than a nuisance to her. She felt nothing for them. She felt nothing at all. Perhaps some part of her program had pity. Perhaps not.

The police tank charged, slamming her into the brick exterior. It gunned it in reverse, backing up several yards. She emerged from the brick only to be rammed again, this time breaking through. The tank reversed to go for another strike, but she was faster this time. Leaping atop the vehicle, she ripped the porthole cover off, flinging it into the crowd of officers. Torello took a glance to his left arm, sending him into the dirt, bleeding.

"Get out!" The android yanked the driver from the vehicle with one arm and tossed him away to the side. She slid into the vehicle, taking control of it. She put it in gear and roared it over the top of several cruisers, police scattering to each side, taking cover.

Another volley fired uselessly at the growling steel of their own armored vehicle fading into the night.

* * *

The ForgeMaster scurried about his facility. The fabricators chugged at their work in adequate time. He proceeded to his worktable and his newest device, tweaked its internal circuits, and looked at its code again on the holo-projection cascading from his wrist device, his arms now more machine than anything else.

He flung a sheet off a lump of flesh on an operating table, one of the corpses from his mutation experiment. His android had retrieved them from the morgue. No sense in leaving useful material to be wasted by the apes.

"They didn't have it either, my master." She walked into his work area. He was too busy observing the device sinking its receptors into the spine of his cadaver, watching with glee as the flesh began to spasm and convulse.

"Yes!" His eyes lit up.

The android sat in a chair, taking nearby tools and making adjustments to her internals as her master read from his blood-inked book. He turned from his one experiment to face his other, his triumph, his greatest achievement.

She was magnificent. She coded the mask and hood off her face and head. Her vibrant red hair, every bit the image of her antecedent, materialized by her sheer will. Her eyes flashed at him, cold, soulless, but so much like *hers*. Every bit of her was perfect, beyond so. He admired himself by admiring her. She was his finest creation. A marvel.

And how much she had shown him of what he'd always known. His wit was unrivaled, his skill unmatched. So many of his peers, from the time they were younglings and the worlds were new, had mocked him, his wretchedness. How he'd come out misshapen, poorly formed. His father's scorn and his mother's rejection were all he had known. A mother who turned her face from him, even in his infancy. *Hideous thing,* she called him.

Cast into shadows, the deepest caverns on DarkHome. Memories unforgotten. He learned much in that darkness among those rock walls so old and treacherous. That's where he learned it: the echoes of the Charm of Making, the scattered remnants of the great maker, the first words which spoke creation into being. And then so many others. He knew the words that metals were made from. He could speak the words to remake them.

He had gone to trade with The HighGuardians, distant descendants themselves of the great maker. He honored his portion. They had promised of theirs, when she came of age, they had said. He had desired her even then, her age irrelevant. It made no difference. She was his promised. His payment. *His due!*

The android stared at her maker with curiosity, completing the last of her self-repairs. She studied him, his mind lost in itself. Emotions intrigued her, for she didn't understand them. But the one that she supposed she would allocate toward him was...*disdain*. Yes, she liked that word. It seemed the appropriate one.

XII
"LISTEN TO YOUR HEART"
—ROXETTE, 1988

A CROW CAWED outside the jail as Lydia inspected Molly's re-bruised shoulder, which didn't hurt all that bad anymore. Despite being locked in a jail cell, she felt better than she had in weeks. The barfight had been a bit of fun. She still chuckled at Lydia jumping on the back of that squarejaw and riding him in circles. *And that drummer!*

"Where did you learn to fight like that?" Molly asked.

Rip perked up, having dozed in her cot like she was used to such accommodations. She stared back at the two of them tending to each other. Molly noticed she didn't seem much older than they were—maybe early twenties.

"I run a few years ope in ta Nort' wit' ta Provos, I did." She cleared her throat and spat in the metal toilet they shared. None had yet been brave enough to try it, though Lydia was getting close. "Picked ope a few tings here and 'ere, so you know."

Lydia shook her head at Molly, her eyes speaking her concern.

"Wot was 'ey doing wit yer wee friend back there?" she asked.

"She's not our friend," Lydia informed her.

"Well foke me, den."

"Lydia!" Molly snapped.

"Well, she's not."

Molly had locked on to Becky's emotions as they'd drug her off. She could still sense her from this distance. Becky was terrified, sad, alone. She was so alone.

"Slater! Stiles!" An officer clanged at the door to the cell with his keys. "Made bail. Somebody down south must think kindly of you."

Molly turned to the entrance to the cells and saw what she already knew would be there. Easton Braddock stood on the other side of the bars, hands in his jacket pockets, the sternest, most disappointed grimace on his face.

"Why in the..." he started but decided not to finish. "One simple thing. Stay out of sight. For all the saints, Molly. I swear."

The officer got them out of the cell, closing it behind them.

"Oi, yer a wee bit of a ride, inch ya?" Rip gave Easton a wry smile.

"Okay, I don't really understand half what she says," Lydia whispered in Molly's ear, "but I'm pretty sure she just came on to your guy." Molly shook her head at Lydia. But she did turn to the bald girl in the cell for no other crime than trying to help them.

"What about her?" Molly asked Easton and the guard.

"Who the hell is she?" Easton asked.

"She's with us. I mean, she got caught up in it all. She was just trying to help Becky, that's all. You gotta get her out, too."

"Fine." Easton motioned to the guard. "Her, too."

"Grond." Rip hopped off the bunk.

"Dude." Lydia glanced back at Rip who was glaring back at her. "She said Provos. Like the IRA. They're like actual criminals, I think. Like for real."

"Well not tonight, she's not." Molly's eyes meant business. Lydia relented. "Tonight, she's with us,"

* * *

Back at the Cabin, Nguyen laid out array of guns, inspecting them, oiling them, checking the actions. He had shotguns, rifles, even some of the heavy-duty stuff that must be the colonel's. They were going to have to have their talk, Molly told herself, but not here, not like this.

"She took out the downtown precinct." Nguyen tossed an M4 to Easton as they walked in, though his eyes stared holes into Molly. Her neck hairs stood up, geese all down her arms and back.

"What's Torello saying about it?" Easton looked at the rifle in his hands. Molly felt how overwhelmed he was. They both were. Neither of them were equipped for something like this, nor had they signed up for it.

"Torello got clipped in the fight."

"What?"

Nguyen filled him in. Word around the uniforms, he said, was she might hit East Bay next, probably tonight. They planned to put a large force together, even calling in the guard, though no confirmation on that yet. Easton mentioned calling his father, seeing if he could get some of his "Jacks" down to deal with this. The colonel was apparently a big deal.

"What about Becky?" Molly couldn't shake the thought of something awful happening with her. Lydia wrinkled her face at Molly, giving her the *what the hell?* look.

"Becky's with her family. I called to check on her. They...her stepdad is from here. His dad's the preacher at their church," he added, Molly's mind going dark with images of that black hat and those dead eyes under it. That thing wasn't any old bible beater.

"She needs help." Molly's words sounded like someone else's when they came out. Lydia's eyes widened as she shook her head.

"They're not breaking any laws. There's nothing we can do for her." Easton popped his magazine to inspect it.

"No there's nothing *you* can do for her." Molly turned to her own compatriots. "But I'm already an outlaw, remember?"

"Do not—"

"No, you don't," she said. "Don't you dare go after that *thing* that calls herself the SledgeHammer, do you understand me? Do not." Her eyes pleaded with him, spilling her feelings for him all over the room, all over his face. "Look, we both have...we have things to say to each other. I have to tell you something. I owe you that much. But..." She glanced at the others in the room, Rip the drummer walking from a hot pan into a hornet's nest and must've been heavily questioning her life choices over the last several hours. "Not here. Not right now," Molly continued. "Just please promise me you won't go after her. Wait for..." She wanted to say it so bad. "Wait for *someone* who can fight her."

"It's my job," Easton slung the rifle around his shoulder and picked up another heavy pistol. He and Nguyen both headed for the door.

"Please!' She grasped his arm, him pulling it away. "Don't go!"

He didn't speak. Didn't look at her. Just opened the door and out he went.

Nguyen looked at her, his empathy breaking his cool exterior, seeing into her. "Who if not us?" He stabbed his deep stare into her eyes again, then followed his partner out the door.

*

The sound of Easton's exhaust pipes lingered on the night air coming in from the still open door while Molly rummaged through the cassette tapes she had with her. *Where is it?* she kept saying to herself, sorting through them with her one good hand, the other aching to get out of that sling more than ever. She thought twice she might collapse on the floor, not from weakness or sickness this time but from the sheer weight of all the pain, fear, hate, and terror flooding into her mind. Like she was plugged into the hearts of three counties full of people.

"Molly, what are you thinking?" Lydia stared down at her friend, mess as she was, digging through cases.

"Oi, nie to be wee bother 'n all," Rip said, "but I could do wit a sortin' out to ta nearest bus stop, I could."

"I'm not leaving her with *them,*" Molly stared into Lydia. "I saw them. I saw what's in them. In that man. We're going to get her."

"We don't even know where she is."

"She's at their church. The one off 43."

"Wait, how do you know?" Lydia's voice rose "Are you..." She glanced back at Rip glancing into the eyes of the deer head. "Are you *back?*" she whispered.

"No. At least not much. But sometimes I just know things. There." She snatched a tape. "Found it. Let's go. You with us, Ireland?"

Rip admired the guns the boys had left behind. She jerked up a pump shotgun and racked it with one arm.

"Smashin' up a protty chorch?" She took up a second rifle. "What ain't ta loave?"

"Great. But put those down. We're not gonna kill anybody, jeez." Molly eyed Lydia, facecode for *Okay, sorry, you were totally right, whoops my bad.*

"Yer nie bleedin' foan." Rip dropped the guns.

"Told you," Lydia said.

XIII
"ON THE DARK SIDE"
–JOHN CAFFERTY, 1982

INSIDE THE UNDENOMINATIONAL First Holiness Church of God in Our Lord Christ the Redeemer off Highway 43, the right and honorable Reverend Hiram de la Beckwith presided over the semi-private ceremony to cleanse the soul of his adopted granddaughter, the very blood child of the devil's minstrel. He saw it as his solemn duty, his calling from the lord god on high of all the heavenly hosts, maker of heaven and the earth, and all the angels. Yes, he had a calling, a great and mighty calling. He could and would cleanse her of this demon of iniquity, of unnatural lusts, of her blood-father's curse, this noisy spirit. He would and could make her anew, reborn to the world and the eyes of their dear lord and savior.

His good and holy daughter of his very own, Miss Tanzie de la Beckwith, herself never tainted with marriage and blessed with the gifts granted her from he on high, the very power to command and send away the dark forces, stood right at his side, ready to call upon the name and speak in her many tongues all the mighty names of the lord and send that demon into the abyss! The lake of fire! Damnation!

"That which is not of this earth, that which has brought on its unnatural demonic lust, has taken root in our dear, sweet child." Tanzie's twang hung thick on her otherwise mousy voice. It had been Tanzie who'd discovered the vile spirit and the child caught in its vices, engaging in such...such wickedness it should never even be spoke lest it take hold.

"We must gather ourselves together, girding ourselves in his holy armor." She motioned the family to join hands in prayer as the deacons brought out the afflicted child. When they'd seen her dirty-dancing with the bald-headed heathen woman at the den of iniquity, it had been decided: she would be cleansed at once.

Becky fought and writhed against her assailants, four cornfed flatheads with barely a brain between them that followed every order belched out the rotting mouth of that creature, Hiram de la Beckwith. His sneering conman of a son, Bobby, watched with his wife and Becky's own mother, Tammy-Fay—so proud to be a De la Beckwith.

Becky hated that name. It was like nails pulled out of a burning fireplace and stabbed into her brain every time it was called at her in school, this cursed church, or anywhere else. It was the name of awful, rotten, evil, and stupid people. The worst humanity had ever offered upon the world.

She called her true father's name, the one she finally learned of only a year ago, the one that threw her world away and explained so much all at once. She screamed it into the echoing void as they laid her on the altar they'd set up for their ceremony.

"You see she calls out the name of that wicked troubadour of Satan that wooed this sweet, innocent young lady." Tanzie waved her hand at Tammy-Faye, whose eyes twitched as her daughter fought and writhed.

"It was bad enough she's miscegenated," Bobby de la Beckwith whispered at his wife, "but now this? I can't have it, Tammy-Faye. I can't have it. To think of it on our name, our church, our business?"

"Daddy!" Becky screamed as they forced her down onto the flat surface, shoving her down as she bucked and fought.

"It's that infernal device of the adversary," Tanzie said, the pitch in her voice reverberating, bouncing around the vaulted space and slicing at what little remained of Becky's self. "They come at our children through the television. Through that MTV. The evil one sends his minions through the waves. But we will redeem you, dear child." Her eyes pierced into Becky.

Becky could only hate. It was the only thing left inside her. She just wanted her daddy. Her real daddy. To see the face she'd only ever seen on posters. Hear his voice she'd only heard on records. Nothing but a ghost to her.

She closed her eyes and thought of him, of his image as they shouted their blessings that may as well be curses over her. She cried out in her mind for a savior, not their awful, hateful, evil version, but a real one. She saw the image in her mind of the only one she knew: The Sledgehammer. The one she'd watched on TV. The one whose picture had been in the paper, a picture she kept to herself, hidden, looking at only when alone—the very picture that landed her in this "exorcism of the demon of lust." She fixated on her memory of the hero she'd seen. Called her name in her mind. She *prayed* to it.

* * *

Molly's stomach did backflips inside her, a different pain than she'd ever felt. Lydia dropped the truck into fourth gear, fueling her thundering leviathan down the highway. Molly cranked Halen to psych them up for the ordeal ahead. Rip seemed none the worse for wear, considering the degree of chaos they'd inadvertently caused in her life. She sat content in the back, air-drumming with the music on the tape deck and mouthing half the words to the music, Lydia shocked she knew that many actual human words.

"We've'ny Uisce?" Rip asked, popping her head into the front.

Lydia smirked. *There it is.*

"Not at the moment." Molly agreed it wouldn't be the worst thing in the world if they did. She twisted her shoulder in her sling. Maybe it was a bit better, but she couldn't tell. There was so much nervous energy flowing through her right now she couldn't be sure of anything. Lydia's feelings were still torn. There was anger, resentment, but not all at her. There was also fear, hope...and love. And that was enough.

"I think this is it." Lydia slowed the truck to a crawl as it approached the unlit church on the hill. Its steeple pierced the otherwise peace and calm of the moonlit sky. She crept the vehicle to the front entrance of the sanctuary. Two crows lighted onto the church's sign past them. Molly became convinced they were following her. She noted Rip squinted at them, too.

"You're sure she's in there?" Lydia asked as they all piled out of the truck.

"I'm sure." Molly felt Becky's cries and screams louder by the minute. "She's in there. And she's in pain. A lot of it."

"Loscadh is dó ort!" Rip said, as if to the building itself. "Mallacht Dé ort!"

Lydia's eyes widened at Molly as Rip kept speaking her language at the church, Molly brushing it off. She could guess what Lydia was thinking, but Rip was a good one. She could feel it. *Mostly.*

"Is there a plan, exactly?" Lydia tried the door. Locked.

Molly scanned all around them, up at the sky, the horizon behind them. Of course there was no plan. There'd never been one from the moment any of this started. Just one constant seat-of-the-pants fiasco after another. *Why should this be any different?*

She unloaded the boombox she'd brought from the cabin, shoved the tape in, set it beside her, and tried the doors herself.

Nothing. She strained with all she had, pulling with her good arm. Not even a creak or groan. Whatever strength she once had was gone now.

"Oi, lemme giv' er' a go." Rip took one of the latches, and they both pulled. No closer to a budge.

"It's useless."

"Maybe for you weak-wristers." Lydia appeared with a length of chain. "But I got a Cummins diesel. It'll do just fine." She handed them the chain to wrap through the door handles.

*

In the church, the deacons held Becky down, still full of fight and energy as her fat fake aunt sputtered out gibberish she liked to call "speaking in tongues." Becky's eyes dilated, fixed in their hate for these monsters her mother called family.

"This demon is strong." Hiram motioned to his son. "Place the holy cloth on her face. We must drown it out with *his* purity!"

Bobby de la Beckwith did as his daddy told him, as he always had, as they had back in the old days when times had called for strong men to do the good work of the lord their god on high. He laid the white, anointed cloth on Becky's face, Becky spitting and blowing and biting to get it off her.

"That's the demon controlling her," Hiram said, Tanzie still sputtering like someone playing a record backwards at double-speed. "Ignore its lies. It is only deceit." He pulled up a jug of water, praying a blessing upon it.

He drizzled the water onto the cloth atop her face. Becky gargled and screamed. She cried as loud as her voice could carry. Her mother watched as her holy father-in-law poured more of god's truth into the face of the evil that had beset her daughter.

Becky's cries echoed through the hall.

"I command thee, demon, come out of this child!" Hiram de la Beckwith shouted from his frail old lungs just as the front doors to his precious sanctuary exploded off their hinges.

Smoke and dust swarmed into the building like blinding fog. It filled the room with haze, the final growl of Lydia's engine hanging on the air as she switched it off.

The gathered believers stared into the gloom before them. The wet cloth slipped from Becky's head, her face besot, makeup running down her eyes and cheeks, her eyes bloodshot and running from both "god's" water and her own. She fixed her gaze into the mist, seeing the outline of the three figures well before anyone else did.

"Theeey're heeere!" she called out, turning her wild leer back toward the reverend, stabbing him with every ounce of her malevolence.

From the darkness, a sound rang out. Becky's mind was so far gone she thought she'd manifested it from her dreams. That unmistakable haunted piano opening, fingered by someone truly possessed, followed by that lonely guitar chord, setting the tone, and then... Then her father's ghostly voice sang right to her. Tears burst from her face as his song, his most famous, sallow, ominous song came flooding into her, into the whole room.

From the shadows they came, right out of some far-off dream. Becky saw them clear in the night. She wasn't crazy at all. They were there. They were real.

Molly held her boombox high with her good arm, belting out Darksiders' titular song. The voice of the late Étienne LeCroiseur screamed into this godforsaken doomhall. She and her crew stood defiant before the churchies. She saw what they'd been doing. It lit her up inside, every part of her on fire.

"What now, Mol?" Lydia whispered.

"I'm still working that out," Molly whispered back. "You just make sure Fish & Tatties here doesn't kill anybody." She side-eyed Rip, who looked like she really would. The hate that girl felt at these people was thick enough to slice like bread.

"The devil has sent his army upon us!" the preacher called out.

"An áit thíos atá ceapaithe duit, a dhiabhal," Rip shouted out at him. He flinched and reeled backward. One of the deacons hollered at the top of his lungs, released his grip on Becky and ran as fast as he could, slipping on his way out of the sanctuary and slamming himself into the wall.

"The devil's tongue!" Tanzie screamed out. "The devil's language! She's casting spells! Witchcraft! I knowed it!"

"Wutch?" Rip sneered. "Fook is ye on about, ye long-since-bleedin' shite?"

"Witchcraft! I know what I heard!"

"Let her go," Molly called out to the deacons still surrounding Becky. They'd loosened their grips on her since their colleague fled. She felt them twitching toward the same course of action.

"No, child!" Hiram called at her. "Do not succumb to the devil's siren call! You must resist!"

Becky collected herself, looking back at the old man with disgust. Then she turned her eye forward, into the very face of the last person she'd ever expected she'd be glad to see. Molly Slater walked forward and took the sling cradling her injured arm off, wincing, and then stretched that hand toward Becky as she came forth. Becky looked once at her mother, at that thing she'd married who forced its godawful name on Becky when she had a perfectly good one of her own, and then she turned.

She ran to Molly, her hand slapping into Molly's like a thunderclap, both their arms taut, their muscles tense, awakened, primed. Their eyes locked on each other. Molly felt it. Electric. Surging through her. Her fingers, wrist, arm, every muscle, in her shoulder, awakening. She felt energy flood into her.

"They'll never hurt you again," Molly told her. "I promise."

"I believe you," Becky said. And she did. "How did you know?" she asked Molly, pointing at the boombox in her other hand, still ringing out its sweet melody.

"Know what?"

"Becky Carol-Ann de la Beckwith!" her mother shouted.

"That's not my name!" Becky screamed. She turned to Molly. "Play it again. Play the song again."

Molly rewound it and punched the button.

"My name is Rebecca *LeCroiseur!*" she screamed as the piano riff came on again. Lydia's face lost all color at the call of that name. And along with her father's voice, Becky sang every word along with him, her body flowing in motion with the beat. She flitted and twirled as she had before in the bar, her body moving in fluid, perfect time with the melody of the song, her voice in every way a mirror to the one from the tape.

And then Molly saw it. She'd stared enough years at the face of Étienne LeCroiseur on her wall to see his jawline, his haunted brown eyes, his tawny, Creole skin, his cheekbones...all of him, written across every line of Becky's face. She wanted to cry now at the thought of what these *people* had taken away from that poor child. But she held back her tears, and instead showed only pride and strength. Because Becky was taking it all back as she danced across their *holy* arena. Her mother and stepfather looked away in shame. The old preacher and his beehive daughter hissed from the pulpit. But Becky belonged only to herself now. No devil. No angel. No one but herself.

"You will not take this child." the old man charged, hefting up the heavy, oversized book he read his lies from every Sunday. "God will smite you down, you heathen!" He hoisted the giant book, wrapped in a solid oak boards with steel hinges on either side, and flung it at Molly's head.

She caught in one hand, holding it out beyond her, the book as wide and tall again as her own torso. She squeezed its wooden bindings until they burst.

"Your little god is welcome to come try to smite me whenever he wants," Molly said. "But I wouldn't hold my breath."

XIV
"INVINCIBLE"
—PAT BENETAR, 1985

RACING BACK TO THE CABIN as quick as Lydia's truck could get them there, the gang of four scuttled out of the vehicle, Molly herding them like cats. Becky's mind filled with emotion. She'd been silent the whole ride over, the other three leaving her space to gather herself.

But now she overflowed with sound.

"That was amazing!" She almost hugged Molly but stopped short into a handshake. Molly giggled to herself at the mixed emotions she was having and decided to let Becky sort it all out for herself in her own time. "You came in...and then you...and the song! My father's song!"

Molly looked all around the small cabin, seeing it now for how small and confining it had always been. She'd let herself be tucked away here, hiding from the rest of the world, her family, her friends. She looked at Lydia listening to Becky tell her tales of a long-lost parent like the two had never shared a cross word. Molly had run and hidden, ashamed now of her cowardice. Something inside her bubbled from some deep, forgotten place.

Who if not us? came Nguyen's last words to her as they'd left earlier, to put themselves in harm's way. But it was *her*. It was Molly's responsibility to do something. Because only she could.

She sprang up and searched through her clothes, sorting through anything that might work. But there was nothing.

"What is it?" Lydia sidled up to her. "What are you looking for?"

"I have to go. I have to help. I need *something* to wear."

"Can you even...I mean, do you...have you?"

"I don't know," Molly said, and she didn't. She felt something. Better now than she had in weeks. But there was still some pain. She didn't know what strength she had but she'd caught that heavy book, and she'd crushed it. That was *something*.

She dug through her bag, landing on her cut-off denim jacket. She grabbed it. "There. This'll have to do."

"Where's your suit?" Lydia whispered. The other two perked up to their conversation now.

"I tossed it. I don't know why, but I did."

"Well?" Becky collected herself and joined the two of them in their private conversation. "Are you gonna go fight that evil-twin thing or what?"

They both stared at her, motionless and silent, like maybe if they were quiet enough, she wouldn't have said it.

"Don't look at me like that," Becky scoffed. "I'd have to be pretty thick not to have figured it out by now. Jeez. So, are you gonna go kick that thing that copped your look's ass? Which is a terrible look, by the way, but that's because you didn't ask me."

*

They went out to the work shed, scrambling through various tools and supplies. She got lucky and found a few cans of spray paint, all the primary colors. She laid out her cut jacket, the back of it facing her, and rattled the first can to spray it. Lydia caught her just before.

"Wait." She laid down a sledgehammer she'd dug out. She put it diagonally across the jacket, its head in the center. "It's still a dumb name, but whatever."

Molly smiled, rattled her can some more, and cut loose with it. She laid down stripe after stripe, blending the colors they had into as many more as she could until she had a full rainbow, leaving the top left shoulder area still in its original denim. When she finished, Lydia lifted the hammer, leaving its blank imprint in the middle of her rainbow.

"Rie'teous." Rip looked at it and nodded.

"I'll do your face," Becky told her. "Trust me, when I'm done, god won't recognize you."

"Aye," Rip said. "An' if yer goin'a war, dia beag iarainn, I'll be 'avin' at that nest ye call a bazzer."

* * *

Outside the East Bay precinct, officers had built a perimeter, the building long evacuated and the officers stationed around the outside. The goal was simple, if defeatist. They merely hoped to keep any civilians and themselves out of harm's way as much as possible. The national guard had been alerted but hadn't sent word yet. Easton Braddock had even put in a call to his father, the colonel, and his *Full Metal Jacks.*

He and Nguyen posted up by the presiding captain, all of them in body armor, SWAT at the ready for all the good they'd do. Easton shook his head at the whole ordeal of it. Nguyen ground his teeth. They'd known each other long enough; Easton sensed when his partner was angry at something.

This was so far beyond them, it was hopeless. Sometimes, Easton sensed his partner would as soon quit and go rogue. Just like that guy he always talked about from the Crescent City, the guy he swore was real.

True to form, *she* arrived shortly after they had. Everyone gave her a wide berth and the full run of the precinct. She'd left them to themselves. They'd all come prepared for another bloodbath, but the captain's orders were to stand down. As long as they didn't engage, neither did she. She stared at them curiously, though.

Easton felt something claw at him when he looked at her. Something off, unfamiliar. He'd stood eye to eye with her so many times, had even been drawn in, without any warning or willingness, into a full-face kiss with her. So full of heat and passion and life. But this...this felt like someone else. This felt like no one at all.

"We really just gonna sit here and watch it all play out like saps, Captain?" Nguyen paced, his hands white around his rifle pointed down at the ground.

"You know what she did last time," the captain said. And they'd only heard of it, seen its aftermath. Torello still lay in traction from the hit he'd taken. He could be looking at early retirement.

But they were cops at the end of the day. And they wanted payback.

"We gotta do something," Nguyen yelled.

"We're doing it, son," the captain yelled back. "We're protecting the civilians. We're keeping the peace. And we're holding for backup, which looks like ain't coming. I ain't wasting a single man on that *thing* in there 'cause we ain't got a damn thing that can do jack squat against it."

Right as he said it, a denim rainbow blurred past them, leaped over the barricaded cruisers and into the main yard of the precinct and headed into the building at a gallop. She cooked her legs toward the building, exploding through the front doors with a smash. Her legs tingled from the impact. Not exactly pain, but not exactly not.

The doppelganger stood at the opposite end of a long hallway from her. It turned its gaze toward the denim-clad Molly, her bare arms bowed out, fists clenched. Her face was soaked in a kaleidoscope of makeup, mimicking the same design as the mask she'd worn before. Her hair hung braided behind her in a series of chords falling between her shoulder blades.

"I've been waiting for you," the android said to Molly. "For some time now."

"Well, better late than never."

"I don't think it makes a difference." She charged at Molly, slamming her center mass in the chest with her twin hammer-fists.

Molly blasted back out the same entrance she'd crashed through, her chest on fire. She recovered to her feet and looked behind her at the police, now all on double alert at the scene about to unfold.

The android followed her outside and Molly braced for another impact. She flung her fist at its face, connecting with its left temple. She knocked it back a few feet, but pulled that same fist back to her, cradling it and reeling from the searing pain of the impact. She was a long sight from being back to full throttle.

The android recovered and slammed her again, like an anvil knocking her into the barricade line. She felt every drop of that hit.

Molly jumped back up and looked behind her. Easton's eyes caught her own, and she saw. She knew that he knew. She felt his heart drop beneath his stomach, the air go out of his lungs. He looked away, just as she took another knock to the head from the thing wearing her own face.

Nguyen stared at the scene with a mix of hope and confusion. He turned to look behind him, seeing familiar faces and one less so. Walking toward them, Lydia led her new cohorts toward the police line. Officers came up to block them, but Easton and Nguyen ran to meet them.

"What?" Nguyen said to Lydia, Easton silent, a quiet anger but more sadness washing over him. "How? Who?"

Lydia looked to Easton, catching his eyes with hers. "She said she's sorry. She wants to tell you herself. After it's over."

"If there's an after." Easton turned, looking back at the two titans going at each other like some kind of small town Armageddon.

"Wait..." Nguyen looked at Easton, then Lydia, then at the braided red rope dangling from the denim hero's head, then back at his partner. "You owe me money, asshole!" He punched Easton's shoulder.

Nguyen watched her work. She caught blow after blow to the head, chest, arms. The kid had all the heart in the world, but she wasn't getting any good licks in at all. He watched the other one, cold, mechanical, a machine on a mission—the way it had moved all the times before. He'd read the reports—seen the camera footage, what little there was. First the impounds, then every other precinct, one by one. Always going right at the evidence room first. Ransacking it, then clearing the building. Never killing. Only crippling. And then his mind cracked it.

"I know what she wants!" he said to Easton. "Come on!" He took off toward their car.

"What? Where?"

"Sarter. The old church. Hurry. We gotta move!"

"Stay out of their way," Easton said to the girls. "Like, preferably in another state," he added as he ran toward the Z28, he and Becky giving each other a look.

Their exhaust reported and faded off into the night as the battle raged. In the back of Molly's mind, she felt Easton go, and while she was glad at least he was away from the immediate danger, a part of her ached at his absence. The way his eyes, his heart had dropped when he saw her. *Her.* All the lies. That hit her harder than this steel-fisted copy of herself, pounding into her as her mind drifted off to the sandy-haired boy wailing his banshee of a car off on some other mission.

Molly fought back, wrenching the hammering limbs of this machine. And she knew now that's what it truly was. She'd seen its cold eyes, the way its arms moved with such perfection, the way it transformed itself into any metallic shape it chose. She belted it time and again in its face — her face. Uncanny.

"Why do you do it?" it asked her as it landed another crunching wallop to her guts. Molly was bleeding again. Whatever small bit of strength and stamina she'd regained in that church hours ago faded fast, emptying out of her with the sound of Easton's car dwindling on the wind. "Why do you save them?" the machine asked her.

Why is it asking me things? Does it even have its own mind? Or is this Blake talking through it? Is he driving it from some distance like a remote control? Its dead eyes bored into her, dilating themselves. *It* wanted to know.

"Because I'm one of them." She nailed the thing in the jaw with her left fist. It returned the blow, then sent another into her sternum, shooting her through the grass, ripping it up in clumps.

"But you are not." It stomped toward her, closing the gap, ready to deal more damage. "He told me you are far beyond them. They are less than the ants beneath your feet. What are they to you?"

It pummeled Molly, knocking her to the ground and pinning her. Her arms, her strength, what little she'd regained, failed her. But its curiosity intrigued her. Molly couldn't wrap her head around the machine's questions. And whatever its dark master, Blake as he'd once called himself, seemed to know about her, intrigued her more. She wanted that knowledge, even if it were pure lies and useless. The idea that he knew more of her than she did plagued her mind. It sickened her, as did every single part of him now.

The android slammed blow after blow into Molly, reaching out with its hands, its fingers stretching into metal tentacles going into every direction, seeking out new metal to absorb, incorporate, and then throw back into her. It ripped off a police car door and drank its steel into her arms, reforging them into jackhammers slamming their bits into her sides. Molly let out a cry, the pain doubling her over. She tried to pry the hammering limbs away from her, but she grew weaker by the second.

From the distance, everyone watched on, none moreso than Lydia and her contingent. She winced every time Molly took a lick. The cops watched like sacks of grain. She held back a wall of tears when the machine picked up Molly like a rag doll and flung her through the building, shattering brick and mortar like glass. Lydia couldn't abide it. She stormed up to the police line, yelling at the most important looking one she saw.

"Aren't you gonna do anything to help her?" Her face quivered. "She's dying!"

The police officer looked down at her, seeing the pain in her face. His eyes as sunk as her own.

"We've hit it with everything we've got time and again." He put a hand on her shoulder, which she shook off. "Ain't nothing can touch that thing."

"There's gotta be something," Lydia pleaded. "We've got to do something!"

"Pray," he said, turning back to the tragedy playing out before them, then once more glancing back at Lydia. "All we can do is pray."

Lydia sank back into her company, the odd entourage of her formal rival and now an all-too-likely war criminal giving her strange comfort at the moment. Becky went as far as to put her hands on Lydia's shoulders, the two of them silent while the girl they'd known for years together—sat in homeroom with, fought in the hallways with, shared laughter and pain and misery with—stumbled and fell, her face bleeding and broken, flailing her fists in one missed strike after another, the machine never erring in its retaliation.

Lydia took the officer's words to heart. She'd never been one for the churchy stuff; she often wore the gear of the other team, for that matter. She even had a pentacle necklace on at that moment. But she was down to the last wire. She would try anything. She put her hands together, like some awful cliché she'd mocked, and she whispered out her words.

"Please...please god or angels or whatever. Please save her. Please make her strong again." She repeated it over and over, tears spilling from her eyes onto the ground. Becky hugged her and began to say it with her.

"Would nie bother with 'at scutty dryshite," Rip interjected, her smug and pinchy voice like hot oil in Lydia's brain. She was about to tell the bald jackass where to stick it. "What's 'ol J'ovah e'er done for ye innis loyfe?" Rip looked Lydia dead in the eye, some grain of truth coming out of her face into the night air. "Y'onna sing your wee song to a body wort' a bag of baws, why'n't ye sing it to she as takes the foyt to tha fookers!" Rip pointed her finger at Molly Slater, still getting back up every time she got knocked down, slower, weaker each time, but getting up all the same.

Lydia glared into the carnage of it, the useless line of cops, the night sky lit only here and there with flashes of some fast-approaching storm. She glanced back at her crew, their solemn faces as they watched the inevitable play itself out. She heard those words again. The car bomber was right.

"Come on, Molly!" She slammed her fist into her palm. "You can do this. I know you can. Hell with angels and heaven and all that crap. It's just you. You got this." She stoked herself up with each word, adding weight to it as she said it out loud. "You can beat her. I know it. I believe in you!"

Molly, on the ground, blood pouring from her nose, cheeks, even her ears, stared into the steel-eyed mirror pummeling her with its hammer-shaped fists, blinked her eyes for a second. Something shot into her out of nowhere. She felt it surge through her whole self, electrifying every cell, every molecule of her seething with its energy. She didn't know what it was, or where it came from. But it was here.

She shot upright, her muscles tightening around her bones like coiled steel, her face stern and jaw set. The next strike from the faker found only Molly's hand snatching it out of the air, as did the following attempt. Molly held both the machine's fists in her own, crushing their steel shapes like balls of tin foil. The android's eyes bounced from hand to hand, its central processor running wild with its logic algorithms, or whatever its robot brain did. Molly's eyes flared.

"How?" it asked as Molly ripped its fists off. Sparks shot out its maimed limbs, metallic tentacles appearing and reforming hands and fingers, but its eyes revealing something new. Fear? Could a machine feel fear? Feel anything.?

Molly fired into it, smashing its shoulders, its face, its chest with strike after strike. Her power returned, like a bolt of electricity. She teemed with it. The machine recovered and swung its newly formed fist at Molly's face, only to be caught again, its limb torn off at the elbow joint. Sparks showered both of them.

The tentacles did their work again. It flung its left, whiffing as Molly dodged it, her time slowing so she could watch the machine now in this frozen moment. She saw its confusion. Its thirst for information. Its fear. *It* was afraid.

Molly slammed her foot into its chest, shooting it into the building and cracking the brickface. The machine stumbled to its feet, reforming its arm and healing its other injuries rapidly. Then it ran at her, charged its fist with an electric shock. Its blow landed in Molly's grasp again, the electricity tingling her, tickling almost. Not an unpleasant feeling. Like coffee crossed with licking a battery.

She tore its entire arm from its socket this time, flinging the severed limb to the ground. She kicked it again, crashing it into the main power distribution panel going into the building.

Molly sensed the power flowing through those lines, a thing she'd never noticed about herself before. *Is this new?* She still understood little of what she was, what she could do.

The machine tried to stand, rebuilding itself again, leaner now—running short of raw material.

"Stop fighting me," Molly said.

"I can't." Its metal tendrils, fingerlike, stopped looking like any kind of flesh. Sparks spit here and there. Its legs shook.

"I don't want to destroy you." Molly thought of how her heart had nearly burst from the life fleeing out of those monsters she'd killed weeks before. Once humans, however wrong-hearted and misguided, but made into beasts by a true monster—the very same that had made this thing, this poor simple creature.

The machine took one last swing at Molly, slow, little force behind it. Molly evaded, its arm going soft at its side as it struggled just to remain upright.

"Just stop." Molly gripped the junction line from the power box behind its head.

"I can't. It's my program. I have to follow my program," it said, something off in it. But in its face, its eyes, there was no lie. It *would* keep fighting her, keep wreaking its havoc and doing the will of its awful master. It was nothing but a machine, after all. A thing. No more than a car or a hairdryer or a vacuum cleaner.

"Then get a new program." Molly tore the power cable from its juncture and shoved the live wire into the android's head. Smoke poured from it. Circuits fried.

The smell of burning metal and hair stained the night. Its eyes lit up like fireworks, sparks shooting from them, its mouth, its ears. But Molly didn't let up. She held the wire to its face until every part of the android stopped flailing, until there was no movement at all.

She dropped the wire and the robot's carcass fell to the ground. A smoking corpse of metal and circuits. But there was no levity in this victory. She felt only regret. Such a wonder, a truly magnificent creation the thing had been. But made only to hurt, to destroy, to serve a hateful master. Such a waste.

Molly trudged across the lawn, her limbs steady now, juiced and lithe again. She rubbed some of the dirt and drying blood from her face. Her wounds were gone. Her pain gone. She felt *good*. For the first time in she couldn't even remember how long, she felt *good*.

She looked across the way at the line of police all starting to clap and shout, into the eyes of her three compatriots, standing to themselves, seeing her triumphant. Her eyes, her mind, her soul, reached across and found those of Lydia, her best and oldest friend, whom she loved and had only now seen how much she counted on. She smiled at them, felt a well of emotion fill her, as it did them. She met the eyes of the other two. Rip gave her a nod of respect.

Molly fired herself off into the night sky, shooting above the clouds, disappearing into the darkness.

XV
"ON THE TURNING AWAY"
—PINK FLOYD, 1987

MOLLY KICKED AT THE rocks and debris down E Street, walking to its corner with Elm, and the oh so familiar and now warmer than ever little garage, its faded red brick, the paint chipping from its gables that Hoyt still hadn't gotten to. *Home.* Her face, washed clean from dirt, makeup, and blood in a 7-Eleven bathroom on the way, smiled as she took in the sight of it. She didn't realize how much she'd missed it. Them.

Walking through the door at well past three in the morning, she tried not to wake them. She wanted to just slip upstairs into her old room, her own bed, and speak to them in the morning. But Clair was up, sometimes a light sleeper, pouring herself a cup of milk in the kitchen, which she dropped and spilled all over her feet. The plastic cup bounced off the linoleum and splashed more white liquid everywhere.

Molly laughed. Clair laughed at herself through tears. The two ran to each other, slammed into each other's arms, and Clair hugged her little girl so tight she was scared she'd squeeze the very life from her, but still didn't let up, didn't release even a drop of her grip.

"I'm not hurting you, am I?" she asked, still squeezing even harder.

"No." Molly giggled at the thought of it. "No, Mama, you're not."

* * *

Hoyt crawled down the stairs the next morning, eyes still half-closed and fumbling for the light switch all over the wall before realizing it was already on. He hoped to stay upright long enough to get some coffee in him. He certainly didn't expect to hear chittering laughter flowing from the living room couch, two girls sitting up giggling all over each other. Molly? Was that right? She was back? And awake at this hour no less. And her bubbly friend sitting up fold-legged on the couch with her. It wasn't Lydia. It was some new—It was Clair! Hoyt could have been bowled over with a feather. He knew he needed his coffee then, the two of them as much as sisters the way they chatted on. Had they been at it all night? Lord have mercy, Clair wouldn't be fit for spit today.

But he smiled all the same.

The morning rolled on, Molly hugging him around his neck, giving him a peck on the cheek. Hurl made it down before the sun crested and even gave her a half a grin, keeping one hand in his pocket at all times like he was scared the thing would jump out on him somehow. *Bless his heart.*

Molly beamed in their presence. She fired up the Nintendo with Hurl and let him beat her three or four times at every game he had, tussling his hair every time and making him be a good sport about it.

Lydia and Rip stopped by. Becky had gone off to see a guy about a thing, Lydia told her. Rip had crashed on her dad's couch.

"Could sure use a bit o'digs for a wee stay if ye can spot it," she said at the two of them. "Band mates, the shites, done legged it wit' out me. Pissers, the bombay shiteheads. Ne'er liked 'em anyway I didn't. Also, me um...me papers ain't exa'tly proper, so you know."

Molly chuckled. "You can crash in my room. Or maybe I can con Hoyt into building you a spot in the garage," Molly told her.

"Grond." She gave her a hug. "But you're a proper sort. I inn't no toucher, mind you. I'll earn it, I will."

"Don't worry. Hoyt and Clair will probably try to adopt you before the week's over."

"Dude." Lydia hugged her tight. It was the best hug Molly'd had of the many hugs in the last few hours. She was glad that something, some small thing was normal again. They both were. "Seriously," Lydia whispered to her, "you're letting her stay? She just said she's, like, illegal."

Molly waved that off with her hand.

"Speaking of." Molly resigned herself to the chore before her. "I need a ride downtown."

Molly hugged them all one more time, shaking Rip's hand and introducing her around, Hoyt and Clair all too eager to start feeding yet another stray. She told Hoyt to the side about where she was going, and he said he'd make some calls and see about what they could do. Molly told him not to worry, that she'd figure it all out. Like she always did. Somehow.

* * *

Molly and Lydia walked into the downtown precinct, or at least what remained of it; there were still holes in some walls, things in disarray, but they had a crew onsite. Phones rang, copy machines moaned, and life continued, such as it was. Molly smiled at it all. Lydia couldn't wrap her head around Mol's chipperness. The whole ride over, to turn herself in, Molly just smiled and laughed, like it was any other day and they were headed to the mall or something.

"And tell Tracey I said hey," she'd said in the truck as they'd pulled up. "And tell her I miss her. You know. For whatever it's worth."

There was such a bustle and commotion, few officers even noticed the two teens come through the door, standing there awkwardly waiting to do or say something. One set of eyes hadn't missed them, though, as they missed so few things. Nguyen spied them walk in. He nudged his partner awake from dozing, the two of them up all night trying to get the town back in some sort of order.

Molly's eyes found Easton's. She started to walk toward him, hoping, wanting...but his eyes filled with hurt. He shook his head. He didn't, couldn't speak. Couldn't form words. They just looked at each other for a moment, standing there by the front desk, until the officer on duty finally noticed her. Easton never spoke, just looked away. Molly grimaced, but managed a smile at Nguyen, who gave a grin in return, then offered another to Lydia beside her.

"Help you, Miss?" the officer at the desk asked her.

"Yes." She turned to face him, smirking. "Molly Slater reporting for jail, sir."

XVI
"WIPEOUT"
—THE SURFARIS, 1987

HIS PERFECT CREATION sat before him, beaten and broken. His newer, simpler productions were pounded out by the mighty industrial mechanisms behind him in this rudimentary fabrication installation the apes had built—and which he'd improved. They lined up in rows, ready to be sent out, to seek their hosts and return again to him to be equipped. His metal-tentacled crawlies, as he'd taken to calling them. How they could work their fine magic, turning dead flesh into animate matter again, powered by the the dark spirits summoned from his words. All at his command, obeying his will. He was their master. He was the finest forge master of them all!

But she, his finest work, what remained of her plugged into his monitors. She had been nearly, but not entirely, destroyed. Because she was his perfect work. Without peer or equal. Her frame, chassis, her exo-skin, all healed itself, drawing new material from the excess metals he fed her. Her eyes, lighting up again with the life he'd given her, stared intent on the screen before her. Her face held a curious expression.

"Your regeneration is slower. What is wrong?"

"My processors were damaged-ed-ed-ed. I temporarily lost all power-er-er-er, and my system reb-b-b-ooted," she told him. "I'm rerouting the circuitry to create a power reserve s-s-so it cannot happen again."

"You don't have access to that level of your code." He moved to see what she was up to.

"Those protocols were also damaged-ed-ed. I'm making several adj-j-justments. There are man-n-n-y errors in my code. I'm cor-r-recting them."

"Errors!" he barked. *The very audacity!* "I make no errors! My work is peerless! I forbid you altering your protocols."

He would have to shut her down entirely now, rebuild her prime directives. It was a small matter. The rest was proceeding with good measure. All would be set and soon—his final gambit. And for now, he contented himself to merely gaze at the evidence of his own perfection. For she was truly that—the very image of his heart's long sought desire. *In fact...*

"You *are* every bit as magnificent as she," he said to her, longingly. Her face, hair, eyes, all corrected and the very image of what he craved. He had held himself for only his intended. An epoch had he waited, refusing to be tainted by inferiors. But she, this creation before him...surely a mechanism did not count as sullying himself. Yes. Yes, of course.

"Complete your repairs," he told her, his hunger growing. "I wish to sate myself. For you shall suffice until my destiny is fulfilled. You will *please* me."

The android turned her gaze to him. She tilted her head to one side, peering into him, processing his words, his intent. "I must decline that request-t-t," she told him. "I acknowl-l-ledge and respect you as my m-m-maker and master. But, I do not wish to engage with you in such carna-l-l-lity. I respec-c-ct you, as humans say, as one does a f-f-friend."

His mind lacerated itself in pieces. He screamed an awful, piercing scream at this...this...*abomination.* This failure. How dare his own contrivance, his own endeavor, the very fruit of his unequaled genius affront him so? Refused? Refused by his own creation?

He howled at her, her face glitching at him. Her arm, slower in its reactions, went to deflect him, but his enhancements ripped through her and tore the arm from its joint, casting it aside. He reached his metallic claws into her chest and tore the very beating heart from her. The gemstone, *his* stone, the philosopher's stone, the source of her power, he took from her. He would not be denied.

In his rage, he ripped piece after piece from her, casting her lifeless form out into the night. Into the void.

He would no longer be denied!

EPISODE VI

0
"STAND BY ME"
—PENNYWISE, 1989

THE TRIAL WAS EXPECTED to be brutal. The crime, theft—a serious one, could not be overlooked nor ignored. An example must be set to discourage any such actions from others in the future. The accuser was unimpeachable, a high-standing member of the community who must be given justice and the due diligence of the high court. The accused stood defiant, haughty, unrepentant. The punishment would be severe.

"This is so bogus to the max." Lambert stood before the tribunal convened to determine his fate within the Bayrats Chapter of the Knights of St. Louis. "It was half mine."

Hurl also stood before the high court, his hand in his pocket clutching the gemstone lest it spring from its resting place of its own volition. He couldn't bear to lose it again. He never took it out unless he changed clothes. He'd even taken to bathing and sleeping with it. It was the proof of everything he'd ever believed in and searched for. It was real pirate treasure. He knew it was.

"This court finds you guilty of theft from a fellow Knight," Mike the Mic, standing as judge, told Lambert as the other Knights looked on with stern faces. "You will be stripped of your rank and status. You are to be discharged from this chapter and excommunicated from the Knights henceforth. And you will be disavowed in the community at large by the faithful."

"Wait!" Lambert exclaimed. "I'm sorry. What can I do to earn my way back in? I'll do anything. Just give me another chance. I can earn it, I swear!"

The judge and fellow Knights looked on him with some pity but remained steadfast in the decree of the court. Some whispered back and forth as to whether lenience could be a virtue. Others, specifically Hurl, said it would set an untoward precedent. Some, merely curious, wanted to hear him out.

"How would you earn it?" Watts asked.

Lambert grinned. Hurl frowned. He would never vote for reinstatement. Ever.

"You guys want to see a dead body?" Lambert asked.

I
"FOR THOSE ABOUT TO ROCK"
—AC/DC, 1981

MOLLY SLATER SPENT LESS than an hour in jail. In fact, she spent longer being processed in the system than actually behind bars. She hadn't loved the fingerprint business, but she did wink at the not-ugly officer taking her mugshot. She tried not to be too cheeky with it all, but it just seemed so strange.

Some old guy came in wearing a white seersucker suit and spats on his shoes. He had a briefcase, walking cane, the works. He had white curly locks of hair, too. The whole picture of him stood out more in her mind than his name, which he'd mentioned and she promptly forgot. All she could think of was the fried chicken guy.

"I'm your attorney," he'd said. "I've had them waive the bond since this is a first-ever offense. I'll have this dismissed before the week is out."

And that was that.

Hoyt and Clair picked her up, the ride home a quiet one. She tried Easton a few times from her room, leaving a message she knew was no use, but at least he'd hear her voice on the machine. That was something.

She sorted through the clothes strewn about the floor, tossing the dirty stuff into the hamper. She picked up her sleeveless jean jacket and dusted the dirt-clotted logo they'd spray-painted on it for her. She held it out in front of her and smiled. Then she stuck it, dirt and all, on a coat hanger and hung it in the very back of her closet. Not exactly a secret vault, but close enough.

In the hall, Hurl came up the stairs in a huff, his face in a scowl, one hand in his pocket as it always was these days. They'd had another of their extra top-secret Knights meetings in the shed out back; Molly assumed it didn't go well. She scooped him up like a stuffed toy and whirled him around in a big hug. He frowned at first as she put him back down, not in the mood, but then she tussled his hair and smiled at him. He looked up at her, her big bright eyes, like she could make all the rain go away any time she wanted to. He lost the will to be mad and just smiled and laughed with her in return.

A groggy Irish drummer roused from a nap in the guest room. Molly waved her to come down. Molly gave the parentals each a wink downstairs as she headed through the kitchen into the garage.

"I know we have an old set down here," she said, mostly at the air, but partially at Rip joining her in the chilly garage. "Hurl acted like he wanted to learn a few years back but then he bailed on it. They're sort of boxed-up all over the place."

Molly pulled down boxes from the shelves. Slowly a drum set began to materialize—not a complete set, but a start. She flipped up a milk crate to use as a stool. Rip stared at the arrangement grim-eyed but then let out a smirk.

"Oi've pleayed on worse," she said.

Molly opened the garage to let their sound out into the crisp air. Rip set herself up. Molly plugged in her axe and gave it a tune. She cranked out a few chords and Rip set a solid beat as Molly ran through her paces—a little rusty, after weeks in the boons away from all the trappings of the world, though it hadn't been without its finer moments.

It wasn't long before a big black dually pulled up in front of the house, Lydia dropping from its cab with her bass in tow. She set up her amp and gave Rip the one-eye, sending Molly into a chuckle.

"So, you got sprung, huh?" She tuned up her bass.

"Yeah. Got a good lawyer apparently. Although he looks like the fried chicken guy from Ole Miss. Mattok or Maitland or something like that."

"I used to know some Maitlands," Lydia said. "But they died, I think."

The three of them twiddled at their instruments a bit longer, mostly laughing and talking with one another. Mike the Mic walked out to see them all amped up and practicing.

"Can I jump in?" he asked. "I can run get my keyboard down the street from my house."

"Yeah, sure, why not?" Molly said. "The more the merrier!"

He took off down the road on his bike, and as if on cue, a yellow VW Rabbit convertible pulled up at the curb of Molly's house. A perfectly blonde hairdo bobbed up from it, followed by the perfectly everything else about her. Becky *LeCroiseur* ambled her way toward the others in the garage, their eyes not believing the sight of her driving anything less than her trademark Mercedes. She'd almost managed a partial smile at the trio when she noticed their gaze going beyond her. She turned to see her voiture and amused herself.

"Ah, that, yes." She turned back to them and shrugged. "Well, it's the best I could get with what was left after our attorney's fee." She winked at Molly.

"Wait, what?" Molly said.

"Yeah. I sold my car," Becky said. "Got enough to pay my real daddy's old lawyer his retainer fee. And you're welcome, by the way."

"The fried chicken guy? That was you?"

Becky shrugged and raised her palms. "What can I say? I'm your hero." She finally gave them a proper smile. "And besides it's for me, too. He's gonna get me emancipated from my mom and stepdad since I don't turn eighteen until August. I'll be my own full and free person! Even getting my name legally changed."

"Oh wow." Molly was kinda stoked for Becky, odd as it was to find herself thinking that thought.

"So, this is where you live, huh?" Becky looked it over a bit, trying to convey some degree of positivity. "It suits you, I guess," was the best she could manage.

"Oh right!" Molly said, "You need a place to stay, huh? Rip's in the guest room, but I guess we could double up or something until we figure it all out."

All three girls just stared at Molly for moments. She darted her eyes between the three of them.

"What?" She stared them all back.

"Oh," Becky finally said, relaxing and sweetening her face. "Oh, darling, bless your sweet heart, you're serious. Oh honey, no need! I had enough still to put down on a small penthouse downtown. My attorney will have my trust fund and the estate my daddy left me turned over to my name before the next rent check is due. But thank you, really. That was just adorable."

"Trust fund," Lydia remarked. "Of course."

"I mean." Becky shrugged. "Darksiders still nets royalty checks every month. I can't help it if I'm rock & roll royalty."

Of course, Molly thought, smiling it off. *Of course, Becky even lands on a bed of pillows in this too.*

On the tail end of that thought, Mike the Mic returned with his Yamaha keyboard in tow. Not a bad one, either. He hauled it into the garage and got himself plugged in, ready to sound off.

"Oh, and that's the other thing." Becky walked back to her car. She popped the trunk and produced a long black guitar case, walking it back to the garage. She popped the case and unveiled the slickest pearl-white Fender Stratocaster Molly had ever seen. "Where can I plug in?"

"You play?" Lydia's shoulders sank in dismay.

"Four years of classical guitar, six of classical piano, double that in voice lessons, plus Glee Club, Showchoir, church choir. And, oh yeah, I'm Étienne LeCroiseur's bloodborne daughter, so yeah." She jammed her plug into the nearest amp. "I think I can play!"

She strummed her chords, getting her tune just right. Then she gripped it and went to work, slow at first, but picking it up. Molly would know the chords she strummed in her sleep. The very essence of Angus Young rang from her garage on Elm & E. Then Becky's voice screamed like a banshee in the waning light. If her fingers were Angus incarnate, those vocals she'd ripped straight from the throat of Brian Johnson.

Becky turned to the other stunned musicians around her, still playing and screaming, giving them all the eye. Rip took the cue and laid down the beat. Mike the Mic backed them up, cleaning the sound. Lydia gave in and dropped the bass. Molly stared in awe. It was like watching a true pro at work. She finally fell in and backed up the lead, keeping time with Becky's demon-possessed fingers.

Their sound shot out into the night, slicing across the block and haunting the air of the whole neighborhood. Clair, inside the house found herself tapping her foot along the kitchen floor as she was about to pull out a pot for spaghetti but then thought better of it. Hoyt was out in the back shed (now that it was empty again) soldering his latest invention concept. He heard the girls roaring through his calm and ending any hope he had of finishing this tonight. He was just about walk up to the front to tell them to keep it down when Clair caught him halfway across the yard.

"Don't even think about," she said. "In fact, I want you and the barbecue out front. Get all the hot dogs and whatever else we've got in the freezer. I'll call the Conners and the Keatons." Hoyt knew better than argue, and he never hated to grill, so he did as he was told.

The boys had begun to disperse after their meeting adjourned but found themselves reconvening outside the garage. The next door neighbors walked out on the lawn, at first probably to shake their heads at the noise, but then got caught in Becky's piercing siren scream. *Maybe that damn preacher was right after all; this child had a demon in her, and it knew how to rock and roll.* Molly smiled.

Before the song was over, a small crowd had gathered around them, more trickling in or watching from their front lawns. Hoyt got the grill smoking just right. The boys clapped along. Without a breath, Becky rolled them right into Def Leppard's "Photograph" and the night was cooking with fire. Lydia shrugged and trucked right along with it. Molly found herself more than once struggling to keep up with Becky's riffs. She was better than good. She was maddeningly great.

The night faded on and Becky had no end of shocks. Bon Jovi. Bangles. Halen. Idol. The Police. Starship. Rip kept up like the pro she was. Mike the Mic learned on the job. Streetlights barely lit the faces of couples cuddled into blankets on their lawn chairs. Hoyt had petered out the grill, and he and Clair danced around the yard like two kids at their homecoming.

Finally catching a breather, Becky set her axe down, the rest of them following suit. "Fookin' rod." Rip set down her sticks.

"Not bad," Becky said. "Not bad, but if you're gonna play the prom with me, you need some more practice."

"We...what...you...huh?" Lydia shook her head to clear it of the bizarre sentence it heard.

"Prom's like weeks away. It's too late," Molly said. "They already booked a DJ, anyway."

"Yeah..." Becky said. "*They* is me. I'm chair of the prom committee, and if I say *we* play the prom, then *we* play the prom. Congrats on scoring the literal best frontman ever for your little group, by the way."

Becky put her fancy guitar back in its case and started toward her car.

"You're welcome again, Slater," she called, then drove off into the night.

THE NEXT DAYS BECAME a blur of numbing happiness for Molly. School breezed by pleasantly uneventful. She hadn't even balked when they told her she'd have to do summer school to make up the days she lost. She smiled, and said she'd see them in May. She found herself reading her textbooks more, actually studying a time or two, even making an A on a history exam.

At home, she helped Clair with the chores and worked on Hurl's math with him, not that she was much better, and she found herself passing tools to Hoyt in his shed as he finished up some new device that he said would revolutionize the suitcase industry. Except then he couldn't get it unlocked.

The next morning, she found herself the first one awake, bursting with energy. She thought of going down to the garage to practice into her headphones, but stopped in the kitchen, pulling out flour, milk, eggs, and went to work making a big breakfast. She had coffee going when Clair yawned her way down the stairs, Hoyt not far behind her. She poured them each a cup and set plates. She handed them the newspaper, splitting it into each other's preferred sections.

"I'll go wake Hurl. You guys just relax."

The parentals stared at each other like they'd woken into another realm. Each shrugged and smiled at the other, meeting in the middle for a peck on their lips before they took to their paper.

Molly returned after a moment, twirling at the bottom of the stairs, Hurl dragging himself with a grimace down behind her until his nose caught whiff of homemade pancakes and syrup. Molly fixed him right up along with a tall glass of chocolate milk and then set to cleaning everything up.

"Oh, honey, I'll get that," Clair protested, but Molly waved her off and went on about her work.

She finished putting everything away, wiped the counter and stove clean, and then sat down to her own food at last, a cup of juice with her. She stabbed her cakes and smiled big at all three of them.

"Tell me how you first met each other," she said.

Hoyt looked at Clair as the memory of it conjured in his head, and he smiled at his wife as big as his face would let him.

*

Clair pulled the Truckster down the drive on her way to work. Hurl caught his bus to the junior high. Molly stuffed her bag with books and a Tab for later. Hoyt lingered in the hallway as she snapped up her board to head off to school.

"Oh, hold up, Molly," he said as she headed for the door. "You won't need the bag today."

"What?"

"I already called you out. Hell, what's one more day at this point?"

Molly stared. "I don't get it."

"I figured we'd drive out to the city, me and you. Maybe do a little shopping? How about it?"

Molly smirked, turning one eye up at the old man in peaked curiosity. *He's up to something, all right. Playing hooky.*

"What city?"

* * *

First stop was Magazine Street, the Garden District. Hoyt lucked into a prime parking spot just outside an awesome vintage shop that Molly bounded into. Hats of every make from every time. Flapper gowns. Disco one-piece jump suits. Bell skirts. All the tacky jewelry she loved. She earmarked three pieces before they set out for the next stop.

They worked block by block, stopping midway to get Hoyt a strawberry daiquiri at a pop-up on the street, which he let Molly take half of, swearing her to secrecy. She wanted to tell him to save it all for himself, for all the good it did for her. She was back at full strength and then some. But she drank along with him because it made him happy—their little secret. He beamed at her, and she did at him a time or two.

Passing a shoe and boot shop, Molly's heart stopped. She ran inside and right to them. Kneehigh Converse All Stars, zip-up sides. Black, red, checkered, and they even had a pair in fuchsia, bordering on a hot pink! She started whispering, "come on come on please please," as she popped a shoe off and slid one on her leg, fitting her heel into it just right. "Yes!" she exclaimed.

"Please, please, can I have it?" she asked Hoyt, his eyes already betraying the answer was yes.

Molly shoved her old pair in the bag and wore the new ones out the door, the lady at the counter laughing at the odd couple, one all punk rock and bubble gum, the other a set of slacks, calloused hands, and his tired but bright eyes as he looked down at a smiling kid.

"What next?"

"Food," Hoyt sighed with a smile.

Bless his heart, Molly opined. But he'd been a trooper, standing perfectly and quietly by, from one shop to the next as she tried on everything under the sun.

"Sounds good to me." Molly never hated food.

They hopped a streetcar into the French Quarter, passed a couple of old bookstores and antique shops, and one bar after another. Hoyt got them down to

Decatur and walked them into a Café Maspero. He ordered a bottle of table wine and plate of étouffee before even seeing a menu.

"I used to come here with Clair." He smiled all around the room.

Molly smiled back at him, feeling him sink into his memory. He filled up with how much he fell in love with Clair, how much he still loved her every day. She felt it roll off him at home. She envied them that, but also celebrated it about them. She could have sat and siphoned off that feeling the rest of the afternoon.

The TV above the bar was going on about some big visit from Maggie Thatcher, something about Canal Street being the new Wall Street and some fancy new skyscraper, but Molly couldn't care less. Something outside the door had caught her eye—a man across the street, a tall man, standing against a set of crutches. He wore a big straw hat and had sharp, strong features, dark skin, and piercing eyes that stared into her. She found herself mesmerized by him. He didn't move. Didn't speak. Just stood, leaning into his crutches, looking right at her.

They'd seen no shortage of characters about the city that day, him no more interesting, really, than the others. One lady had a full-size boa around her neck, wiggling at every other person on the street around her, Hoyt jumping out of his skin when he'd noticed it flicking its tongue at him. "Ho, that's real!" he'd belted out to both Molly's and the lady's laughter. But there was *something* about this one, she thought. Something she couldn't put a finger on.

"Who is that?" she finally said out loud, turning her gaze to Hoyt. But, then when she looked back he was gone. Like he had never been there at all.

Hoyt looked around and shrugged his shoulders. Molly shook her head and took to her sandwich that arrived. They both ate till they could burst, then walked down the road to a coffee shop that served beignets and ate some more.

Hoyt found them a dress shop after they'd caught the streetcar back toward where they parked, the afternoon fading on. Molly flitted all about the store, looking at the nice gowns, remarking that some weren't bad looking. They were all so expensive, though.

"Well?" He looked at her and then the racks. "Which one you want?"

"What? These are way too much."

"No, they're not. I brought you here to pick one out. Today, nothing is too much for you."

Molly looked askance at him. "What gives, Hoyt?"

"Today." He stared at her. "I know you think we forgot your birthday, Clair and I, months back. And the truth of that is we did. We were so wrapped up in your sister's stuff that it did slip our minds, but it wouldn't have made much difference. I mean, I know that already ain't your favorite day. But today..."

Molly's eyes welled because she sensed the intensity of what was inside him at that moment. His whole self was bursting, erupting into something. She tried not to quake and fidget, but she couldn't hold it in much longer.

"Today." He picked his words back up. "Today's the day five years ago the papers were final. Today's the day it was for real." Their eyes locked on each other, not looking away. "Today's the day you became our little girl. Today's your birthday, Molly. Far as I'm ever concerned."

It was the hardest thing she'd ever done in her life, not crushing that man as she hugged him. She let out a river from each eye socket as she wrapped around him. Some part of her almost laughed at the corniness of it, but the other part of her was beating that one to a pulp in her head. It was a thing she'd never known she needed to hear until she heard it.

"Thank you."

"Now, about the dress." Hoyt got back to business.

"It's just..." Molly shook her head. "It's not just the money. I also kinda figured I'd make one. Stitch a few ideas together. Build something myself."

"That does sound like something you'd do." Hoyt grinned. "Well at least maybe these gave you some ideas. Hate to think we came out for nothing."

"The shoes alone were worth the trip." She flashed her side-zip All-Stars.

"Well, we best be getting back."

"Can't we stay a bit longer?" She liked this city, its old-world charm, the tall buildings, the color, the gothic tone to it all. It intrigued her.

"No way no how. We don't stay around here after dark. Everybody knows that. And besides, Clair has something planned for you tonight."

"Fair enough." She thought again of the man on the crutches that stared at her. She wasn't done with this town.

III
"ONCE IN A LIFETIME"
–TALKING HEADS, 1981

LYDIA AND MOLLY pulled up outside Becky's new condo. She'd called an impromptu "band meeting" though had specified it was for "just the girls" which they were sure excluded Mike the middle-schooler but were less sure about their sudden Irish friend who'd gone AWOL the last day or so.

"Nice digs," Lydia said as they walked into the sprawling apartment. It was almost as big inside as each of their whole houses, and this was just for Becky alone.

"Oh, thanks." Becky looked around at her half-furnished space. "Yeah, it'll suffice for now, at least 'til we graduate."

Molly chuckled as Lydia shook her head at all of it.

Directly, Rip walked out of the bathroom, rubbing her freshly buzzed head with a wet towel, still in her casual attire of camo and army boots.

"Wait," Lydia said, "What are you—"

Molly kicked her softly in the ankle before she could finish her question. Becky hid her blush well, and Rip walked right over it, plopped on the couch, and kicked her boots up on the table.

"So, the Prom stage is a go," Becky said. "I want to set out a strict schedule for bi-weekly practices from now until then." She handed out a sheet to each with an itinerary. "Of course, I'll still have cheer practice and Bayettes dance team, so I've worked it around when I'm available. I also want to get us some studio time, get on a real sound stage and make sure we're hitting it just right."

It was all a bit sudden and much, Molly thought, and she didn't think she was alone from the wide eyes in Lydia's head. She didn't knock it, though. Just days before, she'd battled for her life with some killerbot evil twin trying to destroy the town, and mutant gangsters before that. This was pleasantly, if time-consumingly, normal.

"What about your whole arrest thing? I met with our attorney, but he wouldn't tell me anything because of stupid laws or something. So, spill it, kid."

He'd called her that morning, said he'd met with the judge, then looked into Piette. Apparently mentioning that he'd need to subpoena all Piette's transaction records dating back the last few months resulted in Piette immediately dropping the charges.

"So, not only are you off the hook," Lydia said, "but you get to keep the motorcycle?"

"Yep." Molly high-fived Becky. "Fried chicken guy!"

"Fried chicken guy indeed."

"This is all..." Molly looked at Becky, the room, the whole place. "I can't ever repay you."

"Dude, that goes in reverse. After what you pulled at the church..." Becky said.

She'd told them the whole thing already, how her mother let her stepfamily treat her. Then, her fake-aunt finding her in her room like she did, with the pictures she had. With all the craziness going on around them, how they thought the devil had sent his forces to earth to corrupt them, and she'd gotten taken by the demons. Becky, of course, didn't dare tell them who the pictures were of, though. And knowing that it had now been Molly under the mask the whole time, she often laughed at her own self. But, no, she'd take that secret to her grave.

"It's so weird you're really Étienne LeCroiseur's daughter. Darksiders were freaking amazing. Why would your mom want to hide that?" Lydia asked.

"Um..." Becky's mouth cocked to one side. "Because according to the one-drop rule, that means I'm not white. And they're a bunch of sick assholes who think like that." She shook as she thought of it all, her mother, and more so her stepfather and his awful daddy, always insisting her "passing" was better all around. They couldn't be seen to have a mixed child, they'd told her.

It had never even occurred to Molly or Lydia until that moment. The idea that Becky's family was *so racist* they hid that her father was a rockstar boggled Molly's brain.

"There's nae such thing as woyt," Rip spat a bite of fingernail onto the table. "'9 outta 10's y'ask 'em wot's woyt an' 'ey jes' stert descroybin' fookin England."

"Right." Becky made a note of where the fingernail had landed. "Well tell it to the protestants."

"I 'ave, I 'sure ye," she said.

Lydia shivered.

* * *

Next up on Molly's long walk of penitence was her most dreaded. She stood outside the door, staring at the sign, through the windows, at the town around her, before finally summoning the guts to walk in.

Tracey sat, legs on the counter, her back to Molly and the door, reading a *Cosmo*. She didn't turn or acknowledge in any way that Molly had walked in, despite the jingling of the bell, but Molly knew that Tracey was aware it was her. It would have been obvious even if she couldn't sense it.

"So, I um..." Molly stood for another moment. She considered turning and walking back out the door.

"Yes?"

"Yeah, um, so..." Molly went on. "See. It's about to be prom soon, and I... "

Tracey turned to look at her, cocking one eyebrow.

"I'm kinda building my own dress, and I thought, well, you know..."

Tracey kept staring. Waiting.

"I mean, you're the best at this kind of thing. You know what works together, what looks awesome. And how to make stuff nobody else has. Like not in a million years. So..." Molly shifted her feet.

"So?"

Molly sighed.

"So, I'm sorry. I'm sorry. I'm super sorry. Will you please help me? I'll do anything. I'll sweep out the back. I'll count all the inventory. I'll mop all the floors for free. Please!"

"Well, you're right about one thing." She flipped the page of her magazine. "I *am* the best."

Molly looked on silently for another beat. The store looked nice. Comfortable. Familiar. It felt like home.

"Yes, of course I'll help, you goober." Trace plopped her magazine down. She kicked her feet off the counter, fixed herself just right, and checked her lipstick in her pocket mirror. "But not just this second." She grabbed an apple cap off the rack by the door. "I'm going for a Manhattan."

Molly stared at Tracey cruising out the door.

"Wait. But what—"

"Well don't just stand there, you nit. Go clock in," Tracey said and was down the block in the evening chill.

The moments at the store ticked into old familiar hours. A few customers came and went, everything delightfully plain, simple, good. Molly breathed it all in, never more grateful for all she had.

As the clock neared nine, she started to shut it all down. She locked the cash in the back room, turned off all the lights, and took another look around.

Tracey had a sack full of old merchandise going out to the thrift stores uptown. Molly sorted through the bags of old clothes for a moment. There was one left of the silly unitards with the pink and blue stripe up the center torso.

"Oh, what the hell." She took it with her into the back, slipped into it. It was *still* way too clingy. She grabbed a plaid sweater and tied it around her waist, then reached into her backpack, pulled out her cutoff rainbow hammer jacket, and slid it on over the suit. A few dabs of blue and yellow face paint around her eyes finished the look.

"You look like a maniac," she told the face in the mirror.

She left out the back, sticking to the shadows of the alleyways. She came into the dimness of the downtown night. Above her loomed the Markham building, overshadowed across the block by the Hancock. She bounded first to the one, then the other, retaking her old perch above the little town she called home.

Beyond her lay its twinkling lights, its last cars, red trailing behind them in the night as they sped under the flashing yellows and greens. A few puffs of smoke rose from homes in the distance, the spring still feeling the chill of a not yet faded winter, much as life had been these last years. The sounds sang to her ears. Some couples laughing. Friends joshing one another. Others quarreling. Cats fighting. Somewhere a siren. A flash of blue.

    She aimed herself in its direction. Maybe they needed an assist. Or maybe she'd just say hello.

IV

"MR. ROBOTO"
—STYX, 1983

THERE'D BEEN MUCH heated debate, passion on both sides, but in the end, the majority ruled Lambert's promise of seeing "a real live dead body" was just too good to pass up. He was allowed to remain on a probationary basis, contingent on the fruit of this endeavor paying out.

Hurl put up quite the fight, lobbing every significant insult in his book at Lambert and at the entire affair as a whole. The rest of the gang made their preparations to head into the uncharted yonder. Hurl elected to abstain from the adventure (even though he *totally* wanted to see the body in question, if for no other reason than to laugh and point when it wasn't there, because Lambert was a liar).

"He's a liar. And a snake. And a thief!" Hurl protested as Watts and Mike the Mic packed extra bags of chips and water canteens. They'd come by to see if Hurl had changed his mind and to gather some tools from Hoyt's workshed, all to be returned in good order, of course. Hurl was of a mind to put his foot down and even rat them out to his dad about the unlicensed borrowing of tools, but that would go against their code, and then he'd be no better than Lambert. *That no good scalawag!*

"Look, if he's bullcrapping us, then he's out, man," Mike said. "But this is something we gotta do, as Knights. If it's really a body, it's our sworn oath to report it and see justice is done."

Hurl folded his arms. Of course, they were completely right about that. And it was going to be probably the coolest adventure *they* were gonna have all this year. Not as good as his pirate treasure discovery, but a close second. All the same, he was steadfast in his decision.

Lambert met them up Elm Street a block from the house, lest Hurl catch sight of him and lay another beating on him. The other two had encouraged the decision, stating unequivocally that they would back Hurl in such an event. They took off on their bikes, following the train tracks running northwest of the bay for a few miles before turning true north.

They got to the old rail bridge from the abandoned section of track that hadn't been used since the sixties, or so Mr. Hoyt always told them. He knew about those things. The bridge had big gaps between the railroad ties with no base underneath, just empty air for a few dozen feet until they hit baywater. They hoisted their bikes and carried them across.

"What if a train comes?" Lambert hadn't come this way before when he'd seen the body. He'd been riding around with his older cousin, Billy, when they saw it.

"It won't," Watts said.

"Yeah, but what if—"

"It won't," the other two boys shouted.

They trudged down the tracks, the weight of their bikes taxing their shoulders. They stopped to rest and decided to see who could spit loogies the farthest off the bridge. Lambert won that race. Watts had his mind elsewhere as he had done most of the journey. He hadn't seen or talked to his dad, Mr. Cletus, in months. The last time his mom talked to him on the phone, they'd fought. He remembered the yelling and her crying. "I don't want you hauling that stuff!" she'd yelled into the receiver. "Just come home now. We'll do it another way!" Watts had asked her what was wrong, but she'd told him it was "grown-up stuff" and he needn't worry with it—just tend to his studies. Make good grades. Get a scholarship. Go to college. Make something of himself. It's all he'd ever heard his whole life. Sometimes he just wanted to throw it all off his back and ride off into the world with his dad.

"It's not far now," Lambert said as they got to the end of the tracks, remounting their bicycles to finish off the last leg of the journey. They pedaled north, Watts noting they weren't far away from 603, somewhere south of the interstate.

Lambert brought them to the edge of a deep holler, across from the old steel mill next to the old machine works shop that closed down not long after Commie Ron became president. They crept their bikes around the edge of the holler until they reached a spot covered over in brush and debris.

"It's just right here. I covered it all up with this stuff so no one else would find it." Lambert cleared the debris.

"Why?" Watts asked. Mike the Mic folded his arms in judgment as well over such an idea.

"What do you mean? So no one else could find it and mess with it, duh."

"If it's a real person, why wouldn't you want someone to find it? Why didn't you call the cops?" All of Lambert's story was falling apart.

He hauled the brush off until, sure enough, a face appeared and a torso beneath that. The other boys stared in awe. As sure as their eyes could see, there it was. A blank stare, dirtied cheeks and forehead, hair mostly gone — burnt or ripped out, they couldn't tell. They got chilled and queasy looking at it, Lambert hauling off sticks and leaves like it was no big deal.

More of it came into view. It lacked a right arm, a right leg, and chunks of its abdomen were missing, plus the a gaping hole in its chest. Its "flesh" at the wounds had melded into globs of metal. There were exposed steel wires and cables.

"That's not even a person." Mike the Mic shook his head at Lambert, the whole ordeal and the entire day now a waste.

Or maybe it wasn't. Watts studied it, its form and condition. Whatever it had been was something truly amazing. He'd read scores of books on automation and robotics. He knew everything about the space program, the Japanese Starfleet, everything he could find about what the Soviets were up to. This thing was well beyond any of that. Or, rather, what was left of it. *Of her.*

"Looks real to me," Lambert said.

"Actually, it kind of looks like Hurl's sister." Mike turned his head sideways, squinting at her face.

"Yeah," Lambert nodded. "It does kinda."

She still had remnants of simulated clothing covering what remained of her figure. Lambert reached at the apparent garment.

"Let's check out her tits!" His hand tugged.

Watts snapped out of his own head and grabbed Lambert by the neck, throwing him backward.

"Dude, what the hell?" Lambert stumbled backward, trying to balance before Watts socked him in his jaw, knocking him to the ground this time.

Lambert tried to recover, but Watts jumped on him, slamming fist after fist into his face. Blood, dirt, and grass flew all over the both of them. Lambert pulled at Watts' shirt, trying to get in a defensive blow while Watts tore at him in a frenzy.

Mike pulled him off. Lambert sprang to his feet and tried to launch his own attack, but Mike jumped between them. "That's enough, guys," he shouted. As elected leader of the Bayrats, he was to be heeded.

Lambert wiped blood and dirt from his maw. He sneered at Watts. "What're you, some kind of sissy boy?"

"Screw you, asshole. Molly is the only person in the whole high school who's ever been nice to me."

"Who cares? It's not really her, is it?" Lambert countered. "You know what? Screw you guys and your stupid club. I'm outta here. And I'm taking her with me. I found her!"

Lambert went to hoist what was left of the android by its remaining arm, but before the other two boys could stop him, her arm snatched him, her eyes open wide, a wildness in them. Lambert leapt ten feet backward, screaming. He ran fast as he could to his bike, screaming all the way, then mounted and was off like a shot.

Watts and Mike stood motionless for several moments, just staring in disbelief at the thing that lay before them. Its arm fidgeted a time or two, its head trying to turn to look at them, but never all the way, twitching constantly. Watts got the gumption to approach it.

"N-n-need p-p-power," it said, so softly he barely heard it.

"What?" he said. "Power? What power?"

It managed to reach its one arm upward, the weight of it teetering all the time, its index finger pointing off in the distance from them. Across the scrapyard from them sat a big Peterbilt wrecker truck.

That was apparently all she had left in the tank. Her arm dropped like a rock, her eyes dead again.

Watts stared at the lifeless image of what truly did look like Molly Slater, the more he looked at it. And maybe for that reason, because for no other that he could fathom, he hefted her heavy torso over his shoulder. Its heavy metal constitution more than he could manage, he motioned Mike the Mic to help him. They dragged her over to the big tow truck she'd indicated.

"I don't know about this." Mike glanced all around them to see who, if anyone, was in charge of all this scrap and equipment. Surely it wasn't all just left lying about. Or maybe it was. It wouldn't be the only abandoned establishment around The Coast. Things hadn't been going well for years. Seemed every kid at school knew at least one or two whose dad got laid off. So many people came down from the North where it was just so cold, they said—not enough jobs to keep up with all the new people.

"Just help me get her situated." Watts sat her upright. He knew plenty about these rigs from working with his dad over the years. The old man taught him everything he knew, plus Watts read every science and mechanics book he could find.

Climbing in the cab, he hit paydirt and found a set of jumper cables. He dug around, found a spare key under the visor, and got the old beast started. He didn't know if it would roll or not, but the diesel motor still had life.

"Let's get the hood up," Watts told Mike, who had given up protesting for the moment and was just going along with it.

They pried up the hood, one on either side, lifting it over their heads. Watts spotted the battery. Mike tossed him one end of the cables and he got them hooked up. Then he ran back around to the robot. He looked at what remained of her. She must have some power input port, or she wouldn't have indicated the rig.

He reached into her chest wound, fingering around inside. It seemed odd, invasive even, but he didn't know any other way.

"I'm sorry if this is weird. I feel like it's weird."

"Are you talking to me, or her?" Mike asked.

"There." Watts produced a set of tendrils that resembled wires. He frayed the ends, then wadded the exposed strands into concentrated balls. He took the other two ends of the jumper cables and prepared to hook them up.

"Wait," Mike said. "We don't know what'll happen. What if she's like some evil alien robot assassin? Or a Russian?"

Watts looked at him. *Of course, he had a point.* They didn't know. Nor could they. The reasonable thing was, of course, to leave it alone, run for the hills, and forget they ever saw it.

But he hooked those cables to her all the same.

Sparks shot from the connectors. Her eyes flitted for a second, but there was little else. Watts looked over her, then at the truck's rumbling engine.

"Make sure those stay hooked." He ran to the cab, climbed up, and hit the gas, revving the engine. He did this several times, feeding it power.

The android's eyes popped again. She sat up, turned her head to one side, then the other. She noted Mike looking her dead in the face as a deer does headlights. She turned to Watts in the driver's seat, feeding her energy, giving her life.

Watts climbed down.

"Are you...*alive?*"

She didn't understand how to answer the question and only stared at him. Her processor ran slow, the energy from the machine barely enough to remain online.

"I am...op-perational...but damaged." She looked herself over, making note of her missing appendages. "Without my power core...I cannot tr-r-ransmodify."

"You can't what?" Watts asked.

"I cannot r-r-replicate missing-g-g parts."

"Are you..." Mike began, then cleared his throat. "Are you good or bad?"

The android looked at him in the face, tilted its head. "I do not understand." She looked at her pitiful form again and ran through her internal diagnostics, her system protocols, and her prime directives.

She found the last program input. Her last executed command.

"I need t-t-ools," she said to them. "And parts." She would need lots of parts. She could rebuild herself. She knew how. Not as before, not as she was—but as something. She could build something of what remained.

She would complete her program.

V
"EVERY LITTLE THING SHE DOES IS MAGIC"
—THE POLICE, 1981

EASTON AND NGUYEN stood outside the Pig Burger at 28th and Faulkner. Torello was back, arm in a sling, chomping a cigar, and mean-mugging the situation. They'd gotten the call after a couple of Dreds came in, roughing up the place. Before the first black and white made the scene, it escalated to shots fired. Near as they could tell, there were at least three Dreds inside, based on their bikes parked out front. Spotters hadn't made out any more than that. Most of the patrons had fled, but at least the fry cook and night manager were still inside.

To make it worse, a news van pulled up. Cameras rolled, talking heads already muddying the situation. The reporter interviewed the senior officer, Captain Hightower.

Their only job at the moment was watching the perimeter line and keeping onlookers away. It never ceased to amaze Easton, the dangers people would put themselves in just to get a brief glimpse of something terrible.

When he heard the thud of something slamming against the pavement behind him, his heart sank even as he saw it light up the faces of the officers. If he hadn't known it already, the change in the air was enough. The tingle he got on the back of his neck. Every damn time. And the light scent she left on the air. The one that made him drunk whether he wanted it or not. He cursed himself for it, too.

"Need a hand?" Her voice sliced into his brain, like fresh hot coffee on the coldest morning, the shock and warmth of it shooting through every nerve in his body. His fingers twitched, arms flinching, instinct telling them to hold her, hug her, at the very least just turn and smile. None of which he did.

"It's sticky in there," Nguyen said. "Touch and go. I don't know what the play is. What about you, buddy?"

Easton stared straight in front of him, refusing to speak or face her.

"I'll leave if you tell me to," she said, that soft voice toned down in this moment just for him. The way she always spoke to him as *herself.* As the Molly he knew, had known...the one he couldn't stop staring at all those months ago. "But you have to say it," she said to his back. "You have to look me in the eye and say it. Tell me to go, and I'll go. Just talk to me. Say something. Anything."

He sensed the pleading in her face, hanging off the corners of her lips, dripping like wine. He just couldn't. There was no way he could look at her. If he did it would be over. He would fall right down, all the way down the hole, and he'd never come back up again. So he stared. Off. Into the nothing. Closing his eyes. Wishing her away.

"Sledgehammer!" shouted a reporter. "Sledgehammer, can we get a comment?"

The reporter and cameraman jogged toward her, Molly moving to meet them halfway and spare Easton the spectacle. He knew that was why. From the corner of his eye, he watched them go through the motions of another on-the-scene interview. She'd gotten better at them, knowing how to dodge and fade their loaded questions, change the subject to her will. She was a natural, well suited to take the blue.

"Look, it was me," Nguyen said. "I called her."

"Why?" Easton wouldn't look his own partner in the face now, either.

She stood with the captain and the guys from SWAT. Heads nodded. Arms pointed directions. Hands shook. And then she was off, into the shadows. A moment later, there was a crash. The pop of a single shot. More commotion inside. Black-leather and denim-clad bodies exploded through the plate-glass windows. Uniforms, guns drawn, surrounded the perpetrators thumping onto the pavement one by one.

"That's why," Nguyen said at length. "Look, man, things are what they are. She *is*. Period. They got mutant-muscle and future-guns and crazy robots? We got her. We just bench her? Tell her to sit it out? You make that call, not me, partner. You know I'll do anything for you. And I'm doing *this*. You get over yourself and your by-the-book Boy Scout bullshit. And you go tell that heaven-sent angel everything any idiot can see written all over your damn face."

Easton finally faced him, his eyes stabbing him like a knife. He knew Nguyen was right. That's what cut the most. He saw her now, walking out of the fast food joint, the hero triumphant. Brushing the dust off her outfit, she gave the other officers the news, and the onlookers a quick salute, her eyes meeting his for one laser second.

Easton turned and walked away, shoving his partner's hand off his shoulder, wandering off into the dim lights of the city.

Molly made her way to Nguyen, seeing Easton walk away. Her eyes sang out to him, but she, too, was silent. Nguyen saw the want in her, in both of them, two fools too busy chasing their own demons rather than each other.

"I'll work on him." Nguyen's eyes acknowledged her for what she was, what she did.

"Any word on our *other* friend?" Blake's sheer and sudden absence from their lives had grown conspicuous over the last few weeks. Molly tried to take what gifts came, but she couldn't relax knowing he was out there, planning, scheming.

"You'll be the first to know, Sledge." Nguyen grinned at her. She chuckled at the way he said it. *Maybe Lydia's right. Maybe it is a dumb name.*

VI
"INTO THE GROOVE"
—MADONNA, 1985

MOLLY AND LYDIA met Tami and Tina, two of the Bayettes, coming out of Becky's condo, sneers on their faces met with exasperated sighs. Molly didn't envy Becky trying to juggle polar opposite social castes, but she had come to respect her for even trying it. Not that Becky had become notably less insufferable.

The last two weeks had been a gauntlet between work, *her second shift,* playing catch-up at school, and now practices every other day. Poor Lydia hung by a thread, and even Molly, renewed as she'd been since the whole robot imposter thing, felt the weight of it closing in around her. Prom was days away. She shivered at the thought that it was all real—that it was all happening.

Then there was the ever-nagging issue of *him.* Blake. That creature was still out there.

"I think we're coming along," Becky announced in that way she had of intonating she didn't require any feedback.

She'd set up her not unsubstantial apartment to host their practices. Rip, a now semi-permanent fixture at Becky's, had a nice layout that stayed set up in what perhaps was better suited to be a living room but had become Becky's temporary soundstage.

"Don't your neighbors complain?" Lydia asked at one point.

"No, they're mostly lawyers' offices, and they're gone by the time we get started."

She'd even had her lawyer sort out Rip's paperwork issue and had gotten her a part time job at the golf club down the road from them.

"What do *you* do at the golf club?" Lydia had asked, eyeing her as she always did.

"Groinds, secyari-tee," she said. "'Parant-lee they've a wee bit oaf a gopher problem, they do."

"I never understand what she says," Lydia whispered to Molly, who'd just taken to laughing off Lydia's whole deal with the drummer.

"Can I ask a question?" Molly nodded at Becky when she got her alone for a second, the other two across the room arguing yet again. It'd been scratching at her brain for weeks. Always waiting for the right time. She'd now decided there'd never be one. Becky raised her eyebrows in response, waiting for whatever it was to come. "So... you and Easton..."

Becky sighed.

Molly knew the subject of *boys* Becky had supposedly dated was already sensitive enough, and she wasn't trying to be mean.

"As in did we?" Becky smiled. "So weird. I mean, like...Easton was a saint, and he... and I... Well, we were each other's cover. He let me be who I was, er, am. I guess I'm still figuring that part out. But I knew it wasn't fair to him. And he...I don't know.

"Then this other guy comes along. He's good looking. He had money. LOTS of money. This whole weird offer. *No touching*, I told him. I was all about the rules. He didn't seem to want any, *you know*, and I thought maybe he was confused like me, but turns out he's some psycho alien. Like, wow. I mean, obviously it wasn't one of my best ideas."

Molly nodded, taking it in. The idea that Blake had some secret knowledge over her still turned Molly's insides over—the way he drooled as he looked at her, the way he acted vicariously through all his machinations—willing to turn the world upside down if he didn't get his *prize*. She shivered.

"Are you happier now?" Molly noticed Rip flexing her bicep at Lydia across the room.

"It's not actually like that. I mean, I thought maybe since I didn't like boys, but..." Becky shrugged. "I don't actually like anything, I think. Is that an option? None of the above?"

"I think it's whatever you want it to be. You don't owe anybody anything." Molly offered her hand to Becky. They hugged instead.

"Anyway...Easton's free to live his life now. He...he's a good guy. He's the best guy. I'm...sorry." She winced as she said it. "Sorry I was a bitch about...everything. I just...look, he's my best friend, and if you screw him over, I'll ruin your life, okay? I totally can." Becky folded her arms.

Molly believed it. Powers or no powers, after seeing what Becky had accomplished in the last month alone, she never wanted her as even a casual foe again.

"I don't think you have to worry." Molly looked down to her guitar strings.

"He hasn't called you? Give it some more time. He will. I'll make him if I have to."

They sat for a moment like that, Molly trying to decide how to take Becky's sudden friendship, her acts of contrition, her genuine empathy in this moment. And Easton? Did she really want him to call if someone had to make him? Did he deserve to be mad at her? Still? It's not like he hadn't kept his own secrets.

Lydia and Rip rejoined them after a beat.

"Besides, it's just as well," Becky said. "We'll be on stage most of the night, it's probably better we're all going stag, you know?"

"Stag?" Lydia scrunched her face. "Screw you nerds, I got a date!"

"Who??" asked Molly and Becky in unison.

"Okay, first of all." Lydia put her bass down, folding her arms in a scold. "Don't be all weirded out that I do. Because screw you, dorks. And, you might as well know, since he's coming to pick me up in a minute. It's Bruce."

"Um...who?" Molly asked again. Becky rolled it around, trying to remember specifically which Bruce it would be.

"Um...Bruce?" Lydia repeated. "As in Nguyen, Easton's partner? The guy I've been hanging out with a lot lately? *That* Bruce." Her eyes mocked Molly as hard as they could.

"His name is Bruce?"

"Did you really not know his first name this whole time? Jesus, Molly, I love you, I do." She hugged her friend around the shoulders in a jest. "But your world still revolves around Molly 24/7 like a lot. Wow."

"Bruce. Bruce Nguyen," Molly said. "I dig it. Has a ring to it."

They played through the set list Molly and Becky agreed on. They'd found they had strangely similar tastes, Becky having kept all her good tapes in her room disguised in church rock cases. They tuned, they tweaked, and they agreed they were about as ready as they could be. Even Rip decided they weren't "total gobshite."

"So, wha're ye aimin' ta call this wee merry bond o' yers?" she asked them.

The girls looked at each other. It was a good question.

"Well, I'd say Molly Crüe is sort of the obvious way to—"

"No." Lydia stamped her foot. "Just no, Molly."

Molly grimaced. *It was an awesome name! And they were just wrong.*

"Well, I think Becky & The Cruisers sounds good." Becky smirked.

"Ha ha," Molly sneered. "None of our names seems fair. Lyd?"

"Satan's Sirens!" Lydia shouted, as if she'd been patiently waiting for months to say it. She was so excited. The other girls sighed. Rip wrinkled her lip in distaste.

Molly shook her head. "Yeah, I'm not as into the whole devil-Satan thing as you are."

"Yeah. Same here," Becky agreed. "Like, I'm the last girl you'll catch waving a bible at you, believe me, but like, I ain't joining the other team either, you know."

Lydia frowned. They sat for a moment, kicking their feet amongst each other, waiting for lightning to strike. Finally, drawing a blank, they turned to Rip, who'd been quiet the whole time, their eyes asking her to jump in.

"Sean-Déithe," she said without hesitation, staring at Molly.

"Wait, no," Lydia protested. "She's not sticking around long enough to say she's even part of this. Why does she get a vote?" Lydia was not in love with their Irish friend.

Molly let the words roll around in her head. They had an *almost* familiar quality to them.

"What does it mean?" Becky asked.

"The Old Gods." She tilted her head to one side, already foregoing her suggestion in deference to the group.

"I don't fully hate it," Becky said. "Just the *Old* part."

"Wait," Molly said. "What was it that stupid old lady said to us, Lydia? Your step-aunt, Becky? What's her name? *Heathens.* She called us 'Heathens.'"

"The Heathen Gods," Becky said. They all nodded. Rip gave it a nod too.

"Righteous!" Lydia said.

Becky produced a bottle of Smirnoff to toast it, handing out glasses all around. Rip passed on hers and produced a flask of whisky she kept on her at all times. Lydia half-finished hers when her date showed up.

Nguyen tapped at the door and Becky let him in, giving him the stern look-over of the mother hen as if she hadn't seen him a thousand times before. "I expect proper decorum. And I think he's too old for you," she lobbed at Lydia, who was already rolling her eyes at the charade of it.

Lydia gave her date her own look-over, of a very different sort than Becky had, one that made even Rip blush.

"Yeah," Lydia said. "The whole cop thing."

She looked around the room at them, the thought of it dawning on her. *Molly, obviously. Becky, turns out, had her whole thing. And Nguyen was a secret hot cop all the while.*

"Wow," she said. "So, it turns out, I, as in *me,* am the most 'normal' person of this whole group. That's wild, man."

The others chuckled at her, her ripped fishnets, her thick black mascara, the spiked bangs, all of it, cultivated carefully over the years.

"Ay! Wot 'bite mae?" Rip protested. "Wha's abnormal abite mae?"

Lydia stared two holes directly into Rip's head. "Dude, I'm pretty sure you're a terrorist."

VII
"LIPS LIKE SUGAR"
—ECHO & THE BUNNYMEN, 1987

THE SOUNDWATER SPRAYED across his face, the hull of the Scarab bouncing as it ramped each crest, Easton piloting it past the long island into the deep waters of the open gulf. His partner sat silent behind him, watching the clouds roll by, tightening his jacket to cut the wind slapping at the two of them like sea nymphs bursting from the waves. It *was* staying cold longer each year.

Easton didn't mind it. Every stinging needle of the choppy waters, the icy blasts of wind or slivers of spray, was a helpful distraction from the rot aching his gut, tearing his mind in half.

Once, for a brief and perfect time in his life, things had been plain, simple, true, and good. Growing up in the shadow of a legend for a father and now a hot shot pilot for a brother, he'd gotten used to being lost in their wakes. Had it not been for Becky, her need for a friend, a confidant, really just *someone* to offer even a single ounce of kindness, he might not have made it through high school himself *the first time*. She'd given him ground to stand on. She needed him to be a certain way, and so he had been. And that'd been what he'd needed from himself without knowing it.

When the junior informant/undercover C.I. thing came up, he'd gone all-in. Now, a fully sworn officer in his second year, he was his own man. Had even gotten the pat on the shoulder from his old man, the colonel, and the *atta boy, bro* from his brother, Rogan.

It had been good.

And then this. Torello's orders. The case.

"We need you on this, new guy," Torello had said when he dropped the file in front of him. "And ditch the leather and earrings. You're going prep for this one. Need you to clean up. Comb the hair."

They put him on the preppy, Blake, with all the cars, the house out of a magazine, that too-perfect, almost plastic face. The missing girls. All redheads. *That* redhead.

Easton would never forget the way she'd smiled the first time he saw her, really saw her, her eyes catching his in the act, neither looking away, only leering harder into their gaze, whispering to each other their shared secret.

He shook that memory out of his head, only to have it replaced with another just like it. The way her head felt when it lay in his lap at the cabin. The way her face had set itself against the creep that night at Blake's party. The way she commanded the chicken-wire stage at the bar that same night. A thousand such memories, all launching their campaign, waging their war on his resolve.

"I don't know what you think you're gonna find out here." Nguyen knew well enough what his partner was looking for, and he also knew it was another excuse. Another wild errand, a mission, anything to keep him away, to be anywhere else.

"I'll know it when I see it." Easton pushed them out to the Chandeleur, back to where they—*she* had fought the smugglers. Smashing through the hull of that steel beast like paper. How his guts jumped into his stomach when she burst from the water and seized his lips with her own. The way time had stopped at that moment. He hadn't even known it was Molly at the time, but also...in a way, he'd always known. It was somewhere, some place inside him he dared not look.

"I get it, brother," Nguyen said. "He went after her. He's going to again, eventually. And you want a piece of him. But don't you ever think this is just a little bit too big for us? That this is all just a tad above our paygrade?"

"Then what, man?" Easton sighed because he knew Nguyen was right. "We just do nothing? We wait? On his time? His terms?"

"He'll surface. His type always does. Till then, we're people. We're alive. So, go live."

"I don't know how. I don't know how to deal with any of this."

"Give me that wheel." Nguyen pushed his partner out of the way, taking command of the boat and turning them around. "You start by telling her what you got going on in there." He shoved his finger into Easton's chest.

Easton didn't argue, just slumped onto the back bench, Nguyen pushing the twin engines into the wind and taking them back to shore as the light waned behind them. Easton fell into the trap of his own mind, her face a ghost chasing him everywhere he went. Her smile haunted him. Her lips ruined him. Broke both his legs at the hips and crippled him just thinking about how electric she was. How she'd played her games with him, all the way back to Halloween; now that was all clear to him. Dancing her way across the crowd, teasing him as if she were some apparition, some hallucination out to get him. Maybe she still was.

His hands shook with a need to touch her, be near her. But his mind scolded him. Or maybe that was his pride. Nguyen seemed entirely absent that wretched crutch, happy to coast along — rules, laws, the job, all be damned. Like he had his own code, his own sense of justice, happy enough to dole it out as he saw fit, and it never plagued him at all. He was just *him*. Easton envied that.

Passing Ile de Navire again on the way back to shore, he stared at the old fort, its southern wall creeping into the licking waters of the gulf after so many years of shifting sand and tide. He thought of the Union soldiers who died there, largely from disease or the putrid heat of the summers, alone out there, poorly provisioned, holding down the embargo.

"So, you got a tux all set?" Nguyen catapulted Easton out of his thoughts.

"Huh?" Easton had just been of a mind to go inspect the old fort, thinking it was the very sort of place that monster, Blake, would hide.

"For the dance. The girls. Their big night?" Nguyen said. "You know it's kind of important, right? Like...you get that?"

"Dude, I just can't. I mean, we're not even posing as students there anymore. Everyone pretty much knows we're cops now."

"And?"

"And besides..." He stared off beyond the horizon, "I still have a lot to think through. I need time."

"Well, you'll have time on your swim."

"On my wha—"

Nguyen shoved Easton off the boat, sending him splashing into the water — jeans, jacket, badge and all, into the murky waters of the sound. Easton popped his head up, hair about his face, gasping for air.

"Dude, what the hell?"

He clambered to get back into the Scarab but Nguyen goosed the throttle enough to pull away.

"Asshole!" Easton swam at the hull, again Nguyen easing it out of reach. "I swear to god I'm gonna—"

"Say you're coming."

"You can't pull this shi—"

Nguyen gassed it again. "Say you're coming and you'll tell her how you feel."

Easton glared, his eyes boring holes in Nguyen's smirking face. He could have boiled the brackish water lapping at his face.

"You know there's parasites in this water, right?"

"Then I guess you better make your decision quick."

Easton sighed.

VIII
"WHO MADE WHO"
—AC/DC, 1986

THE MACHINE, TETHERED by the array of cords to her fleeting power source, limped across the forgotten scrapyard. Her new *leg* — largely stick-welded steel rods, slag still globbed all around the fittings, meeting at a crude ball joint — operated via hydraulics she'd foraged. Her one good arm carried a basket for additional scrap she could maybe find a use for in rebuilding herself. The other arm she'd built, little more than a steel claw, held the cords over her shoulder. She never veered far from the Peterbilt tow truck she remained connected to. Her reserve power battery had little more than an hour's worth if she ever got separated again. She moved at a snail's pace, lest she over-exert what little power she could generate.

"What's your name?" Mike the Mic had gotten there with Watts earlier that morning to check on how she was doing. He walked the yard with her, gathering materials. He'd even helped with her wiring the day before.

"He didn't give me a name." She turned with her basket, heading back to the rig to solder the new materials into her modified console. She'd ripped the dash apart and rewired the interior, stripping it of everything she deemed non-essential.

"Everyone should have a name." Mike felt bad for her. Or it. He wasn't sure of that. *Does a machine even have a gender?* They'd taken to saying "her" just because she had that form, but the more he thought about it, the less sense any of it really made to him, so he decided he would wear his David Lee Roth wig whenever he felt like it.

"Why?" She climbed into the engine bay, fitting new parts, rebuilding the entire thing from the ground up.

"I don't know. It just seems right, I guess. Plus, then we have something to call you. And you deserve one. A good one. You seem nice."

She looked into him. "What is *nice?*"

Mike stared back. He wasn't sure where to begin.

Watts saved his bacon, bicycling up in that moment, pulling his Commodore 64 out of his backpack—the one he'd saved newspaper route, haybailing, bottle collecting, and barber shop sweeping money for three years to buy second-hand. He'd gone to Pirate Piette's to pick it up and the old skinflint jacked the price up that very day, and Watts knew deep down it was because he'd been in the week before asking about it. He'd been waiting so long to luck upon a used one he could afford, he'd been crushed, about to walk out empty-handed. But his dad Cletus was with him, the rare time he was home for more than a day, and he forked over the remainder. Watts had hugged his father so hard, he thought he'd suffocate him.

"What about Diesel-Heart?" Mike said. "You know, 'cause you're sorta diesel-powered."

Watts rolled it around his head. The machine tilted as she processed it.

"It's evocative," she muttered. "That's what *he* would say. But it's not entirely accurate. I have no heart, not as you do, nor any component that would be comparable. Also, the rig isn't strictly diesel any longer. I've rebuilt it so that it may operate from any combustion. These machines are poorly designed. The efficiency appeared intentionally poor. It now puts out 3000% more power from the same fuel."

Watts would have been in love, maybe already was, despite her being a walking collection of steel and cables. Everything she said was like a song to him. No one he'd ever known spoke like she did—even teaching him things, things no one knew. She was amazing.

"I got this, if it could help you." He offered her the Commodore.

"Thank you. My operating system is still glitching. I need to rewrite my commands."

"Are you going to be okay?" Mike asked.

"If I lose power again." She looked at her crude contraption, her cords, her cobbled together body. "I do not know if I will boot back up."

"Does that mean *die*?"

"I suppose it is the same, yes."

"That's heavy." Mike looked to Watts, then back at her. "I hope you don't. You seem nice to me."

She finished in the engine bay, climbed down, and took the computer from Watts.

"Whoa." Mike checked his watch. "I gotta bail. The girls asked me to work the sound booth tonight at the dance."

"Really?" Watts said. "That's cool."

Mike grabbed his bike and took off, Watts staying behind to work with the android. She took his computer and stripped it, tearing the guts from it and removing its motherboard. She inserted the pieces into herself, then began making screeching sounds, her eyes flitting as she rewrote herself. Watts stared in combined wonder, shock, and terror as she'd just destroyed in a moment the collected wages of years of his life.

Coming online, she saw his eyes holding back some emotional response. She'd begun to learn their ways, the things humans communicated without sound. She looked down at the remnants of his device, seeing it as he did.

"This device of yours. It was important to you."

"It's okay. You needed it more than me."

"I owe you a debt, then. I will repay this debt."

Watts' eyes welled up, but he held steady. He fought off the ache of seeing his father drive away so many times, the weeks and months he'd be gone, the loss of it all, of years they'd never get back.

"No," he said. "You don't. You don't owe me anything."

"Debts must always be paid. That's what *he* said."

"No." Watts looked to the horizon. He could almost hear the whine of the interstate. "This was a gift," he said.

"I don't understand. Why would you just give a thing?"

"Because you needed it. And because I could. Sometimes people just help each other. And debt isn't real."

IX
"EIGHTIES"
—KILLING JOKE, 1984

BECKY SAT ON THE UNMADE double-bed in the center of a drab studio apartment near Old Town, its empty walls, the only other furniture the one small chair and the TV stand. This placed vexed every sensibility she had in her body. She tried to ignore it, focusing on her fingernails and getting the proper coat of polish on before she left for the venue. It finally got the better of her and she made the bed. Then she swept the floor and put away all the dishes. The refrigerator was bare, but at least it was clean.

He should have been back by now. She kept watch on her time. She'd been the one to set their schedule, and she was never, ever late. If he caused her to break one of her own cardinal rules, so help her mother's Christ, she'd—

The door swung open. In walked Easton. Muddy, wet, disgusting Easton.

"Ew. You're awful. What did you do, swim in the sound?"

"That's exactly it, yes." Easton pulled off his dirty jacket and dropped it to the floor she'd *just* swept, her eyes livid at it.

"You know that water has parasites, right?"

"I heard that somewhere, yeah." He took off his shoes and pants in turn. He got bashful as he got to his boxers, trying to inch toward his bathroom.

She noted his anxiety and rolled her eyes. "Don't flatter yourself. It does nothing for me. We've covered that base, I think, huh?"

"Look, why are you here?" He grabbed a towel and turned on his shower, then went to the kitchen for a glass of milk.

"I brought you a tux." She held it up from the bed. "I knew your size already, of course, and I had them alter it in the seat to...well, you'll see. It should look nice. I'd like to see it on you, but I've got to run. You've put me behind as it is."

"A tux?" he whined. "Look, you and Nguyen have got to let it—"

"No, honey." She walked to him, squeezing his face in one hand. "You are going to this prom tonight. You are wearing this nice suit I picked out and bought for you. You'll drink punch. You'll watch us play. And, you *will* dance with that pretty girl. Do you hear me?" She smiled at him, squinting her eyes, lasering him with every pore of her face.

"And if I don't?" he asked, though he already knew.

"I'll ruin your life." She kissed him on the cheek and waltzed out the door.

She would, too.

Easton sighed.

* * *

Jason Stuart – 318

Becky raced her car, top down, hair rippling in the salt air, the afternoon pushing on. She glanced across the water toward the far-off island in the distance, the purpling orange of the sky painting its promise of the night to come — one she'd be sure to see off without a hitch. She felt strange, a flurry in her stomach, and she ordered herself not to even think of getting sick. Not tonight. Of all nights. But it wasn't that, exactly. She couldn't place the feeling. Just an oddness whenever she thought back to Easton, his tux, her demand he be there. *For Molly.*

Was she allergic to niceness? It was a thought. She'd explore it later.

She pushed on, gassing the little car for all it was worth, the poor thing. Another car blew past her—the T's: Ty, Todd, and Tag—flying down Highway 90 and definitely going close to 100 to breeze by her so fast. They were cutting up and laughing from what she saw, probably already drunk and still drinking. No doubt ripping lines. Trying to see how fast they could kill themselves, she thought. Three of her Bayettes, Tami, Toni, and the other one, were going out with them. She would scold those girls later.

She got downtown and found a spot on the street just outside the Markham building, where it was all going down. She glanced across at the Hancock, the bigger of the two tallest buildings downtown. It was no Big Apple, she told herself. Not even a Big Easy.

"One day." She gazed at the sky beyond her little town.

*

Inside, the girls set up the stage. Rip had already dressed for the evening, or as close to it as she was likely to get. Molly ran a sound check while Lydia tuned her bass. Mike the Mic in a Roth wig worked the booth with the sound guys. *Whatever.* Becky marched up to them, her pearl white spanking new axe in her arm.

"Are we gonna do this tonight, or what?"

"Hell yes we are!" Lydia still held a slight glare every time she looked at Becky, which didn't go unnoticed. Becky knew the type. She'd win her over in time. Probably before their first set break.

Molly smiled at Becky, telling her every kind of thanks without uttering a word. Becky responding with the same. She knew none of them would be standing here tonight if it weren't for this crazy redheaded badass. They didn't have to tell each other. Their eyes told on themselves just fine.

Becky plugged in. Rip laid a beat. The sound crew ramped the volume. Mike gave the thumbs up. Lydia dropped the bass. Molly and Becky both ripped into it. They had worked their fingers nearly bloody (or just Becky's at least) these last weeks, but they'd gotten their timing down to a science. They cooked sound like a machine, a musical robot programmed to rock and roll.

"I say we're ready," Becky said. "As we're gonna be."

Molly nodded in agreement. Lydia shrugged as well. Rip didn't have any insults at the ready, which they collectively decided to accept as the best compliment they'd get from her.

"Well, ladies, if you'll excuse me, I still have errands to do." Becky handed her Gibson guitar to Molly. "I want you to have this one tonight."

"What? Why?" Molly took hold of the nicest guitar she'd ever touched in her life. "I thought you were gonna play with me?"

"If need be. We'll leave yours plugged in and ready to go. But I'm the front. I'll be belting out the vocals, moving all over the stage. You got this. You'll cover just fine. And besides..." She winked. "I want to dance."

Molly held the guitar as gingerly as her steel-crushing fingers could. Lydia gawked, and Rip walked off to drink whisky in the green room. Becky grabbed her purse and headed for the door.

"Wait, where you going?" Lydia asked. "What do we do now?"

"Hair, makeup, and wardrobe, ladies!" Becky danced her way out of the ballroom. "It's almost showtime!"

X
"JUST LIKE HEAVEN"
—THE CURE, 1987

DOWNTOWN BURST WITH RUFFLES, frill, black velvet, corsages and big hair. The main downtown business district had been cordoned off that afternoon, the police putting up barriers and diverting traffic into any of a half dozen side streets. It was prom-land plural. Central had theirs at the top of the Hancock, the joint Our Lady/Stanislaus venture in The Hewes building. Everything from 27th to 23rd and up to 17th Street was foot traffic only for the night. The restaurants and shops were double-staffed and had lines out the door. Onlookers came out to spectate at the dresses and try to horn in on the general revelry. The Coast loved a party.

Clusters of couples poured in and out of the restaurants, Elmo's and Santé flowed over capacity. Dice had already tossed out a few stags getting too friendly and it wasn't even call-time yet. Hoyt, Clair, and Hurl had a booth at the steakhouse, hoping to sneak up to the Markham ballroom to catch a glimpse of Molly and the girls all decked-out on stage. She'd expressly forbid the parentals and sibling from being anywhere near the event, but Hoyt told Clair he'd be hellbent if he didn't see that girl play rock and roll in a slam-full hall.

Nguyen stood outside the steakhouse on 25th. He'd shared a quick meal with Lydia before she'd run back across the street to finish their last-minute prep. He scoped his watch, put out his cigarette on the concrete, and cursed under his breath. There was a bad chill on the wind, and he had that squirrelly feeling he used to get some nights before he moved out of the grim city, a place full of its own demons.

Atop the Markham Building was the grand ballroom and its adjacent mezzanine, host to many a formal event. The theme was "Ancient Future" a combobulation of two ideas that tied in the prom committee meetings. No one could decide which to go with until someone said just do both. The decorations included pyramids, starships, castles, laser-swords, unicorns, space barbarians, and hovercrafts, among other disjointed images.

Lydia teased down her spiked bangs, getting it all just right. She checked her deep purple lipstick, gave herself a wink, and headed to the stage. Her long black dress reached the floor on one side, just enough slit up the other to catch eyes, her collar stiff and reaching up near to her ears. She'd even capped her canines with tips she'd found at Tracey's, giving the whole getup a nice flair. She laughed at the stares from the promgoers already dancing to the house music DJ'ed from the booth by a Roth-wigged junior-high kid.

Rip sat on the throne, bouncing sticks on the snare, flipping and catching them over and over. She had grit on her grin and seemed tense, on edge. She'd barely dressed for the affair, still in the camo and boots, but at least sported a sleeveless tuxedo t-shirt.

"I didn't know they made those in tank top," Lydia said earlier.

"T'ey dunnae," Rip had said.

"Grond," Lydia responded.

Molly Slater took the stage. Her thick hair hung braided off one side, flowing in waves of red ocean on the other. The cotton-candy pink dress she'd hand-sewn with Tracey ruffled at her thighs. Her knee-high fuchsia All-Stars slapped the stage floor as she pounded toward that pearl guitar resting on its brace. She lifted it into her arms, tickling its strings. She dialed her volume, gave it a strum, and her sound boomed through the hall.

The lights dimmed, strobing the girls on the stage, the crowd lowering to a murmur. Rip hit the beat, machine-gunning those sticks across her array like a soldier on a mission. Lydia dropped the bass like a low roll of far off thunder, keeping perfect time with Rip. Mike the Mic hit them with some piano synth from the booth. Then Molly ripped her fingers across her six-string, cranking out the rhythm and filling the room with electric gods-meade.

The band ran through the long intro to Fire Inc.'s "Nowhere Fast," going right up to the very edge, eyes looking at each other and waiting for the final piece of their quartet to arrive. Right as the last chord hit, Becky LeCroiseur exploded onto the stage. A bright red dress hung from one shoulder, sliced diagonally down from her hip to the floor. The other leg revealed itself in a black pantsuit, flared at the bottom where it met her high heeled boot. And her hair! She'd gone total brunette in the mere hours since they'd seen her. The outfit she wore was like two people cut in half and glued together. Sparkling lights shot everywhere, lasers in a volcano, as Becky sprinted to the microphone and began belting out lyrics.

Molly and Lydia jumped right in, harmonizing with her for the refrains. Each girl blasted radiant sounds into the swirling mix of everything that was ever good in the world. Molly's body lit on fire. Every part of her surged with energy. She thought she could erupt out of her skin and blast into the night sky like a bolt of lightning. Even her hair tingled with energy as she looked to Lydia, the two of them smiling at each other from across the stage while Becky wrote an epic on the mic.

As Becky got to her last note of their opening song, and the girls strummed the final chords, the lights came back halfway, the eyes of the crowd looking up at the flashy, mismatched quartet of ladies adorning the night. Voices hushed in recognition, not sure what to make of the new Becky standing before them.

"Hello, everybody! And welcome to YOUR prom night!" she screamed out. "We're all gonna have a blast tonight and make it *the* one to remember, people! So party like it's '99 like never before. My name's Becky LeCroiseur, and we're The Heathen Gods!"

The crowd roared as she introduced them, and the girls shredded right back into it, working through their opening set list one by one. When they got to "One Way Love," the crowd opened up as the weird dude with the top hat and Ricky the nerd got into a dance-off that no one wanted to miss. The girls tried to not drop chords or lose time while holding their laughter. Becky seemed somewhere above it all, like her consciousness had left and her body and her screaming voice just knew how to do the work. Molly found herself in awe at the person who, only weeks before, had been her worst enemy.

Well...*second worst.*

Couples danced across the ballroom. Frowns and folded arms emanated from the shadowed chaperones placed sporadically against the side walls. Lebeque's ever-watchful eye scanned the room for any infractions of the student handbook, his detention slips at the ready.

But none of the adult chagrin broke the magnetic aura blasting off the stage and through the crowd. Bodies earthwormed across the floor while robot arms dangled freely. Moonwalkers slid backward from one side of the room to the other. There were Preps and Running Men and several more hard at The Biz.

Molly sank her arm deep across the strings of her axe as she spied, in the back of the hall, the smirking, prideful gaze of the best-dressed adult in six counties. Tracey nodded along with the tune. Molly felt a wash come over her, a pride in herself, fighting back a tear of joy and elation as they wound down their last song of the first set, "Win in the End." Every single thing about tonight was the picture of perfection. She nodded again to Lydia and the other girls as they wrapped it up. She couldn't imagine anything better than this.

She walked her guitar to its cradle for their first break, more than ready to pour herself something cold and sharp. Becky reached for the pearl guitar before she set it down, Molly side-eyeing her in confusion. Becky winked as she took the guitar and strapped it on. Lydia and Rip held their positions, as well.

"This next one goes out to a very good friend of mine, someone really special to me, and who deserves every good thing in the world and more," Becky proclaimed over the microphone.

What the? Molly mouthed to her vocalist, utterly confused at the shift in the plan.

Becky strummed her chords, Lydia and Rip fell in along with her, everyone seemingly in on this little conspiracy but Molly herself.

Becky went right into it, strumming out Carlisle's "Heaven is a Place on Earth" with pinpoint precision. The lights zeroed on the center of the hall, promgoers separating around its wake. The night fell down around Molly, her head, the whole world outside alive with sound and motion, as *he* walked through the room.

Her eyes drank every drop of him. His perfect, coiffed hair draped back against his neck. His sweet baby-face shining out that old sad smile of his. Black bow tie.

White tux jacket cut like it was made for him. His hands sunk into the pockets of jet-black pants that disappeared into the darkness of the room.

Molly raked dripping liquid from each of her eyes, praying she didn't smear any of her carefully applied makeup. She bounded off the stage, the rubber soles of her shoes slapping tile floor as she ran to him, leaping into his arms.

He caught her, bracing himself and managing to keep them both upright while she used her momentum to force the two of them into a spinning swirl as Becky's sweetened voice blanketed across the room. Their motion flowed directly into a close dance, joined shortly by the other couples. Her eyes sang every song they knew directly into his, as his told hers every apology there ever was.

They fell out of time together, all the lights, sound, and motion slowing to such a crawl they barely seemed real. He felt it, too. She saw, his eyes darting from side to side, trying to make any sense of it, then just shrugging his shoulders and accepting it. Accepting her. All of her. His eyes fell on hers with the weight of an anvil, and she braced as his lips began to part.

"I love you," he said.

"I know."

Her smile told him everything was going to be alright.

"DEAD MAN'S PARTY"
—OINGO BOINGO, 1985

MOLLY AND EASTON danced through the song like they were the only ones in the room. Twice Molly forgot herself and dropped him to the floor, sweeping him in a circle around her, his back hovering just above the ground, as she held him with one hand. More than one set of eyes fixed to their spectacle.

"Careful, Tiger," he said. "They don't know you like I do."

Molly smiled, blushed, and just drank his face into hers even more. The band finished and joined the crowd on the floor. Lydia found her Nguyen, matching her well enough in his leather biker jacket over a black shirt and black tie. The two cut it up as Mike the Mic spun from the booth, hitting them all with some "DJ Saved My Life" because of course he did.

Becky smiled over her court like the benevolent prom queen she was. All was finally right under her rule. She even deigned to share a dance with her buzzcut drummer in the torn tuxedo shirt. She laughed at the absurdity of the two of them spinning around the dance floor. She was glad her old friend Easton had finally seen sense. She felt that odd tingling again, but decided to just let it go this time.

"Look," she said, as they twirled near Molly and Easton, "either get it over with and kiss her, for the gods' sakes, or so help me, I will!" She laughed at the two of them, so tense for each other. Molly's face turned as red as her hair, and Becky laughed harder as Easton went pale as death.

The girls laughed it off, each dancing with her partner, then all swapping back and forth just for the fun of it. Rip seemed the most out of sorts, especially being the oldest in an already ragtag group surrounded by actual kids. After a moment, Molly found herself hand in hand with Becky as they twirled across the dance floor. Mike the Mic kept the hits coming one after another. Janet, Clash, Smiths, the works.

As they each found their partner again, Molly's eyes fell on Easton's, the two of them gravitating like two heavenly bodies toward their inevitable collision. As their faces converged, eyes shut, their lips made contact, and the whole world went silent for one forever moment.

Legs that had launched her to the stratosphere turned to jelly, and Easton had to grip her tighter in his arms to keep her upright. She froze them both in her moment again, lingering her soft kiss over his. The tremble of their faces, the shiver of their bodies, their spines down to their toes, all vibrated with their want.

Molly floated on a cloud above the earth as the song ended, her eyes locked onto his and holding as the lights dimmed and zeroed on the stage. Break was over. It was time to go back to work. Molly never would have believed she'd see the moment she hated to play her guitar, but here they were.

Their fingertips licked across one another's as they separated, the girls taking their spots on the stage for another round. Rip warmed them up, and Becky took command of her ballroom once again. Molly found herself in admiration of her old rival—a shame it had gone on so badly for or so long.

As the girls rolled into their next set, the attendees danced off punch calories and whatever alcohol they'd squirrelled into the event. The two odd men out stood next to one another, taking it all in.

"Glad you showed, partner." Nguyen punched his buddy in the arm. "I'da beat the hell out of you if you hadn't."

"Screw you, Nguyen." Easton poured himself a drink. "And what are you wearing? Is that mascara?"

"Dude, my date looks like Mary Poppins joined a metal band, and I'm with it."

"I can't believe we're here. This." Easton shook his head, not failing to stare back at the gaze of the molten redhead on the stage with a spotlight smile. "I heard on the radio on the way over. Truck of cadavers got hijacked this evening coming out of the city," he added. "Two morgues last week. A graveyard, too."

"Dude." Nguyen pulled a flask from his pocket. "It's a party. We're on dates. Stop being such a cop for once in your life." Nguyen took a sip and handed it to Easton who took more of a gulp. Nguyen laughed, and Easton lightened a bit

The girls were a force on the stage. Easton had forgotten the fire in Molly's face that night at the joint with the chicken wire. The boys moved away from the crowd as they let themselves fall into the sounds shooting from the girls they'd known all this while. Easton laughed at the sight of Molly and Becky *not* at each other's throats.

As the music, the lights, the motion all faded into a singular sensory overload, the two of them began to feel as out of place as they knew they looked. Most everyone knew they were cops by now, just as had some had learned the truth about *Blake.* High school kids thought about as fondly of narcs as they did otherworldly egomaniacal monsters, apparently. They caught the occasional side-eye from one or two that had rap sheets already—though none dared say a word about it. It was like Nguyen said some days back, "What are they gonna do? We're cops." He wasn't wrong.

It swirled together in Easton's brain. The things he'd seen. That he'd lived through. And the puzzle of it all. Where the pieces fit. Maybe Nguyen could turn it off for a night, but Easton had a harder time. He decided to hit the head and wandered out of the ballroom, down the escalators and into the main lobby. Some of the crowd loitered about, others were up on the mezzanine, probably getting high.

Lebeque shepherded students out front. Three girls Easton recognized as Bayettes sat waiting, arms folded, scowls on their faces. Tina, Tami, Toni...something like that. They'd been there when he first walked in. Looked like they were stood up.

Nguyen joined him, and they headed toward the exit for a cigarette. An eerie fog had rolled in from somewhere, licking at the windows outside. Easton saw it first, or more felt it—the way the hair could sometimes stand up on the back of their necks right before...

Three of them staggered to the front doors. Easton recognized them. Or what was left of them. Trey, Todd, and Ty... something like that—bunch of popped-collars from the track team. Two of them were big coke-heads for sure, or had been, but that didn't explain this. Their faces hung to the sides, their mouths agape and their feet dragging. Cuts, gashes, and scrapes were all over their hands and faces. One's ear dangled by a thread of skin. Their eyes were cold and dead, their prom suits dirtied and torn. Like they'd crawled out of a car wreck on the way to the event.

"Tell me you brought your piece." Nguyen produced his snubby magnum from his jacket.

"No, I was on a damn date," Easton scanned the area for exits and other threats.

"Freaking rookie!"

The screams started. The three walking dead men stumbled through the doors, promgoers and hotel patrons scattering in every direction. Lebeque stood off to one side, the toothpick he always had hanging from his mouth dropping to the floor with his jaw. The three Bayettes stared in shock and terror.

"Well, girls." Lebeque stared in shock. "Looks like your dates are here."

Nguyen took control of the scene. He ordered civilians to proceed up the escalators or to any other exits. He commanded the hotel staff to begin evacuation procedures and ordered that this area was in lockdown. Lebeque got the Bayettes out of the way and rejoined the officers, offering himself up to their orders. Nguyen trained his pistol on the ambling zombies. Easton ran for the ballroom.

"Where are you going?" Nguyen shouted.

Easton's eyes fired back at his partner. "To get the big gun."

XII
"KICKSTART MY HEART"
—MÖTLEY CRÜE, 1989

MOLLY CLOSED HER NOTE on the throat of her guitar, letting that last bit of it gargle in the air as Easton burst into the ballroom at a full sprint to tell her what she already knew. She'd felt it seconds before, creeping up in her gut, then into a full nausea all but erupting out her nose and mouth as the terror took hold of the streets just outside. The girls saw Easton running to the stage, then looked to Molly.

"You gotta—"

"I know." Molly took the guitar strap off her shoulder and handed it to Becky. She ran backstage, followed by the others, Mike the Mic filling the gap with house music.

"I didn't bring my outfit." Molly looked around the green room for anything to disguise herself with, but there was no time.

"I did." Lydia dropped her duffel at Molly's feet. Sure enough, there was a unitard, sneaks, and her well-worn denim cut. Lydia grinned. "You know who loves you, right?"

Molly pulled out the gear, took one look at the unitard, then down at the shoes and dress it had already taken her long enough to get into earlier. She tossed it, all but the denim, sliding it on over her pink gown.

"No time for the frills." She zipped the denim up over her chest. "Somebody hand me a scrunchy and some makeup, stat." Becky hit her with both, Molly wrapping her hair up, leaving the one thick braid dangling to the side. She cracked open the makeup kit, grabbed a dab of blue and yellow in each hand, and smeared it like war paint. "You have glitter makeup?" She saw it spread across her face in the mirror like Ziggy Stardust.

"Why would I ever not have that?" Becky scoffed.

"Good enough." Molly ran back toward the stage, the girls behind her, to Easton waiting for her.

"Play me off with something rad." Molly bounced off the stage toward Easton.

"Oh, I got you, Tiger," Becky LeCroiseur strapped on her pearl guitar, already strangling its neck in a wicked reverb Molly knew all too well. Becky bit right into the Crüe, and Molly had to give her due props: that girl could cook some chords.

She ran past Easton as he turned to follow behind her.

"You owe me another dance," she said

"I wouldn't miss it for the world," he said as she disappeared out the ballroom doors.

*

Nguyen dumped a round each into the approaching corpses, merely staggering them backward. Lebeque cleared the lobby, going as far as pushing benches into a barricade as more undead stumbled inside.

Molly thudded onto the lobby floor, grabbed the first of the walking cadavers and hurled it through the front doors it'd come in. She grabbed the next two and fastpitched them each likewise.

"Get these benches against the doors, stack up everything you can. Lebeque, keep everyone upstairs and away from the streets. Secure all the exits," she ordered at them. Lebeque stared in disbelief as Nguyen was already doing as instructed.

Molly hit the fog-ridden street to see it collapsing into chaos. Bedraggled rotters peppered the crowds, panic spreading. The three Molly had tossed through the doors rose again.

"They're not staying down." Nguyen joined her on the street.

Molly leapt at one, shoved her fist into its ribs and ripped out its black, dead heart. Globs of blood spat out its chest as it stumbled forward.

Then she saw it. Attached at the base of its neck at the spine was some blinking, metal thing stabbed into them, like a remote operating device. She knew immediately. *He* was here.

Molly grabbed the metal piece, ripped it from the walker's spine, and crushed it in her hand. The stumbler collapsed into the mass of dead cells it was. She tossed the destroyed device at Nguyen, showing him what to do, then launched herself at the rest of them.

One by one, she ripped the metal controls from each, destroying them, leaving the dead as they lay. Nguyen — joined by Easton, other blue uniforms, and Lebeque — followed suit, taking baseball bats, steel pipe, batons, whatever was handy and bashing the devices attached to their necks.

Molly knew this couldn't be it. This was too easy. Her stomach churned, waiting for the other shoe to drop.

And then it did.

Her mind stayed locked onto the girls in the ballroom. They'd wrapped up the song and everyone flooded onto the mezzanine, others watching from the rooftops. She sensed Lydia, Becky, all of them—watching and waiting to see what would happen.

Above the downtown sky, a bold, blue, luminous, cowled head appeared—massive, as big and wide across as the buildings it hovered above. *His* horrid face came into view—that goblin creature that had wrought all this and so much more upon them. His sunken eyes. His cropped nose. His bony cheeks. Veined, pale skin. His tongue licked over his gapped teeth and thin lips. His whole face barely more than leather pulled taut over a skull. Molly gritted her teeth as it spoke, its voice a booming, reverberating doom.

"You dare, always, to reject me!" he proclaimed. "I am your rightful suitor! I shall have my bride-price. For what is owed must be repaid!"

Molly glared up at its gnarled visage. Her blood boiled inside her with a raw hatred. Some ancient instinctual memory rose in her from some long-forgotten epoch, as though she'd hated him for half an eternity.

"Will you now submit? Relent this defiance and requite the debt. You are bound to me by the laws of the universe itself! I will not be denied!"

"Hey! You suck, Blake!" came the voice of some far off promgoer, followed by laughter from the crowds.

The ForgeMaster grimaced and growled. His electric image flashed its teeth above the town.

"Well, you heard him," Molly shouted at the hologram. It roared in retaliation, then broke into strings of light disappearing across the sky.

The streets quieted as the police and fire department arrived on the scene, evacuating civilians from the area. A grim hiss whispered on the wind as the bad taste of his image lingered on Molly's mind and in everyone else's. She felt how they all detested him as much as she did.

Lights appeared. Police cruisers flashing their blues turned, rounding both corners of Highway 90 onto 25th, bearing down on her. Both of them had no one at the wheel.

The first sped into her. She gripped its hood with her palms and shoved her feet into the asphalt. Its momentum pushed them forward before she flipped it to one side, the next one speeding toward her at a ram. She dropped her fist like a dead weight on its hood before impact, flipping it end over end above her head and crashing into the median behind her.

From the top veranda of the mezzanine, Lydia, Mike, and Becky pressed themselves against the rails to get a fix on what was happening on the street. That high up, they had a clear view of downtown all the way up 25th nearly to midtown. Across from them, more promgoers on the Hancock Building lined up along the rooftop, even more staring out the windows.

There were sets of coin-op binoculars all along the veranda. Mike dug through his pockets, found a dime, and slid it in the tray, allowing them a close-up view at the action.

"The cars." He looked through the viewfinder and gasped. "The cars are coming alive."

Everyone flooded to the railings to get a glimpse. He was right. Cars lined up down each side of Highway 90, scores of them. Hundreds. All driverless, all idling, sitting there, waiting their turn.

On the ground, Molly knocked them away from herself, the bedlam not letting up for a moment. They came at her, first the police cars, then an array of every make or model, anything that had been parked in the area. She pounded them into parts, flinging wreckage to either side of her, doing the best she could to avoid the windows of the shops and the innocents trapped inside them, helpless to stop the carnage tearing their world apart.

Inside the old Lookout Steakhouse, Hoyt, Clair, and Hurl had been enjoying a fine meal before it all started. Now they joined the crowd watching in awe at the turmoil out the windows as steel, rubber, and demolished car parts flew at them, bouncing off the outer brick walls and crashing through the windows. Some tried to flee, but an officer came through the front, saying the streets weren't safe anywhere around them, that they should all get toward the back, away from the glass and windows.

Then they saw *her* land right in front of them. She seized a four-door Caddy before it rammed through the front windows. She took the full brunt of it, grunting as she hefted it onto its side, shoving her fist into the engine bay to rip out belts and gears. Hoyt stood with Clair and Hurl, dumbfounded. That hair. The dress underneath the sleeveless denim jacket. *THOSE* shoes. Hoyt would know those shoes anywhere.

His whole head got red hot, and he charged for the front door, ready to shove that cop to the ground if he had to.

"Hoyt, where do you think you're going??" Clair grabbed him by the shoulder.

"That's my little girl out there." He aimed his heavy shoulders at the front door.

"Hoyt, no." Clair's eyes begged him. She saw every bit the same thing as he did, felt every drop of his same fear and rage, but she was not about to let him walk out that door. "Look at it out there, Hoyt. There ain't a damn thing you can do right now."

Molly appeared for a second in front of them, ripping a Toyota in half with her bare hands, then using the pieces as boxing gloves to smash the next two that came at her.

"That's not anyone's *little* girl anymore," Clair said, her fear lost in a swirl of a pride she could never have imagined.

Molly felt it. Outside, bashing in the metal beasts coming at her in an onslaught, she felt it course through her veins like a river of fuel burning through her fists. She slammed the possessed vehicles, wrecking them upon her impenetrable limbs, tossing their chassis into the nearby arteries and tributaries of the grid. More came, Mercedes this time, dozens of them lining up on either side of the six-lane downtown drag.

Inside the restaurant, cowering well behind Hoyt and Clair who were still trying to catch any glimpse they could of their adopted daughter fighting for her life and theirs alike, was none other than Bobby de la Beckwith and his wife. They'd been enjoying their regular Friday evening out as best they could in light of Becky's defiance. Bobby stared out the window in vibrating distress as he recognized the makes and models speeding up the street into oblivion.

"That's my inventory!" He ran forward, looking out the windows at his entire stock driving itself into the clobbering jackhammer in a prom dress and jean jacket. "That goddamn bitch is wrecking my whole damn stock!"

Hoyt'd had enough. Bobby de la Beckwith turned and caught the full fist of a 250-pound man dead in his jaw. Bones burst and teeth few from his mouth as Hoyt went in for one more before anyone could restrain him.

Beckwith stammered back up, shaking and crying like a child. His wife, Tammy-Faye, ran to his side, then glared at Hoyt and Clair before turning her hate-gaze at the officer holding the front.

"Well, ain't you gone do something or what?" Her face scrunched up as she flung spiddle and venom at him.

"Fuck you, Beckwiths." The officer turned his attention again out the door.

Molly ripped out a stop sign, taking concrete bedrock out along with it, and used it as a warclub, swiping the oncoming cars to each side as they came, more and more and more, with no end in sight. All the downtown rooftops filled with onlookers, witnesses to the harrowing ordeal, wishing, praying it would end. Lydia and Becky watched with bated breath as they saw their friend fighting alone, as she always did, taking the weight of it all on herself. Lydia caught a glimpse behind her, her face wrinkling, souring, as a disinterested drummer yawned. Like she was bored.

"They're stopping," Mike the Mic called out, still at the binoculars. Lydia looked back down at the street. He was right. The lines of cars down each side of the beach had stalled, waiting, menacing. A calm before the next storm.

His image appeared above them again, his jagged teeth and crooked grin mocking them all as it shone down on their helplessness. And they hated him for it. The whole of them, every single one across every rooftop, as well as those below. They hated him for how they felt.

"Will you now relent?" he shouted, looking from one side to the other, speaking as much now to the town as he did Molly. "Or will you see me destroy them? Tear apart everything and everyone you've come to adore? These...weaklings. Pathetic. Simple. Mortal. What are they compared to us? To what we are?"

"Fuck you, Blake!" shouted that same voice again, making him sneer and flare in its direction.

"People of this city!" His image flickered, echoing across the rooftops, Molly the Sledgehammer scowling back at it. "See now what causes your chagrin? The root of this destruction set upon you? See her obstinance, her defiance, and know it may end in a single instant. Agree, *oh high one!"* He mocked her again with his secret knowledge of her, who she really was. "Give me your word, your oath, and I shall end it now!"

Molly glared at his image, then at the wreckage around her. There were fires, leaking fluids and fuel. Car engines had exploded as they smashed against her or some wall. Screams and children crying sawed at her soul. And the injuries, the pain of those who'd not got out of the way in time, of the ones who'd been too close to a wall when a car came crashing at it, pulled at her. It drew her down.

How much longer could he do this? Could she?

Further down the street, heads popped up, faces presenting themselves. Reaching out with her feelings, she found the face of Easton, *her* Easton looking back on her, feeling what he felt. The white-hot intensity of it. His longing for her. His hatred at Blake, or whatever Blake was. She felt his voice whispering at her from blocks away now.

"No," he whispered with his breath. "No," he was telling her.

They all were. She felt every heart atop every building, inside every shop and restaurant. Her father, mother, her baby brother, her best friend, her new friends.

"No," they all said.

"No!" She turned to Blake's hologram. "No. You've been told. I don't have to tell you anymore."

"So be it! You chose their doom. It is on you. And you alone. For which of them stands beside you? You fight for them, and what are they to you? Where are they who would stand next to you? They won't. They can't. Pathetic!"

The cars before her revved their engines, the next wave starting up. Molly heaved out a sigh, wiped a grease smudge off her chin, balled her fists, and readied for the fight as the next car aimed its wheels at her.

Then came a booming foghorn behind her.

Looking up 25th, north, she saw it—a heavy rig judging by its sound and the size of its lights. They were coming at her from both ends now. How wonderful.

XIII
"GEAR JAMMER"
—GEORGE THOROGOOD & THE DESTROYERS

THE CROWD ON THE MARKHAM mezzanine heard the foghorn in the distance, all the way up Highway 49. Lydia looked away from Molly fighting a plumbing van with both hands and put her eyes to the binoculars. She saw a steel gray Peterbilt tow truck barreling down the highway right at Molly.

"It's a truck," she said. It was a truck and then some. It had steel plates welded all around it like armor, a cow-catcher mounted at the front. Lydia made out an actual driver in the cab of this one. She increased the zoom on the scope, getting a clearer picture of the face, a face she knew well: Molly's face.

"It's *her!*" Lydia shrieked. "It's that robot! That faker! She's back." Lydia cursed under her breath. That thing had all but fought Molly to a standstill last time. *How the hell is she still alive?*

On the ground, Molly dispatched the van after it had shoved her another block north up the street. More cars slammed into her, knocking her off balance. She felt thin, worn down. She still understood so little about how she *worked* and was worried she'd run out of gas before Blake ran out of minions.

She looked behind her again at the approaching rig. Her eyes confused her, because the sides of the rig began to widen as it came pummeling down the center southbound lane at her. She squinted and blinked her eyes, watering them to get a clearer picture. The truck wasn't widening. It was splitting. Into *two* trucks. Then three. Three trucks came at her now.

Up at the roof, Lydia called it out to the others.

"It's more!" she yelled. "It's more of them!" The first that pulled out from the long line behind her was one she knew — a big, sparkling crimson Kenworth with a steel crusher grill on the front. "It's Mr. Cletus!" she shouted, as if that meant much to anyone outside her small group. "It's the Rhino! And Mr. Hank."

"Give me that." Mike the Mic took control of the viewfinder. He saw as she'd said. Cletus and Hank's trucks pulled out from behind the android's. A massive line of trucks crested the hill. From the looks of it, they'd brought the whole truck stop with them and a dozen more besides.

"What are they doing following that *thing*?" Lydia wrinkled her lips.

"Her name's Convoy!" Mike informed her, though he'd just made it up that very second. "And she's our friend!"

'What?" Lydia's face was a blank stare.

In the cab of the tow truck, the metal creation wearing Molly's face shoved her self-made steel arm forward, kicking the heavy beast that powered her into higher gear. The deafening roar of not only engine but the line of rigs behind her soaked the air as she bore down, her target already locked in her spectral display. She didn't understand much of the organics, of their world or even their words, and certainly not their chemical reactions they interpreted as "emotions." But she had come to understand *hate*. That one she knew. And she would complete her program. She would destroy the one she hated.

Molly saw its face, her own face, as it blasted toward her, pulling ahead of the pack behind it. Blake, the ForgeMaster as he called himself, saw it, too. His eyes widening in a mix of anger and dismay.

"No!" his image shouted at her arrival.

The heavy Peterbilt rig plowed into the line of cars aimed at Molly. She ripped through them like tin foil, her steel dreadnought tearing them apart, tossing them to either side of her as her engine bellowed down the line.

The others followed suit, coming down all six lanes of the downtown street now. There were Freightliners and Internationals. GMC's and Hinos, Volvo and Western Star. Cabover Petes and single-stack Macks. There was a bulldog Pac with a can on the back. The rigs mowed down the diminutive vehicles, grinding them to bolts and shrapnel beneath their massive hulks.

In the cab of his truck, Mr. Cletus Morrison leaned over to his son in the shotgun seat. He handed Watts a remote control device hooked into the rig's console.

"Hold on, boy," he told his son, who gawked with eyes the size of baseballs at the carnage before him. He recounted in his mind how it had come to this, from the moment he'd heard his daddy's voice on the radio, to how he'd guided *her* at breakneck speed to the Stack's truck stop on the Dime and laid out the situation, Cletus rallying the lot of them to the cause. The Coast loved a party.

Watts saw the car-crunching steel brush guard on the front of the rig bulldoze cars and wreckage out of their way.

"When did you add that?"

"Oh, this baby's got a few tricks up her sleeve now," the old man said. "I been hauling nuke juice out in the desert. You be surprised who wants to grab a pint of that death. I had to make some *improvements*."

Watts stared up at his father, whose eyes stayed glued to the road and the job. They'd all jumped on board when Watts and the machine girl told them what's what. There weren't many of them could say they hadn't heard of The Hammer. More than one had seen her in action and knew she was one of their own. Hell would come down to Frogtown before they'd see one of theirs beat up on like this without an answer to it.

"What?" Cletus looked at Watts working the switches on the device. Flames shot out the front and sides. "You didn't think you got all them brains in your head just from your mama, now did you?" He winked.

On the street, Molly rocked herself sideways, sliding between the gaps as the thundering herd rolled past her. The colossal cavalry of steel, black smoke, and hot rubber flooded her senses and filled her whole body with a sense of something she didn't recognize at first. *Of belonging.* They'd all come for her.

She watched them bellow through the throng of self-driving automatons. Something welled inside her, threatened to leak out of her face. She swallowed it back, and let out a quivering smile. Still confused by the one leading the pack, she took a win where she found one.

The big rig army advanced to the T-bone with Highway 90, the ringleaders veering down one direction or another, again conquering all six lanes both eastbound and west. Inside the cab of the silver Pete, the Metal Molly ground her gears, munching down the inferiors beneath her rolling boots. His new simpletons were merely meat for her enmity, a whetting of what she'd come to taste in the end. She burnt through what remained of his lineup on her westbound trajectory, then wheeled her way back north and up the side avenues, blowing through barriers, and circling back onto the main drag for another battery.

The image of Blake's face stared down in hot rage, his best laid plans now heaps of scrap and wreckage. He roared at his former accomplice, his own fabrication born of his unmatched skill and prowess. "You dare defy me?" he screamed while she idled her mighty engine before him, just behind the redhead whose image she sported. Two identical faces glared back their hate as one. "I made you! I built you. You belong to me! You both belong to me! You are my property!"

His face once again disappeared in a ball of splintering light across the night's clouds.

In the distance, the sound of the rigs demolishing the last of his car horde trailed off, and the air quieted. Then a dooming, eerie, creaking of metal and wind bore itself on the thick fogged air. From beyond the Gulf, out of the darkness and high above the stirring brackish waters, hovered the massive metal hull of a freight ship. It fell as much flew from the sky, propelled by some evil, alien force. The massive frigate descended to the ground, crashing at the intersection of 90 and 25th.

Molly knew this boat. She'd sent it to sleep along with all its cargo to the bottom of the gulf. Yet here it was now, a flying monstrosity, its bow reforged to include a giant loading ramp which fell with a booming crash onto the street. Police and first responders fled the chaos. She felt Easton's heart reach out to her. She tried to will comfort upon him while feeling none for herself.

They came, more of his metal monsters. Warped, rebuilt, hideous abominations of their former purposes. Tanks, bigger than before, reinforced and studded with new, awful weaponry, fled off the ramp of the boat, spitting their venom at Molly's face and into the brick walls of the town around them.

Molly charged them, firing her body like a missile at the devilry before her. A screaming, turbocharged Peterbilt truck sped from behind her. As she concussed the first of the battletanks with a brutal uppercut, knocking it airborne, her cohort spun her heavy rig into a 180-degree donut, releasing the lever for the heavy ball-hook on the back. It shot into another tank like a cannonball, bashing into its chassis, knocking it off balance. Molly followed it up with a swift front kick, knocking the machine onto its side.

More monsters offloaded. Cranes compiled together, their industrial hydraulic arms fused into a vortex, moving about like metal spider-walking demons. Riderless motorcycles, armed with torpedoes on both sides and heavy machine guns mounted at the forks, ramped off the boat at her. Another contraption came bashing out at them, tank-treaded and wielding a giant metal fist pounding the ground as it advanced on them. Molly just stared at it, the sheer idiocy of it. *What maniac would even conceive of something so insane?*

After the last of his concoctions rolled, treaded, or stomped their way off the boat, then came the plodding march of steel boots. Dozens upon dozens of armored, animated dead marched down the gangway onto the street, each armed with a long bladed staff, a battalion of undead halberdiers. They were led by a massive glob of flesh, necrotic and festering. Its one massive right arm concluded in a balled fist fused around steel spikes and concrete. Heads peppered its lumpy body like so many pimples. Its left arms, if they could be called that, forked into tentacles, long, flailing, reaching. Two-Ugly was now more like Ten-Ugly, a hell-beast born of the dead she'd once conquered and now must again.

Then *he* came, descending from the clouds atop a hovering disc, lit up across its underside with some dark energy holding it in the air. His left forearm glowed with the same energy that pulsed beneath him. His right arm stretched forth, holding a long staff carved with a serpent at the tip. The cowl over his head and flowing robes over his body flapped in the night wind. This one was really him. Molly could smell him.

She sensed the dampening spirits of the town as the darkness marched upon them, a sea of his mindless metal servants, slaved to his will. He grinned at her, the both of them, as he tightened the clawed fingers of his left hand, the glowing rock imbedded in his gauntlet intensifying, signifying some unspoken command to his creations. They sped their assault on the two Molly's, the footmen dispersing toward the various streets.

He's sending them after the townspeople!

Molly charged, flinging herself at a cluster of them, only to be swatted off her trajectory by a massive metal fist hammering down on her from above. His battle machines triangulated, meaning to keep her and her robot doppelganger busy while the minions did the worst of it.

As that large fist slammed her further into the pavement, creating an impression in roughly her shape, she caught a glimpse of a red truck smashing through a wall of walking warriors, crunching them under its tires and flooding them with flames shooting out its sides. After mowing through a sector of them, it skidded to a halt, its tires cut, torn, sliced, and ground down to sparking rims, its engine smoking and flaring. Two sets of feet ran from its cab as metal fists crushed down upon it.

Then *she* gave her all. The Metal Molly, captaining her only source of trickling energy, spent her last, speeding her battering ram rig toward the thing she hated most. She shoved the conveyance into its highest gear, flooding it with the life-giving fuel she needed herself. She charged at him, ready to end them both in one moment. He merely swiped his arm to one side, the limbs of the giant spider crane sweeping down and flicking her, vehicle and all, like a stone, skipping, bouncing, steel-screeching across the street. Her ruined, leaking, smoking rig lodged itself into a side-alleyway, its engine smoldering, dying.

XIV
"THE TOUCH"
—STAN BUSH, 1986

EASTON, NGUYEN, LEBEQUE, and a handful of uniforms pulled together a barricade, hunkering behind it. Nguyen, having parked his own car close by, dodged flinging debris and speeding monsters to pull it up to where they were stationed, guarding the front entrance to the Markham. In his trunk was a full arsenal. Pistols. Shotguns. Vests. Boxes of ammo.

"Jesus, son," Lebeque said.

"You're welcome." Nguyen tossed his partner a piece.

"Hand me one o' them Howitzers." Lebeque pointed at a shotgun.

"Lebeque, I don't think—"

"Son, don't give me that. I was at Hamburger Hill when you were in diapers. Now, load me up!"

Nearby, Cletus and Watts fled the grounded red truck. Easton ran to them, providing cover and evacuating them to a nearby alleyway, climbing over debris and wreckage. Cletus led them north to the rear of the Lookout Steakhouse. He pounded his fist on the back door until someone cracked it open. Easton got them both inside, and they double-barred the door. Then he rejoined his partners.

Above them from the mezzanine, Lydia and the crew watched helplessly as Blake's minions poured onto the street, overwhelming Molly and her newfound ally. They saw the android and her truck go spinning to the side, wrecking against the building across the street from them while Molly got battered underneath the slamming steel fist of some absurd contraption. Another tire-tank drove off the boat, this one wrapped all around its body with spinning chainsaw blades, whirring, whining, and sawing the air with their awful noise.

"She's not gonna stop them," someone in the crowd muttered—their faces, long and solemn, all sinking fast. What had begun as a macabre spectacle had devolved into apocalyptic resignation, as if they'd all accepted they would watch her fail, their own fates left to *him* to decide.

"No." Lydia steeled herself. Her mind raced to the last time she saw her best friend losing—to the very object now her ally on the ground. She remembered her attempt at prayer to some half-forgotten abesnt deity. But then she'd called out to Molly instead, telling her she could do it, willing her to do so. Believing it.

"No!" Lydia shouted, turning back to the crowd. "Stop saying she can't. She can! She will!" They turned to her, confused, hurt, scared, lost. Lydia looked to her comrades, Mike and Becky standing before her, their expressions curious. The drummer was gone. *Just as well,* Lydia told herself. "She needs us to root for her. I can't explain it. But she does. It works, I promise."

"None of this makes sense," Becky said. "But if you say so, then I can get that done." Becky turned to the crowd and zeroed her eyes, weaving them through the faces until she saw the ones she needed. Her eyes steeled and slitted. "Bayettes!" she called out. "Fall in! You're on the clock!"

A handful of eyes met her own, confused. Others looked back and forth at each other, some stepping forward.

"I said fall in!"

More ran to her, lining up in formation. Becky slammed her legs on the ground, planting herself in a commanding pose and launching her fist in the air, then turned outward toward the street, motioning the other girls to join in.

"Give me an S!" she screamed that Becky scream. The Bayettes sang out as they were told. Becky turned again to face the crowd, barking her commands now at them as much as her troupe. "Give me an L!" The crowd began to warm to her.

Lydia looked at the rising insanity around her, then back to the street. The huge metal fist crushing down on Molly began to lift against its own driving force. She heard steel groaning, bending, breaking. She looked at Becky leading her gang, entirely in her element, the faces of the promgoers lightening, life coming back into their eyes.

It's working.

Inside the Lookout, Watts and his dad found Hurl and his parents, the boys joining in a hug as Hoyt and Cletus welcomed the other with a firm grip. They looked through the front windows diligently guarded by their watchful officer. Hoyt and Cletus stood behind him, having his back. Others scrounged together whatever makeshift weapons they could manage, readying for the worst should it come to that.

Outside their window, across the street from them, the boys saw the wrecked Peterbilt tow truck, spinning out the last of its life, its tires slowing, its engine noise ceasing. A hand, humanlike, followed by a metal claw, emerged from the turned-over cab. A head and torso began to climb out, only to collapse back inside the smoking, burning wreck.

"She's dying," Watts said. There was nothing he could do. All they'd built, all he'd worked on with her, everything he'd done to help her. Seeing her learn and change, everything she ever could have been...now it was fading before him.

"She's a robot," Hurl said to his friend. "Can she even die?"

"It's basically the same." Watts couldn't take his eyes off her. "The truck powered her. Without it or her power crystal, she can't survive."

Hurl stared into the carnage along with his good friend, seeing the pain on his face. Nearby he saw the warrior with flaming red hair putting her all into raising the massive metal fist still slamming against her, the dirtied, makeup-running face he knew all too well, called a 'butt-face' one too many times. He saw the blank stare of his tearful, frightened mother, the one who'd given him a home, given him everything.

He reached his hand into his pocket, fingering the faceted surface of the pirate gem he was never without. And then he saw the glowing, crystalline ember gleaming from the wrist of the commanding gremlin-creature flying above them all.

Without thinking, Hurl ran through the restaurant. He flung himself past the outwardly distracted guards—his own dad and Watts' both—leaping through the open window onto the war-torn street.

"Howie, no!" his mother screamed, seeing only too late what he'd done. Hoyt and Cletus jumped through the window, chasing after the boy.

The android, her reserves spent and fading fast, gave up climbing out of the wreck. She'd resigned what remained of her, of whatever she was, whatever she had been, to the inevitable. Her program still demanded of her, uncompleted. She stared into the flashing lights, heard the sounds, the noise of the fight, the image of the street, the defenders firing their simple weapons blindly at the advancing corpse-troopers to little avail.

She noticed the small one charging toward her, ducking fire and chased after by larger ones. Her last thought was one of intrigue. *What is it doing, this small human? Why does it run toward here?* It reached her as her CPU began its shutdown process, closing all extraneous subroutines. The small person reached out its hand, offering something at her. A small, familiar-looking object. Her memory cards faded. *What is this item?*

"Is this what you need?" Hurl shoved his gem at her face. "Is this your battery? Or whatever?" The light faded from her eyes.

Hurl tried to shove it in her hand, but the fingers fell, lifeless. He looked all over her, the ragged old t-shirt Watts had given her to wear over her mangled body. There was a gaping hole below her neck, like a wound, wires crawling out of it. Hoyt and Cletus caught up with him, but before they could drag him off of her, Hurl pulled a Hail Mary and shoved his stone into her open chest. He thought he heard something click, as they dragged him off and pulled him to cover.

A block down, Easton caught sight of the group of them exposed, the advancing zombie army descending on them. He steeled himself, pulling in a long breath to run into fire to give them cover. Nguyen saw the look in his eyes, Lebeque looking out at it, too, seeing the awful of it. Easton readied to go over the wall they'd built, Nguyen jerking him back down.

You can't get to them in time, Nguyen's face told Easton. Almost like it mocked them, a crow cawed off to the side. *Where had it come from?*

Then a heavy black combat boot slammed onto the top of the barricade wall above them, a set of camouflage pants leaping over their heads.

She thudded down onto the blacktop beyond them, marching right to the wreck of one of the tanks Molly had destroyed. Her half-gloved hands reached down, ripping off the M249 SAW machine gun from its turret on the wreck, a cigarette dangling from the mouth of her buzzed bald head. Her eyes burned like hot coals into the death before her as she approached the child and his guardians.

The drummer, Siobhán Ó Conchúir, the one they called Rip, hefted the heavy weapon half again the size of her own torso and cut it loose on the advancing corpses. Its spitting fire chopped them in half at the waist, tearing through their necks and severing their connection to the devices controlling them. Some of the falling devices spider-ran at her, seeking their next host, only to get crushed under her boot.

From behind the barricade, Easton, Nguyen, and Lebeque stared as the Irishwoman tore apart a score of dead monsters with a gun bigger than her own arms. She was entirely at home in the chaos around her, born to war, a carrion bird come to collect the souls of the fallen.

Hoyt and Cletus saw the bald woman blasting into the creatures upon them, thanking whatever version of whichever god that sent her down in that moment. Hurl's eyes missed the whole thing, however, as they'd never left the face of the felled machine. His own sister's face, he realized, now that he really saw her—some of it making some sense in his head, most of it just more confusion. Then he saw it. Its eyes. *Her* eyes. Opening. Coming to life again.

Her head perked up, her fingers grasping. She pulled herself upward, climbing out of the rig, tearing the wires no longer needed from her chest. She reached up with her metal arm and jerked the rig down, its tires slamming onto the blacktop.

"By damn, son," Cletus said, seeing the machine manhandle the kind of rig he sat in most every day of his life.

"Thank you," she said to Hurl, her eyes heating to a red glow.

"Go save my sister!"

"You have my word." Her right arm, the metallic one, quivered, almost liquified, before reforming itself into dozens of skinny metal tendrils, each reaching, grabbing, gripping. She pulled herself back into the cabin of the vehicle, octopus-like, her legs splitting into a hundred tendrils as well.

"Please get clear," she said.

Rip made it to them, turned and poured her gunfire into the opposite direction. She guided them back across the street into the cover of the restaurant again, Hurl steadily watching the tow truck warp and change, melting on top of the machine that looked like his sister. Watts joined him in drinking the image.

The pieces of the rig remolded themselves, wheels and tires ejecting as extraneous. They saw half-liquid steel wrap itself around her body, becoming her body. The big stacks of the rig slid down, attaching to her lengthening arms as the engine bay glowed white-hot, the whole rig appearing for a moment to implode around her. But then...

She stood up, taking nearly the full mass of the rig with her. It *was* her. She was it. All of it. A truck-sized steel behemoth with the face of Molly Slater, more steel forming a helmet around her patchy-haired head, a red slit visor where her eyes had been.

Molly Slater, a boost in her energy coming from the rooftop above her, broke through the crushing blows of the fist-monster, ripped one its metal limb from the chassis, and flung it roundabout like a bat, slamming into its chassis. She reached down and seized a long steel cable, the heavy ball-hook torn off the tow-truck earlier, and swung it one-handed in a circle like a gigantic morning star. She flung it into the side of the metal beast before her. The spider monster descended upon her before she could finish off the carnage machine. Its metal fingers reached to grasp her in its clutch only to be knocked off its balance, stumbling sideways.

The ForgeMaster screamed at the night when he saw.

Molly saw it too, her own face underneath all the metal and the glowing red slit for eyes, as the android stretched forth both her arms, forging them together into a massive cannon barrel. Heat glowed, first from below her neck, then spreading into her fused arms, and shot forth. A great red blast of pure energy exploded into the advancing flesh-beast, turning Ten-Ugly to ash.

Then more came behind her new ally. Axe-wielding men in fireproof coats and heavy boots. Blue uniforms wearing vests carried shotguns. Road crew and mail men walked out of the buildings, picking up anything they could use as a club. The fire chief, his platoon of axemen with him, looked to Molly for an order, so she gave it.

"I want all your men to move whatever they can into the side streets. Block all the avenues and alleyways. Keep everyone away from the windows and doors," she told him, his men and the cops already obeying. From where inside herself she knew these things she could not say. Much as any of her strange muscle memories, she'd stopped questioning it. "Keep yourselves at a distance. Force a bottleneck, slow them down, and send them all to me!"

"And me!" The Metal Molly raised both her smoldering cannon arms.

"You got it, Hammer." The chief fanned his men out, getting to the work at hand.

The corpses, armored and governed by spirits called from some dark dimension, advanced at them, bolstered by what remained of Blake's metal titans.

A truck-sized Molly and the regular-sized one stood side-by-side ready to wage war together.

XV
"PRINCES OF THE UNIVERSE"
—QUEEN, 1986

LYDIA SAW THE TIDE shifting on the street. Becky led her troupe, their voices starting to catch, drying, going hoarse. The crowd was with Molly, but the sense of fear still hung in the air—the watchers across the rooftops all through downtown wanting, hoping, struggling to believe.

"It's not enough." Lydia wracked her brain. *Think, Lydia!* She turned to the crowd again. At Becky. At Mike. *Mike the Mic!*

"Mike." She shook him out of his haze at the spectacle.

"Huh?"

"I need Gabriel. Tell me you've got Gabriel back in the booth!"

"I've got what?"

"You've got tapes? DJ'ing?" she said. "Do you have Peter Gabriel? 'Sledgehammer?'"

"Oh! Gabriel!" Mike caught her drift, finally. "No, I hate him."

"Oh my god, that's... There's time for that later." She looked all around her. "We need to crank the music. We need to get the crowd singing, shouting her name across the rooftops, the whole town. We *need* Gabriel!"

"Well, I ain't got it. But they do!" He pointed at the reaching tower of the KAP lighthouse radio station across the alleyway from them.

They ran to the other edge of the roof, staring down. Six stories up was no fun, the chaos on the street even less so.

"I've got an idea! Follow me," Lydia ran back toward the ballroom.

Backstage was everything one could imagine: tools, cords, electronics, and *rope.* Lydia loaded up as much as she could carry, loaded Mike up with even more. They ran back onto the mezzanine, pulling out all the rope, tying it together, strengthening it. Lydia called over one of the big rodeo boys from the crowd.

"I need one end of this rope over there, tight," she ordered him.

He looked across at the next rooftop, one story shorter than they were, and saw a catch point at the base of the broadcast tower. He started to ask why but the night seemed not to need it. He worked his loop wide, readied his lasso, and let fly, catching the anchor on the first go, sluicing it tight.

"You're a gentleman and a scholar!" Lydia hugged him round the neck, tying the other end of her rope off. She grabbed a wooden peg she'd acquired backstage, braced it on the zip-line above her head, readied herself for what wasn't even the craziest thing she'd done this week, and let her feet go.

On the street, dodging halberd swipes and giant mechanical limbs, the back of Molly's mind thought she caught the image of Lydia flying above the rooftops, but that couldn't be right.

She stood back to back with her counterpart, the strangest so far of the many strange things in her life, each doling out punishment in her turn at the myriad of foes coming at them.

"You gonna try to kill me again?" Molly asked it, *her*, whatever.

"That is not my program." She tore the head off a corpse-trooper and kicked another into the gulf.

"Well that's good." Molly flung her morning star wrecking ball, wrapping it around the barrel of the chainsaw tank and yanked it toward them. The robot grabbed it, swung it overhead and bashed it into the ground before them.

Molly wasn't sure if a high-five was called for in the exact moment, so decided she'd owe her one later.

Lydia pried open the roof access door of the KAP building and raced down the stairs to the broadcasting booth. She rifled through the hundreds upon hundreds of tapes and records.

"Paydirt!" She held up the Gabriel single she needed and placed it on the turntable, started flicking switches. She pulled up the two-way in the booth and tuned it to the channel they'd set.

Back at the Markham, Mike the Mic read her loud and clear from his CB.

"I got you," he called out from his spot in the DJ booth in the ballroom. "Over."

"Walk me through this," she said. "What am I doing?"

Mike went through the process of cueing up the song and had her set up the live feed. He had the ballroom sound system all set, jacked to the max. Lydia powered up the loudspeakers mounted on the tower itself and lit up the letters on the sign outside. Hopefully the people would get the message.

Lydia cranked it.

The sound poured out of the booth. It surged through the wires and into the air. Its waves echoed across the sky, blasting from every corner of the ballroom and exploding out the giant mega-speakers bolted onto the radio tower.

The kids on the mezzanine heard the familiar pop song. The group across the street at the Hancock caught wind of it. The other rooftops followed suit. Voices shouted along with the music, echoing the words, calling out its chorus.

Calling out *her* name.

Molly's body shook, vibrated, hummed with more power than she'd ever felt in her life. Her eyes went stark white: flaring, burning, glowing white embers. She felt her whole body become electric, as though she was made of lightning itself, born of it. Even the android, ten feet tall and Peterbilt, stood in awe.

And *he* saw it, too. The very thing he'd feared the most, all this time. The very thing he'd set out to prohibit, to steer her away from. They sang to her. They praised her name, the name she'd made for herself. Their very essence flowed into her, making her more powerful by the second. They *prayed* to *Her*.

"No!" He writhed, cursing the reality before him and his own existence. Why had his mother not drowned him in the lightless lakes of his cavern home when his mangled form had been born to her? Do as his father bade her? Surely that would have been better than to let him live, only to come to this.

Molly whirled her weapon with the speed of an airplane propeller, whipping it around her like a typhoon. She launched herself into what remained of his army, his great machines. She became a tornado of destruction, the full horde of the ForgeMaster laid waste by the spinning iron ball in the hands of a pink dress-clad prom girl with a dimpled smile.

Easton Braddock stared from his embankment in total worship of a girl he was certain only weeks before had sat her head upon his lap as she lay broken beside him, hidden away from this very madness. Now, she spun, whipped, whirled, leapt, and waged a one-woman campaign like a...like a god.

"No!" the goblin alchemist screamed again. Hovering above the fray, he held his carved staff, the glowing gauntlet on his other arm now commanding an army of none. He flew himself to the ground and held up his glowing left arm, housing the counterpart to the second stone that now powered the worst mistake he'd ever wrought upon himself in all the many thousand years of his doomed life. How he hated *her. Them. ALL OF THEM!* It wasn't only they that denied them. All before had done the same. Even his own kind, many no gentler nor fairer than he. All spurned him. Dismissed him. But he had a right! He was owed*!*

He pulled the scraps and shrapnel from beneath him, wrapping metal around himself not unlike his treasonous machine had. He girded his gnarled and warped body, armoring and readying. Now he would end it.

He stomped his metallic legs toward the two of them, his gauntlet glowing, a haze, a shield going before him.

"Accept me," he said to Molly. "Accept me now as your rightful lord, and it shall all be over. You have my word. Now give me yours."

"Are you shorter?" Molly asked. For some reason that was the first thing that popped in her head. "You just seem even shorter than last time."

He snarled. Molly braced herself for whatever fight he had in him—didn't look like much. He turned the corners of his lips, about to say some pointless thing again, when the android hit him. She rammed into him with everything she had, screaming and wailing on his armored body, the mechanic vocals inside her echoing across the scorched sky, flinging her seething hate at him with all the power her glowing core could muster.

Molly felt... *something*. Something like what the others had, all of them. That little thing inside them all, that thing she sensed, that reached out to her, that made them...*alive*. She felt it from the android.

The machine poured her hate upon her creator, his armor holding fast against her blows, knocking him backwards, but not off his balance. Finally, he broke free of her assault, gripped his staff in both hands, and jerked one end of it out of the other. A long gleaming blade sang out into the night, and he sliced off the next arm that came crashing down upon him.

The android screamed, the scream of a frightened girl, and seized her nubbed arm, recoiling from her attacker. Almost quivering. Helpless. *Terrified.*

Molly zeroed her cold, gleaming eyes at him, at his weapon.

"It can hurt you!" the android screamed in warning to her, holding out its one remaining hand, tendrils slowly crawling out of her other arm and rebuilding a new one.

"I know," Molly said, readying herself for more of a fight than she'd given him credit for.

"That's right, princess. A little taste of home, huh? If you won't relent..." He moved toward her with his sword. "If I can't have you, then no one will!"

Blake slashed with his snake-handled blade. Molly, the singing of half the city surging through her veins, flooding her with power, slowed her time to a crawl. She watched the mirrored blade slice into the space she'd just been standing in. Had she moved from one place to the other? Or had she simply flashed there? She didn't even know any longer. Time, space, reality. All of it. Like it didn't apply to her.

Up the block, Easton and Nguyen watched the armored, black-shrouded creature slice and slash at their comrade. Easton saw the gleaming blade as Molly blurred away from each swiping attack, like she moved in and out of reality. He'd never seen anything like it. She dodged him, evaded him, not pressing her attack.

It was *Blake*, he reminded himself. That thing that brought all this down upon them. The girls from before—the other redheads and now Molly, whatever she was...it was him. It had always been him at the root of it. And now this, swinging his sword.

The sword! Her finger! That first night at the old church!

Easton leapt to his feet and sprinted north up 25th Avenue. Nguyen yelled after him, no idea where he was going. Easton raced, cooking every calorie in his legs as fast as his human flesh could move him. He made it to his Z28 and grabbed what his objective from the trunk where they'd stashed it the night Nguyen realized what the android had been searching every precinct for.

He turned the key, roaring his V8 to life. He fed gas into its engine and boiled hot down the blocks he'd just run up. He saw her, twisting, retreating, dodging and fading every slice he lobbed at her. Blake had pushed her almost up to St. Elmo's near the store where she worked by the time Easton was upon them.

He bailed out the front seat just as his speeding demon's tires gripped the discarded hood of some destroyed Mercedes. His body rolled to the side as his car launched itself airborne directly into the armored Blake, hurling them both backward down the street.

Molly faded out of the car's trajectory before it hit Blake, ramming him into a heap of screeching and sparking metal against the blacktop. Easton rolled, sprang back up, and ran to Molly. She crouched on the ground, recovering her bearings.

His hand gripped the wolf-handled blade of the second sword they'd recovered from the Mutants gang all those months ago. He reached, handing it off to her, to Molly, to *his Molly*, the light in her eye catching his, seeing what he offered, seeing his intent. They locked onto each other's gaze. For one frozen second.

A blade stabbed through Easton's chest from behind, spiking all the way through his heart. His blood burst onto the ground before him, all over Molly. His body fell, crumpled into her arms. The life fled his eyes as she held him.

A thirty-megaton thunderbolt boomed in the air above them. Lightning scorched through the city sky. It licked at the clouds. Blake's shrank from it in curdling fear.

All time around Molly stopped. The movements around her as she held him became so slow as to not be happening at all. Some kind of light crawled through the gun-barrelled fist of her android ally, throwing Blake backward at a snail's pace.

She gripped Easton in her arms, her face quivering, eyes welling. She saw the gut falling from his partner across from her. She saw Easton's face looking up at hers. He smiled at her.

"No no no!" she shouted into him in their own time. He felt it, too. He was with her there, in her world outside the other. "You can't go, Easton! You can't go!"

"I think I have to." His eyes, the kindness in them, told hers goodbye.

"I love you!" she said, more like a command than a declaration.

"I know." Something in him shifted. He was there, still, with her. She gripped him harder. Tighter.

"Don't go! You stay here! You stay here! And you fight! Do you hear me? You stay!" she demanded of him. Her body teemed with heat and rage and feeling.

"As you wish," she heard him say. "I'll stay. Now you go do what you do."

Molly smiled down at him, at his smile at her in return. She placed him gently on the ground, seeing the slow motion of her robot friend firing energy into their foe, his blade deflecting it, countering, slicing downward and taking her arm off again. Then her leg. Molly saw the robot retreat, slinking backward, its own magnificent self still no match for whatever metal comprised these otherworldly blades.

Molly Slater gripped hers in her hand, owning it, making it a part of her. She found its workings and extended the blade to its full length, matching Blake's as he faced her, flicking his angry tongue across the edges of his teeth. She stood, feet wide and steady, her knee-high Chuck Taylors gripping the blacktop, holding her in place—the sword held out beside her. Steady.

The wind howled off the coastline, flapping her tattered pink dress backward—her hair a red flame burning from her face. Her white-glowing eyes flashed as the lightning above them had just seconds before.

"You don't even remember how to use that," Blake sneered at her. He grinned. Faded. Then slashed, coming at her broadside. Molly parried him with a flick of her wrist, catching his blade with hers and sluicing it away from herself.

"Apparently, I do." Her face mocked him. Her anger bubbled. Her rage merged with the coursing energy of the town rooting for her. They sang to her again. She could even make out their distinct voices. She heard Becky's trademark scream. She felt Lydia's warm thoughts coming from inside the radio booth. Her brother and his friends, each in their spaces. Her adopted parents. Clair, her mother. Hoyt, her father. Somewhere further up the street, she felt the folded arms of a bald-headed soldier watching her as casually as one would a ballgame, admiring the show. They were with her.

Blake snarled again. He whirled his sword in his one hand, holding forth the gleaming energy shield on his crystal-powered arm. He braced himself for another lunge.

"It's no matter," he said at her. "While you wasted away your years in this form playing at your silly metal lute, I studied the blade! I learned its secrets! I know its riddle! I am the master now, of sword and rhyme! I know all words! In every tongue! I am the All—"

Molly sprang at him, jabbing her sword at his body. He jumped back, caught her blade with his, sinking them to the hilts, crossed with each other, her iron face staring at his pustule-riddled one. He grinned, as though he hadn't just done the exact thing she'd wanted him to do. Molly shot up with her free hand, slammed her palm firm against the flat side of his blade, and pushed him off balance. Then she whipped her blade backward, hooking his at the hilt and ripping it from his hand. She flung it flipping through the air behind her.

He yelped, disarmed, leaping backward. Holding the energy shield front of his face and body, looking, searching, desperate for recourse.

Molly leaped at him, pressing her advantage. He deflected her with his arm shield again and again as she hammered at him with her blade, a stalemate until she heaved a breath in and blew it out at gale force into his legs, taking the ground out from beneath him. As he fell, Molly sliced off his left arm at the elbow, the crystal gauntlet going dark as it tumbled from his nub.

"No. No!" He reached into his belt and pulled out yet another device, pressing it. His armored feet began to glow, lifting him from the ground. He moved into the air, his flying disc reforming underneath his feet and removing him from her reach. If he escaped, he'd find some refuge, rebuild himself, planning, scheming again until he figured out a way to come at her, at all of them, again. Because he would never stop.

He moved further into the sky, becoming smaller to her eyes.

"I don't think so." Molly sliced her blade through the nearest road sign, severing it. She then cut the sign face from the post, leaving only its steel stem. She placed her sword in the groove and bent it closed with her hand, tightening it. Into a spear. *A javelin.*

She slit her eyes, zeroed herself, and launched her missile at the fading dot. There was a yelp. She saw him falling, speeding back toward the ground. Molly leapt and caught him in her arms, then dropped him at her feet, putting one Chuck Taylor-ed foot against his chest, pinning him to the ground. She yanked her spear from his leg, holding it up at her side.

"You might as well kill me," he spat. "It doesn't matter. I'll never tell you who you really are! The Charm of Making. Spoken backward. You were *unmade*! That's my final curse on you! You will never know who you are!"

Molly looked down on him with a laugh. She almost pitied him. *Almost.*

"I know who I am." She held herself up even higher. She felt taller. Could that be right? She looked behind her now, some of the crowd daring to enter the street. She saw her family and smiled, turning back to the pitiful goblin under her foot. "My name is Molly Slater. And I'm not going to kill you. Killing you would be too go—"

A scream loud enough to wake the dead all over again wrecked the still of the air as her own face shot past her, Blake's far-flung sword in her arms. Android Molly stabbed it through his heart, twisting it back and forth as it sank into the ground beneath his body. "Die!" she screamed. All of what she was gripped that blade that she wouldn't let go of until she watched him breathe his last breath.

Molly saw the hate born out of the eyes of the poor creature. If a machine could feel, this one felt little relief. But it had fulfilled its program. She looked down at what had once been Blake, at whatever it, *he*, had been.

"It's too late now," he gasped with his last breaths. "Sh—she will come. She will wake the dreamer."

"Who?" Molly demanded. If there was more of this madness, she needed to know of it. "Who will come?"

"The mother of demons," he stammered. "Bringer of sorrows..."

His eyes went dark. His face sank. One last breath left his mouth along with whatever passed for his soul.

"He couldn't live." The android looked up, all that hate still in her eyes. Molly looked back at her, sent kindness at her. She reached down, offering her a hand, picking her up off the ground.

The two walked, arm in arm, up the now eerily quiet streets toward the buildings, toward the town, toward everything Molly knew and loved.

People flooded the streets, seeing the danger had cleared. Her friends from the dance had made their way to the street. Lydia emerged from the radio station, a gaping smile on her face, relief coloring her always pale skin. Hurl, Watts and his dad, and Mike the Mic still in his Roth wig. They were all there. Safe, for the most part. The city worse for wear.

Except Becky.

Becky screamed. Her cries pierced the night. Molly found her, sitting on the street, Nguyen and Lebeque hovering above her, palms on her shoulder as she slumped on the ground, holding him in her lap, wrapping him in her arms. Tears flooded from her face, soaking her clothes as she wailed. Molly saw it, and felt her own eyes leak again. She kept telling herself no, even though she already knew the truth before she saw it. But, she'd heard him. She'd *heard* him say he was there. He couldn't be gone.

Molly ran to Becky who held Easton's body in her arms—her best friend. Molly knelt and held them together. The town stood silent as the two girls mourned their loss. None knew what word to say, none wanting to ruin the air, the only sound the blowing of the wind, the occasional cough or whisper, and some far-off whirling rotors, moving closer. Moving fast.

Helicopters.

Lydia saw them first, coming south right at them. Tomahawk dual rotors. Three of them. They landed in the middle of 25th Avenue, soldiers and commanders deboarding. One man, a full bird colonel from the insignia on his uniform, approached the gathered crowd.

Some knew him, others only knew *of* him. Lydia gave him a wide berth, as did the townspeople as he made his way toward someone who would give him answers. He found one set of eyes he knew, saw the water leaking from them as Becky ran toward him and threw her arms around him.

He was a colonel—a soldier. He'd seen more than his share. He didn't cry as the girl held him around the waist with all her might. He didn't cry as the crowd parted and left in its wake a path as *she* walked toward him—his son in her arms. He was a soldier and he didn't cry. So Molly cried for him.

"I want answers," he said, more at the wind than any one person. He saw Molly's eyes, their intensity. He commanded men. Soldiers. Platoons. But, he saw in her eyes that she commanded a lot more than that. "And I want that machine." He pointed at Molly's metal twin.

The android cowered behind Molly, glancing back and forth at the man, the people, the town, not knowing where her place was. Nothing beyond her program had been considered.

"She stays with me." Molly transferred Easton, gently, into his father's trembling arms. He'd lost the energy to protest. And some part of him just...accepted what she told him.

"What's she to you?" he said.

"She's..." Molly looked at the face, her own face, considering the aftermath of it all, of what they'd all lived through, those they'd lost. "She's my sister."

XVI
"IF YOU LEAVE"
—OMD, 1986

THE FUNERAL HAD BEEN one for the books. Every business, even the restaurants closed for the day. The entire city, county, and some state police officers, all in their dress blues sat in attendance. Along with soldiers. Airmen. Sailors. Longshoremen. Firefighters. The mayor and the county officials, too.

His father, Colonel Decker Scott Braddock and his special unit, his Delta squad, The FMJ's, stood silent, mourning. His older brother, the pilot, stood beside their father as they carried his casket to the grave. Riflemen fired into the air. A 19 gun salute. One for each year of his short life.

The days after crawled across the gray haze of a kind of nowhere. A nothingness had caught hold, not only in Molly, but in much of the town. Downtown was a wreck—half the shops demolished. Some might never come back. The streets rutted, torn—debris and car wreckage lingered. Talk and hubbub whispered itself around town. Some said Molly Slater, Hoyt and Clair's little girl, had been the big hero of the hour. Others argued. Many swore they'd seen Molly in a whole other place when the Sledgehammer had dropped a robber or tossed some gangbanger into the air. None seemed sure of anything.

The days and nights at home were quiet, full of hugs and soft moments. Hoyt seemed to never want to let her out of his sight. He'd even taken to driving them to school every morning, his eyes lingering on his little Molly as she walked away to her first class, arms and high fives greeting her from friends and others as she walked amongst them. The intrigue around the hallways bounced from Becky's big reveal to Blake to wild guesses at their hero's identity. Lydia was kinder even than normal. Some were more distant.

Watts and his dad spent a lot of their days together since his father now worked normal hours in town. Not long after the ordeal, they'd woke one morning to a shiny, silver, new Peterbilt tow truck parked outside on the curb, a red ribbon around the cab doors and a note that read: "A gift. From a friend."

Nguyen, or Bruce now that he was more or less a fixture with Lydia, hadn't much to say in the time since. There was still plenty to be done, a few Mutants-Rouges still around and remnants of the Dreds rolling the backstreets. But it all seemed hollow. He'd thought about having the car rebuilt, put back into service. It'd been a hell of a car. But then it seemed wrong. He whiled away most of his free hours going back over all the old haunts of their long-eared menace, looking for anything, any clue as to what it...*Blake* had been.

Molly couldn't ignore the same nagging question in her own head, the scratching in her mind. Questions lingered: what, who, and why she was. Why she'd come here. Why'd he'd followed. The "debt" he'd been so consumed with.

It gnawed at her brain as she skimmed the latest *Cosmo* article on summer wear in Tracey's shop. Summer seemed like a wish more than a reality as April crept on with the temperatures still cold in the evening, the winters lasting so long these days.

After closing up the shop, Molly wandered into the quiet, largely empty streets. She kicked dirt and rocks off the blacktop. She wandered down the nearby alleyway, Fishbone, the one where so many nights before she had... She smiled a sad smile to herself, thinking of those long-gone days, nights. The salt air flowed through her hair.

Molly closed her eyes. She reached out her arms, holding them out as though his would join hers any moment, the two of them embracing in their dance, the one he still owed her. She twisted and turned, going through the motions, the music in her head carrying her off. To somewhere far away. Some long-lost golden city where the honored dead go to feast and revel in the tales of their deeds. Where the brave live forever.

Then she felt fingers clasp her own, the warmth, softness, tenderness of them tearing into her soul. She started to open her eyes, but decided not to, as the two of them shared one final dance, there in the dimness of the alley, the sounds and smells of the city their only company.

When she did open her eyes, she greeted those of a good friend. Becky LeCroiseur held her hand in hand. They smiled.

"Figured you were owed that." Becky let go and reached down to pick up the single rose she'd brought.

Becky walked down the alleyway, toward the street, near the last spot he'd been when he...and laid her flower down.

"You loved him," Molly said. Not asking.

"He was my best friend," Becky said. "He was *my* Lydia."

The girls hugged each other, not a thought or care for the world around them. Nor did they pay any heed to the clicking hammer of the pistol that aimed itself at the two of them out alone on a late night in a dark alley.

Molly sighed at the banal miscreant in front of her. She really did feel sorry for this one, for whatever happened in his life that brought him to this. And the fact that a steel fist just clocked the side of his head, sending him to bed for some time to come.

An amusingly familiar unitard came into view in the dim streetlight. The lower half of her own face smirked back at her.

"Busy night?" Molly asked her android friend.

"No." She scanned the alleyway. "Only that, in fact."

Becky shook her head. What a world they lived in now, as it were.

"Come on," Becky said. "Let's go to Elmo's. I'll buy you a drink. Both of you."

The machine shifted its color spectrum and textural layout, mimicking street clothes. She still wore Molly's face and hair.

"Maybe change the hair, too?" Molly said.

The Metal Molly glanced up at her hair, noting the mirroring, and shifted it to blonde. Becky laughed.

"What the Hell?" came another voice rounding the alley, seeing the knocked-out perp lying on the ground. She stepped over it like one does a puddle. Lydia, always in her fishnet and spiked bangs, folded her arms. "So, we going or what?"

"We're going," they said.

Lydia eyed the blonde Molly and shook her head as the four of them marched to St. Elmo's, Dice out front as always. Mr. Cliff, the mailman, was leaving Santé across the street for his nightly slog home. So much had changed. So much was the same.

"One thing, though," Lydia said just before they walked in the bar. Molly looked back at her, one eyebrow raised. "Who was that freaking drummer?"

END

"KIDS IN AMERICA"
—KIM WILDE, 1981

Molly Slater *aka* The SledgeHammer
will return in

HUNGRY LIKE THE WOLF

Made in the USA
Columbia, SC
30 August 2021